**WARRIORS AND LOVERS,
CRIMINALS AND LAWMEN:
ELMORE LEONARD BRINGS
THEIR WORLD ALIVE . . .**

"The Tonto Woman": The lines burned into her face were the bars that held her prisoner. Then an outlaw rode into her life—and vowed to set her free.

"Blood Money": The five men had come together to rob a bank. Now they were cornered, and getting picked off one by one. But one believed he could make it out alive.

"The Boy Who Smiled": A vicious and unjust act would scar his soul. And while his enemies were not looking, he started down the long trail of revenge.

"The Captives": The outlaws proved that they would kill in a heartbeat. For a woman who must accept her betrayal and a man who saw it all along, there was only one chance to survive.

"You Never See Apaches . . .": They were searching for a rock formation that looked like a Spanish hat. But between them and the lost gold mine was a trigger-happy kid—and the trouble he would sow.

AND 14 MORE SUPERB STORIES

ALSO BY ELMORE LEONARD

The Bounty Hunters
The Law at Randado
Escape from Five Shadows
Last Stand at Saber River
Hombre
The Big Bounce
The Moonshine War
Valdez Is Coming
Forty Lashes Less One
Mr. Majestyk
Fifty-two Pickup
Swag
Unknown Man No. 89
The Hunted
The Switch
Gunsights
Gold Coast
City Primeval
Split Images
Cat Chaser
Stick
LaBrava
Glitz
Bandits
Touch
Freaky Deaky
Killshot
Get Shorty
Maximum Bob
Rum Punch
Pronto
Riding the Rap
Out of Sight
Cuba Libre

ELMORE LEONARD

THE TONTO WOMAN

AND OTHER WESTERN STORIES

A Delta Book
Published by
Dell Publishing
a division of
Bantam Doubleday Dell Publishing Group, Inc.
1540 Broadway
New York, New York 10036

"The Tonto Woman," *Western Writers of America Anthology Roundup*, 1982; "The Captives," *Argosy*, 1955; "Only Good Ones," *Western Writers of America Anthology Roundup*, 1961; "You Never See Apaches . . . ," *Dime Western*, 1952; "The Colonel's Lady," *Zane Grey's Western Magazine*, 1952; "The Kid," *Western Short Stories*, 1956; "The Big Hunt," *Western Story Magazine*, 1953; "Apache Medicine," *Dime Western*, 1952; "No Man's Guns," *Western Story Roundup*, 1955; "Jugged," *Western Magazine*, 1955; "The Hard Way," *Zane Grey's Western Magazine*, 1953; "Blood Money," *Western Story Magazine*, 1953; "Three-Ten to Yuma," *Dime Western*, 1953; "The Boy Who Smiled," *Gunsmoke*, 1953; " 'Hurrah for Capt. Early,' " *New Trails: Western Writers of America Anthology*, 1994; "Moment of Vengeance," *Saturday Evening Post*, 1956; "Saint with a Six-Gun," *Argosy*, 1954; "The Nagual," *Two-Gun Western*, 1956; "Trouble at Rindo's Station," *Argosy*, 1953.

Library of Congress Cataloging in Publication Data
Leonard, Elmore, 1925–
The Tonto woman and other western stories / Elmore Leonard.
p. cm.
"A Delta book."
ISBN 0-385-32386-7 (Delacorte). —ISBN 0-385-32387-5 (Delta)
I. Title.
PS3562.E55T64 1998

813'.54—dc21 98-21566
CIP

Manufactured in the United States of America
Published simultaneously in Canada
October 1998
10 9 8 7 6 5 4 3 2 1
BVG

Contents

The Tonto Woman

A time would come, within a few years, when Ruben Vega would go to the church in Benson, kneel in the confessional, and say to the priest, "Bless me, Father, for I have sinned. It has been thirty-seven years since my last confession. . . . Since then I have fornicated with many women, maybe eight hundred. No, not that many, considering my work. Maybe six hundred only." And the priest would say, "Do you mean bad women or good women?" And Ruben Vega would say, "They are all good, Father." He would tell the priest he had stolen, in that time, about twenty thousand head of cattle but only maybe fifteen horses. The priest would ask him if he had committed murder. Ruben Vega would say no. "All that stealing you've done," the priest would say, "you've never killed anyone?" And Ruben Vega would say, "Yes, of course, but it was not to commit murder. You understand the distinction? Not to *kill* someone to take a life, but only to save my own."

Even in this time to come, concerned with dying in a state of sin, he would be confident. Ruben Vega knew himself, when he was right, when he was wrong.

* * *

NOW, in a time before, with no thought of dying, but with the same confidence and caution that kept him alive, he watched a woman bathe. Watched from a mesquite thicket on the high bank of a wash.

She bathed at the pump that stood in the yard of the adobe, the woman pumping and then stooping to scoop the water from the basin of the irrigation ditch that led off to a vegetable patch of corn and beans. Her dark hair was pinned up in a swirl, piled on top of her head. She was bare to her gray skirt, her upper body pale white, glistening wet in the late afternoon sunlight. Her arms were very thin, her breasts small, but there they were with the rosy blossoms on the tips and Ruben Vega watched them as she bathed, as she raised one arm and her hand rubbed soap under the arm and down over her ribs. Ruben Vega could almost feel those ribs, she was so thin. He felt sorry for her, for all the women like her, stick women drying up in the desert, waiting for a husband to ride in smelling of horse and sweat and leather, lice living in his hair.

There was a stock tank and rickety windmill off in the pasture, but it was empty graze, all dust and scrub. So the man of the house had moved his cows to grass somewhere and would be coming home soon, maybe with his sons. The woman appeared old enough to have young sons. Maybe there was a little girl in the house. The chimney appeared cold. Animals stood in a mesquite-pole corral off to one side of the house, a cow and a calf and a dun-colored horse, that was all. There were a few chickens. No buckboard or wagon. No clothes drying on the line. A lone woman here at day's end.

From fifty yards he watched her. She stood looking this way now, into the red sun, her face raised. There was something strange about her face. Like shadow marks on it, though there was nothing near enough to her to cast shadows.

He waited until she finished bathing and returned to the house before he mounted his bay and came down the wash to the pasture.

Now as he crossed the yard, walking his horse, she would watch him from the darkness of the house and make a judgment about him. When she appeared again it might be with a rifle, depending on how she saw him.

Ruben Vega said to himself, Look, I'm a kind person. I'm not going to hurt nobody.

She would see a bearded man in a cracked straw hat with the brim bent to his eyes. Black beard, with a revolver on his hip and another beneath the leather vest. But look at my eyes, Ruben Vega thought. Let me get close enough so you can see my eyes.

Stepping down from the bay he ignored the house, let the horse drink from the basin of the irrigation ditch as he pumped water and knelt to the wooden platform and put his mouth to the rusted pump spout. Yes, she was watching him. Looking up now at the doorway he could see part of her: a coarse shirt with sleeves too long and the gray skirt. He could see strands of dark hair against the whiteness of the shirt, but could not see her face.

As he rose, straightening, wiping his mouth, he said, "May we use some of your water, please?"

The woman didn't answer him.

He moved away from the pump to the hardpack, hearing the ching of his spurs, removed his hat and gave her a little bow. "Ruben Vega, at your service. Do you know Diego Luz, the horse-breaker?" He pointed off toward a haze of foothills. "He lives up there with his family and delivers horses to the big ranch, the Circle-Eye. Ask Diego Luz, he'll tell you I'm a person of trust." He waited a moment. "May I ask how you're called?" Again he waited.

"You watched me," the woman said.

Ruben Vega stood with his hat in his hand facing the woman, who was half in shadow in the doorway. He said, "I waited. I didn't want to frighten you."

"You watched me," she said again.

"No, I respect your privacy."

She said, "The others look. They come and watch."

He wasn't sure who she meant. Maybe anyone passing by. He said, "You see them watching?"

She said, "What difference does it make?" She said then, "You come from Mexico, don't you?"

"Yes, I was there. I'm here and there, working as a drover." Ruben Vega shrugged. "What else is there to do, uh?" Showing her he was resigned to his station in life.

"You'd better leave," she said.

When he didn't move, the woman came out of the doorway into light and he saw her face clearly for the first time. He felt a shock within him and tried to think of something to say, but could only stare at the blue lines tattooed on her face: three straight lines on each cheek that extended from her cheekbones to her jaw, markings that seemed familiar, though he could not in this moment identify them.

He was conscious of himself standing in the open with nothing to say, the woman staring at him with curiosity, as though wondering if he would hold her gaze and look at her. Like there was nothing unusual about her countenance. Like it was common to see a woman with her face tattooed and you might be expected to comment, if you said anything at all, "Oh, that's a nice design you have there. Where did you have it done?" That would be one way—if you couldn't say something interesting about the weather or about the price of cows in Benson.

Ruben Vega, his mind empty of pleasantries, certain he would never see the woman again, said, "Who did that to you?"

She cocked her head in an easy manner, studying him as he studied her, and said, "Do you know, you're the first person who's come right out and asked."

"Mojave," Ruben Vega said, "but there's something different. Mojaves tattoo their chins only, I believe."

"And look like they were eating berries," the woman said. "I told them if you're going to do it, do it all the way. Not like a blue dribble."

It was in her eyes and in the tone of her voice, a glimpse of the rage she must have felt. No trace of fear in the memory, only cold anger. He could hear her telling the Indians—this skinny woman, probably a girl then—until they did it her way and marked her good for all time. Imprisoned her behind the blue marks on her face.

"How old were you?"

"You've seen me and had your water," the woman said, "now leave."

It was the same type of adobe house as the woman's but with a great difference. There was life here, the warmth of family: children sleeping now, Diego Luz's wife and her mother cleaning up after the meal as the two men sat outside in horsehide chairs and smoked and looked at the night. At one time they had both worked for a man named Sundeen and packed running irons to vent the brands on the cattle they stole. Ruben Vega was still an outlaw, in his fashion, while Diego Luz broke green horses and sold them to cattle companies.

They sat at the edge of the ramada, an awning made of mesquite, and stared at pinpoints of light in the universe. Ruben Vega asked about the extent of graze this season, where the large herds were that belonged to the Maricopa and the Circle-Eye. He had been thinking of cutting out maybe a hundred—he wasn't greedy—and driving them south to sell to the mine companies. He had been scouting the Circle-Eye range, he said, when he came to the strange woman. . . .

The Tonto woman, Diego Luz said. Everyone called her that now.

Yes, she had been living there, married a few years, when she went to visit her family, who lived on the Gila above Painted Rock. Well, some Yavapai came looking for food. They clubbed her parents and two small brothers to death and took the girl north with them. The Yavapai traded her to the Mojave as a slave. . . .

"And they marked her," Ruben Vega said.

"Yes, so when she died the spirits would know she was Mojave and not drag her soul down into a rathole," Diego Luz said.

"Better to go to heaven with your face tattooed," Ruben Vega said, "than not at all. Maybe so."

During a drought the Mojave traded her to a band of Tonto Apaches for two mules and a bag of salt and one day she appeared at Bowie with the Tontos that were brought in to be sent to Oklahoma. Among the desert Indians twelve years and returned home last spring.

"It put age on her," Ruben Vega said. "But what about her husband?"

"Her husband? He banished her," Diego Luz said, "like a leper. Unclean from living among the red niggers. No one speaks of her to him, it isn't allowed."

Ruben Vega frowned. There was something he didn't understand. He said, "Wait a minute—"

And Diego Luz said, "Don't you know who her husband is? Mr. Isham himself, man, of the Circle-Eye. She comes home to find her husband a rich man. He don't live in that hut no more. No, he owns a hundred miles of graze and a house it took them two years to build, the glass and bricks brought in by the Southern Pacific. Sure, the railroad comes and he's a rich cattleman in only a few years."

"He makes her live there alone?"

"She's his wife, he provides for her. But that's all. Once a month his segundo named Bonnet rides out there with supplies and has someone shoe her horse and look at the animals."

"But to live in the desert," Ruben Vega said, still frowning, thoughtful, "with a rusty pump . . ."

"Look at her," Diego Luz said. "What choice does she have?"

IT was hot down in this scrub pasture, a place to wither and die. Ruben Vega loosened the new willow-root straw that did not yet conform to his head, though he had shaped the brim to curve down on one side and rise slightly on the other so that the brim slanted across the vision of his left eye. He held on his lap a nearly flat cardboard box that bore the name *L. S. Weiss Mercantile Store.*

The woman gazed up at him, shading her eyes with one hand. Finally she said, "You look different."

"The beard began to itch," Ruben Vega said, making no mention of the patches of gray he had studied in the hotel-room mirror. "So I shaved it off." He rubbed a hand over his jaw and smoothed down the tips of his mustache that was still full and seemed to cover his mouth. When he stepped down from the bay and approached the woman standing by the stick-fence corral, she looked off into the distance and back again.

She said, "You shouldn't be here."

Ruben Vega said, "Your husband doesn't want nobody to look at you. Is that it?" He held the store box, waiting for her to answer. "He has a big house with trees and the San Pedro River in his yard. Why doesn't he hide you there?"

She looked off again and said, "If they find you here, they'll shoot you."

"They," Ruben Vega said. "The ones who watch you bathe? Work for your husband and keep more than a close eye on you, and you'd like to hit them with something, wipe the grins from their faces."

"You better leave," the woman said.

The blue lines on her face were like claw marks, though not as wide as fingers: indelible lines of dye etched into her flesh with a cactus needle, the color worn and faded but still vivid against her skin, the blue matching her eyes.

He stepped close to her, raised his hand to her face, and touched the markings gently with the tips of his fingers, feeling nothing. He raised his eyes to hers. She was staring at him. He said, "You're in there, aren't you? Behind these little bars. They don't seem like much. Not enough to hold you."

She said nothing, but seemed to be waiting.

He said to her, "You should brush your hair. Brush it every day. . . ."

"Why?" the woman said.

"To feel good. You need to wear a dress. A little parasol to match."

"I'm asking you to leave," the woman said. But didn't move from his hand, with its yellowed, stained nails, that was like a fist made of old leather.

"I'll tell you something if I can," Ruben Vega said. "I know women all my life, all kinds of women in the way they look and dress, the way they adorn themselves according to custom. Women are always a wonder to me. When I'm not with a woman I think of them as all the same because I'm thinking of one thing. You understand?"

"Put a sack over their head," the woman said.

"Well, I'm not thinking of what she looks like then, when I'm out in the mountains or somewhere," Ruben Vega said. "That part of her doesn't matter. But when I'm *with* the woman, ah, then I realize how they are all different. You say, of course. This isn't a revelation to you. But maybe it is when you think about it some more."

The woman's eyes changed, turned cold. "You want to go to bed with me? Is that what you're saying, why you bring a gift?"

He looked at her with disappointment, an expression of weariness. But then he dropped the store box and took her to him gently, placing his hands on her shoulders, feeling her small bones in his grasp as he brought her in against him and his arms went around her.

He said, "You're gonna die here. Dry up and blow away."

She said, "Please . . ." Her voice hushed against him.

"They wanted only to mark your chin," Ruben Vega said, "in the custom of those people. But you wanted your own marks, didn't you? *Your* marks, not like anyone else. . . . Well, you got them." After a moment he said to her, very quietly, "Tell me what you want."

The hushed voice close to him said, "I don't know."

He said, "Think about it and remember something. There is no one else in the world like you."

HE reined the bay to move out and saw the dust trail rising out of the old pasture, three riders coming, and heard the woman say, "I told you. Now it's too late."

A man on a claybank and two young riders eating his dust, finally separating to come in abreast, reined to a walk as they reached the pump and the irrigation ditch. The woman, walking from the corral to the house, said to them, "What do you want? I don't need anything, Mr. Bonnet."

So this would be the Circle-Eye foreman on the claybank. The man ignored her, his gaze holding on Ruben Vega with a solemn expression, showing he was going to be dead serious. A chew formed a lump in his jaw. He wore army suspenders and sleeve garters, his shirt buttoned up at the neck. As old as you are, Ruben Vega thought, a man who likes a tight feel of security and is serious about his business.

Bonnet said to him finally, "You made a mistake."

"I don't know the rules," Ruben Vega said.

"She told you to leave her be. That's the only rule there is. But you bought yourself a dandy new hat and come back here."

"That's some hat," one of the young riders said. This one held a single-shot Springfield across his pommel. The foreman, Bonnet, turned in his saddle and said something to the other rider, who unhitched his rope and began shaking out a loop, hanging it nearly to the ground.

It's a show, Ruben Vega thought. He said to Bonnet, "I was leaving."

Bonnet said, "Yes, indeed, you are. On the off end of a rope. We're gonna drag you so you'll know the ground and never cross this land again."

The rider with the Springfield said, "Gimme your hat, mister, so's you don't get it dirty."

At this point Ruben Vega nudged his bay and began moving in on the foreman, who straightened, looking over at the roper, and said, "Well, tie on to him."

But Ruben Vega was close to the foreman now, the bay taller than the claybank, and would move the claybank if the man on his back told him to. Ruben Vega watched the foreman's eyes moving and knew the roper was coming around behind him. Now the foreman turned his head to spit and let go a stream that spattered the hard-pack close to the bay's forelegs.

"Stand still," Bonnet said, "and we'll get her done easy. Or you can run and get snubbed out of your chair. Either way."

Ruben Vega was thinking that he could drink with this ramrod and they'd tell each other stories until they were drunk. The man had thought it would be easy: chase off a Mexican gunnysacker who'd come sniffing the boss's wife. A kid who was good with a rope and another one who could shoot cans off the fence with an old Springfield should be enough.

Ruben Vega said to Bonnet, "Do you know who I am?"

"Tell us," Bonnet said, "so we'll know what the cat drug in and we drug out."

And Ruben Vega said, because he had no choice, "I hear the

rope in the air, the one with the rifle is dead. Then you. Then the roper."

His words drew silence because there was nothing more to be said. In the moments that Ruben Vega and the one named Bonnet stared at each other, the woman came out to them holding a revolver, an old Navy Colt, which she raised and laid the barrel against the muzzle of the foreman's claybank.

She said, "Leave now, Mr. Bonnet, or you'll walk nine miles to shade."

There was no argument, little discussion, a few grumbling words. The Tonto woman was still Mrs. Isham. Bonnet rode away with his young hands and a new silence came over the yard.

Ruben Vega said, "He believes you'd shoot his horse."

The woman said, "He believes I'd cut steaks, and eat it too. It's how I'm seen after twelve years of that other life."

Ruben Vega began to smile. The woman looked at him and in a few moments she began to smile with him. She shook her head then, but continued to smile. He said to her, "You could have a good time if you want to."

She said, "How, scaring people?"

He said, "If you feel like it." He said, "Get the present I brought you and open it."

HE came back for her the next day in a Concord buggy, wearing his new willow-root straw and a cutaway coat over his revolvers, the coat he'd rented at a funeral parlor. Mrs. Isham wore the pale blue-and-white lace-trimmed dress he'd bought at Weiss's store, sat primly on the bustle, and held the parasol against the afternoon sun all the way to Benson, ten miles, and up the main street to the Charles Crooker Hotel where the drummers and cattlemen and railroad men sitting in their front-porch rockers stared and stared.

They walked past the manager and into the dining room before Ruben Vega removed his hat and pointed to the table he liked, one against the wall between two windows. The waitress in her starched uniform was wide eyed taking them over and getting them seated. It was early and the dining room was not half filled.

"The place for a quiet dinner," Ruben Vega said. "You see how quiet it is?"

"Everybody's looking at me," Sarah Isham said to the menu in front of her.

Ruben Vega said, "I thought they were looking at me. All right, soon they'll be used to it."

She glanced up and said, "People are leaving."

He said, "That's what you do when you finish eating, you leave."

She looked at him, staring, and said, "Who are you?"

"I told you."

"Only your name."

"You want me to tell you the truth, why I came here?"

"Please."

"To steal some of your husband's cattle."

She began to smile and he smiled. She began to laugh and he laughed, looking openly at the people looking at them, but not bothered by them. Of course they'd look. How could they help it? A Mexican rider and a woman with blue stripes on her face sitting at a table in the hotel dining room, laughing. He said, "Do you like fish? I know your Indian brothers didn't serve you none. It's against their religion. Some things are for religion, as you know, and some things are against it. We spend all our lives learning customs. Then they change them. I'll tell you something else if you promise not to be angry or point your pistol at me. Something else I could do the rest of my life. I could look at you and touch you and love you."

Her hand moved across the linen tablecloth to his with the cracked, yellowed nails and took hold of it, clutched it.

She said, "You're going to leave."

He said, "When it's time."

She said, "I know you. I don't know anyone else."

He said, "You're the loveliest woman I've ever met. And the strongest. Are you ready? I think the man coming now is your husband."

It seemed strange to Ruben Vega that the man stood looking at him and not at his wife. The man seemed not too old for her, as he had expected, but too self-important. A man with a very serious demeanor, as though his business had failed or someone in his family had passed away. The man's wife was still clutching the hand with the gnarled fingers. Maybe that was it. Ruben Vega was going to lift her hand from his, but then thought, Why? He said as pleasantly as he was able, "Yes, can I help you?"

Mr. Isham said, "You have one minute to mount up and ride out of town."

"Why don't you sit down," Ruben Vega said, "have a glass of wine with us?" He paused and said, "I'll introduce you to your wife."

Sarah Isham laughed; not loud but with a warmth to it and Ruben Vega had to look at her and smile. It seemed all right to release her hand now. As he did he said, "Do you know this gentleman?"

"I'm not sure I've had the pleasure," Sarah Isham said. "Why does he stand there?"

"I don't know," Ruben Vega said. "He seems worried about something."

"I've warned you," Mr. Isham said. "You can walk out or be dragged out."

Ruben Vega said, "He has something about wanting to drag people. Why is that?" And again heard Sarah's laugh, a giggle now that she covered with her hand. Then she looked up at her husband, her face with its blue tribal lines raised to the soft light of the dining room.

She said, "John, look at me. . . . Won't you please sit with us?"

Now it was as if the man had to make a moral decision, first consult his conscience, then consider the manner in which he would pull the chair out—the center of attention. When finally he was seated, upright on the chair and somewhat away from the table, Ruben Vega thought, All that to sit down. He felt sorry for the man now, because the man was not the kind who could say what he felt.

Sarah said, "John, can you look at me?"

He said, "Of course I can."

"Then do it. I'm right here."

"We'll talk later," her husband said.

She said, "When? Is there a visitor's day?"

"You'll be coming to the house, soon."

"You mean to see it?"

"To live there."

She looked at Ruben Vega with just the trace of a smile, a sad one. Then said to her husband, "I don't know if I want to. I don't know you. So I don't know if I want to be married to you. Can you understand that?"

Ruben Vega was nodding as she spoke. He could understand it. He heard the man say, "But we *are* married. I have an obligation to you and I respect it. Don't I provide for you?"

Sarah said, "Oh, my God—" and looked at Ruben Vega. "Did you hear that? He provides for me." She smiled again, not able to hide it, while her husband began to frown, confused.

"He's a generous man," Ruben Vega said, pushing up from the table. He saw her smile fade, though something warm remained in her eyes. "I'm sorry. I have to leave. I'm going on a trip tonight, south, and first I have to pick up a few things." He moved around the table to take one of her hands in his, not caring what the husband thought. He said, "You'll do all right, whatever you decide. Just keep in mind there's no one else in the world like you."

She said, "I can always charge admission. Do you think ten cents a look is too high?"

"At least that," Ruben Vega said. "But you'll think of something better."

He left her there in the dining room of the Charles Crooker Hotel in Benson, Arizona—maybe to see her again sometime, maybe not—and went out with a good conscience to take some of her husband's cattle.

The Captives

CHAPTER ONE

He could hear the stagecoach, the faraway creaking and the muffled rumble of it, and he was thinking: It's almost an hour early. Why should it be if it left Contention on schedule?

His name was Pat Brennan. He was lean and almost tall, with a deeply tanned, pleasant face beneath the straight hat-brim low over his eyes, and he stood next to his saddle, which was on the ground, with the easy, hip-shot slouch of a rider. A Henry rifle was in his right hand and he was squinting into the sun glare, looking up the grade to the rutted road that came curving down through the spidery Joshua trees.

He lowered the Henry rifle, stock down, and let if fall across the saddle, and kept his hand away from the Colt holstered on his right leg. A man could get shot standing next to a stage road out in the middle of nowhere with a rifle in his hand.

Then, seeing the coach suddenly against the sky, billowing dust hanging over it, he felt relief and smiled to himself and raised his arm to wave as the coach passed through the Joshuas.

As the pounding wood, iron, and three-team racket of it came swaying toward him, he raised both arms and felt a sudden helplessness as he saw that the driver was making no effort to stop the teams. Brennan stepped back quickly, and the coach rushed past him, the driver, alone on the boot, bending forward and down to look at him.

Brennan cupped his hands and called, "*Rintoooon!*"

The driver leaned back with the reins high and through his fingers, his boot pushing against the brake lever, and his body half turned to look back over the top of the Concord. Brennan swung the saddle up over his shoulder and started after the coach as it ground to a stop.

He saw the company name, HATCH & HODGES, and just below it, *Number 42* stenciled on the varnished door; then from a side window, he saw a man staring at him irritably as he approached. Behind the man he caught a glimpse of a woman with soft features and a small, plumed hat and eyes that looked away quickly as Brennan's gaze passed them going up to Ed Rintoon, the driver.

"Ed, for a minute I didn't think you were going to stop."

Rintoon, a leathery, beard-stubbled man in his mid-forties, stood with one knee on the seat and looked down at Brennan with only faint surprise.

"I took you for being up to no good, standing there waving your arms."

"I'm only looking for a lift a ways."

"What happened to you?"

Brennan grinned and his thumb pointed back vaguely over his shoulder. "I was visiting Tenvoorde to see about buying some yearling stock and I lost my horse to him on a bet."

"Driver!"

Brennan turned. The man who had been at the window was now leaning halfway out of the door and looking up at Rintoon.

"I'm not paying you to pass the time of day with"—he glanced at Brennan—"with everybody we meet."

Rintoon leaned over to look down at him. "Willard, you ain't even part right, since you ain't the man that pays me."

"I chartered this coach, and you along with it!" He was a young man, hatless, his long hair mussed from the wind. Strands of it hung over his ears, and his face was flushed as he glared at Rintoon. "When I pay for a coach I expect the service that goes with it."

Rintoon said, "Willard, you calm down now."

"Mr. Mims!"

Rintoon smiled faintly, glancing at Brennan. "Pat, I'd like you to meet Mr. Mims." He paused, adding, "He's a bookkeeper."

Brennan touched the brim of his hat toward the coach, seeing the woman again. She looked to be in her late twenties and her eyes now were wide and frightened and not looking at him.

His glance went to Willard Mims. Mims came out of the doorway and stood pointing a finger up at Rintoon.

"Brother, you're through! I swear to God this is your last run on any line in the Territory!"

Rintoon eased himself down until he was half sitting on the seat. "You wouldn't kid me."

"You'll see if I'm kidding!"

Rintoon shook his head. "After ten years of faithful service the boss will be sorry to see me go."

Willard Mims stared at him in silence. Then he said, his voice calmer, "You won't be so sure of yourself after we get to Bisbee."

Ignoring him, Rintoon turned to Brennan. "Swing that saddle up here."

"You hear what I said?" Willard Mims flared.

Reaching down for the saddle horn as Brennan lifted it, Rintoon answered, "You said I'd be sorry when we got to Bisbee."

"You remember that!"

"I sure will. Now you get back inside, Willard." He glanced at Brennan. "You get in there, too, Pat."

Willard Mims stiffened. "I'll remind you again—this is *not* the passenger coach."

Brennan was momentarily angry, but he saw the way Rintoon was taking this and he said calmly, "You want me to walk? It's only fifteen miles to Sasabe."

"I didn't say that," Mims answered, moving to the coach door. "If you want to come, get up on the boot." He turned to look at Brennan as he pulled himself up on the foot rung. "If we'd wanted company we'd have taken the scheduled run. That clear enough for you?"

Glancing at Rintoon, Brennan swung the Henry rifle up to him and said, "Yes, sir," not looking at Mims; and he winked at Rintoon as he climbed the wheel to the driver's seat.

A moment later they were moving, slowly at first, bumping and swaying; then the road seemed to become smoother as the teams pulled faster.

Brennan leaned toward Rintoon and said, in the noise, close to the driver's grizzled face, "I wondered why the regular stage would be almost an hour early, Ed, I'm obliged to you."

Rintoon glanced at him. "Thank Mr. Mims."

"Who is he, anyway?"

"Old man Gateway's son-in-law. Married the boss's daughter. Married into the biggest copper claim in the country."

"The girl with him his wife?"

"Doretta," Rintoon answered. "That's Gateway's daughter. She was scheduled to be an old maid till Willard come along and saved her from spinsterhood. She's plain as a 'dobe wall."

Brennan said, "But not too plain for Willard, eh?"

Rintoon gave him a side glance. "Patrick, there ain't nothing plain about old man Gateway's holdings. That's the thing. Four years ago he bought a half interest in the Montezuma Copper Mine for two hundred and fifty thousand dollars, and he's got it back triple since then. Can you imagine anyone having that much money?"

Brennan shook his head. "Where'd he get it, to start?"

"They say he come from money and made more by using the brains God gave him, investing it."

Brennan shook his head again. "That's too much money, Ed. Too much to have to worry about."

"Not for Willard, it ain't," Rintoon said. "He started out as a bookkeeper with the company. Now he's general manager—since the wedding. The old man picked Willard because he was the only one around he thought had any polish, and he knew if he waited much longer he'd have an old maid on his hands. And, Pat"—Rintoon leaned closer—"Willard don't talk to the old man like he does to other people."

"She didn't look so bad to me," Brennan said.

"You been down on Sasabe Creek too long," Rintoon glanced at him again. "What were you saying about losing your horse to Tenvoorde?"

"Oh, I went to see him about buying some yearlings—"

"On credit," Rintoon said.

Brennan nodded. "Though I was going to pay him some of it cash. I told him to name a fair interest rate and he'd have it in two years. But he said no. Cash on the line. No cash, no yearlings. I needed three hundred to make the deal, but I only had fifty. Then when I was going he said, 'Patrick'—you know how he talks—'I'll give you a chance to get your yearlings free,' and all the time he's eyeing this claybank mare I had along. He said, 'You bet your mare and your fifty dollars cash, I'll put up what yearlings you need, and we'll race your mare against one of my string for the winner.' "

Ed Rintoon said, "And you lost."

"By a country mile."

"Pat, that don't sound like you. Why didn't you take what your fifty would buy and get on home?"

"Because I needed these yearlings plus a good seed bull. I could've bought the bull, but I wouldn't have had the yearlings to build on. That's what I told Mr. Tenvoorde. I said, 'This deal's as good as the stock you're selling me. If you're taking that kind of money for a seed bull and yearlings, then you know they can produce. You're sure of getting your money.' "

"You got stock down on your Sasabe place," Rintoon said.

"Not like you think. They wintered poorly and I got a lot of building to do."

"Who's tending your herd now?"

"I still got those two Mexican boys."

"You should've known better than to go to Tenvoorde."

"I didn't have a chance. He's the only man close enough with the stock I want."

"But a bet like that—how could you fall into it? You know he'd have a pony to outstrip yours."

"Well, that was the chance I had to take."

They rode along in silence for a few minutes before Brennan asked, "Where they coming from?"

Rintoon grinned at him. "Their honeymoon. Willard made the agent put on a special run just for the two of them. Made a big fuss while Doretta tried to hide her head."

"Then"—Brennan grinned—"I'm obliged to Mr. Mims, else I'd still be waiting back there with my saddle and my Henry."

Later on, topping a rise that was thick with jack pine, they were suddenly in view of the Sasabe station and the creek beyond it, as they came out of the trees and started down the mesquite-dotted sweep of the hillside.

Rintoon checked his timepiece. The regular run was due here at five o'clock. He was surprised to see that it was only ten minutes after four. He remembered then, his mind picturing Willard Mims as he chartered the special coach.

Brennan said, "I'm getting off here at Sasabe."

"How'll you get over to your place?"

"Hank'll lend me a horse."

As they drew nearer, Rintoon was squinting, studying the three adobe houses and the corral in back. "I don't see anybody," he said. "Hank's usually out in the yard. Him or his boy."

Brennan said, "They don't expect you for an hour. That's it."

"Man, we make enough noise for somebody to come out."

Rintoon swung the teams toward the adobes, slowing them as Brennan pushed his boot against the brake lever, and they came to a stop exactly even with the front of the main adobe.

"Hank!"

Rintoon looked from the door of the adobe out over the yard. He called the name again, but there was no answer. He frowned. "The damn place sounds deserted," he said.

Brennan saw the driver's eyes drop to the sawed-off shotgun and Brennan's Henry on the floor of the boot, and then he was looking over the yard again.

"Where in hell would Hank've gone to?"

A sound came from the adobe. A boot scraping—that or something like it—and the next moment a man was standing in the open doorway. He was bearded, a dark beard faintly streaked with gray and in need of a trim. He was watching them calmly, almost indifferently, and leveling a Colt at them at the same time.

He moved out into the yard and now another man, armed with a shotgun, came out of the adobe. The bearded one held his gun on the door of the coach. The shotgun was leveled at Brennan and Rintoon.

"You-all drop your guns and come on down." He wore range clothes, soiled and sun bleached, and he held the shotgun calmly as if doing this was not something new. He was younger than the bearded one by at least ten years.

Brennan raised his revolver from its holster and the one with the shotgun said, "Gently, now," and grinned as Brennan dropped it over the wheel.

Rintoon, not wearing a handgun, had not moved.

"If you got something down in that boot," the one with the shotgun said to him, "haul it out."

Rintoon muttered something under his breath. He reached down and took hold of Brennan's Henry rifle lying next to the sawed-off shotgun, his finger slipping through the trigger guard. He came up with it hesitantly, and Brennan whispered, barely moving his lips, "Don't be crazy."

Standing up, turning, Rintoon hesitated again, then let the rifle fall.

"That all you got?"

Rintoon nodded. "That's all."

"Then come on down."

Rintoon turned his back. He bent over to climb down, his foot reaching for the wheel below, and his hand closed on the sawed-off shotgun. Brennan whispered, "Don't do it!"

Rintoon mumbled something that came out as a growl. Brennan leaned toward him as if to give him a hand down. "You got two shots. What if there're more than two of them?"

Rintoon grunted, "Look out, Pat!" His hand gripped the shotgun firmly.

Then he was turning, jumping from the wheel, the stubby scattergun flashing head-high—and at the same moment a single revolver shot blasted the stillness. Brennan saw Rintoon crumple to the ground, the shotgun falling next to him, and he was suddenly aware of powder smoke and a man framed in the window of the adobe.

The one with the shotgun said, "Well, that just saves some time," and he glanced around as the third man came out of the adobe. "Chink, I swear you hit him in midair."

"I was waiting for that old man to pull something," said the one called Chink. He wore two low-slung, crossed cartridge belts and his second Colt was still in its holster.

Brennan jumped down and rolled Rintoon over gently, holding

his head off the ground. He looked at the motionless form and then at Chink. "He's dead."

Chink stood with his legs apart and looked down at Brennan indifferently. "Sure he is."

"You didn't have to kill him."

Chink shrugged. "I would've, sooner or later."

"Why?"

"That's the way it is."

The man with the beard had not moved. He said now, quietly, "Chink, you shut your mouth." Then he glanced at the man with the shotgun and said, in the same tone, "Billy-Jack, get them out of there," and nodded toward the coach.

CHAPTER TWO

Kneeling next to Rintoon, Brennan studied them. He watched Billy-Jack open the coach door, saw his mouth soften to a grin as Doretta Mims came out first. Her eyes went to Rintoon, but shifted away quickly. Willard Mims hesitated, then stepped down, stumbling in his haste as Billy-Jack pointed the shotgun at him. He stood next to his wife and stared unblinkingly at Rintoon's body.

That one, Brennan was thinking, looking at the man with the beard—that's the one to watch. He's calling it, and he doesn't look as though he gets excited. . . . And the one called Chink. . . .

Brennan's eyes went to him. He was standing hip-cocked, his hat on the back of his head and the drawstring from it pulled tight beneath his lower lip, his free hand fingering the string idly, the other hand holding the long-barreled .44 Colt, pointed down but cocked.

He wants somebody to try something, Brennan thought. He's itching for it. He wears two guns and he thinks he's good. Well, maybe he is. But he's young, the youngest of the three, and he's anxious. His gaze stayed on Chink and it went through his mind: Don't even reach for a cigarette when he's around.

The one with the beard said, "Billy-Jack, get up on top of the coach."

Brennan's eyes raised, watching the man step from the wheel hub to the boot and then kneel on the driver's seat. He's number-three man, Brennan thought. He keeps looking at the woman. But don't bet him short. He carries a big-gauge gun.

"Frank, there ain't nothing up here but an old saddle."

The one with the beard—Frank Usher—raised his eyes. "Look under it."

"Ain't nothing there either."

Usher's eyes went to Willard Mims, then swung slowly to Brennan. "Where's the mail?"

"I wouldn't know," Brennan said.

Frank Usher looked at Willard Mims again. "You tell me."

"This isn't the stage," Willard Mims said hesitantly. His face relaxed then, almost to the point of smiling. "You made a mistake. The regular stage isn't due for almost an hour." He went on, excitement rising in his voice, "That's what you want, the stage that's due here at five. This is one I chartered." He smiled now. "See, me and my wife are just coming back from a honeymoon and, you know—"

Frank Usher looked at Brennan. "Is that right?"

"Of course it is!" Mims's voice rose. "Go in and check the schedule."

"I'm asking this man."

Brennan shrugged. "I wouldn't know."

"He don't know anything," Chink said.

Billy-Jack came down off the coach and Usher said to him, "Go in and look for a schedule." He nodded toward Doretta Mims. "Take that woman with you. Have her put some coffee on, and something to eat."

Brennan said, "What did you do with Hank?"

Frank Usher's dull eyes moved to Brennan. "Who's he?"

"The station man here."

Chink grinned and waved his revolver, pointing it off beyond the main adobe. "He's over yonder in the well."

Usher said, "Does that answer it?"

"What about his boy?"

"He's with him," Usher said. "Anything else?"

Brennan shook his head slowly. "That's enough." He knew they were both dead and suddenly he was very much afraid of this dull-eyed, soft-voiced man with the beard; it took an effort to keep himself calm. He watched Billy-Jack take Doretta by the arm. She looked imploringly at her husband, holding back, but he made no move to help her. Billy-Jack jerked her arm roughly and she went with him.

Willard Mims said, "He'll find the schedule. Like I said, it's due at five o'clock. I can see how you made the mistake"—Willard was smiling—"thinking we were the regular stage. Hell, we were just going home . . . down to Bisbee. You'll see, five o'clock sharp that regular passenger-mail run'll pull in."

"He's a talker," Chink said.

Billy-Jack appeared in the doorway of the adobe. "Frank, five o'clock, sure as hell!" He waved a sheet of yellow paper.

"See!" Willard Mims was grinning excitedly. "Listen, you let us go and we'll be on our way"—his voice rose—"and I swear to God we'll never breathe we saw a thing."

Chink shook his head. "He's somethin'."

"Listen, I swear to God we won't tell *anything*!"

"I know you won't," Frank Usher said. He looked at Brennan and nodded toward Mims. "Where'd you find him?"

"We just met."

"Do you go along with what he's saying?"

"If I said yes," Brennan answered, "you wouldn't believe me. And you'd be right."

A smile almost touched Frank Usher's mouth. "Dumb even talking about it, isn't it?"

"I guess it is," Brennan said.

"You know what's going to happen to you?" Usher asked him tonelessly.

Brennan nodded, without answering.

Frank Usher studied him in silence. Then, "Are you scared?"

Brennan nodded again. "Sure I am."

"You're honest about it. I'll say that for you."

"I don't know of a better time to be honest," Brennan said.

Chink said, "That damn well's going to be chock full."

Willard Mims had listened with disbelief, his eyes wide. Now he said hurriedly, "Wait a minute! What're you listening to him for? I told you, I swear to God I won't say one word about this. If you don't trust him, then keep him here! I don't know this man. I'm not speaking for him, anyway."

"I'd be inclined to trust him before I would you," Frank Usher said.

"He's got nothing to do with it! We picked him up out on the desert!"

Chink raised his .44 waist high, looking at Willard Mims, and said, "Start running for that well and see if you can make it."

"Man, be reasonable!"

Frank Usher shook his head. "You aren't leaving, and you're not going to be standing here when that stage pulls in. You can scream and carry on, but that's the way it is."

"What about my wife?"

"I can't help her being a woman."

Willard Mims was about to say something, but stopped. His eyes went to the adobe, then back to Usher. He lowered his voice and all the excitement was gone from it. "You know who she is?"

He moved closer to Usher. "She's the daughter of old man Gateway, who happens to own part of the third richest copper mine in Arizona. You know what that amounts to? To date, three quarters of a million dollars." He said this slowly, looking straight at Frank Usher.

"Make a point out of it," Usher said.

"Man, it's staring you right in the face! You got the daughter of a man who's practically a millionaire. His only daughter! What do you think he'd pay to get her back?"

Frank Usher said, "I don't know. What?"

"Whatever you ask! You sit here waiting for a two-bit holdup and you got a gold mine right in your hands!"

"How do I know she's his daughter?"

Willard Mims looked at Brennan. "You were talking to that driver. Didn't he tell you?"

Brennan hesitated. If the man wanted to bargain with his wife, that was his business. It would give them time; that was the main thing. Brennan nodded. "That's right. His wife is Doretta Gateway."

"Where do you come in?" Usher asked Willard Mims.

"I'm Mr. Gateway's general manager on the Montezuma operation."

Frank Usher was silent now, staring at Mims. Finally he said, "I suppose you'd be willing to ride in with a note."

"Certainly," Mims quickly replied.

"And we'd never see you again."

"Would I save my own skin and leave my wife here?"

Usher nodded. "I believe you would."

"Then there's no use talking about it." Mims shrugged and, watching him, Brennan knew he was acting, taking a long chance.

"We can talk about it," Frank Usher said, "because if we do it, we do it my way." He glanced at the house. "Billy-Jack!" Then to Brennan, "You and him go sit over against the wall."

Billy-Jack came out, and from the wall of the adobe Brennan and Willard watched the three outlaws. They stood in close, and Frank Usher was doing the talking. After a few minutes Billy-Jack went into the adobe again and came out with the yellow stage schedule and an envelope. Usher took them and, against the door of the Concord, wrote something on the back of the schedule.

He came toward them folding the paper into the envelope. He sealed the envelope and handed it with the pencil to Willard Mims. "You put Gateway's name on it and where to find him. Mark it personal and urgent."

Willard Mims said, "I can see him myself and tell him."

"You will," Frank Usher said, "but not how you think. You're going to stop on the main road one mile before you get to Bisbee and give that envelope to somebody passing in. The note tells Gateway you have something to tell him about his daughter and to come alone. When he goes out, you'll tell him the story. If he says no, then he never sees his daughter again. If he says yes, he's to bring fifty thousand in U.S. script divided in three saddlebags, to a place up back of the Sasabe. And he brings it alone."

Mims said, "What if there isn't that much cash on hand?"

"That's his problem."

"Well, why can't I go right to his house and tell him?"

"Because Billy-Jack's going to be along to bring you back after you tell him. And I don't want him someplace he can get cornered."

"Oh. . . ."

"That's whether he says yes or no," Frank Usher added.

Mims was silent for a moment. "But how'll Mr. Gateway know where to come?"

"If he agrees, Billy-Jack'll give him directions."

Mims said, "Then when he comes out you'll let us go? Is that it?"

"That's it."

"When do we leave?"

"Right this minute."

"Can I say good-bye to my wife?"

"We'll do it for you."

Brennan watched Billy-Jack come around from the corral, leading two horses. Willard Mims moved toward one of them and they both mounted. Billy-Jack reined his horse suddenly, crowding Mims to turn with him, then slapped Mims's horse on the rump and spurred after it as the horse broke to a run.

Watching them, his eyes half closed, Frank Usher said, "That boy puts his wife up on the stake and then he wants to kiss her good-bye." He glanced at Brennan. "You figure that one for me."

Brennan shook his head. "What I'd like to know is why you only asked for fifty thousand."

Frank Usher shrugged. "I'm not greedy."

CHAPTER THREE

Chink turned as the two horses splashed over the creek and grew gradually smaller down the road. He looked at Brennan and then his eyes went to Frank Usher. "We don't have a need for this one, Frank."

Usher's dull eyes flicked toward him. "You bring around the horses and I'll worry about him."

"We might as well do it now as later," Chink said.

"We're taking him with us."

"What for?"

"Because I say so. That reason enough?"

"Frank, we could run him for the well and both take a crack at him."

"Get the horses," Frank Usher said flatly, and stared at Chink until the gunman turned and walked away.

Brennan said, "I'd like to bury this man before we go."

Usher shook his head. "Put him in the well."

"That's no fit place!"

Usher stared at Brennan for a long moment. "Don't push your luck. He goes in the well, whether you do it or Chink does."

Brennan pulled Rintoon's limp body up over his shoulder and carried him across the yard. When he returned, Chink was coming around the adobe with three horses already saddled. Frank Usher stood near the house and now Doretta Mims appeared in the doorway.

Usher looked at her. "You'll have to fork one of these like the rest of us. There ain't no lady's saddle about."

She came out, neither answering nor looking at him.

Usher called to Brennan, "Cut one out of that team and shoo the rest," nodding to the stagecoach.

Minutes later the Sasabe station was deserted.

They followed the creek west for almost an hour before swinging south toward high country. Leaving the creek, Brennan had thought: Five more miles and I'm home. And his eyes hung on the long shallow cup of the Sasabe valley until they entered a trough that climbed winding ahead of them through the hills, and the valley was no longer in view.

Frank Usher led them single file—Doretta Mims, followed by Brennan, and Chink bringing up the rear. Chink rode slouched, swaying with the movement of his dun mare, chewing idly on the drawstring of his hat, and watching Brennan.

Brennan kept his eyes on the woman much of the time. For almost a mile, as they rode along the creek, he had watched her body shaking silently and he knew that she was crying. She had very nearly cried mounting the horse—pulling her skirts down almost desperately, then sitting, holding on to the saddle horn with both hands, biting her lower lip and not looking at them. Chink had sidestepped his dun close to her and said something, and she had turned her head quickly as the color rose from her throat over her face.

They dipped down into a barranca thick with willow and cottonwood and followed another stream that finally disappeared into the rocks at the far end. And after that they began to climb again. For some time they rode through the soft gloom of timber, following switchbacks as the slope became steeper, then came out into the open and crossed a bare gravelly slope, the sandstone peaks above them cold pink in the fading sunlight.

They were nearing the other side of the open grade when Frank Usher said, "Here we are."

Brennan looked beyond him and now he could make out, through the pines they were approaching, a weather-scarred stone-and-log hut built snugly against the steep wall of sandstone. Against one side of the hut was a hide-covered lean-to. He heard Frank Usher say, "Chink, you get the man making a fire and I'll get the woman fixing supper."

There had not been time to eat what the woman had prepared at the stage station and now Frank Usher and Chink ate hungrily, hunkered down a dozen yards out from the lean-to where Brennan and the woman stood.

Brennan took a plate of the jerky and day-old pan bread, but Doretta Mims did not touch the food. She stood next to him, half turned from him, and continued to stare through the trees across the bare slope in the direction they had come. Once Brennan said to her, "You better eat something," but she did not answer him.

When they were finished, Frank Usher ordered them into the hut.

"You stay there the night . . . and if either of you comes near the door, we'll let go, no questions asked. That plain?"

The woman went in hurriedly. When Brennan entered he saw her huddled against the back wall near a corner.

The sod-covered hut was windowless, and he could barely

make her out in the dimness. He wanted to go and sit next to her, but it went through his mind that most likely she was as afraid of him as she was of Frank Usher and Chink. So he made room for himself against the wall where they had placed the saddles, folding a saddle blanket to rest his elbow on as he eased himself to the dirt floor. Let her try and get hold of herself, he thought; then maybe she will want somebody to talk to.

He made a cigarette and lit it, seeing the mask of her face briefly as the match flared, then he eased himself lower until his head was resting against a saddle, and smoked in the dim silence.

Soon the hut was full dark. Now he could not see the woman, though he imagined that he could feel her presence. Outside, Usher and Chink had added wood to the cook fire in front of the lean-to and the warm glow of it illuminated the doorless opening of the hut.

They'll sit by the fire, Brennan thought, and one of them will always be awake. You'd get about one step through that door and *bam.* Maybe Frank would aim low, but Chink would shoot to kill. He became angry thinking of Chink, but there was nothing he could do about it and he drew on the cigarette slowly to make himself relax, thinking: Take it easy: you've got the woman to consider. He thought of her as his responsibility and not even a doubt entered his mind that she was not. She was a woman, alone. The reason was as simple as that.

He heard her move as he was snubbing out the cigarette. He lay still and he knew that she was coming toward him. She knelt as she reached his side.

"Do you know what they've done with my husband?"

He could picture her drawn face, eyes staring wide open in the darkness. He raised himself slowly and felt her stiffen as he touched her arm. "Sit down here and you'll be more comfortable." He moved over to let her sit on the saddle blanket. "Your husband's all right," he said.

"Where is he?"

"They didn't tell you?"

"No."

Brennan paused. "One of them took him to Bisbee to see your father."

"My father?"

"To ask him to pay to get you back."

"Then my husband's all right." She was relieved, and it was in the sound of her voice.

Brennan said, after a moment, "Why don't you go to sleep now? You can rest back on one of these saddles."

"I'm not tired."

"Well, you will be if you don't get some sleep."

She said then, "They must have known all the time that we were coming."

Brennan said nothing.

"Didn't they?"

"I don't know, ma'am."

"How else would they know about . . . who my father is?"

"Maybe so."

"One of them must have been in Contention and heard my husband charter the coach. Perhaps he had visited Bisbee and knew that my father . . ." Her voice trailed off because she was speaking more to herself than to Brennan.

After a pause Brennan said, "You sound like you feel a little better."

He heard her exhale slowly and he could imagine she was trying to smile.

"Yes, I believe I do now," she replied.

"Your husband will be back sometime tomorrow morning," Brennan said to her.

She touched his arm lightly. "I *do* feel better, Mr. Brennan."

He was surprised that she remembered his name. Rintoon had

mentioned it only once, hours before. "I'm glad you do. Now, why don't you try to sleep?"

She eased back gently until she was lying down and for a few minutes there was silence.

"Mr. Brennan?"

"Yes, ma'am."

"I'm terribly sorry about your friend."

"Who?"

"The driver."

"Oh. Thank you."

"I'll remember him in my prayers," she said, and after this she did not speak again.

Brennan smoked another cigarette, then sat unmoving for what he judged to be at least a half hour, until he was sure Doretta Mims was asleep.

Now he crawled across the dirt floor to the opposite wall. He went down on his stomach and edged toward the door, keeping close to the wall. Pressing his face close to the opening, he could see, off to the right side, the fire, dying down now. The shape of a man wrapped in a blanket was lying full length on the other side of it.

Brennan rose slowly, hugging the wall. He inched his head out to see the side of the fire closest to the lean-to, and as he did he heard the unmistakable click of a revolver being cocked. Abruptly he brought his head in and went back to the saddle next to Doretta Mims.

CHAPTER FOUR

In the morning they brought Doretta Mims out to cook; then sent her back to the hut while they ate. When they had finished they let Brennan and Doretta come out to the lean-to.

Frank Usher said, "That wasn't a head I seen pokin' out the door last night, was it?"

"If it was," Brennan answered, "why didn't you shoot at it?"

"I about did. Lucky thing it disappeared," Usher said. "Whatever it was." And he walked away, through the trees to where the horses were picketed.

Chink sat down on a stump and began making a cigarette.

A few steps from Doretta Mims, Brennan leaned against the hut and began eating. He could see her profile as she turned her head to look out through the trees and across the open slope.

Maybe she *is* a little plain, he thought. Her nose doesn't have the kind of a clean-cut shape that stays in your mind. And her hair—if she didn't have it pulled back so tight she'd look a little younger, and happier. She could do something with her hair. She could do something with her clothes, too, to let you know she's a woman.

He felt sorry for her, seeing her biting her lower lip, still staring off through the trees. And for a reason he did not understand, though he knew it had nothing to do with sympathy, he felt very close to her, as if he had known her for a long time, as if he could look into her eyes—not just now, but anytime—and know what she was thinking. He realized that it was sympathy, in a sense, but not the feeling-sorry kind. He could picture her as a little girl, and self-consciously growing up, and he could imagine vaguely what her father was like. And now—a sensitive girl, afraid of saying the wrong thing; afraid of speaking out of turn even if it meant wondering about instead of knowing what had happened to her husband. Afraid of sounding silly, while men like her husband talked and talked and said nothing. But even having to listen to him, she would not speak against him, because he was her husband.

That's the kind of woman to have, Brennan thought. One that'll stick by you, no matter what. And, he thought, still looking at her, one that's got some insides to her. Not just all on the surface. Probably you would have to lose a woman like that to really appreciate her.

"Mrs. Mims."

She looked at him, her eyes still bearing the anxiety of watching through the trees.

"He'll come, Mrs. Mims. Pretty soon now."

Frank Usher returned and motioned them into the hut again. He talked to Chink for a few minutes and now the gunman walked off through the trees.

Looking out from the doorway of the hut, Brennan said over his shoulder, "One of them's going out now to watch for your husband." He glanced around at Doretta Mims and she answered him with a hesitant smile.

Frank Usher was standing by the lean-to when Chink came back through the trees some time later. He walked out to meet him.

"They coming?"

Chink nodded. "Starting across the slope."

Minutes later two horses came into view crossing the grade. As they came through the trees, Frank Usher called, "Tie up in the shade there!" He and Chink watched the two men dismount, then come across the clearing toward them.

"It's all set!" Willard Mims called.

Frank Usher waited until they reached him. "What'd he say?"

"He said he'd bring the money."

"That right, Billy-Jack?"

Billy-Jack nodded. "That's what he said." He was carrying Rintoon's sawed-off shotgun.

"You didn't suspect any funny business?"

Billy-Jack shook his head.

Usher fingered his beard gently, holding Mims with his gaze. "He can scare up that much money?"

"He said he could, though it will take most of today to do it."

"That means he'll come out tomorrow," Usher said.

Willard Mims nodded. "That's right."

Usher's eyes went to Billy-Jack. "You gave him directions?"

"Like you said, right to the mouth of that barranca, chock full of willow. Then one of us brings him in from there."

"You're sure he can find it?"

"I made him say it twice," Billy-Jack said. "Every turn."

Usher looked at Willard Mims again. "How'd he take it?"

"How do you think he took it?"

Usher was silent, staring at Mims. Then he began to stroke his beard again. "I'm asking you," he said.

Mims shrugged. "Of course, he was mad, but there wasn't anything he could do about it. He's a reasonable man."

Billy-Jack was grinning. "Frank, this time tomorrow we're sitting on top of the world."

Willard Mims nodded. "I think you made yourself a pretty good deal."

Frank Usher's eyes had not left Mims. "You want to stay here or go on back?"

"What?"

"You heard what I said."

"You mean you'd let me go . . . now?"

"We don't need you anymore."

Willard Mims's eyes flicked to the hut, then back to Frank Usher. He said, almost too eagerly, "I could go back now and lead old man Gateway out here in the morning."

"Sure you could," Usher said.

"Listen, I'd rather stay with my wife, but if it means getting the old man out here faster, then I think I better go back."

Usher nodded. "I know what you mean."

"You played square with me. By God, I'll play square with you."

Mims started to turn away.

Usher said, "Don't you want to see your wife first?"

Mims hesitated. "Well, the quicker I start traveling, the better. She'll understand."

"We'll see you tomorrow then, huh?"

Mims smiled. "About the same time." He hesitated. "All right to get going now?"

"Sure."

Mims backed away a few steps, still smiling, then turned and started to walk toward the trees. He looked back once and waved.

Frank Usher watched him, his eyes half closed in the sunlight. When Mims was almost to the trees, Usher said, quietly, "Chink, bust him."

Chink fired, the .44 held halfway between waist and shoulders, the long barrel raising slightly as he fired again and again until Mims went down, lying still as the heavy reports faded into dead silence.

CHAPTER FIVE

Frank Usher waited as Billy-Jack stooped next to Mims. He saw Billy-Jack look up, nodding his head.

"Get rid of him," Usher said, watching now as Billy-Jack dragged Mims's body through the trees to the slope and there let go of it. The lifeless body slid down the grade, raising dust, until it disappeared into the brush far below.

Frank Usher turned and walked back to the hut.

Brennan stepped aside as he reached the low doorway. Usher saw the woman on the floor, her face buried in the crook of her arm resting on one of the saddles, her shoulders moving convulsively as she sobbed.

"What's the matter with her?" he asked.

Brennan said nothing.

"I thought we were doing her a favor," Usher said. He walked over to her, his hand covering the butt of his revolver, and touched her arm with his booted toe. "Woman, don't you realize what you just got out of?"

"She didn't know he did it," Brennan said quietly.

Usher looked at him, momentarily surprised. "No, I don't guess she would, come to think of it." He looked down at Doretta Mims and nudged her again with his boot. "Didn't you know that boy was selling you? This whole idea was his, to save his own skin." Usher paused. "He was ready to leave you again just now . . . when I got awful sick of him way down deep inside."

Doretta Mims was not sobbing now, but still she did not raise her head.

Usher stared down at her. "That was some boy you were married to, would do a thing like that."

Looking from the woman to Frank Usher, Brennan said, almost angrily, "What he did was wrong, but going along with it and then shooting him was all right!"

Usher glanced sharply at Brennan. "If you can't see a difference, I'm not going to explain it to you." He turned and walked out.

Brennan stood looking down at the woman for a few moments, then went over to the door and sat down on the floor just inside it. After a while he could hear Doretta Mims crying again. And for a long time he sat listening to her muffled sobs as he looked out at the sunlit clearing, now and again seeing one of the three outlaws.

He judged it to be about noon when Frank Usher and Billy-Jack rode out, walking their horses across the clearing, then into the trees, with Chink standing looking after them.

They're getting restless, Brennan thought. If they're going to stay here until tomorrow, they've got to be sure nobody's followed their sign. But it would take the best San Carlos tracker to pick up what little sign we made from Sasabe.

He saw Chink walking leisurely back to the lean-to. Chink looked toward the hut and stopped. He stood hip-cocked, with his thumbs in his crossed gun belts.

"How many did that make?" Brennan asked.

"What?" Chink straightened slightly.

Brennan nodded to where Mims had been shot. "This morning."

"That was the seventh," Chink said.

"Were they all like that?" he asked.

"How do you mean?"

"In the back."

"I'll tell you this: Yours will be from the front."

"When?"

"Tomorrow before we leave. You can count on it."

"If your boss gives you the word."

"Don't worry about that," Chink said. Then, "You could make a run for it right now. It wouldn't be like just standing up gettin' it."

"I'll wait till tomorrow," Brennan said.

Chink shrugged and walked away.

After a few minutes Brennan realized that the hut was quiet. He turned to look at Doretta Mims. She was sitting up, staring at the opposite wall with a dazed expression.

Brennan moved to her side and sat down again. "Mrs. Mims, I'm sorry—"

"Why didn't you tell me it was his plan?"

"It wouldn't have helped anything."

She looked at Brennan now pleadingly. "He could have been doing it for all of us."

Brennan nodded. "Sure he could."

"But you don't believe that, do you?"

Brennan looked at her closely, at her eyes puffed from crying. "Mrs. Mims, you know your husband better than I did."

Her eyes lowered and she said quietly, "I feel very foolish sitting here. Terrible things have happened in these two days, yet all I can think of is myself. All I can do is look at myself and feel very foolish." Her eyes raised to his. "Do you know why, Mr. Brennan? Because I know now that my husband never cared for me; because I know that he married me for his own interest." She paused. "I saw an innocent man killed yesterday and I can't even find the decency within me to pray for him."

"Mrs. Mims, try and rest now."

She shook her head wearily. "I don't care what happens to me."

There was a silence before Brennan said, "When you get done feeling sorry for yourself I'll tell you something."

Her eyes came open and she looked at him, more surprised than hurt.

"Look," Brennan said. "You know it and I know it—your husband married you for your money; but you're alive and he's dead and that makes the difference. You can moon about being a fool till they shoot you tomorrow, or you can start thinking about saving your skin right now. But I'll tell you this—it will take both of us working together to stay alive."

"But he said he'd let us—"

"You think they're going to let us go after your dad brings the money? They've killed four people in less than twenty-four hours!"

"I don't care what happens to me!"

He took her shoulders and turned her toward him. "Well, I care about me, and I'm not going to get shot in the belly tomorrow because you feel sorry for yourself!"

"But I can't help!" Doretta pleaded.

"You don't know if you can or not. We've got to keep our eyes open and we've got to think, and when the chance comes we've got to take it quick or else forget about it." His face was close to hers and he was still gripping her shoulders. "These men will kill. They've done it before and they have nothing to lose. They're going to kill us. That means we've got nothing to lose. Now, you think about that awhile."

He left her and went back to the door.

Brennan was called out of the hut later in the afternoon, as Usher and Billy-Jack rode in. They had shot a mule deer and Billy-Jack carried a hindquarter dangling from his saddle horn. Brennan was told to dress it down, enough for supper, and the rest to be stripped and hung up to dry.

"But you take care of the supper first," Frank Usher said, adding that the woman wasn't in fit condition for cooking. "I don't want burned meat just 'cause she's in a state over her husband."

After they had eaten, Brennan took meat and coffee in to Doretta Mims.

She looked up as he offered it to her. "I don't care for anything."

He was momentarily angry, but it passed off and he said, "Suit yourself." He placed the cup and plate on the floor and went outside to finish preparing the jerky.

By the time he finished, dusk had settled over the clearing and the inside of the hut was dark as he stepped inside.

He moved to her side and his foot kicked over the tin cup. He stooped quickly, picking up the cup and plate, and even in the dimness he could see that she had eaten most of the food.

"Mr. Brennan, I'm sorry for the way I've acted." She hesitated. "I thought you would understand, else I'd never have told you about—about how I felt."

"It's not a question of my understanding," Brennan said.

"I'm sorry I told you," Doretta Mims said.

He moved closer to her and knelt down, sitting back on his heels. "Look. Maybe I know how you feel, better than you think.

But that's not important. Right now you don't need sympathy as much as you need a way to stay alive."

"I can't help the way I feel," she said obstinately.

Brennan was momentarily silent. He said then, "Did you love him?"

"I was married to him!"

"That's not what I asked you. While everybody's being honest, just tell me if you loved him."

She hesitated, looking down at her hands. "I'm not sure."

"But you wanted to be in love with him, more than anything."

Her head nodded slowly. "Yes."

"Did you ever think for a minute that he loved you?"

"That's not a fair question!"

"Answer it anyway!"

She hesitated again. "No, I didn't."

He said, almost brutally, "Then what have you lost outside of a little pride?"

"You don't understand," she said.

"You're afraid you can't get another man—is that what it is? Even if he married you for money, at least he married you. He was the first and last chance as far as you were concerned, so you grabbed him."

"What are you trying to do, strip me of what little self-respect I have left?"

"I'm trying to strip you of this foolishness! You think you're too plain to get a man?"

She bit her lower lip and looked away from him.

"You think nobody'll have you because you bite your lip and can't say more than two words at a time?"

"Mr. Brennan—"

"Listen, you're as much woman as any of them. A hell of a lot more than some, but you've got to realize it! You've got to do something about it!"

"I can't help it if—"

"Shut up with that I-can't-help-it talk! If you can't help it, nobody can. All your life you've been sitting around waiting for something to happen to you. Sometimes you have to walk up and take what you want."

Suddenly he brought her to him, his arms circling her shoulders, and he kissed her, holding his lips to hers until he felt her body relax slowly and at the same time he knew that she was kissing him.

His lips brushed her cheek and he said, close to her, "We're going to stay alive. You're going to do exactly what I say when the time comes, and we're going to get out of here." Her hair brushed his cheek softly and he knew that she was nodding yes.

CHAPTER SIX

During the night he opened his eyes and crawled to the lighter silhouette of the doorway. Keeping close to the front wall, he looked out and across to the low-burning fire. One of them, a shadowy form that he could not recognize, sat facing the hut. He did not move, but by the way he was sitting Brennan knew he was awake. You're running out of time, Brennan thought. But there was nothing he could do.

The sun was not yet above the trees when Frank Usher appeared in the doorway. He saw that Brennan was awake and he said, "Bring the woman out," turning away as he said it.

Her eyes were closed, but they opened as Brennan touched her shoulder, and he knew that she had not been asleep. She looked up at him calmly, her features softly shadowed.

"Stay close to me," he said. "Whatever we do, stay close to me."

They went out to the lean-to and Brennan built the fire as Doretta got the coffee and venison ready to put on.

Brennan moved slowly, as if he were tired, as if he had given up hope; but his eyes were alive and most of the time his gaze stayed with the three men—watching them eat, watching them make cigarettes as they squatted in a half circle, talking, but too far away for their voices to be heard. Finally, Chink rose and went off into the trees. He came back with his horse, mounted, and rode off into the trees again but in the other direction, toward the open grade.

It went through Brennan's mind: He's going off like he did yesterday morning, but this time to wait for Gateway. Yesterday on foot, but today on his horse, which means he's going farther down to wait for him. And Frank went somewhere yesterday morning. Frank went over to where the horses are. He suddenly felt an excitement inside of him, deep within his stomach, and he kept his eyes on Frank Usher.

A moment later Usher stood up and started off toward the trees, calling back something to Billy-Jack about the horses—and Brennan could hardly believe his eyes.

Now. It's now. You know that, don't you? It's now or never. God help me. God help me think of something! And suddenly it was in his mind. It was less than half a chance, but it was something, and it came to him because it was the only thing about Billy-Jack that stood out in his mind, besides the shotgun. *He was always looking at Doretta!*

She was in front of the lean-to, and he moved toward her, turning his back to Billy-Jack sitting with Rintoon's shotgun across his lap.

"Go in the hut and start unbuttoning your dress." He half whispered it and saw her eyes widen as he said it. "Go on! Billy-Jack will come in. Act surprised. Embarrassed. Then smile at him." She hesitated, starting to bite her lip. "Damn it, go on!"

He poured himself a cup of coffee, not looking at her as she walked away. Putting the coffee down, he saw Billy-Jack's eyes following her.

"Want a cup?" Brennan called to him. "There's about one left."

Billy-Jack shook his head and turned the sawed-off shotgun on Brennan as he saw him approaching.

Brennan took a sip of the coffee. "Aren't you going to look in on that?" He nodded toward the hut.

"What do you mean?"

"The woman," Brennan said matter-of-factly. He took another sip of the coffee.

"What about her?" Billy-Jack asked.

Brennan shrugged. "I thought you were taking turns."

"What?"

"Now, look, you can't be so young. I got to draw you a map—" Brennan smiled. "Oh, I see. . . . Frank didn't say anything to you. Or Chink. . . . Keeping her for themselves. . . ."

Billy-Jack's eyes flicked to the hut, then back to Brennan. "They were with her?"

"Well, all I know is Frank went in there yesterday morning and Chink yesterday afternoon while you were gone." He took another sip of the coffee and threw out what was left in the cup. Turning, he said, "No skin off my nose," and walked slowly back to the lean-to.

He began scraping the tin plates, his head down, but watching Billy-Jack. Let it sink through that thick skull of yours. But do it quick! Come on, move, you animal!

There! He watched Billy-Jack walk slowly toward the hut. God, make him move faster! Billy-Jack was out of view then beyond the corner of the hut.

All right. Brennan put down the tin plate he was holding and moved quickly, noiselessly, to the side of the hut and edged along the rough logs until he reached the corner. He listened first before he looked around. Billy-Jack had gone inside.

He wanted to make sure, some way, that Billy-Jack would be looking at Doretta, but there was not time. And then he was moving again—along the front, and suddenly he was inside the hut, seeing the back of Billy-Jack's head, seeing him turning, and a glimpse of Doretta's face, and the sawed-off shotgun coming around. One of his hands shot out to grip the stubby barrel, pushing it, turning it up and back violently, and the other hand closed over the trigger guard before it jerked down on Billy-Jack's wrist.

Deafeningly, a shot exploded, with the twin barrels jammed under the outlaw's jaw. Smoke and a crimson smear, and Brennan was on top of him wrenching the shotgun from squeezed fingers, clutching Billy-Jack's revolver as he came to his feet.

He heard Doretta gasp, still with the ringing in his ears, and he said, "Don't look at him!" already turning to the doorway as he jammed the Colt into his empty holster.

Frank Usher was running across the clearing, his gun in his hand.

Brennan stepped into the doorway leveling the shotgun. "Frank, hold it there!"

Usher stopped dead, but in the next second he was aiming, his revolver coming up even with his face, and Brennan's hand squeezed the second trigger of the shotgun.

Usher screamed and went down, grabbing his knees, and he rolled to his side as he hit the ground. His right hand came up, still holding the Colt.

"Don't do it, Frank!" Brennan had dropped the scattergun and now Billy-Jack's revolver was in his hand. He saw Usher's gun coming in line, and he fired, aiming dead center at the half-reclined figure, hearing the sharp, heavy report, and seeing Usher's gun hand raise straight up into the air as he slumped over on his back.

Brennan hesitated. Get him out of there, quick. Chink's not deaf!

He ran out to Frank Usher and dragged him back to the hut, laying him next to Billy-Jack. He jammed Usher's pistol into his belt. Then, "Come on!" he told Doretta, and took her hand and ran out of the hut and across the clearing toward the side where the horses were.

They moved into the denser pines, where he stopped and pulled her down next to him in the warm sand. Then he rolled over on his stomach and parted the branches to look back out across the clearing.

The hut was to the right. Straight across were more pines, but they were scattered thinly, and through them he could see the sand-colored expanse of the open grade. Chink would come that way, Brennan knew. There was no other way he could.

CHAPTER SEVEN

Close to him, Doretta said, "We could leave before he comes." She was afraid, and it was in the sound of her voice.

"No," Brennan said. "We'll finish this. When Chink comes we'll finish it once and for all."

"But you don't know! How can you be sure you'll—"

"Listen, I'm not sure of anything, but I know what I have to do." She was silent and he said quietly, "Move back and stay close to the ground."

And as he looked across the clearing his eyes caught the dark speck of movement beyond the trees, out on the open slope. There he was. It had to be him. Brennan could feel the sharp knot in his stomach again as he watched, as the figure grew larger.

Now he was sure. Chink was on foot leading his horse, not coming straight across, but angling higher up on the slope. He'll come in where the trees are thicker, Brennan thought. He'll come out beyond the lean-to and you won't see him until he turns the corner of the hut. That's it. He can't climb the slope back of the hut, so he'll have to come around the front way.

He estimated the distance from where he was lying to the front of the hut—seventy or eighty feet—and his thumb eased back the hammer of the revolver in front of him.

There was a dead silence for perhaps ten minutes before he heard, coming from beyond the hut, "Frank?" Silence again. Then, "Where the hell are you?"

Brennan waited, feeling the smooth, heavy, hickory grip of the Colt in his hand, his finger lightly caressing the trigger. It was in his mind to fire as soon as Chink turned the corner. He was ready. But it came and it went.

It went as he saw Chink suddenly, unexpectedly, slip around the corner of the hut and flatten himself against the wall, his gun pointed toward the door. Brennan's front sight was dead on Chink's belt, but he couldn't pull the trigger. Not like this. He watched Chink edge slowly toward the door.

"Throw it down, boy!"

Chink moved and Brennan squeezed the trigger a split second late. He fired again, hearing the bullet thump solidly into the door frame, but it was too late. Chink was inside.

Brennan let his breath out slowly, relaxing somewhat. Well, that's what you get. You wait, and all you do is make it harder for yourself. He could picture Chink now looking at Usher and Billy-Jack. That'll give him something to think about. Look at them good. Then look at the door you've got to come out of sooner or later.

I'm glad he's seeing them like that. And he thought then: How long could you stand something like that? He can cover up Billy-Jack and stand it a little longer. But when dark comes . . . If he holds out till dark he's got a chance. And now he was sorry he had not pulled the trigger before. You got to make him come out, that's all.

"Chink!"

There was no answer.

"Chink, come on out!"

Suddenly gunfire came from the doorway and Brennan, hugging the ground, could hear the swishing of the bullets through the foliage above him.

Don't throw it away, he thought, looking up again. He backed up and moved over a few yards to take up a new position. He'd be on the left side of the doorway as you look at it, Brennan thought, to shoot on an angle like that.

He sighted on the inside edge of the door frame and called, "Chink, come out and get it!" He saw the powder flash, and he fired on top of it, cocked and fired again. Then silence.

Now you don't know, Brennan thought. He reloaded and called out, "Chink!" but there was no answer, and he thought: You just keep digging your hole deeper.

Maybe you did hit him. No, that's what he wants you to think. Walk in the door and you'll find out. He'll wait now. He'll take it slow and start adding up his chances. Wait till night? That's his best bet—but he can't count on his horse being there then. I could have worked around and run it off. And he knows he wouldn't be worth a damn on foot, even if he did get away. So the longer he waits, the less he can count on his horse.

All right, what would you do? Immediately he thought: I'd count shots. So you hear five shots go off in a row and you make a break out the door, and while you're doing it the one shooting picks up another gun. But even picking up another gun takes time.

He studied the distance from the doorway to the corner of the hut. Three long strides. Out of sight in less than three seconds. That's if he's thinking of it. And if he tried it, you'd have only that long to aim and fire. Unless . . .

Unless Doretta pulls off the five shots. He thought about this for some time before he was sure it could be done without endangering her. But first you have to give him the idea.

He rolled to his side to pull Usher's gun from his belt. Then, holding it in his left hand, he emptied it at the doorway. Silence followed.

I'm reloading now, Chink. Get it through your cat-eyed head. I'm reloading and you've got time to do something.

He explained it to Doretta unhurriedly—how she would wait about ten minutes before firing the first time; she would count to five and fire again, and so on until the gun was empty. She was behind the thick bole of a pine and only the gun would be exposed as she fired.

She said, "And if he doesn't come out?"

"Then we'll think of something else."

Their faces were close. She leaned toward him, closing her eyes, and kissed him softly. "I'll be waiting," she said.

Brennan moved off through the trees, circling wide, well back from the edge of the clearing. He came to the thin section directly across from Doretta's position and went quickly from tree to tree, keeping to the shadows until he was into thicker pines again. He saw Chink's horse off to the left of him. Only a few minutes remained as he came out of the trees to the off side of the lean-to, and there he went down to his knees, keeping his eyes on the corner of the hut.

The first shot rang out and he heard it *whump* into the front of the hut. One . . . then the second . . . two . . . he was counting them, not moving his eyes from the front edge of the hut . . . three . . . four . . . be ready. . . . Five! Now, Chink!

He heard him—hurried steps on the packed sand—and almost immediately he saw him cutting sharply around the edge of the hut, stopping, leaning against the wall, breathing heavily but thinking he was safe. Then Brennan stood up.

"Here's one facing you, Chink."

He saw the look of surprise, the momentary expression of shock, a full second before Chink's revolver flashed up from his side and Brennan's finger tightened on the trigger. With the report Chink lurched back against the wall, a look of bewilderment still on his face, although he was dead even as he slumped to the ground.

Brennan holstered the revolver and did not look at Chink as he walked past him around to the front of the hut. He suddenly felt tired, but it was the kind of tired feeling you enjoyed, like the bone weariness and sense of accomplishment you felt seeing your last cow punched through the market chute.

He thought of old man Tenvoorde, and only two days ago trying to buy the yearlings from him. He still didn't have any yearlings.

What the hell do you feel so good about?

Still, he couldn't help smiling. Not having money to buy stock seemed like such a little trouble. He saw Doretta come out of the trees and he walked on across the clearing.

Only Good Ones

Picture the ground rising on the east side of the pasture with scrub trees thick on the slope and pines higher up. This is where everybody was. Not all in one place but scattered in small groups: about a dozen men in the scrub, the front-line men, the shooters who couldn't just stand around. They'd fire at the shack when they felt like it or, when Mr. Tanner passed the word, they would all fire at once. Other people were up in the pines and on the road which ran along the crest of the hill, some three hundred yards from the shack across the pasture. Those watching made bets whether the man in the shack would give himself up or get shot first.

It was Saturday and that's why everybody had the time. They would arrive in town that morning, hear about what had happened, and, shortly after, head out to the cattle-company pasture. Almost all of the men went out alone, leaving their families in town: though there were a few women who came. The other women waited. And the people who had business in town and couldn't leave waited. Now and then somebody came back to have a drink or their dinner and would tell what was going on. No, they hadn't got him yet. Still inside the line shack and not showing his face.

But they'd get him. A few more would go out when they heard this. Also a wagon from De Spain's went out with whiskey. That's how the saloon was set up in the pines overlooking the pasture and why nobody went back to town after that.

Barely a mile from town those going out would hear the gunfire, like a skirmish way over on the other side of a woods, thin specks of sound, and this would hurry them. They were careful, though, topping the slope, looking across the pasture, getting their bearings, then peering to see who was present. They would see a friend and ask about this Mr. Tanner and the friend would point him out.

The man there in the dark suit: thin and bony, not big but looking like he was made of gristle and hard to kill, with a mustache and a thin nose and a dark dusty hat worn square over his eyes. That was him. Nobody had ever seen him before that morning. They would look at Mr. Tanner, then across the pasture again to the line shack three hundred yards away. It was a little bake-oven of a hut, wood framed and made of sod and built against a rise where there were pines so the hut would be in shade part of the day. There were no windows in the hut, no gear lying around to show anybody lived there. The hut stood in the sun now with its door closed, the door chipped and splintered by all the bullets that had poured into it and through it.

Off to the right where the pine shapes against the sky rounded and became willows, there in the trees by the creek bed, was the man's wagon and team. In the wagon were the supplies he had bought that morning in town before Mr. Tanner spotted him.

Out in front of the hut, about ten or fifteen feet, was something on the ground. From the slope three hundred yards away nobody could tell what it was until a man came who had field glasses. He looked up and said, frowning, it was a doll: one made of cloth scraps, a stuffed doll with buttons for eyes.

The woman must have dropped it, somebody said.

The woman? the man with the field glasses said.

A Lipan Apache woman who was his wife or his woman or just with him. Mr. Tanner hadn't been clear about that. All they knew was she was in the hut with him and if the man wanted her to stay and get shot, that was his business.

Bob Valdez, twenty years old and town constable for three weeks, carrying a shotgun and glad he had something to hold on to, was present at the Maricopa pasture. He arrived about noon. He told Mr. Tanner who he was, speaking quietly and waiting for Mr. Tanner to answer. Mr. Tanner nodded but did not shake hands and turned away to say something to an R. L. Davis, who rode for Maricopa when he was working. Bob Valdez stood there and didn't know what to do.

He watched the two men. Two of a kind, uh? Both cut from the same stringy hide and looking like father and son: Tanner talking, never smiling, hardly moving his mouth; R. L. Davis standing hip-cocked, posing with his revolver and rifle and a cartridge belt over his shoulder and the funneled, pointed brim of his sweaty hat nodding up and down as he listened to Mr. Tanner, smiling at what Mr. Tanner said, laughing out loud while still Mr. Tanner did not even show the twitch of a lip. Bob Valdez did not like R. L. Davis or any of the R. L. Davises he had met. He was civil, he listened to them, but, God, there were a lot of them to listen to.

A Mr. Beaudry, who leased land to the cattle company, was there. Also Mr. Malsom, manager of Maricopa, and a horsebreaker by the name of Diego Luz, who was big for a Mexican but never offensive and he drank pretty well.

Mr. Beaudry, nodding and also squinting so he could picture the man inside the line shack, said, "There was something peculiar about him. I mean having a name like Orlando Rincon."

"He worked for me," Mr. Malsom said. He was looking at Mr. Tanner. "I mistrusted him and I believe that was part of it, his name being Orlando Rincon."

"Johnson," Mr. Tanner said.

"I hired him two, three times," Mr. Malsom said. "For heavy work. When I had work you couldn't kick a man to doing."

"His name is Johnson," Mr. Tanner said. "There is no fuzz-head by the name of Orlando Rincon. I'm telling you, this one is a fuzz-head from the Fort Huachuca Tenth fuzz-head cavalry and his name was Johnson when he killed James C. Baxter a year ago and nothing else."

He spoke as you might speak to young children to press something into their minds. This man had no warmth and he was probably not very smart. But there was no reason to doubt him.

Bob Valdez kept near Mr. Tanner because he was the center of what was going on here. They would discuss the situation and decide what to do. As the law-enforcement man he, Bob Valdez, should be in on the discussion and the decision. If someone was to arrest Orlando Rincon or Johnson or whatever his name was, then he should do it; he was town constable. They were out of town maybe, but where did the town end? The town had moved out here now; it was the same thing.

Wait for Rincon to give up. Then arrest him.

If he wasn't dead already.

"Mr. Malsom." Bob Valdez stepped toward the cattle-company manager, who glanced over but looked out across the pasture again, indifferent.

"I wondered if maybe he's already dead," Valdez said.

Mr. Malsom, standing heavier and taller and twenty years older than Bob Valdez, said, "Why don't you find out?"

"I was thinking," Valdez said, "if he was dead we could stand here a long time."

R. L. Davis adjusted his hat, which he did often, grabbing the funneled brim, loosening it on his head and pulling it down close to his eyes again and shifting from one cocked hip to the other.

"This constable here's got better things to do," R. L. Davis said. "He's busy."

"No," Bob Valdez said. "I was thinking of the man, Rincon. He's dead or he's alive. He's alive maybe he wants to give himself up. In there he has time to think, uh? Maybe—" He stopped. Not one of them was listening. Not even R. L. Davis.

Mr. Malsom was looking at the whiskey wagon; it was on the road above them and over a little ways with men standing by it, being served off the tailgate. "I think we could use something," Mr. Malsom said. His gaze went to Diego Luz the horsebreaker, and Diego straightened up; not much, but a little. He was heavy and very dark and his shirt was tight across the thickness of his body. They said that Diego Luz hit green horses on the muzzle with his fist and they minded him. He had the hands for it; they hung at his sides, not touching or fooling with anything. They turned open, gestured, when Mr. Malsom told him to get the whiskey and as he moved off, climbing the slope, one hand held his holstered revolver to his leg.

Mr. Malsom looked up at the sky, squinting and taking his hat off and putting it on again. He took off his coat and held it hooked over his shoulder by one finger, said something, gestured, and he and Mr. Beaudry and Mr. Tanner moved a few yards down the slope to a hollow where there was good shade. It was about two or two-thirty then, hot, fairly still and quiet considering the number of people there. Only some of them in the pines and down in the scrub could be seen from where Bob Valdez stood wondering whether he should follow the three men down to the hollow. Or wait for Diego Luz, who was at the whiskey wagon now, where most of the sounds that carried came from: a voice, a word or two that was suddenly clear, or laughter, and people would look up to see what was going on. Some of them by the whiskey wagon had lost interest in the line shack. Others were still watching, though: those farther along the road sitting in wagons and buggies. This was a day, a date, uh? that people would remember and talk about. Sure, I was there, the man in the buggy would be saying a year from now in a saloon over in Benson or St. David or somewhere. The day they got that army deserter, he had a Big-Fifty Sharps and an old Walker and I'll tell you it was ticklish business.

Down in that worn-out pasture, dusty and spotted with desert growth, prickly pear and brittlebush, there was just the sun. It showed the ground cleanly all the way to just in front of the line shack where now, toward the midafternoon, there was shadow coming out from the trees and from the mound the hut was set against.

Somebody in the scrub must have seen the door open. The shout came from there, and Bob Valdez and everybody on the slope was looking by the time the Lipan Apache woman had reached the edge of the shade. She walked out from the hut toward the willow trees carrying a bucket, not hurrying or even looking toward the slope.

Nobody fired at her; though this was not so strange. Putting the front sight on a sod hut and on a person are two different things. The men in the scrub and in the pines didn't know this woman. They weren't after her. She had just appeared. There she was; and no one was sure what to do about her.

She was in the trees a while by the creek, then she was in the open again, walking back toward the hut with the bucket and not hurrying at all: a small figure way across the pasture almost without shape or color, with only the long skirt reaching to the ground to tell it was the woman.

So he's alive, Bob Valdez thought. And he wants to stay alive and he's not giving himself up.

He thought about the woman's nerve and whether Orlando Rincon had sent her out or she had decided this herself. You couldn't tell about an Indian woman. Maybe this was expected of her. The woman didn't count; the man did. You could lose the woman and get another one.

Mr. Tanner didn't look at R. L. Davis. His gaze held on the Lipan Apache woman, inched along with her toward the hut; but must have known R. L. Davis was right next to him.

"She's saying she don't give a goddamn about you and your rifle," Mr. Tanner said.

R. L. Davis looked at him funny. Then he said, "Shoot her?" Like he hoped that's what Mr. Tanner meant.

"Well, you could make her jump some," Mr. Tanner said.

Now R. L. Davis was onstage and he knew it and Bob Valdez could tell he knew it by the way he levered the Winchester, raised it, and fired all in one motion, and as the dust kicked behind the Indian woman, who kept walking and didn't look up, R. L. Davis fired and fired and fired as fast as he could lever and half aim and with everybody watching him, hurrying him, he put four good ones right behind the woman. His last bullet socked into the door just as she reached it and now she did pause and look up at the slope, staring up like she was waiting for him to fire again and giving him a good target if he wanted it.

Mr. Malsom laughed out loud. "She still don't give a goddamn about your rifle."

It stung R. L. Davis, which it was intended to do. "I wasn't aiming at her!"

"But she doesn't know that." Mr. Malsom was grinning, turning then and reaching out a hand as Diego Luz approached them with the whiskey.

"Hell, I wanted to hit her she'd be laying there, you know it."

"Well, now, you go tell her that," Mr. Malsom said, working the cork loose, "and she'll know it." He took a drink from the bottle and passed it to Mr. Beaudry, who drank and handed the bottle to Mr. Tanner. Mr. Tanner did not drink; he passed the bottle to R. L. Davis, who was standing, staring at Mr. Malsom. Finally R. L. Davis jerked the bottle up, took a long swallow, and that part was over.

Mr. Malsom said to Mr. Tanner, "You don't want any?"

"Not today," Mr. Tanner answered. He continued to stare out across the pasture.

Mr. Malsom watched him. "You feel strongly about this army deserter."

"I told you," Mr. Tanner said, "he killed a man was a friend of mine."

"No, I don't believe you did."

"James C. Baxter of Fort Huachuca," Mr. Tanner said. "He come across a *tulapai* still this nigger soldier was working with some Indians. The nigger thought Baxter would tell the army people, so he shot him and ran off with a woman."

"And you saw him this morning."

"I had come in last night and stopped off, going to Tucson," Mr. Tanner said. "This morning I was getting ready to leave when I saw him; him and the woman."

"I was right there," R. L. Davis said. "Right, Mr. Tanner? Him and I were on the porch by the Republic and Rincon goes by in the wagon. Mr. Tanner said, 'You know that man?' I said, 'Only that he's lived up north of town a few months. Him and the woman.' 'Well, I know him,' Mr. Tanner said. 'That man's a army deserter wanted for murder.' I said, 'Well, let's go get him.' He had a start on us and that's how he got to the hut before we could grab on to him. He's been holed up ever since."

Mr. Malsom said, "Then you didn't talk to him."

"Listen," Mr. Tanner said, "I've kept that man's face before my eyes this past year."

Bob Valdez, somewhat behind Mr. Tanner and to the side, moved in a little closer. "You know this is the same man, uh?"

Mr. Tanner looked around. He stared at Valdez. That's all he did—just stared.

"I mean, we have to be sure," Bob Valdez said. "It's a serious thing."

Now Mr. Malsom and Mr. Beaudry were looking up at him. "We," Mr. Beaudry said. "I'll tell you what, Roberto. We need help we'll call you. All right?"

"You hired me," Bob Valdez said, standing alone above them. He was serious but he shrugged and smiled a little to take the edge off the words. "What did you hire me for?"

"Well," Mr. Beaudry said, acting it out, looking past Bob Valdez and along the road both ways, "I was to see some drunk Mexicans I'd point them out."

A person can be in two different places and he will be two different people. Maybe if you think of some more places the person will be more people, but don't take it too far. This is Bob Valdez standing by himself with the shotgun and having only the shotgun to hold on to. This is one Bob Valdez. About twenty years old. Mr. Beaudry and others could try and think of a time when Bob Valdez might have drunk too much or swaggered or had a certain smart look on this face, but they would never recall such a time. This Bob Valdez was all right.

Another Bob Valdez inside the Bob Valdez at the pasture that day worked for the army one time and was a guide when Crook chased Chato and Chihuahua down into the Madres. He was seventeen then, with a Springfield and Apache moccasins that came up to his knees. He would sit at night with the Apache scouts from San Carlos, eating with them and talking some as he learned Chiricahua. He would keep up with them all day and shoot the Springfield one hell of a lot better than any of them could shoot. He came home with a scalp but never showed it to anyone and had thrown it away by the time he went to work for Maricopa. Shortly after that he was named town constable at twenty-five dollars a month, getting the job because he got along with people: the Mexicans in town who drank too much on Saturday night like him and that was the main thing.

The men with the whiskey bottle had forgotten Valdez. They stayed in the hollow where the shade was cool watching the line shack and waiting for the army deserter to realize it was all up with him. He would realize it and open the door and be cut down as he came outside. It was a matter of time only.

Bob Valdez stayed on the open part of the slope that was turning to shade, sitting now like an Apache and every once in a while making a cigarette and smoking it slowly as he thought about himself and Mr. Tanner and the others, then thinking about the army deserter.

Diego Luz came and squatted next to him, his arms on his knees and his big hands that he used for breaking horses hanging in front of him.

"Stay near if they want you for something," Valdez said. He was watching Beaudry tilt the bottle up. Diego Luz said nothing.

"One of them bends over," Bob Valdez said then, "you kiss it, uh?"

Diego Luz looked at him, patient about it. Not mad or even stirred up. "Why don't you go home?"

"He says Get me a bottle, you run."

"I get it. I don't run."

"Smile and hold your hat, uh?"

"And don't talk so much."

"Not unless they talk to you first."

"You better go home," Diego said.

Bob Valdez said, "That's why you hit the horses."

"Listen," Diego Luz said, scowling a bit now. "They pay me to break horses. They pay you to talk to drunks on Saturday night and keep them from killing somebody. They don't pay you for what you think or how you feel, so if you take their money, keep your mouth shut. All right?"

Diego Luz got up and walked away, down toward the hollow. The hell with this kid, he was thinking. He'll learn or he won't learn, but the hell with him. He was also thinking that maybe he could get a drink from that bottle. Maybe there'd be a half inch left nobody wanted and Mr. Malsom would tell him to kill it.

But it was already finished. R. L. Davis was playing with the bottle, holding it by the neck and flipping it up and catching it as it came down. Beaudry was saying, "What about after dark?" Looking at Mr. Tanner, who was thinking about something else and didn't notice. R L. Davis stopped flipping the bottle. He said, "Put some men on the rise right above the hut; he comes out, bust him."

"Well, they should get the men over there," Mr. Beaudry said, looking at the sky. "It won't be long till dark."

"Where's he going?" Mr. Malsom said.

The others looked up, stopped in whatever they were doing or thinking by the suddenness of Mr. Malsom's voice.

"Hey, Valdez!" R. L. Davis yelled out. "Where do you think you're going?"

Bob Valdez had circled them and was already below them on the slope, leaving the pines now and entering the scrub brush. He didn't stop or look back.

"Valdez!"

Mr. Tanner raised one hand to silence R. L. Davis, all the time watching Bob Valdez getting smaller, going straight through the scrub, not just walking or passing the time but going right out to the pasture.

"Look at him," Mr. Malsom said. There was some admiration in the voice.

"He's dumber than he looks," R. L. Davis said. Then jumped a little as Mr. Tanner touched his arm.

"Come on," Mr. Tanner said. "With a rifle." And started down the slope, hurrying and not seeming to care if he might stumble on the loose gravel.

Bob Valdez was now halfway across the pasture, the shotgun pointed down at his side, his eyes not leaving the door of the line shack. The door was probably already open enough for a rifle barrel to poke through. He guessed the army deserter was covering him, letting him get as close as he wanted; the closer he came, the easier to hit him.

Now he could see all the bullet marks in the door and the clean inner wood where the door was splintered. Two people in that little bake-oven of a place. He saw the door move.

He saw the rag doll on the ground. It was a strange thing, the woman having a doll. Valdez hardly glanced at it but was aware of the button eyes looking up and the discomforted twist of the red wool mouth. Then, just past the doll, when he was wondering if he would go right up to the door and knock on it and wouldn't that be a crazy thing, like visiting somebody, the door opened and the Negro was in the doorway, filling it, standing there in pants and boots but without a shirt in that hot place and holding a long-barreled Walker that was already cocked.

They stood ten feet apart looking at each other, close enough so that no one could fire from the slope.

"I can kill you first," the Negro said, "if you raise that."

With his free hand, the left one, Bob Valdez motioned back over his shoulder. "There's a man there said you killed somebody a year ago."

"What man?"

"Said his name is Tanner."

The Negro shook his head, once each way.

"Said your name is Johnson."

"You know my name."

"I'm telling you what he said."

"Where'd I kill this man?"

"Huachuca."

The Negro hesitated. "That was some time ago I was in the Tenth. More than a year."

"You a deserter?"

"I served it out."

"Then you got something that says so."

"In the wagon, there's a bag there my things are in."

"Will you talk to this man Tanner?"

"If I can hold from hitting him one."

"Listen, why did you run this morning?"

"They come chasing. I don't know what they want." He lowered the gun a little, his brown-stained-looking tired eyes staring intently at Bob Valdez. "What would you do? They came on the run. Next thing I know they a-firing at us. So I pop in this place."

"Will you come with me and talk to him?"

The Negro hesitated again. Then shook his head. "I don't know him."

"Then he won't know you, uh?"

"He didn't know me this morning."

"All right," Bob Valdez said. "I'll get your paper says you were discharged. Then we'll show it to this man, uh?"

The Negro thought it over before he nodded, very slowly, as if still thinking. "All right. Bring him here, I'll say a few words to him."

Bob Valdez smiled a little. "You can point that gun some other way."

"Well . . ." the Negro said, "if everybody's friends." He lowered the Walker to his side.

The wagon was in the willow trees by the creek. Off to the right. But Bob Valdez did not turn right away in that direction. He backed away, watching Orlando Rincon for no reason that he knew of. Maybe because the man was holding a gun and that was reason enough.

He had backed off six or seven feet when Orlando Rincon

shoved the Walker down into his belt. Bob Valdez turned and started for the trees.

This was when he looked across the pasture. He saw Mr. Tanner and R. L. Davis at the edge of the scrub trees but wasn't sure it was them. Something tried to tell him it was them, but he did not accept it until he was off to the right, out of the line of fire, and by then the time to yell at them or run toward them was past, for R. L. Davis had the Winchester up and was firing.

They say R. L. Davis was drunk or he would have pinned him square. As it was the bullet shaved Rincon and plowed past him into the hut.

Bob Valdez saw him half turn, either to go inside or look inside, and as he came around again saw the man's eyes on him and his hand pulling the Walker from his belt.

"They weren't supposed to," Bob Valdez said, holding one hand out as if to stop Rincon. "Listen, they weren't supposed to do that!"

The Walker was out of Rincon's belt and he was cocking it. "Don't!" Bob Valdez yelled. "Don't!" Looking right in the man's eyes and seeing it was no use and suddenly hurrying, jerking the shotgun up and pulling both triggers so that the explosions came out in one big blast and Orlando Rincon was spun and thrown back inside.

They came out across the pasture to have a look at the carcass, some going inside where they found the woman also dead, killed by a rifle bullet. They noticed she would have had a child in a few months. Those by the doorway made room as Mr. Tanner and R. L. Davis approached.

Diego Luz came over by Bob Valdez, who had not moved. Valdez stood watching them and he saw Mr. Tanner look down at Rincon and after a moment shake his head.

"It looked like him," Mr. Tanner said. "It sure looked like him."

He saw R. L. Davis squint at Mr. Tanner. "It ain't the one you said?"

Mr. Tanner shook his head again. "I've seen him before, though. Know I've seen him somewheres."

Valdez saw R. L. Davis shrug. "You ask me, they all look alike." He was yawning then, fooling with his hat, and then his eyes swiveled over at Bob Valdez standing with the empty shotgun.

"Constable," R. L. Davis said, "you went and killed the wrong coon."

Bob Valdez started for him, raising the shotgun to swing it like a club, but Diego Luz drew his revolver and came down with it and Valdez dropped to the ground.

Some three years later there was a piece in the paper about a Robert Eladio Valdez who had been hanged for murder in Tularosa, New Mexico. He had shot a man coming out of the Regent Hotel, called him an unprintable name, and shot him four times. This Valdez had previously killed a man in Contention and two in Sands during a bank holdup, had been caught once, escaped from the jail in Mesilla before trial, and identified another time during a holdup near Lordsburg.

"If it is the same Bob Valdez used to live here," Mr. Beaudry said, "it's good we got rid of him."

"Well, it could be," Mr. Malsom said. "But I guess there are Bob Valdezes all over."

"You wonder what gets into them," Mr. Beaudry said.

You Never See Apaches . . .

By nature Angsman was a cautious man. From the shapeless specks that floated in the sky miles out over the plain, his gaze dropped slowly to the sand a few feet from his chin, then rose again more slowly, to follow the gradual slope that fell away before him. He rolled his body slightly from its prone position to reach the field glasses at his side, while his eyes continued to crawl out into the white-hot nothingness of the flats. Sun glare met alkali dust and danced before the slits of his eyes. And, far out, something moved. Something darker than the monotonous tone of the flats. A pinpoint of motion.

He put the glasses to his eyes and the glare stopped dancing and the small blur of motion cleared and enlarged as he corrected the focus. Two ponies and two pack animals. The mules were loaded high. He made that out right away, but it was minutes before he realized the riders were women. Two Indian women. Behind them the scavenger birds floated above the scattered animal carcasses, circling lower as the human figures moved away.

Angsman pushed himself up from the sand and made his way back through the pines that closed in on the promontory. A few dozen yards of the darkness of the pines and then abruptly the glare was forcing against sand again where the openness of the trail followed the shoulder of the hill. He stopped at the edge of the trees, took his hat off, and rubbed the red line where the sweatband had stuck. His mustache drooped untrimmed toward dark, tight cheeks, giving his face a look of sadness. A stern, sun-scarred sadness. It was the type of face that needed the soft shadow of a hat brim to make it look complete. Shadows to soften the gaunt angles. It was an intelligent, impassive face, in its late thirties. He looked at the three men by the horses and then moved toward them.

Ygenio Baca sat cross-legged in the dust smoking a cigarette, drawing deep, and he only glanced at Angsman as he approached. He drew long on his cigarettte, then held it close to his eyes and examined it as some rare object as the smoke curled from his mouth. Ygenio Baca, the mozo, had few concerns.

Ed Hyde's stocky frame was almost beneath his horse's head, with a hand lifted to the horse's muzzle. The horse's nose moved gently against the big palm, licking the salty perspiration from hand and wrist. In the other arm Hyde cradled a Sharps rifle. His squinting features were obscure beneath the hat tilted close to his eyes. Sun, wind, and a week's beard gave his face a puffy, raw appearance that was wild, but at the same time soft and hazy. There was about him a look of sluggishness that contrasted with the leanness of Angsman.

Billy Guay stood indolently with his thumbs hooked in his gun belts. He took a few steps in Angsman's direction and pushed his hat to the back of his head, though the sun was beating full in his face. He was half Ed Hyde's age, a few years or so out of his teens, but there was a hardness about the eyes that contrasted with his soft features. Features that were all the more youthful, and even feminine, because of the long blond hair that covered the tops of his ears and hung unkempt over his shirt collar. Watching Angsman, his mouth was tight as if daring him to say something that he would not agree with.

Angsman walked past him to Ed Hyde. He was about to say something, but stopped when Billy Guay turned and grabbed his arm.

"The dust cloud was buffalo like I said, wasn't it?" Billy Guay asked, but there was more statement of fact than question in his loud voice.

Angsman's serious face turned to the boy, but looked back to Ed Hyde when he said, "There're two Indian women out there cleaning up after a hunting party. The dust cloud was the warriors going home. I suspect they're the last ones. Stragglers. Everyone else out of sight already."

Billy Guay pushed in close to the two men. "Dammit, the cloud could have still been buffalo," he said. "Who says you know so damn much!"

Ed Hyde looked from one to the other like an unbiased spectator. He dropped the long buffalo rifle stock-down in front of him. His worn black serge coat strained tight at the armpits as he lifted his hands to pat his coat pockets. From the right one he drew a half-chewed tobacco plug.

For a moment Angsman just stared at Billy Guay. Finally he said, "Look, boy, for a good many years it's been my business to know so damn much. Now, you'll take my word that the dust cloud was a Indian hunting party and act on it like I see fit, or else we turn around and go back."

Ed Hyde's grizzled head jerked up suddenly. He said. "You're dead right, Angsman. There ain't been buffalo this far south for ten years." He looked at the boy and spoke easier. "Take my word for it, Billy." He smiled. "If anybody knows it, I do. Those Indians most likely ran down a deer herd. But hell, deer, buffalo, what's the difference? We're not out here for game. You just follow along with what Angsman here says and we all go home rich men. Take things slow, Billy, and you breathe easier."

"I just want to know why's he got to give all the orders," Billy

Guay said, and his voice was rising. "It's us that own the map, not him. Where'd he be without us!"

Angsman's voice was the same, unhurried, unexcited, when he said, "I'll tell you. I'd still be back at Bowie guiding for cavalry who ride with their eyes open and know how to keep their mouths shut in Apache country." He didn't wait for a reply, but turned and walked toward the dun-colored mare. "Ygenio," he called to the Mexican still sitting cross-legged on the ground, "hold the mules a good fifty yards behind us and keep your eyes on me."

EIGHT days out of Willcox and the strain was beginning to tell. It had been bad from the first day. Now they were in the foothills of the Mogollons and it was no better. Angsman had thought that as soon as they climbed from the dust of the plains the tension would ease and the boy would be easier to handle, but Billy Guay continued to grumble with his thumbs in his gun belts and disagree with everything that was said. And Ed Hyde continued to say nothing unless turning back was mentioned.

Since early morning their trail had followed this pine-covered crest that angled irregularly between the massive rock peaks to the south and east and the white-gold plain to the west. Most of the ways the trail had held to the shoulder, turning, twisting, and falling with the contour of the hillcrest. And from the west the openness of the plains continued to cling in glaring monotony. Most of the time Angsman's eyes scanned the openness, and the small black specks continued to crawl along in his vision.

The trail dipped abruptly into a dry creek basin that slanted down from between rocky humps looming close to the right. Angsman reined his mount diagonally down the bank, then at the bottom kicked hard to send the mare into a fast start up the opposite bank. The gravel loosened and fell away as hooves dug through the dry crust to clink against the sandy rock. Momentarily the horse began to fall back, but Angsman spurred again and grunted something close to her ear to make the mare heave and kick up over the bank.

He rode on a few yards before turning to wait for the others.

Billy Guay reached the creek bank and yelled across, without hesitating. "Hey, Angsman, you tryin' to pick the roughest damn trail you can find?"

The scout winced as the voice slammed against the towering rock walls and drifted over the flats, vibrating and repeating far off in the distance. He threw off and ran to the creek bank. Billy Guay began to laugh as the echo came back to him. "Damn, Ed. You hear that!" His voice carried clear and loud across the arroyo. Angsman put a finger to his mouth and shook his head repeatedly when he saw Ed Hyde looking his way. Then Hyde leaned close and said something to the boy. He heard Billy Guay swear, but not so loud, and then there was silence.

Now, ten days from the time the message had brought him to the hotel in Willcox, he wasn't so sure it was worth it.

In the hotel room Hyde had come to the point immediately. Anxiety showed on his face, but he smiled when he asked the point-blank question "How'd you like to be worth half a hundred thousand dollars?" With that he waved the piece of dirty paper in front of Angsman's face. "It's right here. Find us the picture of a Spanish sombrero and we're rich." That simply.

Angsman had all the time in the world. He smoked a cigarette and thought. Then he asked, "Why me? There're a lot of prospectors around here."

Hyde did something with his eye that resembled a wink. "You're well recommended here in Willcox. They say you know the country better than most. And the Apaches better than anybody," Hyde said with a hint of self-pride for knowing so much about the scout. "Billy here and I'll give you a equal share of everything we find if you can guide us to one little X on a piece of paper."

Billy Guay had said little that first meeting. He half-sat on the small window ledge trying to stare Angsman down when the scout looked at him. And Angsman smiled when he noticed the boy's two low-slung pistols, thinking a man must be a pretty poor shot with one pistol that he'd have to carry another. And when Billy Guay tried to stare him down, he stared back with the half smile and it made the boy all the madder; so mad that often, then, he interrupted Hyde to let somebody know that he had something to say about the business at hand.

Ed Hyde told a story of a lost mine and a prospector who had found the mine, but was unable to take any gold out because of Indians, and who was lucky to get out with just his skin. He referred to the prospector always as "my friend," and finally it turned out that "my friend" was buffalo hunting out of Tascosa in the Panhandle, along with Ed Hyde, raising a stake to try the mine again, when he "took sick and died." The two of them were out on a hunt when it happened and he left the map to Hyde, "since I saw him through his sickness." Ed Hyde remained silent for a considerable length of time after telling of the death of his friend.

Then he added, "I met Billy here later on and took to him 'cause he's got the nerve for this kind of business." He looked at Billy Guay as a man looks at a younger man and sees his own youth. "Just one thing more, mister," he added. "If you say yes and look at the map, you don't leave our sight."

In the Southwest, lost-mine stories are common. Angsman had heard many, and knew even more prospectors who chased the legends. He had seen a few become rich. But it wasn't so much the desire for gold that finally prompted him to go along. Cochise had promised peace and Geronimo had scurried south to the Sierra Madres. All was quiet in his territory. Too quiet. He had told himself he would go merely as an escape from boredom. Still, it was hard to keep the wealth aspect from cropping into the thought. Angsman saw the years slipping by with nothing to show for them but a scarred Spanish saddle and an old-model Winchester. All he had to do was lead them to a canyon and a rock formation that looked like a Spanish hat.

Two days to collect the equipment and round up a mozo who wasn't afraid to drive mules into that part of Apacheria where there was no peace. For cigarettes and a full belly Ygenio Baca would drive his mules to the gates of hell.

IT was almost a mile past the arroyo crossing that Angsman noticed his black specks had disappeared from the open flats. For the past few hundred yards his vision to the left had been blocked by dense pines. Now the plains yawned wide again, and his glasses inched over the vastness in all directions, then stopped where a spur jutted out from the hillside ahead to cut his vision. The Indian women had vanished.

Hyde and Billy Guay sat their mounts next to Angsman, who, afoot, swept his glasses once more over the flat. Finally he lowered them and said, more to himself than to the others, "Those Indian women aren't nowhere in sight. They could have moved out in the other direction, or they might be so close we can't see them."

He nodded ahead to where the trail stopped at thick scrub brush and pine and then dipped abruptly to the right to drop to a bench that slanted toward the deepness of the valley. From where they stood, the men saw the trail disappear far below into a denseness of trees and rock.

"Pretty soon the country'll be hugging us tight; and we won't see anything," Angsman said. "I don't like it. Not with a hunting party in the neighborhood."

Billy Guay laughed out. "I'll be go to hell! Ed, this old woman's afraid of two squaws! Ed, you hear—"

Ed Hyde wasn't listening. He was staring off in the distance, past the treetops in the valley to a towering, sand-colored cliff with flying rock buttresses that walled the valley on the other side. He slid from his mount hurriedly, catching his coat on the saddle horn and ripping it where a button held fast. But now he was too excited to heed the ripped coat.

"Look! Yonder to that cliff." His voice broke with excitement. "See that gash near the top, like where there was a rock slide? And look past to the mountains behind!" Angsman and Billy Guay squinted at the distance, but remained silent.

"Dammit!" Hyde screamed. "Don't you see it!" He grabbed his horse's reins and ran, stumbling, down the trail to where it leveled again at the bench. When the others reached him, the map was in his hand and he was laughing a high laugh that didn't seem to belong to the grizzled face. His extended hand held the dirty piece of paper . . . and he kept jabbing at it with a finger of the other hand. "Right there, dammit! Right there!" His pointing finger swept from the map. "Now look at that gold-lovin' rock slide!" His laughter subsided to a self-confident chuckle.

From where they stood on the bench, the towering cliff was now above them and perhaps a mile away over the tops of the trees. A chunk of sandrock as large as a two-story building was gouged from along the smooth surface of the cliff top, with a gravel slide trailing into the valley below; but massive boulders along the cliff top lodged over the depression, forming a four-sided opening. It was a gigantic frame through which they could see sky and the flat surface of a mesa in the distance. On both sides the mesa top fell away to shoulders cutting sharp right angles from the straight vertical lines, then to be cut off there, in their vision, by the rock border of the cliff frame. And before their eyes the mesa turned into a flat-topped Spanish sombrero.

Billy Guay's jaw dropped open. "Damn! It's one of those hats like the Mex dancers wear! Ed, you see it?"

Ed Hyde was busy studying the map. He pointed to it again. "Right on course, Angsman. The flats, the ridge, the valley, the hat." His black-crested fingernail followed wavy lines and circles over the stained paper. "Now we just drop to the valley and follow her up to the end." He shoved the map into his coat pocket and reached up to the saddle horn to mount. "Come on, boys, we're good as rich," he called, and swung up into the saddle.

Angsman looked down the slant to the darkness of the trees. "Ed, we got to go slow down there," he tried to caution, but Hyde was urging his mount down the grade and Billy Guay's paint was kicking the loose rock after him. His face tightened as he turned quickly to his horse, and then he saw Ygenio Baca leaning against his lead mule vacantly smoking his cigarette. Angsman's face relaxed.

"Ygenio," he said. "Tell your mules to be very quiet."

Ygenio Baca nodded and unhurriedly flicked the cigarette stub down the grade.

They caught up with Hyde and Billy Guay a little way into the timber. The trail had disappeared into a hazy gloom of tangled brush and tree trunks with the cliff on one side and the piney hill on the other to keep out the light.

Angsman rode past them and they stopped and turned in the saddle. Hyde looked a little sheepish because he didn't know where the trail was, but Billy Guay stared back defiantly and tried to look hard.

"Ed, you saw some bones out there on the flats a while back," Angsman said. "Likely they were men who had gold fever." That was all he said. He turned the head of the mare and continued on.

Angsman moved slowly, more cautiously now than before, and every so often he would rein in gently and sit in the saddle without moving, and listen. And there was something about the deep silence that made even Billy Guay strain his eyes into the dimness and not say anything. It was a loud quietness that rang in their ears and seemed unnatural. Moving at this pace, it was almost dusk when they reached the edge of the timber.

The pine hill was still on their left, but higher and steeper. To the right two spurs reached out from the cliff wall that had gradually dropped until now it was just a hump, but with a confusion of rocky angles in the near distance beyond. And ahead was a canyon mouth, narrow at first, but then appearing to open into a wider area.

As they rode on, Angsman could see it in Ed Hyde's eyes. The map was in his hand and he kept glancing at it and then looking around. When they passed through the canyon mouth into the open, Hyde called, "Angsman, look! Just like it says!"

But Angsman wasn't looking at Ed Hyde. A hundred feet ahead, where a narrow side canyon cut into the arena, the two Indian women sat their ponies and watched the white men approach.

ANGSMAN reined in and waited, looking at them the way you look at deer that you have come across unexpectedly in a forest, waiting for them to bolt. But the women made no move to run. Hyde and Billy Guay drew up next to Angsman, then continued on as Angsman nodged the mare into a walk. They stopped within a few feet of the women, who had still neither moved nor uttered a sound.

Angsman dismounted. Hyde stirred restlessly in his saddle before putting his hands on the horn to swing down, but stopped when Billy Guay's hand tightened on his arm.

"Damn, Ed, look at that young one!" His voice was loud and excited, but as impersonal as if he were making a comment at a girlie show. "She'd even look good in town," he added, and threw off to stand in front of her pony.

Angsman looked at Billy Guay and back to the girl, who was sliding easily from the bare back of her pony. He greeted her in English, pleasantly, and tipped his hat to the older woman, still mounted, who giggled in a high, thin voice. The girl said nothing, but looked at Angsman.

He said, *¿Cómo se llama?* and spoke a few more words in Spanish.

The girl's face relaxed slightly and she said, "Sonkadeya," pronouncing each syllable distinctly.

"What the hell's that mean?" Billy Guay said, walking up to her.

"That's her name," Angsman told him, then spoke to the girl again in Spanish.

She replied with a few Spanish phrases, but most of her words were in a dialect of the Apache tongue. She was having trouble combining the two languages so that the white men could understand her. Her face would frown and she would wipe her hands nervously over the hips of her greasy deerskin dress as she groped for the right words. She was plump and her hair and dress had long gone unwashed, but her face was softly attractive, contrasting oddly with her primitive dress and speech. Her features might have belonged to a white woman—the coloring, too, for that matter—but the greased hair and smoke smell that clung to her were decidedly Apache.

When she finished speaking, Angsman looked back at Hyde. "She's a Warm Springs Apache. A Mimbreño," he said. "She says they're on their way home."

Hyde said, "Ask her if she knows about any gold hereabouts."

Angsman looked at him and his eyes opened a little wider. "Maybe you didn't hear, Ed. I said she's a Mimbre. She's going home from a hunting trip led by her father. And her father's Delgadito," he added.

"Hell, the 'Paches are at peace, ain't they?" Hyde asked indifferently. "What you worried about?"

"Cochise made peace," Angsman answered. "These are Mimbres, not Chiricahuas, and their chief is Victorio. He's never never made peace. I don't want to scare you, Ed," he said looking back to the girl, "but his war lieutenant's Delgadito."

Billy Guay was standing in front of the girl, his thumbs in his gun belts, looking at her closely. "I know how to stop a war," he said, smiling.

"Who's talkin' about war?" Hyde asked. "We're not startin' anything."

"You don't have to stop it, Ed," Angsman said. "You think about finishing it. And you think about your life."

"Don't worry about me thinkin' about my life. I think about it bein' almost gone and not worth a Dixie single. Hell, yes, we're takin' a chance!" Hyde argued. "If gold was easy to come by, it wouldn't be worth nothin'."

"I still know how to stop a war," Billy Guay said idly.

Hyde looked at him impatiently. "What's that talk supposed to mean?" Then he saw how Billy Guay was looking at the girl, and the frown eased off the grizzled face as it dawned on him what Billy Guay was thinking about, and he rubbed his beard.

"You see what I mean, Ed," Billy Guay said, smiling. "We take Miss Indin along and ain't no Delgadito or even U.S. Grant goin' to stop us." He looked up at the old woman on the pony. "Though I don't see any reason for carryin' excess baggage."

Angsman caught him by both arms and spun him around. "You gun-crazy kid, you out of your mind? You don't wave threats at Apaches!" He pushed the boy away roughly. "Just stop a minute, Ed. You got better sense than what this boy's proposing."

"It's worth a chance, Angsman. Any chance. We're not stoppin' after comin' this far on account of some Indin or his little girl," Hyde said. "I'd say Billy's got the right idea. I told you he had nerve. Let him use a little of it."

Billy Guay looked toward Angsman's mount and saw his handgun in a saddle holster, then both pistols came out and he pointed them at the scout.

"Don't talk again, Angsman, 'cause if I hear any more abuse I'll shoot you as quick as this." He raised a pistol and swung it to the side as if without aiming and pulled the trigger. The old Indian woman dropped from the pony without a cry.

There was silence. Hyde looked at him, stunned. "God, Billy! You didn't have to do that!"

Billy Guay laughed, but the laugh trailed off too quickly, as if he just then realized what he had done. He forced the laugh now, and said, "Hell, Ed. She was only an Indin. What you fussin' about?"

Hyde said, "Well, it's done now and can't be undone." But he looked about nervously as if expecting a simple solution to be standing near at hand. A solution or some kind of justification. He saw the mining equipment packed on one of the mules and the look of distress left his eyes. "Let's quit talkin' about it," he said. "We got things to do."

Billy Guay blew down the barrel of the pistol he had fired and watched Sonkadeya as she bent over the woman momentarily, then rose without the trace of an emotion on her face. It puzzled Billy Guay and made him more nervous. He waved a pistol toward Ygenio Baca. "Hey, Mazo! Get a shovel and turn this old woman under. No sense in havin' the birds tellin' on us."

THE scout rode in silence, knowing what would come, but not knowing when. His gaze crawled over the wildness of the slanting canyon walls, brush trees, and scattered boulders, where nothing moved. The left wall was dark, the shadowy rock outlines obscure and blending into each other; the opposite slope was hazy and cold in the dim light of the late sun. He felt the tenseness all over his body. The feeling of knowing that something is close, though you can't see it or hear it. Only the quietness, the metallic clop of hooves, then Billy Guay's loud, forced laughter that would cut the stillness and hang there in the narrowness until it faded out up-canyon. Angsman knew the feeling. It went with campaigning. But this time there was a difference. It was the first time he had ever led into a canyon with such a strong premonition that Apaches were present. Yet, with the feeling, he recognized an eager expectancy. Perhaps fatalism, he thought.

He watched two chicken hawks dodging, gliding in and out, drop toward a brush tree halfway up the slanting right wall, then, just as they were about to land in the bush, they rose quickly and soared out of sight. Now he was more than sure. They were riding into an ambush. And there was so little time to do anything about it.

He glanced at Hyde riding next to him. Hyde couldn't be kept back now. The final circle on his map was just a little figuring from the end of the canyon.

"Slow her down, Ed," Billy Guay yelled. "I can't propose to Miss Indin and canter at the same time." He laughed and reached over to put his hand on Sonkadeya's hip, then let the hand fall to her knee.

He called out, "Yes, sir, Ed, I think we made us a good move."

Sonkadeya did not resist. Her head nodded faintly with the sway of her pony, looking straight ahead. But her eyes moved from one canyon wall to the other and there was the slightest gleam of a smile.

Angsman wondered if he really cared what was going to happen. He didn't care about Hyde or Billy Guay; and he didn't know Ygenio Baca well enough to have a feeling one way or the other. From the beginning Ygenio had been taking a chance like everyone else. He thought of his own life and the odd fact occurred to him that he didn't even particularly care about himself. He tried to picture death in relation to himself, but he would see himself lying on the ground and himself looking at the body and knew that couldn't be so. He thought of how hard it was to take yourself out of the picture to see yourself dead, and ended up with: If you're not going to be there to worry about yourself being dead, why worry at all? But you don't stay alive not caring, and his eyes went back to the canyon sides.

He watched Hyde engrossed in his map and looked back at Billy Guay riding close to Sonkadeya with his hand on her leg. They could be shot from their saddles and not even see where it came from. Or, they could be taken by surprise. His head swung front again and he saw the canyon up ahead narrow to less than fifty feet across. Or they could be taken by surprise!

He flicked the rein against the mare's mane, gently, to ease her toward the right canyon wall. He made the move slowly, leading the others at a very slight angle, so that Hyde and Billy Guay, in their preoccupation, did not even notice the edging. Either to be shot in the head or not at all, Angsman thought.

Now they were riding much closer to the slanting canyon wall. He turned in the saddle to watch Billy Guay, still laughing and moving his hand over Sonkadeya. And when he turned back he saw the half-dozen Apaches standing in the trail not a dozen yards ahead. It was funny, because he was looking at half-naked, armed Apaches and he could still hear Billy Guay's laughter coming from behind.

Then the laughter stopped. Hyde groaned, "Oh, my God!" and in the instant spurred his mount and yanked rein to wheel off to the left. There was the report of a heavy rifle and horse and rider went down.

Angsman's arms were jerked suddenly behind his back and he saw three Apaches race for the fallen Hyde as he felt himself dragged over the rump of the mare. He landed on his feet and staggered and watched one warrior dragging Hyde back toward them by one leg. Hyde was screaming, holding on to the other leg that was bouncing over the rough ground.

Billy Guay had jerked his arms free and stood a little part from the dozen Apaches aiming bows and carbines at him. His hands were on the pistol butts, with fear and indecision plain on his face.

Angsman twisted his neck toward him, "Don't even think about it, boy. You don't have a chance." It was all over in something like fifteen seconds.

Hyde was writhing on the ground, groaning and holding on to the hole in his thigh, where the heavy slug had gone through to take the horse in the belly. Angsman stooped to look at the wound and saw that Hyde was holding the map, pressed tight to his leg and now smeared with blood. He looked up and Delgadito was standing on the other side of the wounded man. Next to him stood Sonkadeya.

DELGADITO was not dressed for war. He wore a faded red cotton shirt, buttonless and held down by the cartridge belt around his waist; and his thin face looked almost ridiculous under the shabby wide-brimmed hat that sat straight on the top of his head, at least two sizes too small. But Angsman did not laugh. He knew Delgadito, Victorio's war lieutenant, and probably the most capable hit-and-run guerilla leader in Apacheria. No, Angsman did not laugh.

Delgadito stared at them, taking his time to look around, then said, "Hello. Angs-mon. You have a cigarillo?"

Angsman fished in his shirt pocket and drew out tobacco and paper and handed it to the Indian. Delgadito rolled a cigarette awkwardly and handed the sack to Angsman, who rolled himself one then flicked a match with his thumbnail and lighted the cigarettes. Both men drew deeply and smoked in silence. Finally, Angsman said, "It is good to smoke with you again, Sheekasay."

Delgadito nodded his head and Angsman went on, "It has been five years since we smoked together at San Carlos."

The Apache shook his head slightly. "Together we have smoked other things since then, Angs-mon," and added a few words in the Mimbre dialect.

Angsman looked at him quickly. "You were at Big Dry Wash?"

Delgadito smiled for the first time and nodded his head. "How is your sickness, Angs-mon?" he asked, and the smile broadened.

Angsman's hand came up quickly to his side, where the bullet had torn through that day two years before at Dry Wash, and now he smiled.

Delgadito watched him with the nearest an Apache comes to giving an admiring look. He said, "You are a big man, Angs-mon. I like to fight you. But now you do something very foolish and I must stop you. I mean you no harm, Angs-mon, for I like to fight you, but now you must go home and stop this being foolish and take this old man before the smell enters his leg. And, Angs-mon, tell this old man what befalls him if he returns. Tell him the medicine he carries in his hand is false. Show him how he cannot read the medicine ever again because of his own blood." For a moment his eyes lifted to the heights of the canyon wall. "Maybeso that is the only way, Angs-mon. With blood."

Angsman offered no thanks for their freedom—gratitude was not an Apache custom—but he said. "On the way home I will impress your words on them."

"Tell my words to the old man," Delgadito replied, then his voice became cold. "I will tell the young one." And he looked toward Billy Guay.

Angsman swallowed hard to remain impassive. "There is nothing I can say."

"The mother of Sonkadeya speaks in my ear, Angs-mon, What could you say?" Delgadito turned deliberately and walked away.

Angsman rode without speaking, listening to Hyde's groans as the saddle rubbed the open rawness of his wound. The groans were beginning to erase the scream that hung in his mind and repeated over and over Billy Guay's scream as they carried him up-canyon.

Angsman knew what he was going to do. He'd still have his worn saddle and old-model carbine, but he knew what he was going to do. Hyde's leg would heal and he'd be back the next year, or the year after; or if not him, someone else. The Southwest was full of Hydes. And as long as there were Hydes, there were Billy Guays. Big talkers with big guns who ended up lying dead, after a while, in a Mimbre rancheria. Angsman would go back to Fort Bowie. Even if it got slow sometimes, there'd always be plenty to do.

The Colonel's Lady

Mata Lobo was playing his favorite game. He stretched his legs stiffly behind him until his moccasined feet touched rock, and then he pushed, writhing his body against the soft, sandy ground, enjoying an animal pleasure from the blistering sun on his naked back and the feel of warm, yielding earth beneath him. His extended hand touched the stock of the Sharps rifle a few inches from his chin and sighted down the barrel for the hundredth time. The target area had not changed.

Sixty yards down the slope the military road came into view from between the low hills, cutting a sharp, treacherous arc to follow the bend of Banderas Creek on the near side and then to continue, paralleling the base of the hill, making the slow climb over this section of the Sierra Apaches. Mata Lobo's front sight was dead on the sudden bend in the road.

He flexed his finger on the trigger and sighted again, taking in the slack, then releasing it. Not long now. In a few minutes he should hear the faint, faraway rattle of the stage as it weaved across the plain from Rindo's Station at the Banderas crossing. Six miles across straight, flat desert. And then louder—with a creaking—a grinding, creaking, jingling explosion of leather, wood, and horseflesh as the Hatch & Hodges Overland began the gradual climb over the woody western end of the Sierra Apaches, and then to drop to another white-hot plain that stretched the twelve miles to Inspiration, the end of the line. The vision in the mind of Mata Lobo shortened the route by a dozen miles.

Every foot of the road was known to him. Especially this sudden bend at the beginning of the climb. He had scouted it for weeks, timing the stage runs, watching the drivers from his niche on the hill. And through his Apache patience he learned many things.

At the bend the driver and the shotgun rider were too busy with the team to be watching the hillside. And the passengers, full and comfortable after a meal at Rindo's, would be suddenly jolted into hanging on with the sway of the bouncing Concord as it swept around the sharp curve, with no thought of looking out the windows.

It was the perfect site for ambush, Apache style. Mata Lobo was sure, for he had done it before.

And then it began. He raised himself on his elbows and cocked his ears to the sound that was still a whisper out on the desert. Two miles away. Then louder, and louder; then the straining pitch to the rattling clamor and the stage was starting up the grade.

The Apache pivoted his rifle on the rocks in front of him, making sure of free motion, and then he lined up again the five brass cartridges arranged on the ground near his right hand.

When he looked back to the road the lead horses were coming into view. He waited until the stage was in full sight, slowed down slightly in the middle of the road, and then he fired, aiming at the closer lead horse.

The horse's momentum carried it along for the space of time it took the Apache to inject another cartridge and squeeze off at the other lead animal. The horses swerved against each other, still going, then four pairs of legs buckled at once, and eight other pairs raced on, trampling the fallen horses, but to be tripped immediately in a wild confusion of thrashing legs and screaming horses and grinding brakes.

Next to the driver the shotgun rider was throwing his boot against the brake lever when the coach jackknifed and twisted over, gouging into the dirt road, sending up a thick cloud of dust to cover the scene.

As the dust began to settle, Mata Lobo saw one figure lying next to the overturned Concord, his face upturned to the two right-side wheels, still turning slowly above him. There was a stir of motion farther ahead as a figure crawled along the ground, got to his feet, stumbled, pulled himself frantically across the road in a wild, reeling motion that finally developed into a crouched run. He was almost to the shelter of the creek bank when the buffalo gun screamed again across the hillsides. The impact threw him over the bank to lie facedown at the edge of the creek.

He aimed the rifle again at the overturned stage in time to see the head appear above the door opening. Mata Lobo's finger almost closed on the trigger, but he hesitated, seeing shoulders appear and then the rest of the body.

The man stopped uncertainly, looking around, cocking his ear to the silence. An odd-looking little man, fat and frightened, but not sure of what to be afraid. He clutched a small black case that singled him out as a drummer of some kind. He clutched it protectingly, shielding his means of existence.

When his gaze swept the hillside, perhaps he saw the glint of the rifle barrel, but if he did, it meant nothing to him. There was no reaction. And a second later it was too late. The .50-caliber bullet tore through his body to spin him off the coach.

Again silence settled. This time, longer. The wheels had stopped moving above the sprawled form of the guard.

Still Mata Lobo waited. His eyes, beneath the red calico headband, were nailed to the overturned Concord. He hadn't moved from his position. He sat stone still and waited. Watched and waited and counted.

He counted three dead: the driver, a passenger, and the guard who was in the road next to the coach—he was undoubtedly dead. But the run usually carried more passengers, at least two more, and that bothered the Apache.

Others might still be inside the coach, dead, wounded, or just waiting. Waiting with a cocked pistol. Either way Mata Lobo had to find out. He hadn't laid this ambush for sport alone. He needed bullets, and a shirt, and any glittering trinkets that might catch his eye. But it was the bullets, more than anything else, that finally made him raise himself and slip quietly down the side of the hill.

His Apache sense led him in a wide circle, so that when he approached the Concord, Banderas Creek was behind him. He walked half crouched, slowly, with short toe-to-heel strides, cat-like, a coiled spring ready to snap. Mata Lobo was a Chiricahua Apache, well schooled in the ways of war.

He passed the baggage strewn about the ground without a side glance and dropped to his hands and knees as he came to the vertical wall that was the top of the coach. He touched the baggage rack lightly, then, pressing his ear against the smooth surface of the coach top, he remained fixed in this position for almost five minutes. Long, silent minutes.

He was about to rise, satisfied the coach was unoccupied, when he heard the sharp, scraping sound from within. Like someone moving a foot across a board.

He froze again, pressing close, then slowly placed his rifle on the ground beside him and lifted a skinning knife from a scabbard at his back.

He inched his body upward until he was standing, placed a foot on a rung of the baggage rack, and pushed his body up until his head was above the coach. He was confident of his own animal stealth. A gun could be waiting, but he doubted it. Only a fool would have moved, knowing he was just outside. A fool, or a child, or a woman.

Nor was he wrong. The woman was crouched against the roof of the coach, her back arched against the smooth surface, holding with both hands a long-barreled pistol that pointed toward the rear window. She was totally unaware of the Apache staring at her a few feet away, lying belly down on the side of the coach. When she saw him it was too late.

Revolver went up as knife came down, but the knife was quicker and the heavy knob on the handle smashed against her knuckles to make her drop the revolver. Dark, vein-streaked arms reached in to drag her up through the door window. She struggled in his grasp, but only briefly, for he flung her from the coach and leapt down to the road after her.

She sat in the road dust and eyed him defiantly, her lips moving slightly, her eyes not wavering from his face. She screamed for the first time as she rose from the dust, but it was not a scream of fear.

She was almost to her feet when the Apache's hand tightened in her hair to fling her off balance back to the ground. He stood over her and looked down into the dust-streaked face. Then he turned back to the stagecoach.

She watched as he rummaged about the wreckage, sitting motionless, knowing that if she tried to run he would probably not hesitate to kill her. Her hands moved to her hair and unhurriedly brushed back the blond wisps that had been pulled from the tight chignon at the nape of her neck. Her hands moved slowly, almost unconsciously, and then down and in the same lifeless manner brushed the heavy dust from the green jersey traveling-dress, as if her movements were instinctive, not predetermined.

But her eyes were not lifeless. They followed the Apache's every move and narrowed slightly into two thin lines that contrasted sharply with her soft face, like fire on water. Her body moved from habit while her mind showed through her eyes.

She was afraid, but only loathing was on the surface. The fear was the stabbing weight in her breast, an emotion she had learned to control. She could have been in her late twenties, but her chin and the lines near her eyes told of at least six additional years.

Every now and then the Apache would glance back in her direction, but he found her always in the same position. She watched him bend over the still form of the guard lying on his back, and her eyes blinked hard as the Indian brought the stock of his rifle down on the man's forehead, but she did not turn her head.

There was no doubt now that all were dead. Mata Lobo was a thorough man, for his people had been slaying the *blanco* since the first war club smashed through the cumbersome armor of the conquistadors. His deeds were known throughout Apacheria; they whispered the name of the bronco Chiricahua with the bloodlust ever in his breast. There would be no survivor to tell of the lone Apache killer.

The sport of the affair had satisfied him, but he was angry. None of the men had been using a Sharps, so there was no ammunition to be had. He picked up the guard's Winchester, slinging the cartridge belt over his shoulder, but he liked the feel of the heavy buffalo rifle better. In the Sharps he had the confidence that comes only after trial. But he had only two cartridges left for it.

He turned his attention to the drummer, who was sprawled awkwardly next to the coach. With his foot he pushed the body over onto its back. A crimson smear spread over the shirtfront. The Apache opened the black satchel next to the man and emptied the contents onto the ground—needles, scissors, paring knives, and thread—and moved on to the horses.

His next act made the woman turn her head slightly, for with his skinning knife he sliced a large chunk of meat from the rump of a disabled horse and stuffed it into the sample case. Then he stepped to the front of the horse and cut the animal's jugular vein.

Soon after, a Chiricahua Apache with a white woman at his

side waded up Banderas Creek along the shallows. The woman dragged her legs through the water stiffly, slowly, as if her reluctance to move quickly was an open act of defiance toward the Indian.

The Chiricahua carried two rifles and a bloodstained satchel and wore a clean shirt, the tail hanging below his narrow hips. With every few steps his glance turned to the cold face of the woman. They disappeared three hundred yards upstream, where the creek cut a bend into the blackness of the pines.

It was the point riders of Phil Langmade's C Troop that found the wrecked stagecoach and the dead men, almost two hours later. Twenty days in the field and a brush with Nachee, and because of it they had missed the stage at Rindo's.

They were returning to the garrison at Inspiration, thighs aching from long, stiff hours in the saddle. Grimy, salt-sweat-white, alkali-caked—both their uniforms and their minds—after days of riding through the savage dust-glare of central Arizona. And of the forty mounts, three had ponchos draped over the saddles, bulging and shapeless. All patrols were not routine.

Langmade sent flankers to climb the ridges on both sides, and then went in. The troopers spread out in a semicircle, watching with hollow, lifeless eyes the flankers on the ridge more than the grisly scene on the road. You get used to the sight of death, but never to expecting it.

Langmade dismounted, but Simon Street, the civilian scout, rode up to the dead driver before throwing off. He walked upstream another hundred yards and then came back, approaching the officer from around the coach. The troopers sat still in their saddles, half-asleep, half-ready to throw up a carbine. Habit.

Langmade said, "I don't know if I want to find her inside the coach or not. If she's there, she's dead."

Street's eyes moved slowly over the scene. "You won't find

her," he said. "There's a little heel print over on the bank. They went upstream. That's sure. If they went down they'd wind up in the open near Rindo's."

Langmade boosted himself onto the side of the stage and came down almost in the same motion. He nodded his head to the scout and kept it moving in an arc along the top of the near ridge.

"Bet they laid up there waiting," Langmade said. "A month's pay they were Apaches."

Street followed his gaze to the ridge. He just glanced at the officer, his face creased-bronze and old beyond its years, crow's feet where eye met temple, his hat tilted low on his forehead, his eyes in shadow. "You're throwin' your money away, soldier," he said. "Apache."

Langmade looked at him quickly. "Only one?"

"That's all the sign says." Street pointed to the butchered horse. "A war party don't cut just one steak."

He turned his attention back to the ridge. He was looking at the exact spot from which the Apache had fired. Then his gaze fell slowly to sweep across the road to Banderas Creek. And he squinted against the glare as his eyes followed the course of the creek to the bend into the pines.

Langmade pushed his field hat back from his forehead, releasing the hot-steel grip of the sweatband, and watched the scout curiously. Langmade was young, in his mid-twenties, but he was good for a second lieutenant. He didn't talk much and he watched. He watched and he learned. And he knew he was learning from one of the best. But the tension was building inside his stomach, and it wasn't just the aftereffects of a twenty-day patrol.

There were three dead men in the road and a woman missing and it had happened because he had failed to bring the patrol in to Rindo's on time. The report would include an account of the brush with Nachee, and that would absolve him of blame. But it wouldn't make it easier for him to face Colonel Darck.

You didn't just look at a stone near your boot toe and say "sorry" to a man whose wife has been carried off by a blood-drunk Apache—even if you weren't to blame.

There it was. Langmade stood motionless, watching the scout. Langmade was in command, a commissioned officer in the United States Army, but he was tired. His bones ached and his mind dragged, weary of fighting the savage country and the elusive Apache who was a part of that country, and always there was so little time.

Learning to fight doesn't come easy with most men. Learning to fight the Apache doesn't come easy with anyone. You watch the veteran until your face takes on the same mask of impassiveness, then you make decisions.

He waited patiently for Street to say something, to give him a lead. He remembered forty troopers who watched the thin gold bars on his shoulders, and he tried to forget his helplessness.

Langmade said, "The colonel was coming from Thomas to meet Mrs. Darck at Inspiration." The scout was aware of this, he knew, but he had to say something. He had to fill the gap until something happened.

Simon Street looked at the officer and a half smile broke the thin line of his mouth. "We'll find her, soldier. It wasn't your fault. People get killed by Apaches every day."

As the words came out, he realized he had said the wrong thing and added, quickly, "Know who this looks like to me?" and then went on when Langmade looked but didn't speak.

"Looks like that bronco Apache we been chasin' on and off for five years. Nochalbestinay. Though the Mexicans named him Mata Lobo. He was a Turkey Creek Chiricahua who'd never get used to reservation life in seven hundred years. Sendin' him to San Carlos was like throwin' a mountain cat a hunk of raw meat and then pullin' all his teeth out."

Street pulled a thin cigar from his pocket and passed his tongue over the crumbling outer layer of tobacco. "You know, at one time there was almost a thousand troops plus a hundred Apache scouts all in the field at one time huntin' him, and no one even saw him. You couldn't ask the dead ones if they saw him or not. An Apache's bad enough, but this one's half devil."

He moved toward the butchered horse. "Boy's got a real yen for steak, ain't he?"

All the time the tension had been building in Langmade. Just standing there with his arms heavy at his sides and the weight pulling down inside his stomach. He had to hesitate until he was sure his voice would come out sounding natural.

"You've got the sign and I've got the men," he said. "Just point the way, Simon. Just point the way."

Street had turned and was walking toward his horse. He stopped and looked back at the officer. "Get your troop back to Inspiration and get a fresh patrol out, soldier."

Street's words were low, directed only to the officer, but Langmade raised his voice almost to a shout when he answered:

"We've got men here—get on his track!"

"I'm not goin' to guide for dead men," the scout answered easily. "If a thousand men can't catch him, you can't count on forty. Maybe just one's the answer. I don't want to tell you how to run your business, son, but if I was you I'd shake it back to Inspiration and get a fresh patrol out."

Street mounted and then looked down at Langmade, who had followed him over to the horse. "The trail's as fresh as you'd want it," he said, nodding toward the butchered horse. "That mare hasn't been dead three hours. And he's got a woman with him to slow him down."

"I've been out longer than that, Simon," Langmade said. "She'll slow him down just so long."

The scout's mouth turned slightly into a smile as he pressed his heels into the mare's flanks. "That's why I got to hurry, soldier."

He walked the mare toward Banderas Creek and kicked her into a gallop as he turned upstream.

AN hour before sunset Simon Street was walking his horse along the winding trail that threaded its way diagonally down the slope of the forest-covered hill that on the western side joined the rocky heights of the Sierra Apaches. This gradual leveling of the sierra was a tangled mass of junipers, gnarled stumps, and rock, rising and falling abruptly from one hillock to the next.

The trail gouged itself laboriously in a general southwesterly direction, fighting rockfalls, pine, and prickly pear, finally to emerge miles to the south at Devil's Flats. From the crest, and occasionally down the path, you could see in the distance the whiteness—the bleak, bone-bleached whiteness—that was the flats.

Street had traveled a dozen-odd miles from the ambush, making his way slowly at first along the creek bank, looking for a particular telltale sign. He knew the Apache had followed the creek, leaving no prints, but somewhere he had to come out.

The Apache would cover his tracks from the creek, but he would be coming out at a particular place for a reason. To pick up his mount. And you can't leave a horse tied in one place for any length of time without also leaving a sign. To recognize the place is something else.

Street saw the low tree branch that had been scarred by the hackamore, and his eyes fell to the particles of horse droppings that had remained after the Apache had swept most of it into the denser scrub brush. He was on the trail. From then on it was just a question of thinking like an Apache.

For the scout, that night, it was the last of his jerked beef and a quarter canteen of cold coffee. No fire. Cold, tasteless rations while he pressed his back against a smooth rock that was still warm from the day's heat and dueled his patience against the black pit that was the night.

His Winchester lay across his lap, and the slight pressure on his thighs was a feeling of reassurance against the loneliness of the night. Dead stillness, then the occasional night sound. He could be the only man in the world. Yet, just a few miles ahead, perhaps less, was a bronco Apache who would kill at the least provocation. And with him was a white woman.

Street rubbed the stock of the Winchester idly.

IN the dusk Amelia Darck watched the Apache. He crouched over the slab of red horsemeat, sitting on his heels, and hacked at the meat with his skinning knife. He cut off a chunk and stuffed it into his mouth, but the cold blood-taste of the raw meat tightened his throat muscles and he swallowed hard to get it down. He would wait.

He cut the slab of meat into thin strips and spread them out separately on a flat shelf of rock. When he had more time he would jerk the meat properly and have plenty to eat.

He looked toward the white woman and saw her staring at him. Always she stared, and always with the same fixed, strange look on her face. The eyes of the Apache and the white woman met, and Mata Lobo turned his attention back to the meat. The woman continued to stare at the Apache.

She sat on the ground with her arms extended behind her, full weight on her arms, propping her body in a rigid position, unmoving. Her legs extended straight out before her, the ankles lashed together with a strip of rawhide. And she continued to watch the Apache.

Amelia Darck saw an Apache for the first time when she was six years old. His face was vivid in her memory. She remembered once somebody had said, ". . . like glistening bacon rind." And always a dirty cloth headband.

Yuma, Whipple Barracks, Fort Apache, and Thomas. Officers' row on a sun-baked parade. Chiricahua, White Mountain, Mescalero, and Tonto. Thigh-high moccasins and a rusted Spencer. Tizwin drunk, then war drums. And only the red sun-slash in the sky after the patrol had faded into the glare three miles west of Thomas. Shapeless ponchos that used to be men. The old story. And she continued to watch the Apache.

Mata Lobo glanced at the woman, then stood up abruptly and walked toward her. He stooped at her feet, hesitated, then placed the blade of the knife between her ankles and jerked up with the blade, severing the rawhide string.

His face was expressionless, smooth and impassive, as he eased his body to the ground. A face that in the dimness was shadow on stone. His hands pushed against her shoulders until her arms bent slowly and her back was flat against the short, sparse grass.

The hands moved from her shoulder and touched her face gently, the fingers moving on her cheeks like a blind man's identifying an object, and his body eased toward hers.

Her face was the same. The eyes open, infrequently blinking. She smelled the sour dirt-smell of the Apache's body. Then she opened her arms and pulled him to her.

SIMON Street was up before dawn. He gave his tightening stomach the last of the cold, stale coffee while he waited for the sun to peel back another layer of the morning darkness. It was cold and damp for that time of the year, and when he again started down the trail, a gray mist hung from the lower branches of the trees and lay softly against the grotesque rock lines.

More often now, the ground fell away to the left, the trail hugging the side of the hill in its diagonal descent; and in the distance was a sheet of milky smoke where the mist clung softly to the flats. The trail was narrow and rocky and lined with dense brush most of the way down.

Less than a mile ahead the grade dropped again steeply to the left of the trail, bare of tree or rock, cutting a smooth swatch twenty yards wide through the pines. The mist had evaporated considerably by then and Street could see almost to the bottom of the slide.

First, it was the faintest blur of motion. And then the sound. A sound that could be human.

Simon Street had been riding half tensed for the past dozen years. There was no abrupt stop. He reined in gently with a soothing murmur into the mare's ear, and slid from the saddle, whispering again to the mare as he tied the reins to a pine branch a foot from the ground.

He made his way along the trail until the slope was again thick with brush and trees, and there he began his descent. A yard at a time, making sure of firm ground before each step, bending branches slowly so there would be no warning swish. And every few yards he would hug the ground and wait, swinging his gaze in every direction—even behind.

He had gone almost a hundred yards when he saw the woman.

He crouched low to the sandy ground and crawled under the full branches of a pine, watching the woman almost thirty yards away. She was sitting on something just off the ground, her back resting against the smoothness of a birch tree.

He was approaching her from the rear and could see only part of her head and shoulder resting against the tree trunk. The brush near her cut off the lower part of her body, but there was something strange about her position—her immobility, the way her shoulder was thrown back so tightly against the roundness of the birch. Street had the feeling she was dead. Time would tell.

He lay motionless under the thick foliage and waited, the Winchester in front of him. And Simon Street had his thoughts. You never get used to the sight of a white woman after an Apache has finished with her. An hour later, a week later, a dozen years later, the picture will flash in your memory, vivid, stark naked of hazy forgetfulness.

And the form of the Apache will be there, too, close like the smothering reek of a hot animal, though you may have never seen him. Then you will be sick if you are the kind. Street wasn't the kind, but he didn't look forward to approaching the woman.

After almost a half hour he again began to work his way toward the woman. In that length of time he had not moved. Nor had the woman. If she was dead, the Apache would probably be gone. But that was guessing, and when you guess, you take a chance.

He crawled all the way, slowly, a foot at a time, until he was directly behind the birch. Then he reached up, his hand sliding along the white bark, and touched her shoulder lightly.

Amelia Darck jumped to her feet and turned in the motion. Her face was powder white, her eyes wide, startled; but when she saw the scout the color seemed to creep through her cheeks and her mouth broke into a fragile smile.

"You're late, Mr. Street. I've waited a good many hours."

The scout was momentarily stunned. He knew his face bore a foolish expression, but there was nothing he could do about it.

The woman's face regained its composure quickly and once again she was the colonel's lady. Though there was a drawn look and a darker shadow about the eyes that could not be wiped away with a polite smile.

Then Street saw the Apache. He was lying belly down in the short grass, close behind Mrs. Darck. Street took a step to her side and saw the handle of the skinning knife sticking straight up from the Apache's back. The cotton shirt was deep crimson in a wide smear around the knife handle.

He looked at her again with the foolish look still on his face.

"Mr. Street, I've been sitting up all night with a dead Indian and I'm almost past patience. Would you kindly take me to my husband."

He looked again at the Apache and then to the woman. Disbelief in his eyes. He started to say something, but Amelia Darck went on.

"I've lived out here most of my life, Mr. Street, as you know. I heard Apache war drums long before I attended my first cotillion, but I have hardly reached the point where I have to take an Apache for a lover."

Simon Street saw a thousand troops and a hundred scouts in the field. Then he looked at the slender woman walking briskly up the grade.

The Kid

I remember looking out the window, hearing the wagon, and saying to Terry McNeil and Delia, "Here comes Repper." And when the wagon came even with the porch, I saw the boy. He was sitting with his legs hanging over the end-gate, but he came forward when Max Repper motioned to him.

That was the first time any of us laid eyes on the boy, and I'll tell you frankly we weren't positive at first it was a boy, even though Max Repper referred to a "him," saying, "Don't let his long hair fool you," and even though up close we could see the features didn't belong to a girl. Still, with the extent of my travel bounded by the Mogollon Rim country, central Sonora, the Pecos River, and the Kofa Mountains—north, south, east, and west respectively—I wasn't going to confine my judgment to this being either just a boy or a girl. There are many things in the world I haven't seen, and the way Terry McNeil was keeping his mouth closed I suspect he was reserving judgment on the same grounds.

Terry was in to buy stores for his prospecting site in the Dragoons. He came in usually about every two weeks, but by the little bit he'd buy it was plain he came for Delia more than for flour and salt-meat.

It was just the three of us in the store when Max Repper came—Terry, taking his time like he was planning to outfit an expedition; Deelie, my girl-child, helping him and hoping he'd take all day; and me. Me being the first line of the sign outside that says PATTERSON GENERAL SUPPLIES. BANDERAS, ARIZONA, TERR.

Now, this Max Repper was a man who saddle-tamed horses on a little place he had a few miles up the creek. He sold them to anybody who needed a horse; sometimes a few to the Cavalry Station at Dos Fuegos, though most often their remounts were all matched and came down from Whipple Barracks. So Max Repper sold mainly to the one hundred and eighty-odd souls who lived in and around Banderas.

He also operated a livery here in the settlement, but even Max admitted it wasn't a paying proposition and ordinarily he wasn't one to come right out and say he was holding a bad guess. Max was a hard-nosed individual, like a man had to be to mustang for a living; but he also had a mile-high opinion of himself, and if any living creature sympathized with him it'd have to have been one of his horse string. Though the way Max broke a horse, the possibility of that was even doubtful.

Repper came in with the boy behind him and he said to me, "Pat, look what the hell I found."

I asked him, "What is it?"

And he said, "Don't let the long hair fool you. It's a boy . . . a *white* boy."

We had to take Max's word for it at first, for that boy cut the strangest figure I ever saw. Maybe twelve years old, he was, with long dark hair hanging to his shoulders Apache style, matted and tangled, but he didn't have on a rag headband and that's why you didn't think of Apache when you looked at him, even though his skin was weathered mahogany and the rest of his getup might have been Indian. His shirt was worn-out cotton and open all the way down, no buttons left; his pants were buckskin, homemade by Indian or Mexican, you couldn't tell which, and he wasn't wearing shoes.

The bare feet made you feel sorry for him even after you looked close and saw something half wild about him. You wondered if the mind was translating what the eyes saw into man-talk or into some kind of gray-shadowed animal understanding.

TERRY McNeil was toward the back, leaning on the counter close to Delia. They were just looking. I got up from the desk (it was by the front window and served as "office" for the Hatch & Hodges Line's Banderas station), but I just stood there, not wanting to go up and gawk at the boy like he was P. T. Barnum's ten cent attraction.

"The good are rewarded," Max Repper said. He grinned showing his crooked yellow teeth, which always took the humor out of anything funny he ever said. "I was thinking about hiring a boy when I found this one." He looked at the boy standing motionless. "He's going to work for me free."

I asked now, "Where'd you find him?"

"Snoopin' around my stores."

"Where's he from?"

"Damn' if I know. He don't even talk."

Max pulled the boy forward by the shoulder right up in front of me and said, "What do you judge his breed to be?" Like the boy was a paint mustang with spots Max hadn't ever seen before.

I asked him again where he'd found the boy and he told how a few nights ago he'd heard something in the lean-to back of his shack, and had eased out there in his sock feet and jabbed a Henry in the boy's back as he was taking down Max's fresh jerky strings.

He kept the boy tied up the rest of the night and fed him in the morning, watched him stuff jerked venison into his mouth, asked him where he came from, and got only grunts for answers.

He put the boy to work watering his corral mounts, and the

way the boy roughed the horses told Max maybe there was Apache in his background. But Max didn't know any Apache words and the boy wasn't volunteering any. Max thought of Spanish. The only trouble was he didn't know Spanish either.

The second night the boy tried to run away and Max (grinning as he told it) beat him blue. The third morning Max decided (reluctantly) he'd have to bring the boy in for shoeing. Shoes cost money, but barefooted a boy don't work so good—not on a south Arizona horse ranch.

I realized then Max was honest-to-goodness planning on keeping the boy, but I mentioned, just to make sure, "I suppose you'll take him to Dos Fuegos and turn him over to the Army."

"What for? He don't belong to them."

"He don't belong to you either."

"He sure as hell does. Long as I feed him."

I told Max, "Maybe the Army can trace where this boy came from."

But Repper said he'd tried for two days to get something out of the boy, and if he couldn't, then no lousy Army man could expect to.

"The kid's had his chance to talk," Max said. "If he don't want to, all right, then. I'll draw him pictures of what to do and push him to'ard it."

Max sat the boy down on a stool and I handed the shoes to him and he jammed them on the boy's feet until he thought he'd found the right size. When Max started to button one of them up the boy yanked his foot away and grunted like it hurt him. Max reached up and swatted the boy across the face and he kept still then.

I remember thinking: He handles the boy like he would a wild mustang, not like a human being. And Terry McNeil must have been thinking the same thing. He came up to us, then knelt down next to the boy, ignoring Max Repper, who was ready to put on the other shoe.

The boy looked at Terry and seemed to back off, maybe just a couple of inches on the outside, but the way he tensed you knew an iron door slammed shut inside of him.

Max said, "What in the name of George H. Hell you think you're doing?" Max had no use for Terry—but I'll tell you about that later.

Terry looked up at Repper and said, "I thought I'd just talk to him."

Max most probably wanted to kick Terry in the teeth, especially now, worn out from trying on shoes, and on general principle besides. Terry was the kind of boy who never let anything bother him, never raised his voice, and I know for a fact that burned Max, especially when they had differences of opinion, which was about every other time they ran into each other.

Max was near the end of his short-sized temper, but he held on and forced out a laugh to show Terry what he thought of him and said to me, "Pat, I'm going to buy myself a drink."

I kept just a couple of bottles for customers who didn't have time to get down to the State House. Serving Max, I watched Terry and the boy.

TERRY was sitting cross-legged in front of him now slipping off the shoe Max had buttoned up. He took another from the pile of shoes and tried it on, the boy letting him, watching curiously, and I could hear Terry saying something in that slow, quiet way he talked. First, I thought it was Spanish, and maybe it was, but the little bit I could hear after that was a low mumble . . . then bit-off crisp words like *sik-isn* and *nakai-yes* and *pesh-klitso*, though not used together. The kind of talk you hear up at the San Carlos Reservation.

Then Terry leaned close to the boy and for a while I couldn't see the boy's face. Terry leaned back and said something else; then he touched the boy's arm, holding it for a moment, and when he stood up the boy's eyes followed him and they no longer had that locked iron door behind them.

Terry came over to us and said, "The boy was taken from the Mexican village of Sahuaripa something like three years ago. He was out watching the men herd cattle when a Chiricahua raiding party hit them. They killed the others and carried off the boy."

Max didn't speak, so I said, "I thought he was white."

Terry nodded his head. "His Mexican father told him that his real parents had died when he was a small boy. The Mexican had hired out to them as a guide, but they both died of a fever on the way to wherever they were going. So the Mexican went home to Sahuaripa and took the boy with him. He explained to the boy that he and his wife had never had a child, but they had prayed, and he believed the boy to be God's answer. They named the boy Regalo."

Max said, "You expect me to believe that?"

Terry shrugged. "Why shouldn't you?"

Max just looked at Terry, then grinned and shook his head slowly like saying: You think I was born last week? Terry might have told him what he thought, but Repper stomped out, dragging the boy and his new shoes with him.

I said to Terry, "The boy really tell you that?"

"Sure he did."

"What about the past three years?"

"He's been with Chiricahuas. Made blood son of Juh, who's chief of the whole red she-bang." Terry said the boy had wandered off on a lone hunt; his horse lamed and he was cutting back home when he came across Max's place.

"Terry," I said, "I imagine a boy could learn a lot of mean things from Chiricahuas."

And Terry said, "That's why I'm almost tempted to feel sorry for old Max."

Terry went back to outfitting for his expedition, but now he actually put his list down and asked Deelie to fill it. He didn't stay more than ten minutes after that, talking to Deelie, telling her what the boy said. And when he was gone I asked Deelie what his big hurry was.

"I never saw a man so eager to get back to a mine camp," I said.

"Terry's anxious to make this one pay," Deelie said. There was a soft smile on her face and she dropped her eyes quick, which was Deelie's way of telling you she had a secret—though I suspected it was something more akin to wishful thinking. Terry McNeil was never too anxious about anything.

He took everything in long, easy strides, even pretty little seventeen-year-old things like Deelie. I know he was taken with her, ever since the first day he set foot here, which was two years ago. He came through on his way to Dos Fuegos, riding dispatch for General Stoneman, and stopped off to buy a pound of Arbuckle's (he said that ration coffee put him to sleep); Deelie waited on him and I remember he looked at her like she was the only woman between Whipple Barracks and the border. Deelie ate it up and stood by the window after he was gone. Three weeks later he showed up again with a shovel, a pick, and boards for a sluice box; and said he'd once seen a likely placer up in the Dragoons and he'd always wanted to test it and now he was going to.

He must have saved his dispatch-riding money, because the first year and a half he paid his store bill cash and carry though he never struck anything likelier than quartz. Lately, he hadn't been buying so much.

I never have disrespected him for not wanting to work steady. That's his business. Max Repper called him a saddle tramp—not to his face—but whenever he referred to Terry. You see, the big war between those two started over Deelie. Max thought he had priority, even though Deelie practically told him right out she didn't care for him. Then Terry came along and Deelie about strained her back putting on extra charm. Max saw this and blamed Terry for stealing her affections. Max himself, being close to pushing forty and with those yellow snag teeth, couldn't have stole her affections with seven hundred Henry rifles.

Maybe Deelie and Terry were closer now than when they first met, but I didn't judge so close as to make Terry *run* back to his diggings to work on the marriage stake. Right after he left, it dawned on me that he would have to pass Repper's place on the way. So that was probably why he left on the run: to look in there. Repper was burning when he left, and a man of his sour nature was likely to take out his anger even on a boy.

Terry came back about three weeks later. He tied his horse, stood on the porch, and took time to stretch the saddle kinks out of his back while Deelie waited behind the counter dying. And when he came in she gave him a smile brighter than the sun flash of a U.S. Army heliograph. Deelie's smile would come right up from her toes.

"Terry!"

He gave her a nice smile.

I told him, "You look happy enough, but not like you're ready to celebrate pay dirt."

"Getting warmer, Mr. Patterson," he said. Which is what he always said.

"Have you seen the boy?" I asked. And was a little surprised when he nodded right away.

"Saw him this morning."

"How so?"

"Well," Terry said, "I was over to Dos Fuegos last week, and you know that big black-haired lieutenant, the married one with the little boy?" I nodded. "He sold me one of his son's shirts. A red one from St. Louis."

"And you gave it to the boy."

Terry nodded. "Regalo."

"You rode all the way over to Dos Fuegos to buy a shirt for the boy."

"A red one—"

"From St. Louis. How'd he like it?"

"He liked it fine."

"How'd Repper like it?"

"He was in the shack."

Terry asked me if I'd seen the boy and I told him no. Repper had kept to his horse camp since the first time he brought the boy in. Terry said the boy looked all right in body, but not in his eyes.

LATER on, after I'd closed up, the three of us were sitting in back having something to eat—Deelie showing off what a good cook she was—when I heard someone at the front door.

Everyone in Banderas knows what time I close; still, it could have been something special, so I walked up front through the dark store and opened the door.

Maybe you've guessed it. I sure didn't. It was the boy, Regalo. He just stood there and I had to take him by the arm and bring him inside. Then, when we reached the light, I saw what was the matter.

He had on the red shirt but the back of it was almost in shreds, and crisscrossing his bare skin were raw welts, ugly red-looking burns like a length of manila had been sanded across his back a couple of dozen times.

Terry was up out of the chair and we eased the boy into it and made him lean forward over the table. Terry knelt down close to him and started to talk in Spanish. Ordinarily I know some, but not the way Terry was running the words together. Then the boy spoke. While he did, Deelie went out and came back with some cocoa butter and she spread it over his back gently without batting an eye. I think right then she advanced seven hundred feet in Terry McNeil's estimation.

The boy said, Terry told us, that Repper had come out of the house and when he saw the new shirt he tried to rip it off the boy, but Regalo ran. That made Repper mad and when he caught him at the barn he reached a hackamore line off a nail and laid it across the boy's back until his arm got tired.

Leaning over the table, the boy didn't cry or whimper, but you knew his back stung like fire.

Terry was saying, let's fix him some eggs, when we heard the door again . . . then heavy footsteps and there was Max Repper in the doorway with his Henry rifle square on us.

"The boy's coming with me." That's all he said. He took Regalo by the arm, yanked him out of the chair, marched him through the front part, and out the door. It happened so fast, I hardly realized Max had been there.

Terry was in the doorway looking up toward the front door. He didn't say a word. Probably he was thinking he should have done something, even if it had happened fast and Max was holding a Henry. Whatever he was thinking, he made up his mind fast. Terry took one last glance at Deelie and was gone.

Of course we knew where he was going. First to the boarding-house for his gun, then to the livery, then to Repper's place. We didn't want him to do it . . . but at the same time, we did. The only thing was, someone else should be there. I figured whatever was going to happen ought to have a witness. So I saddled up and rode out about fifteen minutes behind Terry.

I thought I might catch him on the road, but didn't see a soul and finally I cut off to Repper's. There was Terry's claybank and just over the rump a cigarette glow where Terry was leaning next to the front door.

"He's not here?"

Terry shook his head.

"But we would have passed him on the road," I said.

"Well," Terry said, "he's got to come sooner or later."

As it turned out, it was just after daybreak when we heard the wagon.

Crossing the yard Max looked at us, but he kept on heading the team for the barn. We walked toward him, approaching broadside, then Max turned the team straight on toward the barn door and we could see the wagon bed. Regalo wasn't in it.

Max stepped off the wagon and waited for us with his hands on his hips.

"He ain't here."

Terry asked him, "What happened?"

"He jumped off the wagon and I lost him in the dark."

"And you've been looking for him."

Max grinned that ugly grin of his. "Sure," he said. "A man don't like to lose his top hand."

Then, glancing at Terry, seeing a look on the boy's face I'd never witnessed before, I knew Max Repper was about to lose his top teeth.

Sure enough. Terry took two steps and a little shuffle dance and hit Max square in the mouth. Max went back, but didn't go down and now he came at Terry. Terry had his right cocked, waiting, and he started to throw it. Max put up his guard and Terry held the right, but his left came around wide and clobbered Max on the ear. Then the right followed through, straightening him up, and the left swung wide again and smacked solid against his cheekbone. Max didn't throw a punch. He wanted to at first, then he was kept too busy trying to cover up. I thought Terry's arms would drop off before Max caved in. Then, there it was, for a split second—Max's chin up like he was posing for a profile—and Terry found it with the best-timed, widest-swung roundhouse I've ever seen.

Max went down and he didn't move. Terry stepped inside the

barn and came out with a hackamore. He looked down at Max and started to roll him over with his boot. But then he must have thought, What good will it do— He turned away, dropping the hackamore on top of Repper.

All Terry said was "Long as the boy got away . . . that's the main thing."

AFTER that everything was quiet for a while. Of course what had happened made good conversation, and wherever you'd go somebody would be talking about the half-wild white boy who'd lived with Apaches. And they talked about Max Repper and Terry. Everybody agreed that was a fine thing Terry did, loosening Max's teeth . . . but Terry better watch himself, the way Max holds on to a grudge with both hands and both feet.

Terry went back to his diggings and Deelie wore her tragic look like he was off to the wars. Max would come in about once a week still, but now he didn't talk so much. Ordered what he wanted and got out.

Then one day a man named Jim Hughes came in and told how he'd seen the boy.

Jim had a one-loop outfit a few miles beyond Repper's place. I told him it was probably just a stray reservation buck, but he said no, he came through the willows to the creek off back of his place and there was the boy lying belly down at the side of the creek. The boy jumped up surprised not ten feet away from him, scrambled for his horse, and was gone. And Jim said the boy was wearing a red shirt, the back of it all ripped.

Max heard about it too. The next day he was in asking whether I'd seen the boy. He talked about it like he was just making conversation, but Max wasn't cut out to be an actor. He wanted to find that boy so bad, he could taste it, and it showed through soon as he started talking.

Within the next few days the boy was seen two more times.

First by a neighbor of Jim Hughes's who lived this side of him, then a day later by a cavalry patrol out of Dos Fuegos. They gave chase, but the boy ran for high timber and got away. Both times the boy's red shirt was described.

Now there was something to talk about again; everybody speculating what the boy was up to. The cavalry station received orders from the commandant at Fort Huachuca to bring the boy in and be pretty damn quick about it. It didn't look good to have a boy running around who'd been stolen by the Indians. This was something for the authorities. Down at the State House Saloon they were betting five to one the cavalry would never find him, and they had some takers.

Most people figured the boy was out to get Max Repper and was sneaking around waiting for the right time.

I had the hunch the boy was looking for Terry McNeil. And when Terry finally came in again (it had been almost a month), I told him so.

He was surprised to hear the boy had been seen around here and said he couldn't figure it out. Thought the boy would be glad to get away.

"Why would he want to go back to Apaches?" I asked him.

"He lived with them," Terry said.

"That doesn't mean he liked them," I said. "I could see him going back to those Mexican people, but Sahuaripa's an awful long way off and probably he couldn't find his way back."

Terry shook his head. "But why would he be hanging around here?"

"I still say he's looking for you."

"What for?"

"Maybe he likes you."

Terry said, "That doesn't make sense."

"Maybe he likes red shirts."

"Well," Terry said, "I could look for him."

"It would be easier to let him find you," I said.

"If that's what he wants to do."

"Why don't you just sit here for a while," I suggested. "The boy knows you come here. If he wants you, then sooner or later he'll show up."

Terry thought about it, making a cigarette, then agreed finally that he wouldn't lose anything by staying.

Right in front of me Deelie threw her arms around his neck and kissed him about twelve times. I thought: If that's what having him around just a little while will do, what would happen if he agreed to stay on for life?

DURING the next four days nothing happened. There weren't even claims of seeing the boy. Terry said, well, the boy's probably a hundred miles away now. And I said, Either that or else he's closing in now and playing it more careful. Repper came in once and when he saw Terry he got suspicious and hung around a long time, though acting like Terry wasn't even there.

The night of the sixth day we were sitting out on the porch talking and smoking, like we'd been doing every evening, and I remember saying something about working up energy to go to bed, when Terry's hand touched my arm. He said, "Somebody's standing between those two buildings across the street."

I looked hard, but all I saw was the narrow deep shadow between the two adobes. And I was about to tell Terry he was mistaken when this figure appeared out of the shadows. He stood there for a minute close to one of the adobes, then started across the street, walking slowly.

He came to the steps and hesitated; but when Terry stood up and said, "Regalo," softly, the boy came up on the porch.

Deelie turned the lamp up as we went inside and I heard Terry asking the boy if he was hungry. The boy shook his head. Then we all just stood there not knowing what to say, trying not to stare at the boy. He was wearing the torn red shirt and looking at Terry like he had something to tell him but didn't know the right words.

Then he reached into his shirt, suddenly starting to talk in Spanish. He pulled something out wrapped in buckskin, still talking, and handed it to Terry. Then he stopped and just watched as Terry, looking embarrassed, unwrapped the little square of buckskin.

Terry looked at the boy and then at me, his eyes about to pop out of his head, and I saw what he was holding . . . a raw gold nugget.

It must have been the size of two shot glasses; way, way bigger than any I'd ever had the pleasure of seeing. Terry put it on the counter, stepped back, and looked at it like he was beholding the palace of the king of China.

He just stared, and the boy started talking again in that rapid-fire Spanish like he was trying to say everything at once. Terry looked at the boy and he stared some more until the boy stopped talking.

"What'd he say?" I asked him.

Terry took a minute to look over at me. "He says this is mine and that he'll show me a lot more. A place nobody knows about. . . ."

I could believe that. You don't find nuggets that size out in the road. And it made sense the boy might know of a mine. It was common talk that any Apache could be a rich man, the way he knew the country—the whereabouts of mines worked by the Spanish two and three hundred years ago. Sure Indians knew about them, but they weren't going to tell whites and be crowded off their land quicker than it was already happening. In three years with Chiricahuas, Regalo could have learned plenty.

I said, "Terrence, you and that red shirt have made a valuable friendship."

* * *

TERRY was still about three feet off the ground. He said then, "But he claims he wants to live with me!"

"Well, taking him in is the least you can do, considering—"

"But I can't—"

He stopped there. I turned around to see what Terry was looking at and there was Max Repper in the doorway, with his Henry.

Max was grinning, which he hadn't done in a month, and he came forward keeping the barrel trained at Terry.

"I knew he'd show," Repper said, "soon as I saw you hanging around. I came for two things. Him"—he swung the barrel to indicate the boy—"and my nugget."

"Yours?" I said.

"The boy stole it from me."

"You never saw it before you peeked in that window."

"That's your say," Repper answered.

Terry said, "What do you want with the boy?"

"I got work for him till the reservation people take him away."

"He doesn't belong on a reservation," Terry said.

"That's not my worry." Repper shrugged. "That's what they're saying at Dos Fuegos will happen to him."

Terry shook his head slowly, saying, "That wouldn't be right."

Repper lifted the Henry a little higher. "Just hand me the nugget."

Terry hesitated. Then he said, "You come and take it."

"I can do that too," Repper said. He was concentrating on Terry and started to move toward him. His eyes went to the nugget momentarily, two seconds at best, and as they did the boy went for him. He was at Repper's throat in one lunge, dragging him down. Terry moved then, pushing the rifle barrel up and against Repper's face. Repper went down, the boy on top of him, and then a knife was in Regalo's hand.

Deelie screamed and Terry lifted the boy off of Repper, saying, "Wait a minute!" Then, in Spanish, he was talking more quietly, calming the boy.

Repper sat up with his hand to his face. He had a welt across his forehead where the rifle barrel hit, but he was more mad than hurt. He said, "You think I'm going to let you get away with this?"

Terry was himself again. He said, "I don't think you got a choice."

"I haven't?" Max said. "I'll make damn sure he gets put the hell on that reservation."

"If you can prove he's Indian," Terry answered.

Max gave us his sly look. "Either way," he said. "If he ain't Indian then he's white, with white kin, and no authority's going to let him get adopted by a saddle tramp who ain't worked in two years."

It was a good thing Max was sitting down when he said that. Max was through, and he probably knew it, but if Terry wanted the boy, then he'd sure make it plain hell for Terry to keep him.

I told Repper, "That's up to the authorities. The thing is, this boy's got no recollection of white kin and the only other person who knew his parents is dead. And he's said himself he wants to live with Terry."

Max grinned. "And I imagine Terry wants the boy, and his nugget, to live with him. But like I said, the authorities won't see it that way."

And then Deelie had something to say. She was looking at Max Repper, but I think talking to Terry, and she said, "No, they wouldn't let the boy live with a saddle tramp who hasn't worked in two years . . . but I'm sure they would agree with a successful mining man of Mr. McNeil's character would be more than they could hope for . . . especially since he'll be married within the week."

That was exactly how Deelie did it. I've often wondered if she ever thought Terry married her just so he could raise the boy. I didn't think he did, knowing Terry, and I doubt if Deelie really cared . . . long as she had him.

The Big Hunt

It was a Sharps .50, heavy and cumbrous, but he was lying at full length downwind of the herd behind the rise with the long barrel resting on the hump of the crest so that the gun would be less tiring to fire.

He counted close to fifty buffalo scattered over the grass patches, and his front sight roamed over the herd as he waited. A bull, its fresh winter hide glossy in the morning sun, strayed leisurely from the others, following thick patches of gamma grass. The Sharps swung slowly after the animal. And when the bull moved directly toward the rise, the heavy rifle dipped over the crest so that the sight was just off the right shoulder. The young man, who was still not much more than a boy, studied the animal with mounting excitement.

"Come on, granddaddy . . . a little closer," Will Gordon whispered. The rifle stock felt comfortable against his cheek, and even the strong smell of oiled metal was good. "Walk up and take it like a man, you ugly monster, you dumb, shaggy, ugly hulk of a monster. Look at that fresh gamma right in front of you. . . ."

The massive head came up sleepily, as if it had heard the hunter, and the bull moved toward the rise. It was less than eighty yards away, nosing the grass tufts, when the Sharps thudded heavily in the crisp morning air.

The herd lifted from grazing, shaggy heads turning lazily toward the bull sagging to its knees, but as it slumped to the ground the heads lowered unconcernedly. Only a few of the buffalo paused to sniff the breeze. A calf bawled, sounding *nooooo* in the open-plain stillness.

Will Gordon had reloaded the Sharps, and he pushed it out in front of him as another buffalo lumbered over to the fallen bull, sniffing at the blood, nuzzling the bloodstained hide: and, when the head came up, nose quivering with scent, the boy squeezed the trigger. The animal stumbled a few yards before easing its great weight to the ground.

Don't let them smell blood, he said to himself. They smell blood and they're gone.

He fired six rounds then, reloading the Sharps each time, though a loaded Remington rolling-block lay next to him. He fired with little hesitation, going to his side, ejecting, taking a cartridge from the loose pile at his elbow, inserting it in the open breech. He fired without squinting, calmly, killing a buffalo with each shot. Two of the animals lumbered on a short distance after being hit, glassy eyed, stunned by the shock of the heavy bullet. The others dropped to the earth where they stood.

Sitting up now, he pulled a square of cloth from his coat pocket, opened his canteen, and poured water into the cloth, squeezing it so that it would become saturated. He worked the wet cloth through the eye of his cleaning rod, then inserted it slowly into the barrel of the Sharps, hearing a sizzle as it passed through the hot metal tube. He was new to the buffalo fields, but he had learned how an overheated gun barrel could put a man out of business. He had made sure of many things before leaving Leverette with just a two-man outfit.

Pulling the rod from the barrel, he watched an old cow sniffing at one of the fallen bulls. Get that one quick . . . or you'll lose a herd!

He dropped the Sharps, took the Remington, and fired at the buffalo from a sitting position. Then he reloaded both rifles, but fired the Remington a half-dozen more rounds while the Sharps cooled. Twice he had to hit with another shot to kill, and he told himself to take more time. Perspiration beaded his face, even in the crisp fall air, and burned powder was heavy in his nostrils, but he kept firing at the same methodical pace, because it could not last much longer, and there was not time to cool the barrels properly. He had killed close to twenty when the blood smell became too strong.

The buffalo made rumbling noises in the thickness of their throats, and now three and four at a time would crowd toward those on the ground, sniffing, pawing nervously.

A bull bellowed, and the boy fired again. The herd bunched, bumping each other, bellowing, shaking their clumsy heads at the blood smell. Then the leader broke suddenly, and what was left of the herd was off, from stand to dead run, in one moment of panic, driven mad by the scent of death.

The boy fired into the dust cloud that rose behind them, but they were out of range before he could reload again.

It's better to wave them off carefully with a blanket after killing all you can skin, the boy thought to himself. But this had worked out all right. Sometimes it didn't, though. Sometimes they stampeded right at the hunter.

He rose stiffly, rubbing his shoulder, and moved back down the rise to his picketed horse. His shoulder ached from the buck of the heavy rifles, but he felt good. Lying back there on the plain was close to seventy or eighty dollars he'd split with Leo Cleary . . . soon as they'd been skinned and handed over to the hide buyers. Hell, this was easy. He lifted his hat, and the wind was cold on his sweat-dampened forehead. He breathed in the air, feeling an exhilaration, and the ache in his shoulder didn't matter one bit.

Wait until he rode into Leverette with a wagon full of hides, he thought. He'd watch close, pretending he didn't care, and he'd see if anybody laughed at him then.

HE was mounting when he heard the wagon creaking in the distance, and he smiled when Leo Cleary's voice drifted up the gradual rise, swearing at the team. He waited in the saddle, and swung down as the four horses and the canvas-topped wagon came up to him.

"Leo, I didn't even have to come wake you up." Will Gordon smiled up at the old man on the box, and the smile eased the tight lines of his face. It was a face that seemed used to frowning, watching life turn out all wrong, a sensitive boyish face, but the set of his jaw was a man's . . . or that of a boy who thought like a man. There were few people he showed his smile to other than Leo Cleary.

"That cheap store whiskey you brought run out," Leo Cleary said. His face was beard stubbled, and the skin hung loosely seamed beneath tired eyes.

"I thought you quit," the boy said. His smile faded.

"I have now."

"Leo, we got us a lot of money lying over that rise."

"And a lot of work. . . ." He looked back into the wagon, yawning. "We got near a full load we could take in . . . and rest up. You shooters think all the work's in knocking 'em down."

"Don't I help with the skinning?"

Cleary's weathered face wrinkled into a slow smile. "That's just the old man in me coming out," he said. "You set the pace, Will. All I hope is roaming hide buyers don't come along . . . you'll be wanting to stay out till April." He shook his head. "That's a mountain of back-breaking hours just to prove a point."

"You think it's worth it or not?" the boy said angrily.

Cleary just smiled. "Your dad would have liked to seen this," he said. "Come on, let's get those hides."

Skinning buffalo was filthy, back-straining work. Most hunters wouldn't stoop to it. It was for men hired as skinners and cooks, men who stayed by the wagons until the shooting was done.

During their four weeks on the range the boy did his share of the work, and now he and Leo Cleary went about it with little conversation. Will Gordon was not above helping with the butchering, with hides going for four dollars each in Leverette, three dollars if a buyer picked them up on the range.

The more hides skinned, the bigger the profit. That was elementary. Let the professional hunters keep their pride and their hands clean while they sat around in the afternoon filling up on scootawaboo. Let them pay heavy for extra help just because skinning was beneath them. That was their business.

In Leverette, when the professional hunters laughed at them, it didn't bother Leo Cleary. Maybe they'd get hides, maybe they wouldn't. Either way it didn't matter much. When he thought about it, Leo Cleary believed the boy just wanted to prove a point—that a two-man outfit could make money—attributing it to his Scotch stubbornness. The idea had been Will's dad's—when he was sober. The old man had almost proved it himself.

But whenever anyone laughed, the boy would feel that the laughter was not meant for him but for his father.

Leo Cleary went to work with a frown on his grizzled face, wetting his dry lips disgustedly. He squatted up close to the nearest buffalo and with his skinning knife slit the belly from neck to tail. He slashed the skin down the inside of each leg, then carved a strip from around the massive neck, his long knife biting at the tough hide close to the head. Then he rose, rubbing the back of his knife hand across his forehead.

"Yo! Will . . ." he called out.

The boy came over then, leading his horse and holding a coiled riata in his free hand. One end was secured to the saddle horn. He bunched the buffalo's heavy neck skin, wrapping the free end of line around it, knotting it.

He led the horse out the full length of the riata, then mounted, his heels squeezing flanks as soon as he was in the saddle.

"Yiiiiii!" He screamed in the horse's ear and swatted the rump with his hat. The mount bolted.

The hide held, stretching, then jerked from the carcass, coming with a quick sucking, sliding gasp.

They kept at it through most of the afternoon, sweating over the carcasses, both of them skinning, and butchering some meat for their own use. It was still too early in the year, too warm, to butcher hindquarters for the meat buyers. Later, when the snows came and the meat would keep, they would do this.

They took the fresh hides back to their base camp and staked them out, stretching the skins tightly, flesh side up. The flat ground around the wagon and cook fire was covered with staked-out hides, taken the previous day. In the morning they would gather the hides and bind them in packs and store the packs in the wagon. The boy thought there would be maybe two more days of hunting here before they would have to move the camp.

For the second time that day he stood stretching, rubbing a stiffness in his body, but feeling satisfied. He smiled, and even Leo Cleary wasn't watching him to see it.

At dusk they saw the string of wagons out on the plain, a black line creeping toward them against the sunlight dying on the horizon.

"Hide buyers, most likely," Leo Cleary said. He sounded disappointed, for it could mean they would not return to Leverette for another month.

The boy said, "Maybe a big hunting outfit."

"Not at this time of day," the old man said. "They'd still have their hides drying." He motioned to the creek back of their camp. "Whoever it is, they want water."

Two riders leading the five Conestogas spurred suddenly as they neared the camp and rode in ahead of the six-team wagons. The boy watched them intently. When they were almost to the camp circle, he recognized them and swore under his breath, though he suddenly felt self-conscious.

The Foss brothers, Clyde and Wylie, swung down stiff legged, not waiting for an invitation, and arched the stiffness from their backs. Without a greeting Clyde Foss's eyes roamed leisurely over the staked-out hides, estimating the number as he scratched at his beard stubble. He grinned slowly, looking at his brother.

"They must a used rocks . . . ain't more than forty hides here."

Leo Cleary said, "Hello, Clyde . . . Wylie," and watched the surprise come over them with recognition.

Clyde said, "Damn, Leo, I didn't see you were here. Who's that with you?"

"Matt Gordon's boy," Leo Cleary answered. "We're hunting together this season."

"Just the two of you?" Wylie asked with surprise. He was a few years older than Clyde, calmer, but looked to be his twin. They were both of them lanky, thin through face and body, but heavy boned.

Leo Cleary said, "I thought it was common talk in Leverette about us being out."

"We made up over to Caldwell this year," Clyde said. He looked about the camp again, amused. "Who does the shooting?"

"I do." The boy took a step toward Clyde Foss. His voice was cold, distant. He was thinking of another time four years before when his dad had introduced him to the Foss brothers, the day Matt Gordon contracted with them to pick up his hides.

"And I do skinning," the boy added. It was like What are you going to do about it! the way he said it.

Clyde laughed again. Wylie just grinned.

"So you're Matt Gordon's boy," Wylie Foss said.

"We met once before."

"We did?"

"In Leverette, four years ago." The boy made himself say it naturally. "A month before you met my dad in the field and paid him for his hides with whiskey instead of cash . . . the day before he was trampled into the ground. . . ."

THE Foss brothers met his stare, and suddenly the amusement was gone from their eyes. Clyde no longer laughed, and Wylie's mouth tightened. Clyde stared at the boy and said, "If you meant anything by that, you better watch your mouth."

Wylie said, "We can't stop buffalo from stampedin'."

Clyde grinned now. "Maybe he's drunk . . . maybe he favors his pa."

"Take it any way you want," the boy said. He stood firmly with his fists clenched. "You knew better than to give him whiskey. You took advantage of him."

Wylie looked up at the rumbling sound of the wagon string coming in, the ponderous creaking of wooden frames, iron-rimmed tires grating, and the never-changing off-key leathery rattle of the traces, then the sound of reins flicking horse hide and the indistinguishable growls of the teamsters.

Wylie moved toward the wagons in the dimness and shouted to the first one, "Ed . . . water down!" pointing toward the creek.

"You bedding here?" Leo Cleary asked after him.

"Just water."

"Moving all night?"

"We're meeting a party on the Salt Fork . . . they ain't going to stay there forever." Wylie Foss walked after the wagons leading away their horses.

Clyde paid little attention to the wagons, only glancing in that direction as they swung toward the stream. Stoop shouldered, his hand curling the brim of his sweat-stained hat, his eyes roamed lazily over the drying hides. He rolled a cigarette, taking his time, failing to offer tobacco to the boy.

"I guess we got room for your hides," he said finally.

"I'm not selling."

"We'll load soon as we water . . . even take the fresh ones."

"I said I'm not selling."

"Maybe I'm not asking."

"There's nothing making me sell if I don't want to!"

The slow smile formed on Clyde's mouth. "You're a mean little fella, aren't you?"

"I'm not bothering you . . . just water your stock and get out."

Clyde Foss dropped the cigarette stub and turned a boot on it. "There's a bottle in my saddle pouch." He nodded to Leo Cleary, who was standing off from them. "Help yourself, Leo."

The old man hesitated.

"I said help yourself."

Leo Cleary moved off toward the stream.

"Now, Mr. Gordon . . . how many hides you say were still dryin'?"

"None for you."

"Forty . . . forty-five?"

"You heard what I said." He was standing close to Clyde Foss, watching his face. He saw the jaw muscles tighten and sensed Clyde's shift of weight. He tried to turn, bringing up his shoulder, but it came with pain-stabbing suddenness. Clyde's fist smashed against his cheek, and he stumbled off balance.

"Forty?"

Clyde's left hand followed around with weight behind it, scraping his temple, staggering him.

"Forty-five?"

He waded after the boy then, clubbing at his face and body, knocking his guard aside to land his fists, until the boy was backed against his wagon. Then Clyde stopped as the boy fell into the wheel spokes, gasping, and slumped to the ground.

Clyde stood over the boy and nudged him with his boot. "Did I hear forty or forty-five?" he said dryly. And when the boy made no answer— "Well, it don't matter."

He heard the wagons coming up from the creek. Wylie was leading the horses. "Boy went to sleep on us, Wylie." He grinned. "He said don't disturb him, just take the skins and leave the payment with Leo." He laughed then. And later, when the wagons pulled out, he was laughing again.

Once he heard voices, a man swearing, a never-ending soft thudding against the ground, noises above him in the wagon. But these passed, and there was nothing.

He woke again, briefly, a piercing ringing in his ears, and his face throbbed violently though the pain seemed to be out from him and not within, as if his face were bloated and would soon burst. He tried to open his mouth, but a weight held his jaws tight. Then wagons moving . . . the sound of traces . . . laughter.

It was still dark when he opened his eyes. The noises had stopped. Something cool was on his face. He felt it with his hand— a damp cloth. He sat up, taking it from his face, working his jaw slowly.

The man was a blur at first . . . something reflecting in his hand. Then it was Leo Cleary, and the something in his hand was a half-empty whiskey bottle.

"There wasn't anything I could do, Will."

"How long they been gone?"

"Near an hour. They took all of them, even the ones staked out." He said, "Will, there wasn't anything I could do. . . ."

"I know," the boy said.

"They paid for the hides with whiskey."

The boy looked at him, surprised. He had not expected them to pay anything. But now he saw how this would appeal to Clyde's sense of humor, using the same way the hide buyer had paid his dad four years before.

"That part of it, Leo?" The boy nodded to the whiskey bottle in the old man's hand.

"No, they put three five-gallon barrels in the wagon. Remember . . . Clyde give me this."

The boy was silent. Finally he said, "Don't touch those barrels, Leo."

He sat up the remainder of the night, listening to his thoughts. He had been afraid when Clyde Foss was bullying him, and he was still afraid. But now the fear was mixed with anger, because his body ached and he could feel the loose teeth on one side of his mouth when he tightened his jaw, and taste the blood dry on his lips and most of all because Clyde Foss had taken a month's work, four hundred and eighty hides, and left three barrels of whiskey.

Sometimes the fear was stronger than the anger. The plain was silent and in its darkness there was nothing to hold to. He did not bother Leo Cleary. He talked to himself and listened to the throb in his temples and left Leo alone with the little whiskey he still had. He wanted to cry, but he could not because he had given up the privilege by becoming a man, even though he was still a boy. He was acutely aware of this, and when the urge to cry welled in him he would tighten his nerves and call himself names until the urge passed.

Sometimes the anger was stronger than the fear, and he would think of killing Clyde Foss. Toward morning both the fear and the anger lessened, and many of the things he had thought of during the night he did not now remember. He was sure of only one thing: He was going to get his hides back. A way to do it would come to him. He still had his Sharps.

He shook Leo Cleary awake and told him to hitch the wagon.

"Where we going?" The old man was still dazed, from sleep and whiskey.

"Hunting, Leo. Down on the Salt Fork."

HUNTING was good in the Nations. The herds would come down from Canada and the Dakotas and winter along the Cimarron and the Salt and even down to the Canadian. Here the herds were big, two and three hundred grazing together, and sometimes you could look over the flat plains and see thousands. A big outfit with a good hunter could average over eighty hides a day. But, because there were so many hunters, the herds kept on the move.

In the evening they saw the first of the buffalo camps. Distant lights in the dimness, then lanterns and cook-fires as they drew closer in a dusk turning to night, and the sounds of men drifted out to them on the silent plain.

The hunters and skinners were crouched around a poker game on a blanket, a lantern above them on a crate. They paid little heed to the old man and the boy, letting them prepare their supper on the low-burning cook fire and after, when the boy stood over them and asked questions, they answered him shortly. The game was for high stakes, and there was a pot building. No, they hadn't seen the Foss brothers, and if they had, they wouldn't trade with them anyway. They were taking their skins to Caldwell for top dollar.

They moved on, keeping well off from the flickering line of lights. Will Gordon would go in alone as they neared the camps, and, if there were five wagons in the camp, he'd approach cautiously until he could make out the men at the fire.

From camp to camp it was the same story. Most of the hunters had not seen the Fosses; a few had, earlier in the day, but they could be anywhere now. Until finally, very late, they talked to a man who had sold to the Foss brothers that morning.

"They even took some fresh hides," he told them.

"Still heading west?" The boy kept his voice even, though he felt the excitement inside of him.

"Part of them," the hunter said. "Wylie went back to Caldwell with three wagons, but Clyde shoved on to meet another party up the Salt. See, Wylie'll come back with empty wagons, and by that time the hunters'll have caught up with Clyde. You ought to find him up a ways. We'll all be up there soon . . . that's where the big herds are heading."

They moved on all night, spelling each other on the wagon box. Leo grumbled and said they were crazy. The boy said little because he was thinking of the big herds. And he was thinking of Clyde Foss with all those hides he had to dry . . . and the plan was forming in his mind.

Leo Cleary watched from the pines, seeing nothing, thinking of the boy who was out somewhere in the darkness, though most of the time he thought of whiskey, barrels of it that they had been hauling for two days and now into the second night.

The boy was a fool. The camp they had seen at sundown was probably just another hunter. They all staked hides at one time or another. Seeing him sneaking up in the dark they could take him for a Kiowa and cut him in two with a buffalo gun. And even if it did turn out to be Clyde Foss, then what?

Later, the boy walked in out of the darkness and pushed the pine branches aside and was standing next to the old man.

"It's Clyde, Leo."

The old man said nothing.

"He's got two men with him."

"So . . . what are you going to do now?" the old man said.

"Hunt," the boy said. He went to his saddlebag and drew a cap-and-ball revolver and loaded it before bedding for the night.

In the morning he took his rifles and led his horse along the base of the ridge, through the pines that were dense here, but scattered higher up the slope. He would look out over the flat plain to the south and see the small squares of canvas, very white in the brilliant sunlight. Ahead, to the west, the ridge dropped off into a narrow valley with timbered hills on the other side.

The boy's eyes searched the plain, roaming to the white squares, Clyde's wagons, but he went on without hesitating until he reached the sloping finish of the ridge. Then he moved up the valley until the plain widened again, and then he stopped to wait. He was prepared to wait for days if necessary, until the right time.

From high up on the slope above, Leo Cleary watched him. Through the morning the old man's eyes would drift from the boy and then off to the left, far out on the plain to the two wagons and the ribbon of river behind them. He tried to relate the boy and the wagons in some way, but he could not.

After a while he saw buffalo. A few straggling off toward the wagons, but even more on the other side of the valley where the plain widened again and the grass was higher, green-brown in the sun.

Toward noon the buffalo increased, and he remembered the hunters saying how the herds were moving west. By that time there were hundreds, perhaps a thousand, scattered over the grass, out a mile or so from the boy who seemed to be concentrating on them.

Maybe he really is going hunting, Leo Cleary thought. Maybe he's starting all over again. But I wish I had me a drink. The boy's downwind now, he thought, lifting his head to feel the breeze on his face. He could edge up and take a hundred of them if he did it right. What's he waiting for! Hell, if he wants to start all over, it's all right with me. I'll stay out with him. At that moment he was thinking of the three barrels of whiskey.

"Go out and get 'em, Will," he urged the boy aloud, though he would not be heard. "The wind won't keep forever!"

Surprised, then, he saw the boy move out from the brush clumps leading his horse, mount, and lope off in a direction out and away from the herd.

"You can't hunt buffalo from a saddle . . . they'll run as soon as they smell horse! What the hell's the matter with him!"

HE watched the boy, growing smaller with distance, move out past the herd. Then suddenly the horse wheeled, and it was going at a dead run toward the herd. A yell drifted up to the ridge and then a heavy rifle shot followed by two reports that were weaker. Horse and rider cut into the herd, and the buffalo broke in confusion.

They ran crazily, bellowing, bunching in panic to escape the horse and man smell and the screaming that suddenly hit them with the wind. A herd of buffalo will run for hours if the panic stabs them sharp enough, and they will stay together, bunching their thunder, tons of bulk, massive bellowing heads, horns, and thrashing hooves. Nothing will stop them. Some go down, and the herd passes over, beating them into the ground.

They ran directly away from the smell and the noises that were now far behind, downwind they came and in less than a minute were thundering through the short valley. Dust rose after them, billowing up to the old man, who covered his mouth, coughing, watching the rumbling dark mass erupt from the valley out onto the plain. They moved in an unwavering line toward the Salt Fork, rolling over everything, before swerving at the river—even the two canvas squares that had been brilliant white in the morning sun. And soon they were only a deep hum in the distance.

Will Gordon was out on the flats, approaching the place where the wagons had stood, riding slowly now in the settling dust.

But the dust was still in the air, heavy enough to make Leo Cleary sneeze as he brought the wagon out from the pines toward the river.

He saw the hide buyers' wagons smashed to scrap wood and

shredded canvas dragged among the strewn buffalo hides. Many of the bales were still intact, spilling from the wagon wrecks; some were buried under the debris.

Three men stood waist deep in the shallows of the river, and beyond them, upstream, were the horses they had saved. Some had not been cut from the pickets in time, and they lay shapeless in blood at one end of the camp.

Will Gordon stood on the bank with the revolving pistol cocked, pointed at Clyde Foss. He glanced aside as the old man brought up the team.

"He wants to sell back, Leo. How much, you think?"

The old man only looked at him, because he could not speak.

"I think two barrels of whiskey," Will Gordon said. He stepped suddenly into the water and brought the long pistol barrel sweeping against Clyde's head, cutting the temple.

"Two barrels?"

Clyde Foss staggered and came to his feet slowly.

"Come here, Clyde." The boy leveled the pistol at him and waited as Clyde Foss came hesitantly out of the water, hunching his shoulders. The boy swung the pistol back, and, as Clyde ducked, he brought his left fist up, smashing hard against the man's jaw.

"Or three barrels?"

The hide buyer floundered in the shallow water, then crawled to the bank, and lay on his stomach, gasping for breath.

"We'll give him three, Leo. Since he's been nice about it."

Later, after Clyde and his two men had loaded their wagon with four hundred and eighty hides, the old man and the boy rode off through the valley to the great plain.

Once the old man said, "Where we going now, Will?"

And when the boy said, "We're still going hunting, Leo," the old man shrugged wearily and just nodded his head.

Apache Medicine

Kleecan was three hours out of Cibicu, almost halfway to the Mescalero camp at Chevelon Creek, when he met the Apache.

Ordinarily he welcomed company, for the life of a cavalry scout is lonely enough without the added routine of riding from camp to camp to count reservation heads, and that day the sky was a dismal gray-green to the north, dark and depressing. It made the semidesert surroundings stand out in vivid contrast—the alkali stretches a garish white between low, bleak hills and ghostly, dust-covered mesquite clumps. It was a composite of gray and bright white and dead green that formed a coldness, a penetrating chill that was premature for so early in September, and more than anything else, it made a man feel utterly alone.

But even with the loneliness on him, Kleecan did not welcome the company he saw on the trail ahead. For he had recognized the Apache. It was Juan Pony. And Juan had been drinking mescal.

There wasn't a man in the vicinity of San Carlos who would have blamed Kleecan for not wanting to meet an Apache under such conditions—and especially this one. Juan Pony had a reputation for meanness, and he did everything in his power to keep the reputation alive. And because he was the son of Pondichay, chief of the Chevelon Creek Mescaleros, other Apaches kept out of his way and white men had to use special handling, for Pondichay had a reputation too.

Less than two years before, he had cut a path of fire and blood from Chihuahua to the Little Colorado, and it had taken seven troops of cavalry to subdue thirty-four braves. Twenty-eight civilians and thirteen troopers had been killed during the campaign. Pondichay had lost two men. He was not to be taken lightly; yet the Bureau had merely snatched his carbine from him and given him a few sterile acres of sand along the Chevelon.

Then the Bureau gave the carbine to Kleecan and turned its back, lest Kleecan had to use it to crush the hostile's skull. Pondichay was hungry for war, and he loved his son more than anything on the Apache earth. The least excuse would send Pondichay back on the warpath. That was why men kept out of the way of Juan Pony. But Kleecan had a job to do. He dropped his left elbow to feel the bulge of the handgun under his coat as he reined in before Juan Pony, who had turned his sorrel sideways, blocking the narrow trail.

THE scout could have easily gone around, for the sandy ground was flat on both sides of the trail, but Kleecan had a certain standing to think of. When a man scouts for the cavalry and keeps track of reservation Apaches, he's boss, and he never lets the Apache forget it. Juan Pony had a poor memory, but he had to be reminded with a smile—for his father was still Pondichay.

The scout nodded his head. "*Salmann*, Juan."

Juan Pony shifted his position on the saddle blanket to show full face, but he ignored the scout's greeting of *friend.* Instead, he swung an old Burnside .54 carbine in the scout's direction, aimlessly but with the hint of a threat, and mumbled some words of Mescalero through tight lips. His sharp-featured face was drawn, and his eyes bloodshot, but through his drunkenness it was plain to see what was in his soul. An Apache does not sip mescal like a gentleman. Nor does it have the same effect.

Kleecan caught one of the mumbled words and it was not complimentary. He said, "Juan, you be a good boy and go home. You go on home and I won't report you for tippin' at the mescal."

The Apache nudged the sorrel with his right heel and the horse moved forward and to the side until the naked knee of the Apache was touching the top of the scout's calf-high boot. They were close, two feet separating their faces, and the scout could smell the foulness of the Apache. Rancid body odor and the sour smell of mescal—the result of a three-day binge.

Kleecan wanted to back away, but he sat motionless, his eyes fixed on the Apache's face, his own dark and impassive in the shadow of the narrow-brimmed hat. Kleecan had been smelling mescal and tizwin on the foul breaths of Apaches for almost fifteen years, and it occurred to him that it never did get any sweeter. He noticed a gleam of saliva at the corner of Juan Pony's mouth and he unconsciously passed a knuckle along the bottom of his heavy dragoon mustache.

He said, "I'll ride along with you, Juan. I'm goin' up to Chevelon to see your daddy."

Juan Pony did not answer, but continued to stare at him, his eyes tightening into slits. He leaned closer to the scout until his face and coarse, loose-hanging hair were less than a foot from the scout's. Then Juan Pony cleared his throat and spat, full into the dark face beneath the narrow brim, and with it he sneered the word "*Coche!*" with all the hate in his savage soul.

In the desolate country north of San Carlos, when a man meets a drunken Apache and the Apache spits in his face, he does one of two things: smiles, or shoots him.

KLEECAN smiled. Because he was looking into the future. But with the smile there was a gnawing in his belly, a gnawing and a revulsion and a bitter urge rising within him that he could not stem by simply gritting his teeth. And though he was looking into the future and seeing Pondichay, fifteen years of dealing with the Apache his own way overruled five seconds of logic, and his hand formed a fist and he drove it into the sneering face of Juan Pony.

The Apache went backward off the sorrel, still clutching the carbine, and was out of sight the few seconds it took Kleecan's arm to raise and swing down against the rump of the sorrel. The horse bolted off to the side of the trail with the slap to reveal the Apache pushing himself up with one hand, raising the Burnside with the other. Instinct told Kleecan to draw the handgun, but the ugly, omnipotent face of Pondichay was there again and he flung himself from the saddle in one motion to land heavily on the rising form of Juan Pony. The Apache went backward, landing hard on his back, but his legs were doubled against his body and as he hit, one moccasin shot up between the scout's legs and kicked savagely.

Kleecan's fingers were at the Apache's throat, but the fingers stiffened and spread and he imagined a fire cutting through his body, pushing him away from the Indian. He was on his feet for a moment and then sickness rose from his stomach and almost gagged him so that he fell to his knees and doubled up, holding an arm close to his stomach. Juan Pony twisted his mouth into a smile in his drunkenness and raised the Burnside .54. It would tear a large hole in the white scout. He smiled and began to aim.

His cheek was against the smooth stock when he heard the explosion, and he looked up in surprise, for he was certain he had not yet fired. Then he saw the revolving pistol in the outstretched arm in front of him. Juan Pony had underestimated. It was the last thing he saw in his natural life.

It was said of Kleecan that he never let go. That after he was dead he would still take the time to get the man who had killed him, for Kleecan was not expected to die in bed. He dropped the pistol and rolled to his side with his knees almost touching his chest. The pain cut like a saber and with it was the feeling of sickness. But after a few minutes the saliva eased down from his throat and the sharp pain began to turn to a stiffness. He got to his feet slowly and took the first few steps as if he were walking over broken bottles without boots, but he looked at Juan Pony and the glance snatched him back to reality. And he looked with a grim, troubled face, for he knew what the death of the son of an Apache war chief could mean.

The sky was darker, still gray-green but darker, when Kleecan returned to his mare. He saw the storm approaching and the trouble-look seemed to lift slightly from his dark face. The rain would come and wash away the sign. But it would not wash away the urge for revenge in Pondichay, for the old chief was certain to find the body of his son, buried shallow beneath the rocks and brush off-trail. Pondichay would have no sign to explain to him how it had happened, but that would not hold his hand from its work of vengeance. A revenge on any and all that he chanced to meet. As soon as he discovered the bones of his son.

The scout had one leg up in a stirrup when he saw the small beaded deerskin bag in the road. A leather thong attached to it had been broken, and he realized he had ripped it from the Apache's throat when he had been kicked backward. He picked it up and looked the hundred-odd feet to the mesquite clump where he had buried Juan Pony. He hesitated only for a moment and then stuffed the bag into a side coat pocket. He rode off to the east, leading Juan Pony's sorrel. When he had gone almost three miles, he released the horse with a slap on the rump and set off at a gallop, still toward the east.

He pushed his mount hard, for he wanted to reach the Hatch & Hodges Station at Cottonwood Creek before the rain came. Overhead, the sky was becoming blacker.

* * *

AT a quarter to four Kleecan stopped at the edge of the mesa. In front of him the ground dropped gradually a thousand yards or more to the adobe stagecoach station at Cottonwood Creek. He watched a Hatch & Hodges Concord start to roll, the greasers jump to the sides, and he could faintly hear the shouts of the driver as he reined with one hand and threw gravel at the lead horses with the other. Within a hundred feet the momentum was up and the Concord streaked past the low adobe wall that ringed the station house on four sides. The yells grew fainter and the dust tail stretched and puffed and soon the coach passed from view, following a bend in the Cottonwood, and all that was left was the cylinder of dust that rolled on to the north into the approaching blackness.

Somewhere in the stillness there was the cold-throated howl of a dog coyote. It complemented the dreary blackness pressing from the north like a soul in hell's despair. Kleecan stiffened in the saddle and started to the south into a yellowness that was sun-glare and hazy reflection from the northern storm, and with it the deathlike stillness. Then his eye caught motion. It was a speck, a blur against the yellow-gray, and he knew it to be the dust raised from fast-moving horses. Probably four miles off. Three, four horses. It was hard to tell in the haze. When he reached the bottom of the grade he could no longer see the dust, but he was sure the riders had been heading for the Hatch & Hodges Station.

Art McLeverty, the station agent, came out of the doorway and stood under the front ramada, scratching a massive stomach. His stubby fingers clawed at a soiled expanse of blue-striped shirt, collarless, the neckband frayed, framing a lobster-red neck and above it an even deeper red, puffy face. Kleecan called it the map of Ireland because he had heard the expression somewhere and knew McLeverty thought of it as a compliment.

McLeverty sucked in his stomach and yelled in no particular direction, "Roberto! *¡Aquí, muy pronto!*" And almost at once a small

Mexican boy was in front of the mount, taking the reins from Kleecan.

The station agent led the way through the doorway and then to the right to the small mahogany bar that crossed one side of the narrow room. On the opposite side of the doorway was the long plank table and eight cane-bottomed Douglas chairs where the stage passengers ate, and between bar and table, against the back wall, was the rolltop desk where McLeverty kept his accounts and schedules. Bare, cold to the eye, grimy from sand blowing through the open doorway, it was where Kleecan went for a drink when he had the time.

He leaned on the bar and took off his hat, rubbing the back of his hand over eyes and forehead. Thin, dark hair was smeared against the whiteness of a receding hairline, but an inch above the eyes the face turned tan and weather beaten and the dragoon mustache, waxed at the tips, accentuated a face that could look ferocious as well as kindly. With his hat on, straight over his eyes, the brim cut a shadow of hardness over his face and Kleecan looked stern and cold. Without the hat he looked kindly because the creases at the corners of his eyes cut a perpetual smile in his light blue eyes. He dropped the hat back onto his head, loosely.

"Oh, guess I'll have mescal, Art." He said it slowly, as if after deliberation, though he drank mescal every time he came here.

The station agent reached for the bottle of pale liquid and set it in front of Kleecan, then picked up a thick tumbler and passed it against his shirt before placing it next to the bottle. McLeverty looked as if he was memorizing a speech. He was about to say something, but Kleecan had started to talk.

"If you'd slice up a hen and drop her into the mescal when it's brewin', you'd get a little tone to it. Damn white stuff looks like water." He was pouring as he spoke. He cleared his throat and drank down half a tumblerful.

"I don't make it, I only sell it." McLeverty said it hurriedly. He was almost puffing, so anxious to tell something he knew.

"Listen, Kleecan! Didn't you hear the news—no, I know you didn't. . . ." And then he blurted it out: "The paymaster got robbed and killed this morning! Indians!" He had said it. Now he relaxed.

KLEECAN hadn't looked up. He poured another drink. "I'm not kiddin' with you, Art. You ought to watch the Mexes make it. Throw a few pieces of raw chicken in it and your mescal'll turn kind of a yellow. Makes it look like it's got some body."

"Damn it, Kleecan! I said the paymaster got robbed! The paywagon burned and the paymaster, Major Ulrich, and four of the guards shot and scalped as bald as you please. Passengers going up to Holbrook were all talking about it. They said a cavalry patrol'd stopped them on the road from Apache and told them and then asked them if they'd seen anything. And they were all scared to hell 'cause the cavalry lieutenant told them he was sure it was Juan Pony and some Mescaleros, 'cause no one's seen Juan in almost a week. Damn butchers are probably all up in the hills now."

Kleecan took another drink before looking at the Irishman. "What happened to the other two guards? They always ride at least six."

"They think they were carried away by the 'Paches. What else you think! They weren't around!"

Kleecan put the tumbler down and propped his elbows on the bar.

"Art, there're only two things wrong with your story," he said. "Number one: Mescaleros don't scalp. You been out here long enough to know that. And it wouldn't be Yavapais, Maricopas, or Pimas, 'cause they've been farmin' so long their boys don't know what a scalp knife looks like—and an Arapaho hasn't been down this far in ten years. Number two: Just a little more than three hours ago I shot Juan Pony as dead as you can get. And he was too full of mescal to have taken any paymaster."

Kleecan pushed away from the bar and did a half knee bend. "Damn Indian like to ruined me for life."

McLeverty didn't know what to say. He stood behind the bar with his mouth slightly open and watched his story break up into little pieces.

The scout couldn't help smiling. When news reaches a man in a lonely corner like the Cottonwood station, he will tell it to himself over and over, savoring it, waiting, his jaw aching to tell it to the next man that comes in from an even farther corner. He was a little bit sorry he had spoiled the news-breaking for McLeverty.

Kleecan said, "Tell you what, Art. I'll bet you five to three dollars that there weren't any Indians around and that those two missin' guards are in on the deal."

As he spoke his gaze drifted along the front wall and then stopped at the wide window. There was the flat whiteness, the darkness above it, then in the distance the dust cloud. A few moments later he made out three horsemen. His eyes narrowed from habit, years of squinting into the distance, and he judged that two of the riders could be wearing cavalry blue.

"Get the Army up this way much, Art?"

McLeverty followed the scout's gaze out the window. He squinted for a long time, then his eyes became wider as the riders drew closer, and next they were bulging, for McLeverty seldom enough got a troop of cavalry on patrol up this way—let alone two troopers and a civilian—and it was easy to see he was thinking of what Kleecan had said about the other two guards being a part of the holdup.

And Kleecan was thinking of the same thing. He had been making conversation before. Now he wasn't sure. He told himself it was just the timing that made him think that way.

McLeverty couldn't turn his eyes from the window. He just stared. Finally he said, "God, do you suppose those three—"

"Four," Kleecan said. "I'll add another dollar that there're four of them."

TWO troopers and a civilian, dressed for riding, came into the room slowly and glanced around before walking over to the bar. But even in their slight hesitancy they had smiled. They stood at the bar brushing trail dust from their coats, still smiling, and talked about the coming rain and the dark sky, and they offered to buy the station agent and the scout a drink. Kleecan didn't speak because he was trying to picture the happy world these men were living in. It wasn't cynicism. It was just that men didn't ride into an out-of-the-way stage station covered with the grime of hours on horseback and then suddenly react with a brother-love spirit that belonged to Christmas Eve. A saddle doesn't treat a man that way.

McLeverty was pushing the bottle across the bar to the three men when the back door opened and the fourth one entered. Like the other civilian his coat was open and a pistol hung at his side. McLeverty looked at the man and then to Kleecan and in the look there was a mixture of suspicion, respect, and fear.

The fourth man saw the suspicion.

"Wanted to use your backhouse," he explained. "Afore I came in and had to go right out again," and he ended the words with a meaningless laugh.

He joined the others at the bar and stood next to Kleecan, who lounged against the bar with his back half turned to the four men. The fourth one slapped the two troopers on the shoulders and told them to pour a drink. The troopers were younger than the two civilians. Big, rawboned men, they wore their uniforms slovenly and didn't seem to care. The man who had come in the back way did most of the talking and most of the drinking.

They had been at the bar for almost fifteen minutes when the lull finally came. They had been talking continually during that time. Talking about uninteresting things in loud voices. There were a few words, then prolonged laughter, and after that silence. The four men lifted their glasses to their lips. It was a way of filling the lull while they thought of something else.

Kleecan turned his head slightly in their direction. "Hear about the paymaster gettin' held up?"

When he said it four drinks were still mouth high. There was the clatter of a shot glass hitting the bar. And the strangled coughing as a drink caught halfway down a throat, and the continued coughing as the liquor hung there and burned. But after the coughing there was silence. Kleecan wasn't paying any attention to them.

The fourth man had his coat open and his right hand was on the pistol butt at his hip. The two troopers glanced at each other and then at Kleecan, who had turned his head in their direction, but they dropped the glance to somewhere in front of them. Only the other civilian was completely composed. He hadn't moved a muscle. He was about Kleecan's age, older than the other three, and wore long dragoon mustaches similar to the scout's.

He looked at Kleecan. "No, mister. Tell us about it. Happen near here?" The man's voice was even, and carried a note of curiosity.

"Happened south of Fort Apache," Kleecan said. "That right, Art?"

McLeverty said, "That's right. The major was coming up from Fort Thomas when these—uh—Indians jumped the train and took five scalps and the pay."

"You don't say," the civilian said. "We've just come from Fort McDowell. Left yesterday and been riding ever since. That's why we haven't heard anything, I guess." He smiled, but not with nervousness.

Kleecan didn't smile. He nodded to the troopers. "You soldiers from Whipple?"

"Yes, they're both from Whipple Barracks." The civilian answered before either trooper could say anything. "You see, my partner and I are to join the survey party on the upper Chevelon, and these two gentlemen"—he pointed to the two troopers with a sweep of his arm—"are our guides."

"You could use another guide," Kleecan said. "You're fifteen miles east of Chevelon."

The civilian looked dumbfounded. He pushed his hat back from his forehead. "No! Why I thought it was due north of here!" There was surprise in his voice. "Well, it's a good thing we stopped in here," he said. "You say we have to go back fifteen miles?"

Kleecan didn't answer. He was staring at the troopers, looking at the regiment number on their collars. And as he looked he couldn't help the feeling that was coming over him. "I didn't know the Fifth was over at McDowell," he said.

The civilian shrugged his shoulders. "You know how the Army moves regiments around."

"I ought to," Kleecan said slowly. "I guide for them."

The silence was heavy in the narrow room. Heavy and oppressing, and because no one spoke the silence acted to strip naked the thoughts of the two men who stood at the bar staring into each other's eyes. The civilian knew his pretense was at an end and he shrugged his shoulders again, but looked in Kleecan's face.

Kleecan stared back at him, and all of a sudden there was a god-awful hate in him and he wanted to yell something, swear, and go for his gun—because the Fifth was at Fort Thomas, and the paywagon guards would be men of the Fifth, but they wouldn't wear their forage caps like that, not without the slant across an eye that meant Manassas and Antietam and a thousand miles of blood-red plains between the Rosebud and the Gila, and there was no survey party on the upper Chevelon for he had taken it out ten days before, and two men didn't go into Mescalero country to survey with two others who pretended to be troopers—not without equipment.

The civilian said, matter-of-factly, "What are you going to do about it?"

Kleecan stood motionless and knew he couldn't do anything about it. But he felt the hot anger drain from his face and he was glad of that, for then he wouldn't move rashly. Four to one wasn't gambling odds.

"Well, if you don't know, I'll tell you," the civilian said. "You're going to get on your horse and start guiding, and you're going to guide us over the best trail right out of Arizona, and you'll ride with that feeling that the least little move you make out of line will be your last. If we go, you go, and you don't look like a martyr to me."

THE rain continued to drizzle in the early dusk. They rode single file along the narrow trail that followed the bend of the lower Chevelon, and they rode in silence, each man with his own thoughts. Kleecan was soaked to the skin. One of the troopers had taken his poncho and now rode huddled, his chin bent into the folds of the collar, his body dry. When it had started to grow dark, Kleecan thought they would stop and find some kind of shelter for the night. He had even suggested it, but the outlaw leader had only laughed and said, "Travel when it's raining and there isn't any sign. You ought to know that, Indian scout. We'll keep on long as the rain lasts, even if we ride all night." That had been almost two hours before.

And it was then that the idea had been born. *Even if we ride all night.* He had had two hours to think it out clearly.

When they came to the Chevelon ford it was almost dark. Kleecan dismounted and walked to the bank of the running creek that was now almost waist deep from the continuous rain. The outlaw leader dismounted with him, but the others stayed on their horses, back under the bow of a cottonwood. From there the two men at the creek bank were only dim shadows. And that was what Kleecan was counting on. He looked at the creek and then to the outlaw and nodded his head, but as he turned to go back to his horse his foot slipped on the loose, sandy bank, throwing him off balance and hard against the outlaw. The man pushed Kleecan aside violently and drew his gun in a clean motion—but not before Kleecan's hand had found the side pocket of his coat.

"Don't do that again. We don't need you that bad."

"The darkness is makin' you spooky. I slipped on the bank."

Nothing more was said.

They made the crossing without mishap and picked up the trail again on the other side. In the darkness they made their way haltingly, brushing sharp chaparral and ducking suddenly as the blackness of a tree limb loomed in front of their faces. Kleecan rode silently and gave no warning call when an obstruction came in the trail, then smiled when he'd hear the curse from one of the outlaws whose face had been swatted by a soaked tree branch. The rain continued to drizzle and they rode on. They were a good two miles from the creek ford when Kleecan called back, "Trail goes left." Then he kicked the mare hard and swerved her to the left to follow the sharp turn in the trail.

The outlaws were taken by surprise momentarily. Their heads were down, shielding their faces from the stinging drizzle, but they heard Kleecan's mare break into a gallop, and in a body they spurred their own horses, bunching in confusion at the trail bend, then singling out to kick their mounts into a gallop up a sharp, widening rise. The trail dipped again suddenly and the outlaw chief, in the lead, reined in with a jolting motion, swinging an arm over his head. In the dimness he saw heavy, bulky shapes all around him, round and massive. The outlaws instinctively brought their mounts in close together and looked about, squinting into the darkness. Then one of the outlaws made a noise like a deep sigh. It was a moan and an exclamation. Somebody said, "Oh, God!" and another man cursed, but it sounded like a prayer, for there was a plea in it. On the outer rim they saw the hazy shapes of the wickiups and on four sides of them they looked down into the faces of Mescalero Apaches.

Kleecan had led them into the middle of Pondichay's rancheria.

The scout still sat his mare, but he was beyond the circle of Apaches. Next to him stood Pondichay, old and somber, too polite to ask outright the meaning of the sudden intrusion. Kleecan greeted him in Mescalero and continued to speak in that tongue, but he kept his eyes on the outlaw chief as he spoke.

For Kleecan told the old chief many things. He told him what a great warrior he was and recounted many of Pondichay's deeds, but slowly his voice saddened and finally he told him how sad he had been to hear of Juan Pony. The old Apache looked up, but Kleecan continued. And he told him that Juan Pony had been murdered. He told him that he had worked great medicine and was able to bring right to this camp the murderers of Juan Pony. His voice became cold and he told him how the murderers had committed the greatest sacrilege of all by taking Juan's *hoddentin* sack, which held the sacred pollen to ward off evil. And he told Pondichay that if he did not believe him, why not look in the chief murderer's pocket and see if the medicine bag was not still there—for it is said that an Apache warrior parts with his *hoddentin* bag only when he is dead.

Kleecan wheeled his horse around. He had made his offering to the gods of destruction.

No Man's Guns

As he drew near the mass of tree shadows that edged out to the road he heard the voice, the clear but hesitant sound of it coming unexpectedly in the almost-dark stillness.

"Cliff—"

His right knee touched the booted Springfield and he thought of it calmly, instinctively, drawing it left-handed in his mind, as he slowed the sorrel to a walk. Now at the edge of the shadows he saw a man with a rifle.

The man called uncertainly, "Cliff?"

"You got the wrong party," he answered, and neck-reined the sorrel toward the trees.

Less than twenty feet away the rifle came up suddenly. "Who are you?"

"My name's Mitchell."

The rifle barrel hung hesitantly. "You better light down."

Astride the McClellan saddle, Dave Mitchell didn't move. He sat with his shoulders pulled back, yet he was relaxed. Narrow hips, sun-darkened, thin-lined features beneath the slightly-turned-up forward brim of a faded Stetson and everything about him said *Cavalry*. Everything but the rough-wool gray suit he wore. His coat was unbuttoned and his dark shirt was unmistakably Army issue.

"You're camped back in there?" Mitchell asked, and he was thinking, watching the man studying him: I'm the wrong man and now he doesn't know what to do. The man with the rifle didn't reply and Mitchell said, "I'm ready to camp the night. If you already got a place, maybe I could join you."

For a moment the man didn't answer. Then the rifle, a long-barreled Remington, waved in a short arc. "Light down."

Mitchell let his right rein fall as he came off the sorrel. The rifle waved again. The man stood aside and Mitchell walked past him leading the sorrel. They moved through the trees, thinly scattered aspen, then cottonwood as the ground began to slope gradually, and Mitchell knew there'd be a creek close by. Unexpectedly, then, he saw the broad clearing and a wagon illuminated by firelight.

The ribbed canvas covering of it formed a pale background for the two figures who stood watching him approach. A man, his legs slightly apart and his hand covering the butt of a holstered revolver. A woman was next to him and she watched Mitchell with open curiosity as he entered the clearing.

"Rady's brought us a guest," the woman said.

The man with the rifle was next to Mitchell now. "Hyatt, he says he wants to camp." The woman walked to the fire, but Hyatt, his hand still on the revolver, didn't move. Nor did he answer, and his eyes remained on Mitchell. "He said he was ready to camp the night," Rady added, "so I thought—"

"Open your coat," Hyatt said. "Hold it open."

Slowly Mitchell spread the coat open. "I'm not armed."

"He's got a carbine on the horse," Rady said.

Hyatt glanced at him. "Go back where you were."

* * *

MITCHELL dropped the rein and walked toward the low-burning fire as the woman extended a porcelain cup toward him and said, "Coffee?" Behind him he heard Rady's footsteps in the dry leaves, then fading to nothing, and he felt Hyatt watching him as he took the cup of coffee, his hand momentarily touching the woman's.

"You drink your coffee, then move off," Hyatt said. He was in his early thirties, but a week-old beard stubble darkened his face, adding ten years to his appearance. His face was drawn into tight, sunken cheeks and he looked as if he'd never smiled in his life. To the woman he said, "I'll tell you when we start giving coffee to everybody who goes by."

Mitchell hesitated, letting the sudden tension inside him subside, and he thought, Don't let him rile you. Don't even tell him to go to hell. He said to Hyatt, "I'll leave in a minute."

"You'll leave sooner if I say so."

Maybe you ought to tell him, at that, Mitchell thought. Just to see what he'd do. But he heard the woman say, "Hy, don't talk like that," and he turned to the fire again.

"You shut your mouth!" Hyatt told her.

Mitchell sipped his coffee, his eyes on the woman. Her face was lit by the firelight and it shone warmly and cleanly. He watched her glance at Hyatt but not answer him and he said to her, mildly, "I don't want to start a family argument."

"We'll ignore him, then," the woman said. She smiled and the smile was faintly in her eyes. She'd impressed Mitchell as a woman who smiled little, and the soft radiance that came briefly into her eyes surprised him. Still, she fell into a type in Mitchell's mind: small, frail looking, a woman who picked at her food yet was strong and you wondered what kept her going. Light hair, thin, delicately formed features, and dark shadows beneath the eyes. A serious kind, a woman who loved strongly and simply. A woman who spoke little. This, Mitchell believed, was the most interesting type of all. The most feminine, even while sometimes reminding you of a little boy. At least the most appealing. Perhaps the kind to marry.

She said, "Could I ask where you're going?"

"Home," Mitchell answered. No, she didn't exactly fit the type. She talked too freely.

"Where is that?"

"Banderas. I just left Whipple Barracks yesterday. Discharged."

"I thought so," the woman said. "Just the way you stand."

"I suppose some of it's bound to rub off, after twelve years."

"You don't look that old."

"Older'n you. I'm almost thirty-one."

"Were you an officer?"

"No, ma'am. Sergeant."

"You're going home to your folks?"

"Yes, ma'am. My dad has a place near Banderas."

"They'll be glad to see you."

Mitchell half turned as Hyatt said, "How do we know you're from Whipple?"

"I just told you I was."

"What proof you got?"

"I don't have to show you anything."

Hyatt's hand hung close to his holster. "You don't think so, huh?"

"Look," Mitchell said. "Why don't you quit standing on your nerves."

"Let's see your proof," Hyatt said.

Mitchell glanced at the woman. "You ought to keep him locked up."

The woman half smiled. "Do you have discharge papers?"

Mitchell's hand slipped into his open coat and patted his shirt pocket. "Right here."

"Why don't you show him?" the woman said. "So we'll have a little peace."

MITCHELL shook his head. "It's a matter of principle now." A matter of principle. And a matter of twelve years someone telling you what to do. You can take it when you're being paid to take it. But this one isn't paying, Mitchell thought. Take that handgun off him and bend it over his head? No, just get out. You don't have any business here.

The woman said, "Men are always talking about principle, or honor."

"Well, I'm through talking about it tonight," Mitchell said. He handed the empty cup to her. "Much obliged. I'm moving on now." She looked at him, but said nothing.

He saw her eyes shift suddenly.

Behind you!

It snapped in his mind and he heard the movement and he wheeled, bringing up his arms, throwing himself low at Hyatt who was almost on top of him. His shoulder slammed into Hyatt's knees and he drove forward as the pistol barrel came down against his spine. His arms clamped Hyatt's legs and he came up suddenly, his boots digging into the sand, throwing Hyatt's legs over his shoulder. Hyatt landed on his back, rolling over almost as he struck the ground, frantically reaching for the revolver knocked from his hand, almost touching it as Mitchell dropped on top of him.

They rolled in the sand, Hyatt's fingers tearing through Mitchell's shirt, clawing at his throat. Mitchell's hand found the revolver. He threw it spinning across the sand and his fist came back to slam against Hyatt's face. He pushed himself free, rolling, rising to his feet, and as Hyatt came up he swung hard against his jaw. Hyatt staggered. He started to go down and Mitchell hit him again, holding him momentarily with his left hand as his right clubbed into the upturned face. Hyatt's head snapped back and he went down.

Mitchell turned to the woman. He was breathing heavily and his left hand was pressed to the small of his back. "Are you married to him?" he asked.

She shook her head. "Not really."

Mitchell hesitated. If he turned away he'd never see this woman again. Something made him ask, "Do you love him?"

She looked at him, her face softly impassive in the firelight. "You'd better move along," she said quietly.

For a moment Mitchell's eyes remained on her, as if he were reluctant to leave. He turned to the sorrel, then hesitated again and walked over to Hyatt.

"Mister, you brought this on yourself. Your man out there thought I was somebody named Cliff and he brought me in because he was too scared to do anything else. I don't care who you are. . . . I don't care who Cliff is—" Mitchell broke off. "If you want to know the truth, I think you're crazy." He glanced momentarily at the woman before telling Hyatt, "Maybe you got some good points, but if you do you keep them a secret."

Hyatt's head came up slowly. He watched Mitchell go to his sorrel and mount. He watched him silently, his hand covering a folded piece of paper on the ground beneath him. A square of paper folded four times just to fit into a shirt pocket.

Mitchell urged the sorrel into the trees, letting it have its head, but holding it enough to reach the road farther down from where Rady would be. The woman stayed in his mind: standing in the firelight, her eyes meeting his and not lowering even when he continued to stare at her.

Some woman.

His body came alive as the shot sounded behind him and his hand instinctively went to the booted carbine. He turned in the saddle drawing the Springfield, the sorrel sidestepping nervously, kicking the dry leaves, throwing its head. There were other sounds in the leaves and suddenly a man's voice: "Throw up your hands!" And almost with the words Mitchell was dragged from the saddle. Men were all around him in the darkness, two holding his arms, and as he tried to rise a fist came from nowhere, stinging hard against his face.

A rifle barrel jabbed into his back and he was taken through the trees, a man holding each arm. There were more men at the clearing and the nearest ones stepped aside as Mitchell was brought in. One man was building the fire. Another was climbing the wagon wheel, now looking inside. The rest stood in a semicircle around Hyatt and the woman.

The man holding Mitchell's left arm shouted, "Dyke, we got the other one!"

Mitchell saw one of the men turn and nod his head, then beckon them to come closer. He stood relaxed, a tall man wearing a stiff-brimmed hat low and straight over his eyes, and a tawny tip-twisted mustache that in the firelight blended with the weathered cut of his features. His coat was open, a dark coat . . . and then Mitchell saw it. The deputy star against the dark cloth and everything was suddenly perfectly clear.

Hyatt was saying, "What're you doing! We're camped here and you barge in, shooting—"

A man said, "You scrambled for that gun quick enough."

"How'd I know who you were?"

"You know now." The man laughed. Mitchell looked from this man to the others. There were perhaps a dozen in the group, but only Dyke and two or three more wore deputy stars.

"Listen"—Hyatt's voice calmed—"I think you could've announced yourselves, that's all. You're looking for somebody and you want to ask some questions, that it?"

Dyke shook his head. "I don't have any questions."

Hyatt's eyes shifted along the line of men. "We're on our way down to Tucson. I'm going in business with a man down there."

Dyke said nothing. His eyes were on Hyatt, studying him.

"In the freight business," Hyatt said. "This man's already got contracts."

"Are you through?" Dyke said then.

Hyatt frowned. "What do you mean?"

"I'll tell a story now," Dyke said. "It starts the day before yesterday when the Hatch & Hodges was held up an hour out of Mojave. One of the passengers, Mr. J. A. Hicks, was shot and killed when he raised an objection. Now, this Mr. Hicks was owner of the Mogollon Cattle Company—Slash M—of which I'm foreman. Mr. Hicks, besides being boss, was my best friend . . . which doesn't mean much to the story aside from it's the reason I was deputized to take out a posse."

Hyatt said, "I'm sorry to hear that, but—"

"I'm not finished," Dyke stated. "You see, these holdup men separated after the robbery. We spent a whole day scratching for sign and finally we got on one we were pretty sure of. Last night we caught up with a man named Cliff something. Now, at first he said he didn't know anything about it."

DYKE'S eyes hadn't left Hyatt's. "I hit this man twice. The second one broke his jaw and after that he wrote down what we wanted to know. How he was to meet his friends tonight, and where. A woman and two men posing as travelers. A man named James Rady; another by the name of Hyatt Earl."

"Well?" Hyatt said. His voice was controlled, and it told nothing of what he might be thinking.

Dyke brought a match out of his vest pocket and wedged it into the corner of his mouth, shaking his head as he did. "That's all there is to the story."

Hyatt hesitated. "Now what?"

"Now, Mr. Earl," Dyke said mildly, his eyes lifting then, "we're going to hang you right on that cottonwood over there."

"What're you talking about, hanging! You don't even know—" Hyatt broke off. He looked at Dyke and at his men and for a long moment he was silent, gaining control of himself. He said then, calmly, almost defiantly, "You got to take us to trial. That's what the law says."

The matchstick moved under Dyke's full mustache. "Mr. Earl, are you telling me what I have to do?"

That was it. The futility of arguing showed briefly on Hyatt's face. He asked, "What about the woman?"

Dyke shook his head. "This Cliff said she didn't want any part of it, but you forced her into it. We're not bothered about her. Just you and Rady there." He nodded directly at Mitchell.

Mitchell frowned. Hurriedly then his eyes swept the clearing. Rady wasn't here! He called to Dyke, "I'm not Rady! He's the one with the Remington . . . was out by the road."

Dyke studied him before answering. "There wasn't anybody out there."

"Then he got away, but I sure as hell ain't Rady!"

"Who're you supposed to be?"

"Dave Mitchell. I just rode in a little while ago looking to camp." He saw Hyatt watching him, a grin softening the dark bearded face.

"Rady," Hyatt said, "are you drunk or something?"

Mitchell stared at him with disbelief. "What's the matter with you? Tell them who I am!"

Hyatt shook his head. "There's no use in that, Rady. Let's own up . . . take our medicine like men."

Mitchell's eyes went to Dyke. "Listen. This man's crazy. I suspected it before. Now I'm sure."

"If I was in your shoes," said Dyke, "I might pull the same stunt."

Mitchell paused. "All right"—his glance went to the woman—"ask her."

She looked at Mitchell, then shook her head. "He's not Rady. His name is Mitchell."

Dyke said, "Uh-huh, and you're Mrs. Mitchell."

"I never saw him before this evening."

"Claire," Hyatt said sympathetically, "there's no use. Rady's got to take his medicine just the same way I do."

The woman's face was cold and showed no emotion. "He had a fight with this man Mitchell and lost. That's why he wants to see him hang."

"Claire! . . . Rady and I were just kidding! You thought we really meant it?"

Mitchell looked at Dyke again. "You said that holdup was day before yesterday. I can prove I was at Whipple then. I was just discharged yesterday."

"What's your proof?" Dyke asked.

"Ask anybody at Whipple!"

"Rady," Hyatt said, "delaying it a few days ain't going to help any, they'll still hang you. Let's get it over with."

Mitchell's expression changed suddenly and his hand went to his chest. "My discharge order! It's dated yesterday!"

"Keep your hand out of that coat!" Dyke snapped. He nodded to one of the men near Mitchell. "Take a look."

The man stepped in front of Mitchell. His hand went over the shirt, then to the inside coat pocket. "Nothing," he said over his shoulder.

Mitchell's hand came up. He felt the empty pocket, and the part of his shirt that was torn—

"Listen, while we were fighting my shirt was ripped. The paper fell out, that's what happened. Look around there, right where you're standing!"

Dyke continued to study Mitchell, but some of his men moved about, looking at the ground and scuffing the sand with their boots. A man said, "I don't see nothin'," and another said, "Not around here." Watching them, the tension building and becoming unbearable. Mitchell suddenly tore himself from the men holding him. They started after him and Dyke called, "Let him go!"

Mitchell came on, his eyes searching the ground, then dropped to his hands and knees, his fingers brushing the sand, smoothing it, and carefully he covered the area where the fight had taken place. He came up slowly and sat back on his heels. "It's not here," he said wearily. Then: "Wait! When I was pulled off my horse—" He came to his feet quickly.

Dyke asked, "You ever on the stage?"

"I'm telling you the truth!" Mitchell screamed. "Can't you see that!"

"I see a man fighting awful hard," Dyke replied, "for a life he don't deserve."

"What do you expect me to do!" Mitchell paused then. He breathed in and out and said, more calmly, "I swear to Almighty God I had nothing to do with that holdup."

"That's what this Cliff said," Dyke answered. "Before I broke his jaw."

"Rady," Hyatt spoke up, "you don't want that to happen to you, do you?"

Mitchell ignored him. Still looking at Dyke he said, "Isn't there a doubt in your mind?" Dyke didn't answer and in the silence their eyes held.

Then, behind Mitchell, a man said, "Let's have some coffee first." Dyke's eyes lifted. He nodded and walked toward the fire, finished with Mitchell.

HYATT and the woman were moved over by the wagon. Then Mitchell was brought over. They tied Hyatt's and Mitchell's hands behind their backs and made them sit down, the woman between them.

There was nothing to be said. In silence they watched Dyke's men build another fire close to the cottonwood tree they would use. Two men entered the clearing carrying riatas, uncoiling them as they crossed to the tree. Mitchell saw his sorrel and a bay brought in and the saddles were taken off both horses.

Now what do you do? he thought.

Tell him!

I did tell him! He's hard shelled and mean because Hyatt killed his friend and that's all he can think about. But he's calm about it, isn't he? Judge and jury wrapped into one hard-bitten weathered face. His mind is the law and he can be as calm as he pleases, knowing his way is the only way.

Twelve years of campaigning and you're going to die under another man's name. Nobody knowing . . . no, two people knowing who you are. The woman—Claire—and Hyatt.

Two feet away and you can't even touch him. Get up quick and butt his face in with your head! No . . . come on, think straight now. Now isn't a time to think about revenge. Forget about him. You're going to die and that's all there is to it.

He said it in his mind, feeling each word: I'm going to die. More slowly then: I am going to die.

All right, now you know it. You always knew it, but now you *know* it. Come on, think straight. I *am* thinking straight. Go to hell with that thinking straight business! There's no *straight* way to think when you're going to die. What did you think about the other time? The first and only and supposedly last other time.

Nervous and not liking it, not believing that it was happening to him, but holding himself together nevertheless and thinking over and over again that it was a shame to die alone. Alone, because the Coyotero tracker didn't count. You couldn't talk about last things in sign language. Dos Fuegos had taken out a buckskin pouch in which he carried his *hoddentin*, the sacred pollen made from tule that would ward off evil, and with that he had readied himself.

* * *

CORPORAL Mitchell then, Corporal Mitchell and a Coyotero tracker called Dos Fuegos—the two of them riding point and cut off from the others and their mounts shot from under them. Then holding flat to the ground, lying behind the mound and looking across to the rock-scrambled sand-glaring dead-silent slope where the Mimbres were. Lying unmoving—wondering if the patrol would find them.

The Mimbres came—a few at a time, running, dodging, firing carbines; and they drove them back to cover. The second rush came before they had time to reload—but so did D Company, brought by the firing, and that was that.

Sergeant Mitchell, the next month, and less talkative.

But, Mitchell thought, you really didn't learn anything that time. Not that you could apply to this one. Only that dying is important to you and if you can't do it in bed, sometime far in the future, then have it happen during a heroic act with a great number of people watching. Don't talk foolish. You're going to die, that's all . . . so do it as well as you can.

He thought of his father and mother and for a few minutes he prayed.

The woman touched his arm and he looked up. "I'm sorry . . . I wish there was something I could do."

"I wish there was too," Mitchell answered. "I wonder if you'd do me a favor."

"What is it?"

"Sometime look up my father in Banderas, R. F. Mitchell, and let him know what happened."

She nodded slowly. "All right."

Hyatt leaned forward. "Rady, your folks don't live in Banderas."

"You've got a real sense of humor," Mitchell said, mildly.

Momentarily Hyatt frowned. "You've calmed down some."

Mitchell didn't reply. He saw Dyke, standing by the big cottonwood tree, motion to the men guarding them, and now they were pulled to their feet. Hyatt turned to the woman. "Claire, we say good-bye now."

"Hy, tell them who he is."

Hyatt grinned. "Honey, I did."

"I think I'm glad they're hanging you," she said.

Hyatt shrugged. One of the possemen took Mitchell's arm. He looked at the woman and their eyes held lingeringly. Come on, he thought. You couldn't say it in minutes, so don't say it at all. He turned and followed Hyatt across the clearing and he knew that the woman was watching him.

"Get 'em up," Dyke ordered.

THEY were lifted onto the horses and a mounted man rode between them and adjusted the riata loops over their heads. Dyke looked up at them. "Mr. Rady seems to've lost his fight."

Hyatt grinned. "He's turned honest."

Mitchell looked at him. "You proved your point. Now you're wearing it out."

Hyatt's eyes narrowed. For a moment he was silent and he watched Mitchell curiously. "You ever see a hanging?" he asked then.

Mitchell shook his head. "No."

"If your neck don't bust, you strangle awhile." His eyes stayed on Mitchell. "You scared?"

Mitchell shrugged. "Probably, the same as you are."

A bewildered look crossed Hyatt's face. Apparently he had expected Mitchell to panic now, to lose control of himself pleading for his life, but he was at ease and he sat the sorrel without moving. He leaned closer so that only Mitchell could hear him say, "Rady's ten miles away by now; but in another minute he'll be legally, officially dead."

"I'd say I was doing him some favor." Mitchell answered.

Hyatt hesitated, and the cloud of uncertainty clouded his face again. He wanted to whisper, but his voice rasped. "You're going to *hang*! You understand that? Hang!"

Mitchell nodded. "The same as you are."

Hyatt's teeth clenched. He was about to say more, but he stopped.

Mitchell looked down at Dyke. "He's going to foam at the mouth in a minute."

Dyke shook his head. "He don't have that long."

But now Hyatt was looking at Mitchell calmly, without bewilderment, and without the brooding anger that had been a knife edge inside of him since the fight. That had started to die as they sat by the wagon. He had tried to bring it back by taunting Mitchell, but it was no use. His anger was dead and even the memory of it seemed senseless and unimportant. Mitchell was a man. Give him credit for it.

That's how it happened. That's what caused Hyatt to say, unexpectedly, "Reach in the side of my boot; the right one."

Dyke looked at him. "What for?"

"Just do it!"

Hyatt's eyes returned to Mitchell. "You either got more guts than any man I ever saw . . . or else you're the dumbest."

Dyke's two fingers came out of the boot lifting the folded sheet of paper. He unfolded it and his eyes went over it slowly.

The two granite-faced men, at the very gates of a hot and waiting hell, stared stonily down at the executioner.

Dyke read it completely: the formal phrasing of the discharge order, the written-in-ink portion that described the soldier, and the scrawled, illegible signature at the bottom. He looked at the date again. Then, and only then, did he look at Mitchell.

Their eyes met briefly before Dyke turned away. He said to the men near him, "Take him down and untie him," and started toward the edge of the trees, walking with his head down. He stopped then and turned. "Hyatt Earl too. We're taking him to Mojave."

When his hands were cut loose, Mitchell walked over to Dyke. "Can I have my order now?"

Dyke handed it to him. "Listen, if I tried to tell you I'm sorry—"

Mitchell turned away. Don't listen to that, he thought. You might hit him. Don't even think of Hyatt. He looked over at the woman and saw her watching him. Then stopped. He'd have plenty of time to talk to her. And he thought, feeling the relief, but still holding himself calm: You've carried it this far. Hang on one more minute.

He turned back to Dyke and said, "Don't take it so hard, we all make mistakes."

JUGGED

Stan Cass, his elbows leaning on the edge of the rolltop desk, glanced over his shoulder as he said, "Take a look how I made this one out."

Marshal John Boynton had just come in. He was standing in the front door of the jail office, one finger absently stroking his full mustache. He looked at his regular deputy, Hanley Miller, who stood next to a chair where a young man sat leaning forward looking at his hands.

"What's the matter with him?" Boynton said, ignoring Stan Cass.

Hanley Miller put his hand on the back of the chair. "A combination of things, John. He's had too many, been beat up, and now he's tired."

"He looks tired," Boynton said, again glancing at the silent young man.

Stan Cass turned his head. "He looks like a smart-aleck kid."

Boynton walked over to Cass and picked up the record book from the desk. The last entry read:

NAME: Pete Given

DESCRIPTION: Ninteen. Medium height and build. Brown hair and eyes. Small scar under chin.

RESIDENCE: Dos Cabezas

OCCUPATION: Mustanger

CHARGE: Drunk and disorderly

COMMENTS: Has to pay a quarter share of the damages in the Continental Saloon whatever they are decided to be.

Boynton handed the record book to Cass. "You spelled *nineteen* wrong."

"Is that all?"

"How do you know he has to pay a quarter of the damages?"

"Being four of them," Cass said mock seriously. "I figured to myself: Now, if they have to chip in for what's busted, how much would—"

"That's for the judge to say. What were they doing here?"

"They delivered a string to the stage line," Cass answered. He was a man in his early twenties, clean shaven, though his sideburns extended down to the curve of his jaw. He was smoking a cigarette and he spoke to Boynton as if he were bored.

"And they tried to spend all the profit in one night," Boynton said.

Cass shrugged indifferently. "I guess so."

Boynton's finger stroked his mustache and he was thinking: Somebody's going to bust his nose for him. He asked, civilly, "Where're the other three?"

Cass nodded to the door that led back to the first-floor cell. "Where else?"

Hanley Miller, the regular night deputy, a man in his late forties, said, "John, you know there's only room for three in there. I was wondering what to do with this boy." He tipped his head toward the quiet young man sitting in the chair.

"He'll have to go upstairs," Boynton said.

"With Obie Ward?"

"I guess he'll have to." Boynton nodded to the boy. "Pull him up."

Hanley Miller got the sleepy boy on his feet.

Cass shook his head watching them. "Obie Ward's got everybody buffaloed. I'll be a son of a gun if he ain't got everybody buffaloed."

Boynton's eyes dropped to Cass, but he did not say anything.

"I'm just saying that Obie Ward don't look so tough," Cass said.

"Act like you've got some sense once in a while," Boynton said now. He had hired Cass the week before as an extra night guard—the day they brought in Obie Ward—but he was certain now he would not keep Cass. Tomorrow he would look around for somebody else. Somebody who didn't talk so much and didn't have such a proud opinion of himself.

"All I'm saying is he don't look so tough to me," Cass repeated.

Boynton ignored him. He looked at the young man, Pete Given, standing next to Hanley now with his eyes closed, and he heard his deputy say, "The boy's asleep on his feet."

"He looks familiar," Boynton said.

"We had him here about three months ago."

"Same thing?"

Hanley nodded. "Delivered his horses, then stopped off at the Continental. Remember, his wife come here looking for him. He was here five days because the judge was away and she got here court day. Pretty little thing with light-colored hair? Not more'n seventeen. Come all the way from Dos Cabezas by herself."

"Least he had sense enough to get a good woman," Boynton said. He seemed to hesitate. Then: "You and I'll take him up." He slipped his revolver from its holster and placed it on the desk. He took young Pete Given's arm then and raised it up over his shoulder, glancing at his deputy again. "Hanley, you come behind with your shotgun."

Cass watched them go through the door and down the hall to the back of the jail to the outside stairway, and he was thinking: Won't even wear his gun up there, he's so scared. That's some man to work for, won't even wear his gun when he goes in Ward's cell. He shook his head and said the name again, contemptuously. Obie Ward. He'd pull his tough act on me just once.

PETE Given opened his eyes. Lying on his right side his face was close to the wall and for a moment, seeing the chipped and peeling adobe and smelling the stale mildewed smell of the mattress which did not have a cover on it, he did not know where he was. Then he remembered, and he closed his eyes again.

The sour taste of whiskey coated his mouth and he lay very still, waiting for the throbbing to start in his head. But it did not come. He raised his head and moved closer to the wall and felt the edge of the mattress cool and firm against his cheek. Still the throbbing did not come. There was a dull tight feeling at the base of his skull, but not the shooting sharp pain he had expected. That was good. He moved his toes and could feel his boots still on and there was no blanket covering him.

They just dumped you here, he thought. He made saliva in his mouth and kept swallowing until his mouth did not feel sticky and some of the sour taste went away. Well, what did you expect?

It's about all you deserve, buddy. No, it's more'n you deserve.

You'll learn, huh?

He thought of his wife, Mary Ellen, and his eyes closed tighter and for a moment he tried not to think of anything.

How do I do this? How do I get something good, then kick it away like it's not worth anything?

What'll you tell her this time?

"Mary Ellen, honest to gosh, we just went in to get one drink. We sold the horses and got something to eat and figured one drink before starting back. Then Art said one more. All right, just one, I told him. But, you know, we were relaxed—and laughing. That's hard work running a thirty-horse string for five days. Harry got in a blackjack game. The rest of us were just sitting relaxed. When you're sitting like that the time seems to go faster. We had a few drinks. Maybe four—five at the most. Like I said, we were laughing and Art was telling some stories. You know Art, he keeps talking—then there's a commotion over at the blackjack table and we see Harry haulin' all at this man. And—"

And Mary Ellen will say, "Just like the last time," not raising her voice or seeming mad, but she'll keep looking you right in the eye.

"Honey, those things just happen. I can't help it. And it wasn't just like last time."

"The result's the same," she'll say. "You work hard for three months to earn decent money then pay it all out in fines and damages."

"Not all of it."

"It might as well be all. We can't live on what's left."

"But I can't help it. Can't you see that? Harry got in a fight and we had to help him. It's just one of those things that happen. You can't help it."

"But it seems a little silly, doesn't it?"

"Mary Ellen, you don't understand."

"Doesn't throwing away three months' profit in one night seem silly to you?"

"You don't understand."

You can be married to a girl for almost a year and think you know her and you don't know her at all. That's it. You know how she talks, but you don't know what she's thinking. That's a big difference. But there's some things you can't explain to a woman anyway.

He felt a little better. Facing her would not be pleasant—but it still wasn't his fault.

He rolled over, momentarily studying the ceiling, then he let his head roll on the mattress and he saw the man on the other bunk watching him. He was sitting hunched over, making a cigarette.

Pete Given closed his eyes and he could still see the man. He didn't seem big, but he had a stringy hard-boned look. Sharp cheekbones and dull-black hair that was cut short and brushed forward to his forehead. No mustache, but he needed a shave and it gave the appearance of an almost full-grown mustache.

He opened his eyes again. The man was drawing on the cigarette, still watching him.

"What time you think it is?" Given asked.

"About nine." The man's voice was clear though he barely moved his mouth.

Given said, "If you were one of them over to the Continental I'd just as soon shake hands this morning."

The man did not reply.

"You weren't there, then?"

"No," he said now.

"What've they got you for?"

"They say I shot a man."

"Oh."

"Fact is, they say I shot two men, during the Grant stage holdup."

"Oh."

"When the judge comes tomorrow, he'll set a court date. Give the witnesses time to get here." He stood up, saying this. He was tall, above average, but not heavy.

"Are you"—Given hesitated—"Obie Ward?"

The man nodded, drawing on the cigarette.

"Somebody last night said you were here. I'd forgot about it." Given spoke louder, trying to make his voice sound natural, and now he raised himself on an elbow.

Obie Ward asked, "Were you drinking last night?"

"Some."

"And got in a fight."

Given sat up, swinging his legs off the bunk and resting his elbows on his knees. "One of my partners got in trouble and we had to help him."

"You don't look so good," Ward said.

"I feel okay."

"No," Ward said. "You don't look so good."

"Well, maybe I just look worse'n I am."

"How's your stomach?"

"It's all right."

"You look sick to me."

"I could eat. Outside of that I got no complaint." Given stood up. He put his hands on the small of his back and stretched, feeling the stiffness in his body. Then he raised his arms straight up, stretching again, and yawned. That felt good. He saw Obie Ward coming toward him, and he lowered his arms.

Ward reached out, extending one finger, and poked it at Pete Given's stomach. "How's it feel right there?"

"Honest to gosh, it feels okay." He smiled looking at Ward, to show that he was willing to go along with a joke, but he felt suddenly uneasy. Ward was standing too close to him and Given was thinking: What's the matter with him?—and the same moment he saw the beard-stubbled face tighten.

Ward went back a half step and came forward, driving his left fist into Given's stomach. The boy started to fold, a gasp coming from his open mouth, and Ward followed with his right hand, bringing it up solidly against the boy's jaw, sending him back, arms flung wide, over the bunk and hard against the wall. Given slumped on the mattress and did not move. For a moment Ward looked at him, then picked up his cigarette from the floor and went back to his bunk.

He was sitting on the edge of it when Given opened his eyes—smoking another cigarette, drawing on it and blowing the smoke out slowly.

"Are you sick now?"

Given moved his head, trying to lift it, and it was an effort to do this. "I think I am."

Ward started to rise. "Let's make sure."

"I'm sure."

WARD relaxed again. "I told you so, but you didn't believe me. I been watching you all morning and the more I watched, the more I thought to myself: Now there's a sick boy. Maybe you ought to even have a doctor."

Given said nothing. He stiffened as Ward rose and came toward him.

"What's the matter? I'm just going to see you're more comfortable." Ward leaned over, lifting the boy's legs one at a time, and pulled his boots off, then pushed him, gently, flat on the bunk and covered him with a blanket that was folded at the foot of it. Given looked up, holding his body rigid, and saw Ward shake his head. "You're a mighty sick boy. We got to do something about that."

Ward crossed the cell to his bunk, and standing at one end, he lifted it a foot off the floor and let it drop. He did this three times, then went down to his hands and knees and, close to the floor, called, "Hey, Marshal!" He waited. "Marshal, we got a sick boy up here!" He rose, winking at Given, and sat down on his bunk.

Minutes later a door at the back end of the hallway opened and Boynton came toward the cell. A deputy with a shotgun, his day man, followed him.

"What's the matter?"

Ward nodded. "The boy's sick."

"He ought to be," Boynton said.

Ward shrugged. "Don't matter to me, but I got to listen to him moaning."

Boynton looked toward Given's bunk. "A man that don't know how to drink has got to expect that." He turned abruptly. Their steps moved down the hall and the door slammed closed.

"No sympathy," Ward said. He made another cigarette, and when he had lit it he walked over to Given's bunk. "He'll come back in about two hours with our dinner. You'll still be in bed, and this time you'll be moaning like you got belly cramps. You got that?"

Staring up at him, Given nodded his head stiffly.

At a quarter to twelve Boynton came up again. This time he ordered Ward to lie down flat on his bunk. He unlocked the door then and remained in the hall as the day man came in with the dinner tray and placed it in the middle of the floor.

"He still sick?" Boynton stood in the doorway holding a sawed-off shotgun.

Ward turned his head on the mattress. "Can't you hear him?"

"He'll get over it."

"I think it's something else," Ward said. "I never saw whiskey hold on like that."

"You a doctor?"

"As much a one as you are."

Boynton looked toward the boy again. Given's eyes were closed and he was moaning faintly. "Tell him to eat something," Boynton said. "Maybe then he'll feel better."

"I'll do that," Ward said. He was smiling as Boynton and his deputy moved off down the hall.

Lying on his back, his head turned on the mattress, Given watched Ward take a plate from the tray. It looked like stew.

"Can I have some?" Given said.

Chewing, Ward shook his head.

"Why not?"

Ward swallowed. "You're too sick."

"Can I ask you a question?"

"Go ahead."

"How come I'm sick?"

"You haven't figured it?"

"No."

"I'll give you a hint. We'll get our supper about six. Watch the two that bring it up."

"I don't see what they'd have to do with me."

"You don't have to see."

Given was silent for some time. He said then, "It's got to do with you busting out."

Obie Ward grinned. "You got a head on your shoulders."

Boynton came up a half hour later. He stood in the hall and when his deputy brought out the tray, his eyes went from it to Pete Given's bunk. "The boy didn't eat a bite," Boynton observed.

Ward raised up on his elbow. "Said he couldn't stand the smell of it." He watched Boynton look toward the boy, then sank down on the bunk again as Boynton walked away. When the door down the hall closed, Ward said, "Now he believes it."

It was quiet in the cell after that. Ward rolled over to face the wall and Pete Given, lying on his back, remained motionless, though his eyes were open and he was studying the ceiling.

He tried to understand Obie Ward's plan. He tried to see how his being sick could have anything to do with Ward's breaking out. And he thought: He means what he says, doesn't he? You can be sure of that much. He's going to bust out and you got a part in it and there ain't a damn thing you can do about it. It's that simple, isn't it?

* * *

OBIE Ward was right. At what seemed close to six o'clock they heard the door open at the end of the hall and a moment later Stan Cass and Hanley Miller were standing in front of the cell. Hanley opened the door and stood holding a sawed-off shotgun as Cass came in with the tray.

Cass half turned to face Ward sitting on his bunk, then went down to one knee, lowering the tray to the floor, and he did not take his eyes from Ward. He rose then and turned as he heard groans from the other bunk.

"What's his trouble?"

Ward looked up. "Didn't your boss tell you?"

"He told me," Cass said, "but I believe what I see."

"Help yourself, then."

Cass turned sharply. "You shut your mouth till I want to hear from you!"

"Yes, sir," Ward said. His dark face was expressionless.

Cass stared at him, his thumbs hooked in his gun belt. "You think you're somethin', don't you?"

Ward's head moved from side to side. "Not me."

"I'd like to see you pull somethin'," Cass said. His right hand opened and closed, moving closer to his hip. "I'd just like to see you get off that bunk and pull somethin'."

Ward shook his head. "Somebody's been telling you stories."

"I think they have," Cass said. He hesitated, then walked out, slamming the door shut.

Ward called to him through the bars, "What about the boy?"

"You take care of him," Cass said, moving off. Hanley Miller followed, looking back over his shoulder.

Ward waited until the back door closed, then picked up a plate and began to eat and not until he was almost finished did he notice Given watching him.

"Did you see anything?"

Given came up on his elbow slowly. He looked at the tray on the floor, then at Ward. "Like what?"

"Like the way that deputy acted."

"He wanted you to try something."

"What else?"

Given pictured Cass again in his mind. "He was wearing a gun." Suddenly he seemed to understand and he said, "The marshal wasn't wearing any, but this one was!"

Ward grinned. "And he knows you're sick. First his boss told him, then he saw it with his own eyes." Ward put down the plate and he made a cigarette as he walked over to Given's bunk. "I'll tell you something else," he said, standing close to the bunk. "I've been here seven days. For seven days I watch. I see the marshal. He knows what he's doing and he don't wear a gun when he comes in here. A man out in the hall with a scattergun's enough. Then this other one they call Cass. He walks like he can feel his gun on his hip. He's not used to it, but it feels good and he'd like an excuse to use it. He even wears it in here, though likely he's been told not to. What does that tell you? He's sure of himself, but he's not smart. He wants to see me try something—and he's sure he can get his gun out if I do. For seven days I see this and there's nothing I can do about it—until this morning."

Given nodded thoughtfully, but said nothing.

"This morning I saw you," Ward went on, "and you looked sick. There it was."

Given nodded again. "I guess I see."

"We let the marshal know about it. He tells Cass when he comes on duty. Cass comes up and sure enough, you're sick."

"Yeah?"

"Then Cass comes up the next time—understand it'll be dark outside by then: he brings supper up at six, but he must go out to eat after that because he doesn't come back for the tray till almost eight—and he's not surprised to see you even sicker."

"How does he see that?"

"You scream like your stomach's been pulled out and you roll off the bunk."

"Then what?"

"Then you don't have to do anything else."

Given's eyes held on Ward's face. He swallowed and said, as evenly as he could, "Why should I help you escape?" He saw it coming and he tried to roll away, but it was too late and Ward's fist came down against his face like a mallet.

He was dazed and there was a stinging throbbing over the entire side of his face, but he was conscious of Ward leaning close to him and he heard the words clearly. "I'll kill you. That reason enough?"

After that he was not conscious of time. His eyes were closed and for a while he dozed off. Then, when he opened his eyes, momentarily he could remember nothing and he was not even sure where he was, because he was thinking of nothing, only looking at the chipped and peeling adobe wall and feeling a strange numbness over the side of his face.

His hand was close to his face and his fingers moved to touch his cheekbone. The skin felt swollen hard and tight over the bone, and just touching it was painful. He thought then: Are you afraid for your own neck? Of course I am!

But it was more than fear that was making his heart beat faster. There was an anger inside of him. Anger adding excitement to the fear and he realized this, though not coolly, for he was thinking of Ward and Mary Ellen and himself as they came into his mind, not as he called them there.

Ward said, Roll off the cot. All right.

He heard the back door open and instantly Ward muttered, "You awake?" He turned his head to see Ward sitting on the edge of the bunk, his hands at his sides gripping the mattress. He heard the footsteps coming up the hall.

"I'm awake."

"Soon as he opens the door," Ward said, and his shoulders seemed to relax.

As soon as he opens the door.

He heard Cass saying something and a key rattled in the lock. The squeak of the door hinges—

He groaned, bringing his knees up. His heart was pounding and a heat was over his face and he kept his eyes squeezed closed. He groaned again, louder this time, and doing it he rolled to his side, hesitated at the edge of the mattress, then let himself fall heavily to the floor.

"What's the matter with him!"

Four steps on the plank floor vibrated in his ear. A hand took his shoulder and rolled him over. Opening his eyes, he saw Cass leaning over him.

Suddenly then, Cass started to rise, his eyes stretched open wide, and he twisted his body to turn. An arm came from behind hooking his throat, dragging him back, and a hand was jerking the revolver from its holster.

HANLEY Miller tried to push away from the bars to bring up the shotgun. It clattered against the bars and on top of the sound came the deafening report of the revolver. Hanley doubled up and went to the floor, clutching his thigh.

Cass's mouth was open and he was trying to scream as the revolver flashed over his head and came down. The next moment Ward was throwing Cass's limp weight aside. Ward stumbled, clattering over the tray in the middle of the floor, almost tripping.

Given saw Ward go through the wide-open door. He glanced then at Hanley Miller lying on the floor. Then, looking at Ward's back, the thought stabbed suddenly, unexpectedly, in his mind—

Get him!

He hesitated, though the hesitation was in his mind and it was part of a moment. Then he was on his feet, moving quickly, silently, in his stocking feet, stooping to pick up the sawed-off shotgun, turning and seeing Ward near the door. Now Given was running down the hallway, now swinging open the door that had just closed behind Ward.

Ward was on the back-porch landing, starting down the stairs, and he wheeled, bringing up the revolver as the door opened, as he saw Pete Given on the landing, as he saw the stubby shotgun barrels swinging savagely in the dimness.

Ward fired hurriedly, wildly, the same moment the double barrels slashed against the side of his head. He screamed as he lost his balance and went down the stairway. At the bottom he tried to rise, groping momentarily, feverishly, for his gun. As he came to his feet, Pete Given was there—and again the shotgun cut viciously against his head. Ward went down, falling forward, and this time he did not move.

Given sat down on the bottom step, letting the shotgun slip from his fingers. A lantern was coming down the alley.

Boynton appeared in the circle of lantern light. He looked from Obie Ward to the boy, not speaking, but his eyes remained on Given until he stepped past him and went up the stairs.

A man stooped next to him, extending an already rolled cigarette. "You look like you want a smoke."

Given shook his head. "I'd swallow it."

The man nodded toward Obie Ward. "You took him by yourself?"

"Yes, sir."

"That must've been something to see."

"I don't know—it happened so fast." In the crowd he heard Obie Ward's name over and over—someone asking if he was dead, a man bending over him saying no . . . someone asking, "Who's that boy?" and someone answering, "I don't know, but he's got enough guts for everybody."

Boynton appeared on the landing and called for someone to get the doctor. He came down and Given stood up to let him pass.

The man who was holding the cigarette said, "John, this boy got Obie all by himself."

Boynton was looking at Ward. "I see that."

"More'n I would've done," the man said, shaking his head.

"More'n most anybody would've done," Boynton answered. He looked at Given then, studying him openly. He said then, "I'll recommend to the judge we drop the charges against you."

Given nodded. "That'd be fine."

"Anxious to get home to your wife?"

"Yes, sir."

For a moment Boynton was silent. His expression was mild, but his eyes were fastened on Pete Given's face as if he were trying to read something there, some mark of character that would tell him about this boy.

"On second thought," Boynton said abruptly, "I'll tear your name right out of the record book, if you'll take a deputy job. You won't even have to put a foot in court."

Given looked up. "You mean that?"

"I got two jobs open," Boynton said. He hesitated before adding, "Look, it's up to you. Probably I'll tear your name out even if you don't take the job. Seeing the condition of Obie Ward, I wouldn't judge you're a man who's going to be pressured into anything."

Given's face showed surprise, but it was momentary, his mouth relaxing into a slow grin—almost as if the smile widened as Boynton's words sank into his mind—and he said, "I'll have to go to Dos Cabezas and get my wife."

Boynton nodded. "Will she be happy about this?"

Pete Given was still smiling. "Marshal, you and I probably couldn't realize how happy she'll be."

The Hard Way

Tio Robles stretched stiffly on the straw mattress, holding the empty mescal bottle upright on his chest. His sleepy eyes studied Jimmy Robles going through his ritual. Tio was half smiling, watching with amusement.

Jimmy Robles buttoned his shirt carefully, even the top button, and pushed the shirttail tightly into his pants, smooth and tight with no blousing about the waist. It made him move stiffly the few minutes he was conscious of keeping the clean shirt smooth and unwrinkled. He lifted the gun belt from a wall peg and buckled it around his waist, inhaling slowly, watching the faded cotton stretch tight across his stomach. And when he wiped his high black boots it was with the same deliberate care.

Tio's sleepy smile broadened. "Jaime," he spoke softly, "you look very pretty. Are you to be married today?" He waited. "Perhaps this is a feast day that has slipped my mind." He waited longer. "No? Or perhaps the mayor has invited you to dine with him."

Jimmy Robles picked up the sweat-dampened shirt he had taken off and unpinned the silver badge from the pocket. Before looking at his uncle he breathed on the metal and rubbed its smooth surface over the tight cloth of his chest. He pinned it to the clean shirt, studying the inscription cut into the metal that John Benedict had told him read *Deputy Sheriff.*

Sternly, he said, "You drink too much," but could not help smiling at this picture of indolence sprawled on the narrow bed with a foot hooked on the window ledge above, not caring particularly if the world ended at that moment.

"Why don't you stop for a few days, just to see what it's like?"

Tio closed his eyes. "The shock would kill me."

"You're killing yourself anyway."

Tio mumbled, "But what a fine way to die."

He left the adobe hut and crossed a backyard before passing through the narrow dimness of two adobes that squeezed close together, and when he reached the street he tilted his hat closer to his eyes against the afternoon glare and walked up the street toward Arivaca's business section. This was a part of Saturday afternoon. This leaving the Mexican section that was still quiet, almost deserted, and walking up the almost indiscernible slope that led to the more prosperous business section.

Squat gray adobe grew with the slope from Spanishtown into painted, two-story false fronts with signs hanging from the ramadas. Soon, cowmen from the nearer ranges and townspeople who had quit early because it was Saturday would be standing around under the ramadas, slapping each other on the shoulder thinking about Saturday night. Those who hadn't started already. And Jimmy Robles would smile at everybody and be friendly because he liked this day better than any other. People were easier to get along with. Even the Americans.

Being deputy sheriff of Arivaca wasn't a hard job, but Jimmy Robles was new. And his newness made him unsure. Not confident of his ability to uphold the law and see that the goods and rights of these people were protected while they got drunk on Saturday night.

The sheriff, John Benedict, had appointed him a month before because he thought it would be good for the Mexican population. One of their own boys. John Benedict said you performed your duty "in the name of the law." That was the thing to remember. And it made him feel uneasy because the law was such a big thing. And justice. He wished he could picture something other than that woman with the blindfold over her eyes. John Benedict spoke long of these things. He was a great man.

Not only had he made him deputy, but John Benedict had given him a pair of American boots and a pistol, free, which had belonged to a man who had been hanged the month before. Tio Robles had told him to destroy the hanged man's goods, for it was a bad sign; but that's all Tio knew about it. He was too much *Mexicano.* He would go on sweating at the wagonyard, grumbling, and drinking more mescal than he could hold. It was good he lived with Tio and was able to keep him out of trouble. Not all, some.

His head was down against the glare and he watched his booted feet move over the street dust, lost in thought. But the gunfire from up-street brought him to instantly. He broke into a slow trot, seeing a lone man in the street a block ahead. As he approached him, he angled toward the boardwalk lining the buildings.

SID Roman stood square in the middle of the street with his feet planted wide. There was a stubble of beard over the angular lines of his lower face and his eyes blinked sleepily. He jabbed another cartridge at the open cylinder of the Colt, and fumbled trying to insert it into one of the small openings. The nose of the bullet missed the groove and slipped from his fingers. Sid Roman was drunk, which wasn't unusual, though it wasn't evident from his face. The glazed expression was natural.

Behind him, two men with their hats tilted loosely over their eyes sat on the steps of the Samas Café, their boots stretched out into the street. A half-full bottle was between them on the ramada step. A third man lounged on his elbows against the hitch rack, leaning heavily like a dead weight. Jimmy Robles moved off the boardwalk and stood next to the man on the hitch rack.

Sid Roman loaded the pistol and waved it carelessly over his head. He tried to look around at the men behind him without moving his feet and stumbled off balance, almost going down.

"Come on . . . who's got the money!" His eyes, heavy lidded, went to the two men on the steps. "Hey, Walt, dammit! Put up your dollar!"

The one called Walt said, "I got it. Go ahead and shoot," and hauled the bottle up to his mouth.

Sid Roman yelled to the man on the hitch rack, "You in, Red?" The man looked up, startled, and stared around as if he didn't know where he was.

Roman waved his pistol toward the high front of the saloon across the street. SUPREME, in foot-high red letters, ran across the board hanging from the top of the ramada. "A dollar I put five straight in the top loop of the *P.*" He slurred his words impatiently.

Jimmy Robles heard the man next to him mumble, "Sure, Sid." He looked at the sign, squinting hard, but could not make out any bullet scars near the *P.* Maybe there was one just off to the left of the *S.* He waited until the cowman turned and started to raise the Colt.

"Hey, Sid." Jimmy Robles smiled at him like a friend. "I got some good targets out back of the jail."

Aiming, Sid Roman turned irritably, hot in the face. Then the expression was blank and glassy again.

"How'd you know my name?"

Jimmy Robles smiled, embarrassed. "I just heard this man call you that."

Roman looked at him a long time. "Well you heard wrong," he finally said. "It's Mr. Roman."

A knot tightened the deputy's mouth, but he kept the smile on his lips even though its meaning was gone. "All right, mester. It's all the same to me." John Benedict said you had to be courteous.

The man was staring at him hard, weaving slightly. He had heard of Sid Roman, old man Remillard's top hand, but this was the first time he had seen him close. He stared back at the beard-grubby face and felt uneasy because the face was so expressionless—looking him over like he was a dead tree stump. Why couldn't he get laughing drunk like the Mexican boys, then he could be laughing, too, when he took his gun away from him.

"Why don't you just keep your mouth shut," Roman said, as if that was the end of it. But then he added, "Go on and sweep out your jailhouse," grinning and looking over at the men on the steps.

The one called Walt laughed out and jabbed at the other man with his elbow.

Jimmy Robles held on to the smile, gripping it with only his will now. He said, "I'm just thinking of the people. If a stray shot went inside, somebody might get hurt."

"You saying I can't shoot, or're you just chicken scared!"

"I'm just saying there are many people on the street and inside there."

"You're talking awful damn big for a dumb Mex kid. You must be awful dumb." He looked toward the steps, handling the pistol idly. "He must be awful dumb, huh, Walt?"

Jimmy Robles heard the one called Walt mumble, "He sure must," but he kept his eyes on Roman, who walked up to him slowly, still looking at him like he was a stump or something that couldn't talk back or hear. Now, only a few feet away, he saw a glimmer in the sleepy eyes as if a new thought was punching its way through his head.

"Maybe we ought to learn him something, Walt. Seeing he's so dumb." Grinning now, he looked straight into the Mexican boy's eyes. "Maybe I ought to shoot his ears off and give 'em to him for a present. What you think of that, Walt?"

Jimmy Robles's smile had almost disappeared. "I think I had better ask you for your gun, mester." His voice coldly polite.

Roman's stubble jaw hung open. It clamped shut and his face colored, through the weathered tan it colored as if it would burst open from ripeness. He mumbled through his teeth, "You two-bit kid!" and tried to bring the Colt up.

Robles swung his left hand wide as hard as he could and felt the numbing pain up to his elbow the same time Sid Roman's head snapped back. He tried to think of courtesy, his pistol, the law, the other three men—but it wasn't any of these that drew his hand back again and threw the fist hard against the face that was falling slowly toward him. The head snapped back and the body followed it this time, heels dragging in the dust off balance until Roman was spread-eagled in the street, not moving. He swung on the three men, pulling his pistol.

They just looked at him. The one called Walt shrugged his shoulders and lifted the bottle that was almost empty.

WHEN John Benedict closed the office door behind him, his deputy was coming up the hall that connected the cells in the rear of the jail. He sat down at the rolltop desk, hearing the footsteps in the bare hallway, and swiveled his chair, swinging his back to the desk.

"I was over to the barbershop. I saw you bring somebody in," he said to Jimmy Robles entering the office. "I was all lathered up and couldn't get out. Saw you pass across the street, but couldn't make out who you had."

Jimmy Robles smiled. "Mester Roman. Didn't you hear the shooting?"

"Sid Roman?" Benedict kept most of the surprise out of his voice. "What's the charge?"

"He was drinking out in the street and betting on shooting at the sign over the Supreme. There were a lot of people around—" He wanted to add, "John," because they were good friends, but Benedict was old enough to be his father and that made a difference.

"So then he called you something and you got mad and hauled him in."

"I tried to smile, but he was pointing his gun all around. It was hard."

John Benedict smiled at the boy's serious face. "Sid call you chicken scared?"

Jimmy Robles stared at this amazing man he worked for.

"He calls everybody that when he's drunk." Benedict smiled. "He's a lot of mouth, with nothing coming out. Most times he's harmless, but someday he'll probably shoot somebody." His eyes wandered out the window. Old man Remillard was crossing the street toward the jail. "And then we'll get the blame for not keeping him here when he's full of whiskey."

Jimmy Robles went over the words, his smooth features frowning in question. "What do you mean we'll get blamed?"

Benedict started to answer him, but changed his mind when the door opened. Instead, he said, "Afternoon," nodding his head to the thick, big-boned man in the doorway. Benedict followed the rancher's gaze to Jimmy Robles. "Mr. Remillard, Deputy Sheriff Robles."

Remillard's face was serious. "Quit kidding," he said. He moved toward the sheriff. "I'm just fixing up a mistake you made. Your memory must be backing up on you, John." He was unexcited, but his voice was heavy with authority. Remillard hadn't been told no in twenty years, not by anyone, and his air of command was as natural to him as breathing. He handed Benedict a folded sheet he had pulled from his inside coat pocket, nodding his head toward Jimmy Robles.

"You better tell your boy what end's up."

He waited until Benedict looked up from the sheet of paper, then said, "I was having my dinner with Judge Essery at the Samas when my foreman was arrested. Essery's waived trial and suspended sentence. It's right there, black and white. And kind of lucky for you, John, the judge's in a good mood today." Remillard walked to the door, then turned back. "It isn't in the note, but you better have my boy out in ten minutes." That was all.

John Benedict read the note over again. He remembered the first time one like it was handed to him, five years before. He had read it over five times and had almost torn it up, before his sense returned. He wondered if he was using the right word, *sense.*

"Let him out and give him his gun back."

Jimmy Robles smiled, because he thought the sheriff was kidding. He said, "Sure," and the "John" almost slipped out with it. He propped his hip against the edge of his table-desk.

"What are you waiting for?"

Jimmy Robles came off the table now, and his face hung in surprise. "Are you serious?"

Benedict held out the note. "Read this five times and then let him go."

"But I don't understand," with disbelief all over his face. "This man was endangering lives. You said we were to protect and . . ." His voice trailed off, trying to think of all the things John Benedict had told him.

Sitting in his swivel chair, John Benedict thought, Explain that one if you can. He remembered the words better than the boy did. Now he wondered how he had kept a straight face when he had told him about rights, and the law, and seeing how the one safeguarded the other. That was John Benedict the realist. The cynic. He told himself to shut up. He did believe in ideals. What he had been telling himself for years, though having to close his eyes occasionally because he liked his job.

Now he said to the boy, "Do you like your job?" And Jimmy Robles looked at him as if he did not understand.

He started to tell him how a man elected to a job naturally had a few obligations. And in a town like Arivaca, whose business depended on spreads like Remillard's and a few others, maybe the obligations were a little heavier. It was a cowtown, so the cowman ought to be able to have what he wanted. But it was too long a story to go through. If Jimmy Robles couldn't see the handwriting, let him find out the hard way. He was old enough to figure it out for himself. Suddenly, the boy's open, wondering face made him mad.

"Well, what the hell are you waiting for!"

JIMMY Robles pushed Tio's empty mescal bottle to the foot of the bed and sat down heavily. He eased back until he was resting on his spine with his head and shoulders against the adobe wall and sat like this for a long time while the thoughts went through his head. He wished Tio were here. Tio would offer no assistance, no explanation other than his biased own, but he would laugh and that would be better than nothing. Tio would say, "What did you expect would happen, you fool?" And add, "Let us have a drink to forget the mysterious ways of the American." Then he would laugh. Jimmy Robles sat and smoked cigarettes and he thought.

Later on, he opened his eyes and felt the ache in his neck and back. It seemed like only a few moments before he had been awake, clouded with his worrying, but the room was filled with a dull gloom. He rose, rubbing the back of his neck, and, through the open doorway that faced west, saw the red streak in the gloom over the line of trees in the distance.

He felt hungry, and the incident of the afternoon was something that might have happened a hundred years ago. He had worn himself out thinking and that was enough of it. He passed between the buildings to the street and crossed it to the adobe with the sign

EMILIANO'S. He felt like enchiladas and tacos and perhaps some beer if it was cold.

He ate alone at the counter, away from the crowded tables that squeezed close to each other in the hot, low-ceilinged café, taking his time and listening to the noise of the people eating and drinking. Emiliano served him, and after his meal set another beer—that was very cold—before him on the counter. And when he was again outside, the air seemed cooler and the dusk more restful.

He lighted a cigarette, inhaling deeply, and saw someone emerge from the alley that led to his adobe. The figure looked up and down the street, then ran directly toward him, shouting his name.

Now he recognized Agostino Reyes, who worked at the wagonyard with his uncle.

The old man was breathless. "I have hunted you everywhere," he wheezed, his eyes wide with excitement. "Your uncle has taken the shotgun that they keep at the company office and has gone to shoot a man!"

Robles held him hard by the shoulders. "Speak clearly! Where did he go!"

Agostino gasped out, "Earlier, a man by the Supreme insulted him and caused him to be degraded in front of others. Now Tio has gone to kill him."

He ran with his heart pounding against his chest, praying to God and His Mother to let him get there before anything happened. A block away from the Supreme he saw the people milling about the street, with all attention toward the front of the saloon. He heard the deep discharge of a shotgun and the people scattered as if the shot were a signal. In the space of a few seconds the street was deserted.

He slowed the motion of his legs and approached the rest of the way at a walk. Nothing moved in front of the Supreme, but across the street he saw figures in the shadowy doorways of the

Samas Café and the hotel next door. A man stepped out to the street and he saw it was John Benedict.

"Your uncle just shot Sid Roman. Raked his legs with a Greener. He's up there in the doorway laying half dead."

He made out the shape of a man lying beneath the swing doors of the Supreme. In the dusk the street was quiet, more quiet than he had ever known it, as if he and John Benedict were alone. And then the scream pierced the stillness. "God Almighty somebody help me!" It hung there, a cold wail in the gloom, then died.

"That's Sid," Benedict whispered. "Tio's inside with his pistol. If anybody gets near that door, he'll let go and most likely finish off Sid. He's got Remillard and Judge Essery and I don't know who else inside. They didn't get out in time. God knows what he'll do to them if he gets jumpy."

"Why did Tio shoot him?"

"They say about an hour ago Sid come staggering out drunk and bumped into your uncle and started telling him where to go. But your uncle was just as drunk and he wouldn't take any of it. They started swinging and Sid got Tio down and rubbed his face in the dust, then had one of his boys get a bottle, and he sat there drinking like he was on the front porch. Sitting on Tio. Then the old man come back about an hour later and let go at him with the Greener." John Benedict added, "I can't say I blame him."

Jimmy Robles said, "What were you doing while Sid was on the front porch?" and started toward the Supreme, not waiting for an answer.

John Benedict followed him. "Wait a minute," he called, but stopped when he got to the middle of the street.

On the saloon steps he could see Sid Roman plainly in the square of light under the doors, lying on his back with his eyes closed. A moan came from his lips, but it was almost inaudible. No sound came from within the saloon.

He mounted the first step and stood there. "Tio!"

No answer came. He went all the way up on the porch and looked down at Roman. "Tio! I'm taking this man away!"

Without hesitating he grabbed the wounded man beneath the arms and pulled him out of the doorway to the darkened end of the ramada past the windows. Roman screamed as his legs dragged across the boards. Jimmy Robles moved back to the door and the quietness settled again.

He pushed the door in, hard, and let it swing back, catching it as it reached him. Tio was leaning against the bar with bottles and glasses strung out its smooth length behind him. From the porch he could see no one else. Tio looked like a frightened animal cowering in a dead-end ravine, more pathetic in his ragged and dirty cotton clothes. His rope-soled shoes edged a step toward the doorway, with his body moving in a crouch. The pistol was in front of him, his left hand under the other wrist supporting the weight of the heavy Colt and, the deputy noticed now, trying to keep it steady.

Tio waved the barrel at him. "Come in and join your friends, Jaime." His voice quivered to make the bravado meaningless.

Robles moved inside the door of the long barroom and saw Remillard and Judge Essery standing by the table nearest the bar. Two other men stood at the next table. One of them was the bartender, wiping his hands back and forth over his apron.

Robles spoke calmly. "You've done enough, Tio. Hand me the gun."

"Enough?" Tio swung the pistol back to the first table. "I have just started."

"Don't talk crazy. Hand me the gun."

"Do you think I am crazy?"

"Just hand me the gun."

Tio smiled, and by it seemed to calm. "My foolish nephew. Use your head for one minute. What do you suppose would happen to me if I handed you this gun?"

"The law would take its course," Jimmy Robles said. The words sounded meaningless even to him.

"It would take its course to the nearest cottonwood," Tio said. "There are enough fools in the family with you, Jaime." He smiled still, though his voice continued to shake.

"Perhaps this is my mission, Jaime. The reason I was born."

"You make it hard to decide just which one is the fool."

"No. Hear me. God made Tio Robles to his image and likeness that he might someday blow out the brains of señores Rema-yard and Essery." Tio's laugh echoed in the long room.

Jimmy Robles looked at the two men. Judge Essery was holding on to the table and his thin face was white with fear, glistening with fear. And for all old man Remillard's authority, he couldn't do a thing. An old Mexican, like a thousand he could buy or sell, could stand there and do whatever he desired because he had slipped past the cowman's zone of influence, past fearing for the future.

Tio raised the pistol to the level of his eyes. It was already cocked. "Watch my mission, Jaime. Watch me send two devils to hell!"

He watched fascinated. Two men were going to die. Two men he hardly knew, but he could feel only hate for them. Not like he might hate a man, but with the anger he felt for a principle that went against his reason. Something big, like injustice. It went through his mind that if these two men died, all injustice would vanish. He heard the word in his mind. His own voice saying it. *Injustice.* Repeating it, until then he heard only a part of the word.

His gun came out and he pulled the trigger in the motion. Nothing was repeating in his mind, now. He looked down at Tio Robles on the floor and knew he was dead before he knelt over him.

He picked up Tio in his arms like a small child and walked out of the Supreme into the evening dusk. John Benedict approached him and he saw people crowding out into the street. He walked past the sheriff and behind him heard Remillard's booming voice. "That was a close one!" and a scattering of laughter. Fainter then, he heard Remillard again. "Your boy learns fast."

He walked toward Spanishtown, not seeing the faces that lined the street, hardly feeling the limp weight in his arms.

The people, the storefronts, the street—all was hazy—as if his thoughts covered his eyes like a blindfold. And as he went on in the darkness he thought he understood now what John Benedict meant by justice.

Blood Money

The Yuma Savings and Loan, Asunción Branch, was held up on a Monday morning, early. By eight o'clock the doctor had dug the bullet out of Elton Goss's middle and said if he lived, then you didn't need doctors anymore—the age of miracles was back. By nine Freehouser, the Asunción marshal, had all the facts—even the identity of the five holdup men—thanks to the Centralia Hotel night clerk's having been awake to see four of them come down from their rooms just after sunup. Then, he had tried to make the faces register in his mind, but even squinting and wrinkling his forehead did no good. The fifth man had been in the hotel lobby most of the night and the clerk knew for sure who he was, but didn't at the time associate him with the others. Later, when Freehouser showed him the WANTED dodgers, then he was dead sure about all of them.

Four were desperadoes. Well known, though with beard bristles and range clothes they looked like anybody else. First, the Harlan brothers, Ford and Eugene. Ford was boss: Eugene was too lazy to work. Then Deke, an old hand whose real name was something Deacon, though no one knew what for sure. And the fourth, Sonny Navarez, wanted in Sonora by the *rurales;* in Arizona, by the marshal's office. He, like the others, had served time in the territorial prison at Yuma.

As far as Freehouser was concerned, they weren't going back to Yuma if he caught them. Not with Elton Goss dying and his dad yelling for blood.

The fifth outlaw was identified as Rich Miller, a rider from down by Four Tanks. Those who knew of him said he was weathered good for his age, though not as tough as he thought he was. A boy going on eighteen and getting funny ideas in his brain because of the changing chemistry in his body. The bartender at the Centralia said Rich had been in and out all day, looking like he was mad at somebody. So they judged Rich had gotten drunk and was talked into something that was way over his head.

A hand from F-T Connected, which was out of Four Tanks, said Rich Miller'd been let go the day before, when the old man caught him drunk up at a line shack and not tending his fences. So what the Centralia bartender said was probably true. Freehouser said it was just too damn bad for him, that's all.

Monday afternoon the marshal's posse was in Four Tanks, then heading east toward the jagged andesite peaks of the Kofas. McKelway, the law at Four Tanks, had joined the posse, bringing five men with him, and offering a neighborly hand. But he became hard-to-hold eager when he found out who they were after. The Fords, Deke, and Navarez had dead-or-alive money on them. McKelway knew Rich Miller and said he just ought to have his nose wiped and run off home. But Freehouser looked at it differently.

This was armed robbery. Goss, the bank manager, and his son Elton, who clerked for him, were hauled out of bed by two men—they turned out to be Eugene Harlan and Deke. Ford Harlan and Sonny Navarez were waiting at the rear door of the bank. The robbery would have come off without incident if Elton hadn't gone for a gun in a desk drawer. The elder Goss wasn't sure which one shot him. Then they were gone, with twelve thousand dollars.

They rode around front and Rich Miller came out of the Centralia to join them. He'd been sitting at the window, asleep, the clerk thought, wearing off a drunk. He was used to having riders do that. When the rooms were filled up he didn't care. But Rich Miller suddenly came alive and swung onto a mount the Mexican was leading. So all that time he must have been watching the front to see no one sneaked up on them.

McKelway said a boy ought to be allowed one big mistake before he was called hard on something he'd done. Besides, Rich Miller's name didn't bring any reward money.

Tuesday morning, the twenty-man posse was deep in the Kofas. Gray rock towering on all sides, wild country, and now, no trail. Freehouser decided they would split up, climb to higher ground, and wait. Just look around. He sent a man back to Four Tanks to wire Yuma and Aztec in case the outlaws got through the Kofas. But Freehouser was sure they were still in the mountains, somewhere.

Wednesday morning his hunch paid off. One of McKelway's men spotted a rider, and the posse closed in by means of a mirror-flash system they'd planned beforehand. The rider turned out to be Ford Harlan.

Wednesday afternoon Ford Harlan was dead.

He had led them a chase most of the morning, slipping through the man net, but near noon he turned into a dead-end canyon, a deserted mine site that once had been Sweet Mary No. 1. Ford Harlan had been urging his mount up a slope above the mine works, toward an adobe hut perched on a ledge about three hundred yards up, when Freehouser cupped his hands and called for him to halt. He kept on. A moment later Jim Mission, McKelway's deputy, knocked him out of the saddle with a single shot from his Remington.

Then McKelway and Mission volunteered to bring Ford Harlan down. McKelway tied a white neckerchief to the end of his Sharps for a truce flag and they went up. Freehouser had said if you want to get Ford, you might as well go a few more steps and ask the rest if they want to give up. They were almost to the body when the pistol fire broke from above. They scrambled down fast and when they reached the posse, Freehouser was smiling.

They were all up there, Eugene and Deke and the Mexican and Rich Miller. One of them had lost his nerve and opened up. You could see it on Freehouser's face. The self-satisfaction. They were trapped in an old assay shack with a sheer sandstone wall towering behind it—thin shadow lines of crevices reaching to slender pinnacles—and only one way to come down. The original mine opening was on the same shelf; probably they'd hid their horses there.

Freehouser was a contented man; he had all the time in the world to figure how to pry them out of the 'dobe. He even listened to McKelway and admitted that maybe the kid, Rich Miller, shouldn't be hung with the others—if he didn't get shot first.

Some of the posse went back home, because they had jobs to hold down, but the next day, others came out from Asunción and Four Tanks to see the fun.

IT seemed natural that Deke should take over as boss. There was no discussing it; no one gave it a thought. Ford was dead. Eugene was indifferent. Sonny Navarez was Mexican, and Rich Miller was a kid.

The boy had wondered why Deke wasn't the boss even before. Maybe Deke didn't have Ford's nerve, but he had it over him in age and learning. Still, a man gets old and he thinks of too many what-ifs. And sometimes Deke was scary the way he talked about fate and God pulling little strings to steer men around where they didn't want to go.

He was at the window on the right side of the doorway, which was open because there was no door. Eugene and Deke were at the left front window. He could hear Sonny Navarez behind him moving gear around, but the boy did not take his eyes from the slope.

Deke lounged against the wall, his face close to the window frame, his carbine balanced on the sill. Eugene was a step behind him. He was a heavy-boned man, shoulders stretching his shirt tight, and tall, though Deke was taller when he wasn't lounging. Eugene pulled at his shirt, sticking to his body with perspiration. The sun was straight overhead and the heat pushed into the canyon without first being deflected by the rimrock.

The Mexican drew his carbine from his bedroll and moved up next to Rich Miller, and now the four of them were looking down the slope, all thinking pretty much the same thing, though in different ways.

Eugene Harlan broke the silence. "I shouldn't of fired at them."

It could have gone unsaid. Deke shrugged. "That's under the bridge."

"I wasn't thinking."

Deke did not bother to look at him. "Well, you better start."

"It wasn't my fault. Ford led 'em here!"

"Nobody's blaming you for anything. They'd a got us anyway, sooner or later. It was on the wall."

Eugene was silent, and then he said, "What happens if we give ourselves up?"

Deke glanced at him now. "What do you think?"

Sonny Navarez grinned. "I think they would invite us to the rope dance."

"Ford's the one shot that boy in the bank," Eugene protested. "They already got him."

"How would they know he's the one?" Deke said.

"We'll tell them."

Deke shook his head. "Get a drink and you'll be doing your nerves a favor."

Sonny Navarez and Rich Miller looked at Deke and both of them grinned, but they said nothing and after a moment they looked away again, down the slope, which fell smooth and steep. Slightly to the left, beyond an ore tailing, rose the weathered gray scaffolding over the main shaft; below it, the rickety structure of the crushing mill and, past that, six rusted tanks cradled in a framework of decaying timber. These were roughly three hundred yards down the slope. There was another hundred to the clapboard company buildings straggled along the base of the far slope.

A sign hanging from the veranda of the largest building said SWEET MARY NO. 1—EL TESORERO MINING CO.—FOUR TANKS, ARIZONA TERR. Most of the possemen now sat in the shade of this building.

Deke raised his hat again and passed a hand over his bald head, then down over his face, weathered and beard stubbled, contrasting with the delicate whiteness of his skull. Rich Miller's eyes came back up the slope, hesitating on Ford Harlan's facedown body. Then he removed his hat, passed a sleeve across his forehead, and replaced the curled brim low over his eyes.

He heard Eugene say, "You can't tell what they'll do."

"They won't send us back to Yuma." Deke said. "That's one thing you can count on. And it costs money to rig a gallows. They'd just as lief do it here, with a gun—appeals to the sporting blood."

Sonny Navarez said, "I once shot a mountain sheep in this same canyon that weighed as much as a man."

"Right from the start there were signs," Deke said. "I was a fool not to heed them. Now it's too late. Something's brought us to die here all together, and we can't escape it. You can't escape your doom."

Sonny Navarez said, "I think it was twelve thousand dollars that brought us."

"Sure it was the money, in a way," Deke said. "But we're so busy listening to Ford tell how easy money's restin' in the bank, waitin' to be sent to Yuma, we're not seein' the signs. Things that've never happened before. Like Ford insisting we got to have five—so he picks up this kid—"

Rich Miller said, "Wait a minute!" because it didn't sound right.

Deke held up his hand. "I'm talking about the signs—and Ford all of a sudden gettin' the urge to go on scout when he never done anything like that before. It was all working toward this—and now there's nothing we can do about it."

"I ain't going to get shot up just because you got a crazy notion," Eugene said.

Deke shook his head, wearily. "It's sealed up now. After fate shows how it's going, then it's too late."

"I didn't shoot that man in the bank!"

"You think they'll bother to ask you?"

"Damn it, I'll tell 'em—and they'll have to prove I did it!"

"If you can get close enough to 'em without gettin' shot," Deke said quietly. He brought out field glasses from his saddlebags, which were below the window, and put the glasses to his face, edging them along the men far below in front of the company buildings.

Rich Miller said to him, "What do you see down there?"

"Same thing you do, only bigger."

"I think," Sonny Navarez said to Deke, "that you are right in what you have said, that they will try hard to kill us—but this boy is not one of us. I think if he would surrender, they would not kill him. Prison, perhaps, but prison is better than dying."

"You worry about yourself," Rich Miller said.

"The time to be brave," the Mexican said, "is when they are handing out medals."

"You heard him," Deke said. "Worry about your own hide. The more people we got, the longer we last. There's nothing that says if you're going to get killed, you got to hurry it up."

Rich Miller watched Eugene move back to the table along the rear wall and pick up the whisky bottle that was there. The boy passed his tongue over dry lips, watching Eugene drink. It would be good to have a drink, he thought. No, it wouldn't. It would be bad. You drank too much and that's why you're here. That's why you're going to get shot or hung.

But he could not sincerely believe what Deke had said. That one way of the other, this was the end. Down the slope the posse was very far away—dots of men that seemed too small to be a threat. He did not feel sorry about joining the holdup, because he did not let himself think about it. He did feel something resembling sorry for the man in the bank. But he shouldn't have reached for the gun. I wonder if I would have, he thought.

It wasn't so bad up here in the 'dobe. Plenty of water and grub. Maybe we'll have some fun. Look at that crazy Mexican, talking about hunting mountain sheep.

If you were in jail you could say, all right, you made a mistake; but how do you know if you've made a mistake when you're still alive and got two thousand dollars in your pants? My God, a man can do just about anything with two thousand dollars!

FREEHOUSER sat in the shade, not saying anything. McKelway came to him, biting on his pipe idly, and after a while pointed to the mine-shaft scaffolding and said how a man with a good rifle might be able to draw a bead and throw something in that open doorway if he was sitting way up there on top.

Freehouser studied the ore tailings, furrowed and steep, that extended out from the slope on both sides of the hut. If a man was going up to that 'dobe, he'd have to go straight up, right into their guns. Maybe McKelway had something. Soften them up a bit.

STANDING by the windows, watching the possemen not moving, became tiresome. So one by one they would go back to the table and take a drink. Rich Miller took his turn and it tasted good. But he did not drink much.

Still, the time dragged on—until Eugene thought of something. He went to his gear and drew a deck of cards.

Sonny Navarez said, "I have not played often."

"Stand by the window awhile," Deke told him. "Then somebody'll spell you. You got enough cash to learn with."

Eugene shook his head, thinking of his brother, who had taken twice as much as the others because the holdup had been his idea. "Damn Ford had four thousand in his bags. . . ."

They started playing, using matches for chips, each one worth a dollar. Rich Miller said the stakes were big . . . he'd never played higher than nickel-dime before; but he began winning right off and he changed his tune. Most of the time they played five-card stud. Deke said it separated the men from the boys and he looked at Rich Miller when he said it. Deke played with a dumb face, but would smile after the last card was dealt—as if the last card always twinned the one he had in the hole. And he lost every hand. Eugene and Rich Miller took turns winning the pots, and after a while Deke stopped smiling.

"We're raising the stakes," he said finally. "Each stick's worth ten dollars." Deke's cut was down to a few hundred dollars.

Eugene took a drink and wiped his mouth and grinned. "Ain't you losing it fast enough?"

Rich Miller grinned with him.

Deke said, "Just deal the cards."

* * *

McKELWAY reached the platform on top of the shaft scaffolding and dropped the line to haul up the rifles—his own Sharps and Jim Mission's roll-block Remington. He was glad Jim Mission was coming up with him. Jim was company and could shoot probably better than he could.

When Jim reached the platform the two men nodded and smiled, then loaded their rifles and practice-sighted on the doorway. McKelway said, Try not to hit the boy, though knocking off any of the others would be doing mankind a good turn, and Jim Mission said it was all right with him.

EUGENE got up from the table unsteadily, tipping back his chair; he was grinning and stuffing currency into his pants pockets. In two hours he had won every cent of Deke's and Rich Miller's money. They remained seated, watching him sullenly, thinking it was a damn fool thing to try and win back all your losings in a couple of hands. Eugene took another pull at the bottle and wiped his mouth and looked at them, but he only grinned.

"Sonny!" He called to the Mexican lounging beside the window. "Your turn to get skinned."

The Mexican shook his head. "I could not oppose such luck."

"Come on!"

Sonny Navarez shook his head again and smiled.

Harlan looked at him steadily, frowning. "Are you going to play?"

"Why should I give you my money?"

"You don't come over here, I'll come get you."

The Mexican did not smile now and the room was silent. Rich Miller started to rise, but Deke was up first. "Gene, you want to fight somebody—there's plenty outside."

Eugene ignored him and kept on toward Sonny. The Mexican's hand edged toward his holstered pistol.

"Gene, you sit down now," Deke said tensely.

Eugene stepped into the rectangle of sunlight carpeting in from the doorway. He was stepping out of it when the rifle cracked and sang in the open stillness. Eugene's hands clawed at his face and he dropped without uttering a sound.

McKelway reloaded quickly. He had got one of them, he was sure of that. And it hadn't looked like the boy, else he wouldn't have fired. Jim Mission told him it was good shooting. After that McKelway did some figuring.

From the crest of the ore tailing in front of them, they'd be only about fifty yards from the hut. The only trouble was, they'd be out in the open. He told Jim Mission about it and he said why not go up after dark; then if they didn't see anything they'd still be close enough to shoot at sounds. McKelway said he was just waiting for Jim to say it.

There was no poker the rest of the afternoon. Deke had dragged him by his boots out of the doorway and placed him against a side wall with his hands on his chest, not crossed, but pushed inside his coat. He took the money out of Eugene's pockets—six thousand dollars—and laid it on the table. Then he sat down and looked at it.

Rich Miller pressed close to the wall by the window, studying the slope, wondering where the man with the rifle was. His eyes hung on the weathered shaft scaffolding, and now he wasn't so sure if there'd be any fun.

Once Deke said, "Now it's starting to show itself," but they didn't bother to ask him what.

Sonny Navarez stayed by a window. He would look at Eugene's body, but most of the time he was watching the dying sun. Rich Miller noticed this, but he figured the Mexican was thinking about God—or heaven or hell—because there was a dead man in the room. Sonny had crossed himself when Eugene was cut down, even though he would have killed him himself a minute before.

The sun was below the canyon rim, though the sky still reflected it red and orange, when Sonny Navarez pulled his pistol.

Deke was raising the bottle. He glanced at the Mexican, but only momentarily. He took a long swallow then and extended the bottle to Rich Miller. But the boy was staring at Sonny Navarez. Deke's head turned abruptly. Sonny's long-barreled .44 was pointing toward them.

Deke took his time putting down the bottle. He looked up again. "What's the idea?"

The Mexican said, "When it is dark I'm leaving."

Deke nodded to the pistol. "You think we're going to try and stop you?"

"You might. I am taking the money."

"You're wasting your time."

Sonny Navarez shrugged. "*Qué va*—it's worth a try. From no matter where you die, it's the same distance to hell."

"You wouldn't have a chance," Rich Miller said. "There's somebody out there close with a rifle dead on this place."

"For this money a man will brave many things," the Mexican said. "And—I am not leaving until dark." Then he told them to face the wall, and when they did, he picked up the bundles of oversize bills and stuffed them inside his jacket.

Rich Miller said, "Do you think you'll get through?"

"Probably no."

Deke said, "You're a damn fool."

"If I get out," Sonny Navarez said, "I will visit a priest and give his church part of the money, and not rob again."

"It's too late for that," Deke said. "It's too late for anything."

"No," the Mexican insisted. "I will be very sorry for this crime. With the money that is left after the church I will buy my mother a house in Hermosillo and after that I will recite the rosary every day."

Deke shook his head. "Things are going the way they are for a reason we don't know. But nothing you can do will change it."

The Mexican shrugged and said, "*Qué va*—"

It was almost full dark when Sonny Navarez moved to the doorway. He stood next to the opening and holstered his pistol and lifted his carbine, which was there against the wall. He levered a shell into the breech and stepped into the opening, crouching slightly. He hesitated, as if listening, then turned to the two men at the table and nodded. As he was turning back, the rifle shot rang in the dim stillness and echoed up-canyon. Sonny Navarez doubled, sinking to his knees, and hung there momentarily, as if in prayer, before falling half through the doorway.

LATER, McKelway and Mission climbed down from the ore tailing and reported to Freehouser. The marshal said three out of five men wasn't bad for one day's work. They were sitting on the porch, cigarettes glowing in the darkness, when the rider came in from Asunción. He told them that Elton Goss was going to pull through.

Freehouser laughed and said, well, he guessed the age of miracles was back. A good one on the doctor, eh?

The news made everybody feel pretty good, because Elton was a nice boy. McKelway mentioned that it would also make it a whole lot easier on Rich Miller.

LOOKING out into the night, the boy could just barely make out the shapes of the mine structures and the cyanide vats, which Deke had told him held 250 tons of ore and had to be hauled all the way across the desert from Yuma. How did he say it? The ore'd pour into the crusher—jaws and rollers that'd beat it almost to powder—then pass onto the vats and get leached in cyanide for nine days. Five pounds of cyanide to the ton of water, that was it. He thought, What's the sense in remembering that?

It's a strange thing, Rich Miller thought now, how in two days a man can change from a thirty-a-month rider to an outlaw and not even feel it. Almost like the man has nothing to do with it. Just a rope pulling you into things.

He remembered earlier in the day, being eager, looking forward to doing some long-range shooting, but seeing the situation apart from himself. He wondered how he could have thought this. Now there were two dead men in the room—that was the difference.

Later on, he got to thinking about Eugene breaking the poker game and about one Mexican. It occurred to him that both of them, for a short space of time, had all of the money, and now they were dead. Ford had taken the biggest cut, and he was dead. Toward morning he dozed and when he awoke, Deke was sitting, leaning against the wall below the other window.

Deke was silent and Rich Miller said, for something to say, "When they going to try for us?"

"When they get good and damn ready."

Rich Miller was silent and after a while he said, "We could take a chance and give up—you know, not like surrenderin'—with the idea of gettin' away later on when they ain't a hundred of 'em around."

"You know what I told you."

"But you ain't dead sure about that."

"I'd say I'm a little older than you are."

Rich Miller did not answer. Damn, he hated for someone to tell him that. As if old men naturally knew more than young ones. Taking credit for being older when they didn't have anything to do with it.

"What're you thinking about?" Deke said.

"Giving up."

Deke exhaled slowly. "You saw what happens if you go through that door."

"There's other ways."

"Like what?"

"Wavin' a flag."

"You wave anything out that door," Deke said quietly, "I'll kill you."

HE'S crazy, Rich thought. *He's honest-to-God crazy and doesn't know it. . . .* Deke had butted the table against the wall under the window and now they sat opposite each other, Deke on one side of the window, the boy on the other. Deke had divided the eight thousand dollars between them and said they were going to play poker to keep their minds from blowing away. He placed his pistol on the edge of the table.

They stayed fairly close at first, each winning about the same number of pots, but after a while the boy began to win more often. In the quietness he thought of many things—like not being able to give himself up—and then he remembered something which had occurred to him earlier.

"Deke," the boy said, "you know why Sonny and Eugene got killed?"

"I've been telling you why. 'Cause they were destined to."

"But why?"

"No one knows that."

"I do." The boy watched the older man closely. "Because they had the money." He paused. "Ford had most of it, and he was the first. Eugene had all but Sonny's when he got hit. Then Sonny took all of it and he lasted less than an hour."

Deke said nothing, but his sunken expression seemed more drawn.

They played on in silence and slowly Rich Miller was taking more and more of the money. Deke seemed uncomfortable and he said quietly that he guessed it just wasn't his day. In less than an hour he was down to two hundred and fifty dollars.

"You might clean me out," Deke said.

Rich Miller said nothing and dealt the cards. The first ones down, then a queen to Deke and a jack to himself. He looked at his hole card. A ten of diamonds. Deke bet fifty dollars on the queen.

"You must have twin girls," the boy said.

"You know how to find out."

Rich Miller's next card was a king. Deke's an ace. He bet fifty dollars again. Their fourth cards were low and no help, but Deke pushed in all the money he had.

"That's on a hunch," he said.

Rich Miller dealt the last cards—a queen to Deke, making it an ace, a five, and two queens. He gave himself a second king.

"What you show beats me," Deke said, grinning. He pushed away from the table and stood up. "You got it all, boy. You know what that means."

"It means I'm giving up."

"It's too late. You explained it yourself a while ago—the man who gets the money gets killed!" Deke was grinning deeply. "Now I don't have anything."

"You're dead sure you'll be last."

"As sure as a man can be. It's the handwriting."

"What good'll it do you?"

"Who knows?"

"You're so dead sure, go stand in that doorway."

Deke was silent.

"What about your handwritin'? The pattern says you'll be the last, and even then, who knows? That all the bunk?"

Deke hesitated momentarily, then walked slowly toward the doorway. He stopped next to it, stiffly. Then he moved out.

Rich Miller's eyes stayed on Deke as his hand moved across the table. He lifted Deke's pistol from the table edge and swung it out the window and fired in the direction of the scaffolding.

A high-pitched, whining report answered the shot and hung longer in the air. Deke staggered, turning back into the room, and had time to look at the boy in wide-eyed amazement. Then he was dead.

The boy returned to the window after getting his carbine and, with his bandanna tied to the end of the barrel, waved it in a slow arc back and forth. And as they started up the slope he sat back in the chair and idly turned over his hole card, the ten.

The possemen were drawing closer, up to Ford Harlan's body now. He flipped Deke's hole card. It landed on top of the two queens. Three ladies.

He rose and moved to the doorway as he saw the men nearing the shelf, then glanced down at Deke and shook his head. I sure am crazy, he thought. I never heard before of a man cheating to lose.

He walked through the doorway with his hands above his head.

THREE-TEN TO YUMA

He had picked up his prisoner at Fort Huachuca shortly after midnight and now, in a silent early morning mist, they approached Contention. The two riders moved slowly, one behind the other.

Entering Stockman Street, Paul Scallen glanced back at the open country with the wet haze blanketing its flatness, thinking of the long night ride from Huachuca, relieved that this much was over. When his body turned again, his hand moved over the sawed-off shotgun that was across his lap and he kept his eyes on the man ahead of him until they were near the end of the second block, opposite the side entrance of the Republic Hotel.

He said just above a whisper, though it was clear in the silence, "End of the line."

The man turned in his saddle, looking at Scallen curiously. "The jail's around on Commercial."

"I want you to be comfortable."

Scallen stepped out of the saddle, lifting a Winchester from the boot, and walked toward the hotel's side door. A figure stood in the gloom of the doorway, behind the screen, and as Scallen reached the steps the screen door opened.

"Are you the marshal?"

"Yes, sir." Scallen's voice was soft and without emotion. "Deputy, from Bisbee."

"We're ready for you. Two-oh-seven. A corner . . . fronts on Commercial." He sounded proud of the accommodation.

"You're Mr. Timpey?"

The man in the doorway looked surprised. "Yeah, Wells Fargo. Who'd you expect?"

"You might have got a back room, Mr. Timpey. One with no windows." He swung the shotgun on the man still mounted. "Step down easy, Jim."

The man, who was in his early twenties, a few years younger than Scallen, sat with one hand over the other on the saddle horn. Now he gripped the horn and swung down. When he was on the ground his hands were still close together, iron manacles holding them three chain lengths apart. Scallen motioned him toward the door with the stubby barrel of the shotgun.

"Anyone in the lobby?"

"The desk clerk," Timpey answered him, "and a man in a chair by the front door."

"Who is he?"

"I don't know. He's asleep . . . got his brim down over his eyes."

"Did you see anyone out on Commercial?"

"No . . . I haven't been out there." At first he had seemed nervous, but now he was irritated, and a frown made his face pout childishly.

Scallen said calmly, "Mr. Timpey, it was your line this man robbed. You want to see him go all the way to Yuma, don't you?"

"Certainly I do." His eyes went to the outlaw, Jim Kidd, then back to Scallen hurriedly. "But why all the melodrama? The man's under arrest—already been sentenced."

"But he's not in jail till he walks through the gates at Yuma,"

Scallen said. "I'm only one man, Mr. Timpey, and I've got to get him there."

"Well, dammit . . . I'm not the law! Why didn't you bring men with you? All I know is I got a wire from our Bisbee office to get a hotel room and meet you here the morning of November third. There weren't any instructions that I had to get myself deputized a marshal. That's your job."

"I know it is, Mr. Timpey," Scallen said, and smiled, though it was an effort. "But I want to make sure no one knows Jim Kidd's in Contention until after train time this afternoon."

Jim Kidd had been looking from one to the other with a faintly amused grin. Now he said to Timpey, "He means he's afraid somebody's going to jump him." He smiled at Scallen. "That marshal must've really sold you a bill of goods."

"What's he talking about?" Timpey said.

Kidd went on before Scallen could answer. "They hid me in the Huachuca lockup 'cause they knew nobody could get at me there . . . and finally the Bisbee marshal gets a plan. He and some others hopped the train in Benson last night, heading for Yuma with an army prisoner passed off as me." Kidd laughed, as if the idea were ridiculous.

"Is that right?" Timpey said.

Scallen nodded. "Pretty much right."

"How does he know all about it?"

"He's got ears and ten fingers to add with."

"I don't like it. Why just one man?"

"Every deputy from here down to Bisbee is out trying to scare up the rest of them. Jim here's the only one we caught," Scallen explained—then added, "Alive."

Timpey shot a glance at the outlaw. "Is he the one who killed Dick Moons?"

"One of the passengers swears he saw who did it . . . and he didn't identify Kidd at the trial."

Timpey shook his head. "Dick drove for us a long time. You know his brother lives here in Contention. When he heard about it he almost went crazy." He hesitated, and then said again, "I don't like it."

Scallen felt his patience wearing away, but he kept his voice even when he said, "Maybe I don't either . . . but what you like and what I like aren't going to matter a whole lot, with the marshal past Tucson by now. You can grumble about it all you want, Mr. Timpey, as long as you keep it under your breath. Jim's got friends . . . and since I have to haul him clear across the territory, I'd just as soon they didn't know about it."

Timpey fidgeted nervously. "I don't see why I have to get dragged into this. My job's got nothing to do with law enforcement. . . ."

"You have the room key?"

"In the door. All I'm responsible for is the stage run between here and Tucson—"

Scallen shoved the Winchester at him. "If you'll take care of this and the horses till I get back, I'll be obliged to you . . . and I know I don't have to ask you not to mention we're at the hotel."

He waved the shotgun and nodded and Jim Kidd went ahead of him through the side door into the hotel lobby. Scallen was a stride behind him, holding the stubby shotgun close to his leg. "Up the stairs on the right, Jim."

Kidd started up, but Scallen paused to glance at the figure in the armchair near the front. He was sitting on his spine with limp hands folded on his stomach and, as Timpey had described, his hat low over the upper part of his face. You've seen people sleeping in hotel lobbies before, Scallen told himself, and followed Kidd up the stairs. He couldn't stand and wonder about it.

Room 207 was narrow and high-ceilinged, with a single window looking down on Commercial Street. An iron bed was placed the long way against one wall and extended to the right side of the window, and along the opposite wall was a dresser with washbasin and pitcher and next to it a rough-board wardrobe. An unpainted table and two straight chairs took up most of the remaining space.

"Lay down on the bed if you want to," Scallen said.

"Why don't you sleep?" Kidd asked. "I'll hold the shotgun."

The deputy moved one of the straight chairs near to the door and the other to the side of the table opposite the bed. Then he sat down, resting the shotgun on the table so that it pointed directly at Jim Kidd sitting on the edge of the bed near the window.

He gazed vacantly outside. A patch of dismal sky showed above the frame buildings across the way, but he was not sitting close enough to look directly down onto the street. He said, indifferently, "I think it's going to rain."

There was a silence, and then Scallen said, "Jim, I don't have anything against you personally . . . this is what I get paid for, but I just want it understood that if you start across the seven feet between us, I'm going to pull both triggers at once—without first asking you to stop. That clear?"

Kidd looked at the deputy marshal, then his eyes drifted out the window again. "It's kinda cold too." He rubbed his hands together and the three chain links rattled against each other. "The window's open a crack. Can I close it?"

Scallen's grip tightened on the shotgun and he brought the barrel up, though he wasn't aware of it. "If you can reach it from where you're sitting."

Kidd looked at the windowsill and said without reaching toward it, "Too far."

"All right," Scallen said, rising. "Lay back on the bed." He worked his gun belt around so that now the Colt was on his left hip.

Kidd went back slowly, smiling. "You don't take any chances, do you? Where's your sporting blood?"

"Down in Bisbee with my wife and three youngsters," Scallen told him without smiling, and moved around the table.

There were no grips on the window frame. Standing with his side to the window, facing the man on the bed, he put the heel of his hand on the bottom ledge of the frame and shoved down hard. The window banged shut and with the slam he saw Jim Kidd kicking up off of his back, his body straining to rise without his hands to help. Momentarily, Scallen hesitated and his finger tensed on the trigger. Kidd's feet were on the floor, his body swinging up and his head down to lunge from the bed. Scallen took one step and brought his knee up hard against Kidd's face.

The outlaw went back across the bed, his head striking the wall. He lay there with his eyes open looking at Scallen.

"Feel better now, Jim?"

Kidd brought his hands up to his mouth, working the jaw around. "Well, I had to try you out," he said. "I didn't think you'd shoot."

"But you know I will the next time."

For a few minutes Kidd remained motionless. Then he began to pull himself straight. "I just want to sit up."

Behind the table Scallen said, "Help yourself." He watched Kidd stare out the window.

Then, "How much do you make, Marshal?" Kidd asked the question abruptly.

"I don't think it's any of your business."

"What difference does it make?"

Scallen hesitated. "A hundred and fifty a month," he said, finally, "some expenses, and a dollar bounty for every arrest against a Bisbee ordinance in the town limits."

Kidd shook his head sympathetically. "And you got a wife and three kids."

"Well, it's more than a cowhand makes."

"But you're not a cowhand."

"I've worked my share of beef."

"Forty a month and keep, huh?" Kidd laughed.

"That's right, forty a month," Scallen said. He felt awkward. "How much do you make?"

Kidd grinned. When he smiled he looked very young, hardly out of his teens. "Name a month," he said. "It varies."

"But you've made a lot of money."

"Enough. I can buy what I want."

"What are you going to be wanting the next five years?"

"You're pretty sure we're going to Yuma."

"And you're pretty sure we're not," Scallen said. "Well, I've got two train passes and a shotgun that says we are. What've you got?"

Kidd smiled. "You'll see." Then he said right after it, his tone changing, "What made you join the law?"

"The money," Scallen answered, and felt foolish as he said it. But he went on, "I was working for a spread over by the Pantano Wash when Old Nana broke loose and raised hell up the Santa Rosa Valley. The army was going around in circles, so the Pima County marshal got up a bunch to help out and we tracked Apaches almost all spring. The marshal and I got along fine, so he offered me a deputy job if I wanted it." He wanted to say that he started for seventy-five and worked up to the one hundred and fifty, but he didn't.

"And then someday you'll get to be marshal and make two hundred."

"Maybe."

"And then one night a drunk cowhand you've never seen will be tearing up somebody's saloon and you'll go in to arrest him and he'll drill you with a lucky shot before you get your gun out."

"So you're telling me I'm crazy."

"If you don't already know it."

Scallen took his hand off the shotgun and pulled tobacco and paper from his shirt pocket and began rolling a cigarette. "Have you figured out yet what my price is?"

Kidd looked startled, momentarily, but the grin returned. "No, I haven't. Maybe you come higher than I thought."

Scallen scratched a match across the table, lighted the cigarette, then threw it to the floor, between Kidd's boots. "You don't have enough money, Jim."

Kidd shrugged, then reached down for the cigarette. "You've treated me pretty good. I just wanted to make it easy on you."

The sun came into the room after a while. Weakly at first, cold and hazy. Then it warmed and brightened and cast an oblong patch of light between the bed and the table. The morning wore on slowly because there was nothing to do and each man sat restlessly thinking about somewhere else, though it was a restlessness within and it showed on neither of them.

The deputy rolled cigarettes for the outlaw and himself and most of the time they smoked in silence. Once Kidd asked him what time the train left. He told him shortly after three, but Kidd made no comment.

Scallen went to the window and looked out at the narrow rutted road that was Commercial Street. He pulled a watch from his vest pocket and looked at it. It was almost noon, yet there were few people about. He wondered about this and asked himself if it was unnaturally quiet for a Saturday noon in Contention . . . or if it were just his nerves. . . .

He studied the man standing under the wooden awning across the street, leaning idly against a support post with his thumbs hooked in his belt and his flat-crowned hat on the back of his head. There was something familiar about him. And each time Scallen had gone to the window—a few times during the past hour—the man had been there.

He glanced at Jim Kidd lying across the bed, then looked out the window in time to see another man moving up next to the one at the post. They stood together for the space of a minute before the second man turned a horse from the tie rail, swung up, and rode off down the street.

The man at the post watched him go and tilted his hat against the sun glare. And then it registered. With the hat low on his forehead Scallen saw him again as he had that morning. The man lying in the armchair . . . as if asleep.

He saw his wife, then, and the three youngsters and he could almost feel the little girl sitting on his lap where she had climbed up to kiss him good-bye, and he had promised to bring her something from Tucson. He didn't know why they had come to him all of a sudden. And after he had put them out of his mind, since there was no room now, there was an upset feeling inside as if he had swallowed something that would not go down all the way. It made his heart beat a little faster.

Jim Kidd was smiling up at him. "Anybody I know?"

"I didn't think it showed."

"Like the sun going down."

Scallen glanced at the man across the street and then to Jim Kidd. "Come here." He nodded to the window. "Tell me who your friend is over there."

Kidd half rose and leaned over looking out the window, then sat down again. "Charlie Prince."

"Somebody else just went for help."

"Charlie doesn't need help."

"How did you know you were going to be in Contention?"

"You told that Wells Fargo man I had friends . . . and about the posses chasing around in the hills. Figure it out for yourself. You could be looking out a window in Benson and seeing the same thing."

"They're not going to do you any good."

"I don't know any man who'd get himself killed for a hundred and fifty dollars." Kidd paused. "Especially a man with a wife and young ones. . . ."

Men rode to town in something less than an hour later. Scallen heard the horses coming up Commercial, and went to the window to see the six riders pull to a stop and range themselves in a line in the middle of the street facing the hotel. Charlie Prince stood behind them, leaning against the post.

Then he moved away from it, leisurely, and stepped down into the street. He walked between the horses and stopped in front of them just below the window. He cupped his hands to his mouth and shouted, "*Jim!*"

In the quiet street it was like a pistol shot.

Scallen looked at Kidd, seeing the smile that softened his face and was even in his eyes. Confidence. It was all over him. And even with the manacles on, you would believe that it was Jim Kidd who was holding the shotgun.

"What do you want me to tell him?" Kidd said.

"Tell him you'll write every day."

Kidd laughed and went to the window, pushing it up by the top of the frame. It raised a few inches. Then he moved his hands under the window and it slid up all the way.

"Charlie, you go buy the boys a drink. We'll be down shortly."

"Are you all right?"

"Sure I'm all right."

Charlie Prince hesitated. "What if you don't come down? He could kill you and say you tried to break. . . . Jim, you tell him what'll happen if we hear a gun go off."

"He knows," Kidd said, and closed the window. He looked at Scallen standing motionless with the shotgun under his arm. "Your turn, Marshal."

"What do you expect me to say?"

"Something that makes sense. You said before I didn't mean a thing to you personally—what you're doing is just a job. Well, you figure out if it's worth getting killed for. All you have to do is throw your guns on the bed and let me walk out the door and you can go back to Bisbee and arrest all the drunks you want. Nobody's going to blame you with the odds stacked seven to one. You know your wife's not going to complain. . . ."

"You should have been a lawyer, Jim."

The smile began to fade from Kidd's face. "Come on—what's it going to be?"

The door rattled with three knocks in quick succession. Abruptly the room was silent. The two men looked at each other and now the smile disappeared from Kidd's face completely.

Scallen moved to the side of the door, tiptoeing in his high-heeled boots, then pointed his shotgun toward the bed. Kidd sat down.

"Who is it?"

For a moment there was no answer. Then he heard, "Timpey."

He glanced at Kidd, who was watching him. "What do you want?"

"I've got a pot of coffee for you."

Scallen hesitated. "You alone?"

"Of course I am. Hurry up, it's hot!"

He drew the key from his coat pocket, then held the shotgun in the crook of his arm as he inserted the key with one hand and turned the knob with the other. The door opened—and slammed against him, knocking him back against the dresser. He went off balance, sliding into the wardrobe, going down on his hands and knees, and the shotgun clattered across the floor to the window. He saw Jim Kidd drop to the floor for the gun. . . .

"Hold it!"

A heavyset man stood in the doorway with a Colt pointing out past the thick bulge of his stomach. "Leave that shotgun where it is." Timpey stood next to him with the coffeepot in his hand. There was coffee down the front of his suit, on the door, and on the flooring. He brushed at the front of his coat feebly, looking from Scallen to the man with the pistol.

"I couldn't help it, Marshal—he made me do it. He threatened to do something to me if I didn't."

"Who is he?"

"Bob Moons . . . you know, Dick's brother. . . ."

The heavyset man glanced at Timpey angrily. "Shut your damn whining." His eyes went to Jim Kidd and held there. "You know who I am, don't you?"

Kidd looked uninterested. "You don't resemble anybody I know."

"You didn't have to know Dick to shoot him!"

"I didn't shoot that messenger."

Scallen got to his feet, looking at Timpey. "What the hell's wrong with you?"

"I couldn't help it. He forced me."

"How did he know we were here?"

"He came in this morning talking about Dick and I felt he needed some cheering up; so I told him Jim Kidd had been tried and was being taken to Yuma and was here in town . . . on his way. Bob didn't say anything and went out, and a little later he came back with the gun."

"You damn fool." Scallen shook his head wearily.

"Never mind all the talk." Moons kept the pistol on Kidd. "I would've found him sooner or later. This way everybody gets saved a long train ride."

"You pull that trigger," Scallen said, "and you'll hang for murder."

"Like he did for killing Dick. . . ."

"A jury said he didn't do it." Scallen took a step toward the big man. "And I'm damned if I'm going to let you pass another sentence."

"You stay put or I'll pass sentence on you!"

Scallen moved a slow step nearer. "Hand me the gun, Bob."

"I'm warning you—get the hell out of the way and let me do what I came for."

"Bob, hand me the gun or I swear I'll beat you through that wall."

Scallen tensed to take another step, another slow one. He saw Moons's eyes dart from him to Kidd and in that instant he knew it would be his only chance. He lunged, swinging his coat aside with his hand, and when the hand came up it was holding a Colt. All in one motion. The pistol went up and chopped an arc across Moons's head before the big man could bring his own gun around. His hat flew off as the barrel swiped his skull and he went back against the wall heavily, then sank to the floor.

Scallen wheeled to face the window, thumbing the hammer back. But Kidd was still sitting on the edge of the bed with the shotgun at his feet.

The deputy relaxed, letting the hammer ease down. "You might have made it, that time."

Kidd shook his head. "I wouldn't have got off the bed." There was a note of surprise in his voice. "You know, you're pretty good. . . ."

At two-fifteen Scallen looked at his watch, then stood up, pushing the chair back. The shotgun was under his arm. In less than an hour they would leave the hotel, walk over Commercial to Stockman, and then up Stockman to the station. Three blocks. He wanted to go all the way. He wanted to get Jim Kidd on that train . . . but he was afraid.

He was afraid of what he might do once they were on the street. Even now his breath was short and occasionally he would inhale and let the air out slowly to calm himself. And he kept asking himself if it was worth it.

People would be in the windows and the doors, though you wouldn't see them. They'd have their own feelings and most of their hearts would be pounding . . . and they'd edge back of the door frames a little more. The man out on the street was something without a human nature or a personality of its own. He was on a stage. The street was another world.

Timpey sat on the chair in front of the door and next to him, squatting on the floor with his back against the wall, was Moons. Scallen had unloaded Moons's pistol and placed it in the pitcher behind him. Kidd was on the bed.

Most of the time he stared at Scallen. His face bore a puzzled expression, making his eyes frown, and sometimes he would cock his head as if studying the deputy from a different angle.

Scallen stepped to the window now. Charlie Prince and another man were under the awning. The others were not in sight.

"You haven't changed your mind?" Kidd asked him seriously.

Scallen shook his head.

"I don't understand you. You risk your neck to save my life, now you'll risk it again to send me to prison."

Scallen looked at Kidd and suddenly felt closer to him than any man he knew. "Don't ask me, Jim," he said, and sat down again.

After that he looked at his watch every few minutes.

At five minutes to three he walked to the door, motioning Timpey aside, and turned the key in the lock. "Let's go, Jim." When Kidd was next to him he prodded Moons with the gun barrel. "Over on the bed. Mister, if I see or hear about you on the street before train time, you'll face an attempted murder charge." He motioned Kidd past him, then stepped into the hall and locked the door.

They went down the stairs and crossed the lobby to the front door, Scallen a stride behind with the shotgun barrel almost touching Kidd's back. Passing through the doorway he said as calmly as he could, "Turn left on Stockman and keep walking. No matter what you hear, keep walking."

As they stepped out into Commercial, Scallen glanced at the ramada where Charlie Prince had been standing, but now the saloon porch was an empty shadow. Near the corner two horses stood under a sign that said EAT, in red letters; and on the other side of Stockman the signs continued, lining the rutted main street to make it seem narrower. And beneath the signs, in the shadows, nothing moved. There was a whisper of wind along the ramadas. It whipped sand specks from the street and rattled them against clapboard, and the sound was hollow and lifeless. Somewhere a screen door banged, far away.

They passed the café, turning onto Stockman. Ahead, the deserted street narrowed with distance to a dead end at the rail station—a single-story building standing by itself, low and sprawling, with most of the platform in shadow. The westbound was there, along the platform, but the engine and most of the cars were hidden by the station house. White steam lifted above the roof, to be lost in the sun's glare.

They were almost to the platform when Kidd said over his shoulder, "Run like hell while you're still able."

"Where are they?"

Kidd grinned, because he knew Scallen was afraid. "How should I know?"

"Tell them to come out in the open!"

"Tell them yourself."

"Dammit, *tell* them!" Scallen clenched his jaw and jabbed the short barrel into Kidd's back. "I'm not fooling. If they don't come out, I'll kill you!"

Kidd felt the gun barrel hard against his spine and suddenly he shouted, "Charlie!"

It echoed in the street, but after there was only the silence.

Kidd's eyes darted over the shadowed porches. "Dammit, Charlie—hold on!"

Scallen prodded him up the warped plank steps to the shade of the platform and suddenly he could feel them near. "Tell him again!"

"Don't shoot, Charlie!" Kidd screamed the words.

From the other side of the station they heard the trainman's call trailing off, ". . . Gila Bend. Sentinel, Yuma!"

The whistle sounded loud, wailing, as they passed into the shade of the platform, then out again to the naked glare of the open side. Scallen squinted, glancing toward the station office, but the train dispatcher was not in sight. Nor was anyone. "It's the mail car," he said to Kidd. "The second to last one." Steam hissed from the iron cylinder of the engine, clouding that end of the platform. "Hurry it up!" he snapped, pushing Kidd along.

Then, from behind, hurried footsteps sounded on the planking, and, as the hiss of steam died away—"Stand where you are!"

The locomotive's main rods strained back, rising like the legs of a grotesque grasshopper, and the wheels moved. The connecting rods stopped on an upward swing and couplings clanged down the line of cars.

"Throw the gun away, brother!"

Charlie Prince stood at the corner of the station house with a pistol in each hand. Then he moved around carefully between the two men and the train. "Throw it far away, and unhitch your belt," he said.

"Do what he says," Kidd said. "They've got you."

The others, six of them, were strung out in the dimness of the platform shed. Grim faced, stubbles of beard, hat brims low. The man nearest Prince spat tobacco lazily.

Scallen knew fear at that moment as fear had never gripped him before; but he kept the shotgun hard against Kidd's spine. He said, just above a whisper, "Jim—I'll cut you in half!"

Kidd's body was stiff, his shoulders drawn up tightly. "Wait a minute. . . ." he said. He held his palms out to Charlie Prince, though he could have been speaking to Scallen.

Suddenly Prince shouted, "Go down!"

There was a fraction of a moment of dead silence that seemed longer. Kidd hesitated. Scallen was looking at the gunman over Kidd's shoulder, seeing the two pistols. Then Kidd was gone, rolling on the planking, and the pistols were coming up, one ahead of the other. Without moving Scallen squeezed both triggers of the scattergun.

Charlie Prince was going down, holding his hands tight to his chest, as Scallen dropped the shotgun and swung around drawing his Colt. He fired hurriedly. *Wait for a target!* Words in his mind. He saw the men under the platform shed, three of them breaking for the station office, two going full length to the planks . . . one crouched, his pistol up. *That one! Get him quick!* Scallen aimed and squeezed the heavy revolver and the man went down. *Now get the hell out!*

Charlie Prince was facedown. Kidd was crawling, crawling frantically and coming to his feet when Scallen reached him. He grabbed Kidd by the collar savagely, pushing him on, and dug the pistol into his back. "Run, damn you!"

Gunfire erupted from the shed and thudded into the wooden caboose as they ran past it. The train was moving slowly. Just in front of them a bullet smashed a window of the mail car. Someone screamed, "You'll hit Jim!" There was another shot, then it was too late. Scallen and Kidd leapt up on the car platform and were in the mail car as it rumbled past the end of the station platform.

Kidd was on the floor, stretched out along a row of mail sacks. He rubbed his shoulder awkwardly with his manacled hands and watched Scallen, who stood against the wall next to the open door.

Kidd studied the deputy for some minutes. Finally he said, "You know, you really earn your hundred and a half."

Scallen heard him, though the iron rhythm of the train wheels and his breathing were loud in his temples. He felt as if all his strength had been sapped, but he couldn't help smiling at Jim Kidd. He was thinking pretty much the same thing.

THE BOY WHO SMILED

When Mickey Segundo was fourteen, he tracked a man almost two hundred miles—from the Jicarilla Subagency down into the malpais.

He caught up with him at a waterhole in late afternoon and stayed behind a rock outcropping watching the man drink. Mickey Segundo had not tasted water in three days, but he sat patiently behind the cover while the man quenched his thirst, watching him relax and make himself comfortable as the hot lava country cooled with the approach of evening.

Finally Mickey Segundo stirred. He broke open the .50-caliber Gallagher and inserted the paper cartridge and the cap. Then he eased the carbine between a niche in the rocks, sighting on the back of the man's head. He called in a low voice, "Tony Choddi . . ." and as the face with the wide-open eyes came around, he fired casually.

He lay on his stomach and slowly drank the water he needed, filling his canteen and the one that had belonged to Tony Choddi. Then he took his hunting knife and sawed both of the man's ears off, close to the head. These he put into his saddle pouch, leaving the rest for the buzzards.

A week later Mickey Segundo carried the pouch into the agency office and dropped the ears on my desk. He said very simply, "Tony Choddi is sorry he has caused trouble."

I remember telling him, "You're not thinking of going after McKay now, are you?"

"This man, Tony Choddi, stole stuff, a horse and clothes and a gun," he said with his pleasant smile. "So I thought I would do a good thing and fix it so Tony Choddi didn't steal no more."

With the smile there was a look of surprise, as if to say, "Why would I want to get Mr. McKay?"

A few days later I saw McKay and told him about it and mentioned that he might keep his eyes open. But he said that he didn't give a damn about any breed Jicarilla kid. If the kid felt like avenging his old man, he could try, but he'd probably cash in before his time. And as for getting Tony Choddi, he didn't give a damn about that either. He'd got the horse back and that's all he cared about.

After he had said his piece, I was sorry I had warned him. And I felt a little foolish telling one of the biggest men in the Territory to look out for a half-breed Apache kid. I told myself, Maybe you're just rubbing up to him because he's important and could use his influence to help out the agency . . . and maybe he knows it.

Actually I had more respect for Mickey Segundo, as a human being, than I did for T. O. McKay. Maybe I felt I owed the warning to McKay because he was a white man. Like saying, "Mickey Segundo's a good boy, but, hell, he's half Indian." Just one of those things you catch yourself doing. Like habit. You do something wrong the first time and you know it, but if you keep it up, it becomes a habit and it's no longer wrong because it's something you've always been doing.

McKay and a lot of people said Apaches were no damn good. The only good one was a dead one. They never stopped to reason it out. They'd been saying it so long, they knew it was true. Certainly any such statement was unreasonable, but damned if I wouldn't sometimes nod my head in agreement, because at those times I'd be with white men and that's the way white men talked.

I might have thought I was foolish, but actually it was McKay who was the fool. He underestimated Mickey Segundo.

That was five years ago. It had begun with a hanging.

EARLY in the morning, Tudishishn, sergeant of Apache police at the Jicarilla Agency, rode in to tell me that Tony Choddi had jumped the boundaries again and might be in my locale. Tudishishn stayed for half a dozen cups of coffee, though his information didn't last that long. When he'd had enough, he left as leisurely as he had arrived. Hunting renegades, reservation jumpers, was Tudishishn's job; still, it wasn't something to get excited about. Tomorrows were for work; todays were for thinking about it.

Up at the agency they were used to Tony Choddi skipping off. Usually they'd find him later in some shaded barranca, full of tulapai.

It was quiet until late afternoon, but not unusually so. It wasn't often that anything out of the ordinary happened at the subagency. There were twenty-six families, one hundred eight Jicarillas all told, under my charge. We were located almost twenty miles below the reservation proper, and most of the people had been there long before the reservation had been marked off. They had been fairly peaceful then, and remained so now. It was one of the few instances where the Bureau allowed the sleeping dog to lie; and because of that we had less trouble than they did up at the reservation.

There was a sign on the door of the adobe office which described it formally. It read: D. J. MERRITT—AGENT, JICARILLA APACHE SUBAGENCY—PUERCO, NEW MEXICO TERRITORY. It was a startling announcement to post on the door of a squat adobe sitting all alone in the shadow of the Nacimentos. My Apaches preferred higher ground and the closest jacales were two miles up into the foothills. The office had to remain on the mail run, even though the mail consisted chiefly of impossible-to-apply Bureau memoranda.

Just before supper Tudishishn returned. He came in at a run this time and swung off before his pony had come to a full stop. He was excited and spoke in a confusion of Apache, Spanish, and a word here and there of English.

Returning to the reservation, he had decided to stop off and see his friends of the Puerco Agency. There had been friends he had not seen for some time, and the morning had lengthened into afternoon with tulapai, good talking, and even coffee. People had come from the more remote jacales, deeper in the hills, when they learned Tudishishn was there, to hear news of friends at the reservation. Soon there were many people and what looked like the beginning of a good time. Then Señor McKay had come.

McKay had men with him, many men, and they were looking for Mickey Solner—the squaw man, as the Americans called him.

Most of the details I learned later on, but briefly this is what had happened: McKay and some of his men were out on a hunting trip. When they got up that morning, McKay's horse was gone, along with a shotgun and some personal articles. They got on the tracks, which were fresh and easy to follow, and by that afternoon they were at Mickey Solner's jacal. His woman and boy were there, and the horse was tethered in front of the mud hut. Mickey Segundo, the boy, was honored to lead such important people to his father, who was visiting with Tudishishn.

McKay brought the horse along, and when they found Mickey Solner, they took hold of him without asking questions and looped a rope around his neck. Then they boosted him up onto the horse they claimed he had stolen. McKay said it would be fitting that way. Tudishishn had left fast when he saw what was about to happen. He knew they wouldn't waste time arguing with an Apache, so he had come to me.

When I got there, Mickey Solner was still sitting McKay's chestnut mare with the rope reaching from his neck to the cottonwood bough overhead. His head drooped as if all the fight was out of him, and when I came up in front of the chestnut, he looked at me with tired eyes, watery and red from tulapai.

I had known Solner for years, but had never become close to him. He wasn't a man with whom you became fast friends. Just his living in an Apache rancheria testified to his being of a different breed. He was friendly enough, but few of the whites liked him—they said he drank all the time and never worked. Maybe most were just envious. Solner was a white man gone Indian, whole hog. That was the cause of the resentment.

His son, Mickey the Second, stood near his dad's stirrup looking at him with a bewildered, pathetic look on his slim face. He held on to the stirrup as if he'd never let it go. And it was the first time, the only time, I ever saw Mickey Segundo without a faint smile on his face.

"Mr. McKay," I said to the cattleman, who was standing relaxed with his hands in his pockets, "I'm afraid I'll have to ask you to take that man down. He's under bureau jurisdiction and will have to be tried by a court."

McKay said nothing, but Bowie Allison, who was his herd boss, laughed and then said, "You ought to be afraid."

Dolph Bettzinger was there, along with his brothers Kirk and Sim. They were hired for their guns and usually kept pretty close to McKay. They did not laugh when Allison did.

And all around the clearing by the cottonwood were eight or ten others. Most of them I recognized as McKay riders. They stood solemnly, some with rifles and shotguns. There wasn't any doubt in their minds what stealing a horse meant.

"Tudishishn says that Mickey didn't steal your horse. These

people told him that he was at home all night and most of the morning until Tudishishn dropped in, and then he came down here." A line of Apaches stood a few yards off and as I pointed to them, some nodded their heads.

"Mister," McKay said, "I found the horse at this man's hut. Now, you argue that down, and I'll kiss the behind of every Apache you got living around here."

"Well, your horse could have been left there by someone else."

"Either way, he had a hand in it," he said curtly.

"What does he say?" I looked up at Mickey Solner and asked him quickly, "How did you get the horse, Mickey?"

"I just traded with a fella." His voice shook, and he held on to the saddle horn as if afraid he'd fall off. "This fella come along and traded with me, that's all."

"Who was it?"

Mickey Solner didn't answer. I asked him again, but still he refused to speak. McKay was about to say something, but Tudishishn came over quickly from the group of Apaches.

"They say it was Tony Choddi. He was seen to come into camp in early morning."

I asked Mickey if it was Tony Choddi, and finally he admitted that it was. I felt better then. McKay couldn't hang a man for trading a horse.

"Are you satisfied, Mr. McKay? He didn't know it was yours. Just a matter of trading a horse."

McKay looked at me, narrowing his eyes. He looked as if he were trying to figure out what kind of a man I was. Finally he said, "You think I'm going to believe them?"

It dawned on me suddenly that McKay had been using what patience he had for the past few minutes. Now he was ready to continue what they had come for. He had made up his mind long before.

"Wait a minute, Mr. McKay, you're talking about the life of an innocent man. You can't just toy with it like it was a head of cattle."

He looked at me and his puffy face seemed to harden. He was a heavy man, beginning to sag about the stomach. "You think you're going to tell me what I can do and what I can't? I don't need a government representative to tell me why my horse was stolen!"

"I'm not telling you anything. You know Mickey didn't steal the horse. You can see for yourself you're making a mistake."

McKay shrugged and looked at his herd boss. "Well, if it is, it isn't a very big one—leastwise we'll be sure he won't be trading in stolen horses again." He nodded to Bowie Allison.

Bowie grinned, and brought his quirt up and then down across the rump of the chestnut.

"Yiiiiiiiii . . ."

The chestnut broke fast. Allison stood yelling after it, then jumped aside quickly as Mickey Solner swung back toward him on the end of the rope.

IT was two weeks later, to the day, that Mickey Segundo came in with Tony Choddi's ears. You can see why I asked him if he had a notion of going after McKay. And it was a strange thing. I was talking to a different boy than the one I had last seen under the cottonwood.

When the horse shot out from under his dad, he ran to him like something wild, screaming, and wrapped his arms around the kicking legs trying to hold the weight off the rope.

Bowie Allison cuffed him away, and they held him back with pistols while he watched his dad die. From then on he didn't say a word, and when it was over, walked away with his head down. Then, when he came in with Tony Choddi's ears, he was himself again. All smiles.

I might mention that I wrote to the Bureau of Indian Affairs about the incident, since Mickey Solner, legally, was one of my charges; but nothing came of it. In fact, I didn't even get a reply.

Over the next few years Mickey Segundo changed a lot. He became Apache. That is, his appearance changed and almost everything else about him—except the smile. The smile was always there, as if he knew a monumental secret which was going to make everyone happy.

He let his hair grow to his shoulders and usually he wore only a frayed cotton shirt and breechclout; his moccasins were Apache—curled toes and leggings which reached to his thighs. He went under his Apache name, which was Peza-a, but I called him Mickey when I saw him, and he was never reluctant to talk to me in English. His English was good, discounting grammar.

Most of the time he lived in the same jacal his dad had built, providing for his mother and fitting closer into the life of the rancheria than he did before. But when he was about eighteen, he went up to the agency and joined Tudishishn's police. His mother went with him to live at the reservation, but within a year the two of them were back. Tracking friends who happened to wander off the reservation didn't set right with him. It didn't go with his smile.

Tudishishn told me he was sorry to lose him because he was an expert tracker and a dead shot. I know the sergeant had a dozen good sign followers, but very few who were above average with a gun.

He must have been nineteen when he came back to Puerco. In all those years he never once mentioned McKay's name. And I can tell you I never brought it up either.

I saw McKay even less after the hanging incident. If he ignored me before, he avoided me now. As I said, I felt like a fool after warning him about Mickey Segundo, and I'm certain McKay felt only contempt for me for doing it, after sticking up for the boy's dad.

McKay would come through every once in a while, usually going on a hunt up into the Nacimentos. He was a great hunter and would go out for a few days every month or so. Usually with his herd boss, Bowie Allison. He hunted everything that walked, squirmed, or flew and I'm told his ranch trophy room was really something to see.

You couldn't take it away from the man; everything he did, he did well. He was in his fifties, but he could shoot straighter and stay in the saddle longer than any of his riders. And he knew how to make money. But it was his arrogance that irked me. Even though he was polite, he made you feel far beneath him. He talked to you as if you were one of the hired help.

One afternoon, fairly late, Tudishishn rode in and said that he was supposed to meet McKay at the adobe office early the next morning. McKay wanted to try the shooting down southwest toward the malpais, on the other side of it, actually, and Tudishishn was going to guide for him.

The Indian policeman drank coffee until almost sundown and then rode off into the shadows of the Nacimentos. He was staying at one of the rancherias, visiting with his friends until the morning.

McKay appeared first. It was a cool morning, bright and crisp. I looked out of the window and saw the five riders coming up the road from the south, and when they were close enough I made out McKay and Bowie Allison and the three Bettzinger brothers. When they reached the office, McKay and Bowie dismounted, but the Bettzingers reined around and started back down the road.

McKay nodded and was civil enough, though he didn't direct more than a few words to me. Bowie was ready when I asked them if they wanted coffee, but McKay shook his head and said they were leaving shortly. Just about then the rider appeared coming down out of the hills.

McKay was squinting, studying the figure on the pony.

I didn't really look at him until I noticed McKay's close attention. And when I looked at the rider again, he was almost on us. I didn't have to squint then to see that it was Mickey Segundo.

McKay said, "Who's that?" with a ring of suspicion to his voice.

I felt a sudden heat on my face, like the feeling you get when you're talking about someone, then suddenly find the person standing next to you.

Without thinking about it I told McKay, "That's Peza-a, one of my people." What made me call him by his Apache name I don't know. Perhaps because he looked so Indian. But I had never called him Peza-a before.

He approached us somewhat shyly, wearing his faded shirt and breechclout but now with a streak of ochre painted across his nose from ear to ear. He didn't look as if he could have a drop of white blood in him.

"What's he doing here?" McKay's voice still held a note of suspicion, and he looked at him as if he were trying to place him.

Bowie Allison studied him the same way, saying nothing.

"Where's Tudishishn? These gentlemen are waiting for him."

"Tudishishn is ill with a demon in his stomach," Peza-a answered. "He has asked me to substitute myself for him." He spoke in Spanish, hesitantly, the way an Apache does.

McKay studied him for some time. Finally, he said, "Well . . . can he track?"

"He was with Tudishishn for a year. Tudishishn speaks highly of him." Again I don't know what made me say it. A hundred things were going through my head. What I said was true, but I saw it getting me into something. Mickey never looked directly at me. He kept watching McKay, with the faint smile on his mouth.

McKay seemed to hesitate, but then he said, "Well, come on. I don't need a reference . . . long as he can track."

They mounted and rode out.

McKay wanted prongbuck. Tudishishn had described where

they would find the elusive herds and promised to show him all he could shoot. But they were many days away. McKay had said if he didn't have time, he'd make time. He wanted good shooting.

Off and on during the first day he questioned Mickey Segundo closely to see what he knew about the herds.

"I have seen them many times. Their hide the color of sand, and black horns that reach into the air like bayonets of the soldiers. But they are far."

McKay wasn't concerned with distance. After a while he was satisfied that this Indian guide knew as much about tracking antelope as Tudishishn, and that's what counted. Still, there was something about the young Apache. . . .

"TOMORROW, we begin the crossing of the malpais," Mickey Segundo said. It was evening of the third day, as they made camp at Yucca Springs.

Bowie Allison looked at him quickly. "Tudishishn planned we'd follow the high country down and come out on the plain from the east."

"What's the matter with keeping a straight line," McKay said. "Keeping to the hills is longer, isn't it?"

"Yeah, but that malpais is a blood-dryin' furnace in the middle of August," Bowie grumbled. "You got to be able to pinpoint the wells. And even if you find them, they might be dry."

McKay looked at Peza-a for an answer.

"If Señor McKay wishes to ride for two additional days, that is for him to say. But we can carry our water with ease." He went to his saddle pouch and drew out two collapsed, rubbery bags. "These, from the stomach of the horse, will hold much water. Tomorrow we fill canteens and these, and the water can be made to last five, six days. Even if the wells are dry, we have water."

Bowie Allison grumbled under his breath, looking with distaste at the horse-intestine water sacks.

McKay rubbed his chin thoughtfully. He was thinking of prongbuck. Finally he said, "We'll cut across the lava."

Bowie Allison was right in his description of the malpais. It was a furnace, a crusted expanse of desert that stretched into another world. Saguaro and ocotillo stood nakedly sharp against the whiteness, and off in the distance were ghostly looming buttes, gigantic tombstones for the lava waste. Horses shuffled choking white dust, and the sun glare was a white blistering shock that screamed its brightness. Then the sun would drop suddenly, leaving a nothingness that could be felt. A life that had died a hundred million years ago.

McKay felt it and that night he spoke little.

The second day was a copy of the first, for the lava country remained monotonously the same. McKay grew more irritable as the day wore on, and time and again he would snap at Bowie Allison for his grumbling. The country worked at the nerves of the two white men, while Mickey Segundo watched them.

On the third day they passed two waterholes. They could see the shallow crusted bottoms and the fissures that the tight sand had made cracking in the hot air. That night McKay said nothing.

In the morning there was a blue haze on the edge of the glare; they could feel the land beneath them begin to rise. Chaparral and patches of toboso grass became thicker and dotted the flatness, and by early afternoon the towering rock formations loomed near at hand. They had then one water sack two thirds full; but the other, with their canteens, was empty.

Bowie Allison studied the gradual rise of the rock wall, passing his tongue over cracked lips. "There could be water up there. . . . Sometimes the rain catches in hollows and stays there a long time if it's shady."

McKay squinted into the air. The irregular crests were high and dead still against the sky. "Could be."

Mickey Segundo looked up and then nodded.

"How far to the next hole?" McKay asked.

"Maybe one day."

"If it's got water. . . . Then how far?"

"Maybe two day. We come out on the plain then near the Datil Mountains and there is water, streams to be found."

McKay said, "That means we're halfway. We can make last what we got, but there's no use killing ourselves." His eyes lifted to the peaks again, then dropped to the mouth of a barranca which cut into the rock. He nodded to the dark canyon which was partly hidden by a dense growth of mesquite. "We'll leave our stuff there and go on to see what we can find."

They unsaddled the horses and ground-tied them and hung their last water bag in the shade of a mesquite bush.

Then they walked up-canyon until they found a place which would be the easiest to climb.

They went up and they came down, but when they were again on the canyon floor, their canteens still rattled lightly with their steps. Mickey Segundo carried McKay's rifle in one hand and the limp, empty water bag in the other.

He walked a step behind the two men and watched their faces as they turned to look back overhead. There was no water.

The rocks held nothing, not even a dampness. They were naked now and loomed brutally indifferent, and bone dry with no promise of moisture.

The canyon sloped gradually into the opening. And now, ahead, they could see the horses and the small fat bulge of the water bag hanging from the mesquite bough.

Mickey Segundo's eyes were fixed on the water sack. He looked steadily at it.

Then a horse screamed. They saw the horses suddenly pawing the ground and pulling at the hackamores that held them fast. The three horses and the pack mule joined together now, neighing shrilly as they strained dancing at the ropes.

And then a shape the color of sand darted through the mesquite thicket, so quickly that it seemed a shadow.

Mickey Segundo threw the rifle to his shoulder. He hesitated. Then he fired.

The shape kept going, past the mesquite background and out into the open.

He fired again and the coyote went up into the air and came down to lie motionless.

It only jerked in death. McKay looked at him angrily. "Why the hell didn't you let me have it! You could have hit one of the horses!"

"There was not time."

"That's two hundred yards! You could have hit a horse, that's what I'm talking about!"

"But I shot it," Mickey Segundo said.

When they reached the mesquite clump, they did not go over to inspect the dead coyote. Something else took their attention. It stopped the white men in their tracks.

They stared unbelieving at the wetness seeping into the sand, and above the spot, the water bag hanging like a punctured bladder. The water had quickly run out.

Mickey Segundo told the story at the inquiry. They had attempted to find water, but it was no use; so they were compelled to try to return.

They had almost reached Yucca Springs when the two men died. Mickey Segundo told it simply. He was sorry he had shot the water bag, but what could he say? God directs the actions of men mysteriously.

The county authorities were disconcerted, but they had to be satisfied with the apparent facts.

McKay and Allison were found ten miles from Yucca Springs and brought in. There were no marks of violence on either of them, and they found three hundred dollars in McKay's wallet. It was officially recorded that they died from thirst and exposure.

A terrible way to die just because some damn Apache couldn't shoot straight. Peza-a survived because he was lucky, along with the fact that he was Apache, which made him tougher. Just one of those things.

Mickey continued living with his mother at the subagency. His old Gallagher carbine kept them in meat, and they seemed happy enough just existing.

Tudishishn visited them occasionally, and when he did they would have a tulapai party. Everything was normal.

Mickey's smile was still there but maybe a little different.

But I've often wondered what Mickey Segundo would have done if that coyote had not run across the mesquite thicket. . . .

"HURRAH FOR CAPT. EARLY"

The second banner said HERO OF SAN JUAN HILL. Both were tied to the upstairs balcony of the Congress Hotel and looked down on La Salle Street in Sweetmary, a town named for a copper mine. The banners read across the building as a single statement. This day that Captain Early was expected home from the war in Cuba, over now these two months, was October 10, 1898.

The manager of the hotel and one of his desk clerks were the first to observe the colored man who entered the lobby and dropped his bedroll on the red velvet settee where it seemed he was about to sit down. Bold as brass. A tall, well-built colored man wearing a suit of clothes that looked new and appeared to fit him as though it might possibly be his own and not one handed down to him. He wore the suit, a stiff collar, and a necktie. With the manager nearby but not yet aware of the intruder, the young desk clerk spoke up, raised his voice to tell the person, "You can't sit down there."

The colored man turned his attention to the desk, taking a moment before he said, "Why is that?"

His quiet tone caused the desk clerk to hesitate and look over at the manager, who stood holding the day's mail, letters that had arrived on the El Paso & Southwestern morning run along with several guests now registered at the hotel and, apparently, this colored person. It was hard to tell his age, other than to say he was no longer a young man. He did seem clean and his bedroll was done up in bleached canvas.

"A hotel lobby," the desk clerk said, "is not a public place anyone can make theirself at home in. What is it you want here?"

At least he was uncovered, standing there now hat in hand. But then he said, "I'm waiting on Bren Early."

"*Bren* is it," the desk clerk said. "Captain Early's an acquaintance of yours?"

"We go way back a ways."

"You worked for him?"

"Some."

At this point the manager said, "We're all waiting for Captain Early. Why don't you go out front and watch for him?" Ending the conversation.

The desk clerk—his name was Monty—followed the colored man to the front entrance and stepped out on the porch to watch him, bedroll over his shoulder, walking south on La Salle the two short blocks to Fourth Street. Monty returned to the desk, where he said to the manager, "He walked right in the Gold Dollar."

The manager didn't look up from his mail.

TWO riders from the Circle-Eye, a spread on the San Pedro that delivered beef to the mine company, were at a table with their glasses of beer: a rider named Macon and a rider named Wayman, young men who wore sweat-stained hats down on their eyes as they stared at the Negro. Right there, the bartender speaking to him as he poured a whiskey, still speaking as the colored man drank it and the bartender poured him another one. Macon asked Wayman if he had ever seen a nigger wearing a suit of clothes and a necktie. Wayman said he couldn't recall. When they finished drinking their beer and walked up to the bar, the colored man gone now, Macon asked the bartender who in the hell that smoke thought he was coming in here. "You would think," Macon said, "he'd go to one of the places where the miners drink."

The bartender appeared to smile, for some reason finding humor in Macon's remark. He said, "Boys, that was Bo Catlett. I imagine Bo drinks just about wherever he feels like drinking."

"Why?" Macon asked it, surprised. "He suppose to be somebody?"

"Bo lives up at White Tanks," the bartender told him, "at the Indin agency. Went to war and now he's home."

Macon squinted beneath the hat brim funneled low on his eyes. He said, "Nobody told me they was niggers in the war." Sounding as though it was the bartender's fault he hadn't been informed. When the bartender didn't add anything to help him out, Macon said, "Wayman's brother Wyatt was in the war, with Teddy Roosevelt's Rough Riders. Only, Wyatt didn't come home like the nigger."

Wayman, about eighteen years old, was nodding his head now.

Because nothing about this made sense to Macon, it was becoming an irritation. Again he said to Wayman, "You ever see a smoke wearing a suit of clothes like that?" He said, "Je-sus Christ."

BO Catlett walked up La Salle Street favoring his left leg some, though the limp, caused by a Mauser bullet or by the regimental surgeon who cut it out of his hip, was barely noticeable. He stared at the sight of the mine works against the sky, ugly, but something monumental about it: straight ahead up the grade, the main shaft scaffolding and company buildings, the crushing mill lower down, ore tailings that humped this way in ridges on down the slope to run out at the edge of town. A sorry place, dark and forlorn; men walked up the grade from boardinghouses on Mill Street to spend half their life underneath the ground, buried before they were dead. Three whiskeys in him, Catlett returned to the hotel on the corner of Second Street, looked up at the sign that said HURRAH FOR CAPT. EARLY, and had to grin. THE HERO OF SAN JUAN HILL my ass.

Catlett mounted the steps to the porch, where he dropped his bedroll and took one of the rocking chairs all in a row, the porch empty, close on noon but nobody sitting out here, no drummers calling on La Salle Mining of New Jersey, the company still digging and scraping but running low on payload copper, operating only the day shift now. The rocking chairs, all dark green, needed painting. Man, but made of cane and comfortable with that nice squeak back and forth, back and forth. . . . Bo Catlett watched two riders coming this way up the street, couple of cowboys . . . Catlett wondering how many times he had sat down in a real chair since April twenty-fifth when war was declared and he left Arizona to go looking for his old regiment, trailed them to Fort Assinniboine in the Department of the Dakotas, then clear across the country to Camp Chickamauga in Georgia and on down to Tampa where he caught up with them and Lt. John Pershing looked at his twenty-four years of service and put him up for squadron sergeant major. It didn't seem like any twenty-four years. . . .

Going back to when he joined the First Kansas Colored Volunteers in '63, age fifteen. Wounded at Honey Springs the same year. Guarded Rebel prisoners at Rock Island, took part in the occupation of Galveston. Then after the war got sent out here to join the all-Negro Tenth Cavalry on frontier station, Arizona Territory, and deal with hostile Apaches. In '87 went to Mexico with Lieutenant Brendan Early out of Fort Huachuca—Bren and a contract guide named Dana Moon, now the agent at the White Tanks reservation—brought back a one-eyed Mimbreño named Loco, brought back a white woman the renegade Apache had run off with—and Dana Moon later married—and they all got their pictures in some newspapers. Mustered out that same year, '87 . . . Drove a wagon for Capt. Early Hunting Expeditions Incorporated before going to work for Dana at White Tanks. He'd be sitting on Dana's porch this evening with a glass of mescal and Dana would say, "Well, now you've seen the elephant I don't imagine you'll want to stay around here." He'd tell Dana he saw the elephant a long time ago and wasn't too impressed. Just then another voice, not Dana's, said out loud to him:

"So you was in the war, huh?"

It was one of the cowboys. He sat his mount, a little claybank quarter horse, close to the porch rail, sat leaning on the pommel to show he was at ease, his hat low on his eyes, staring directly at Catlett in his rocking chair. The other one sat his mount, a bay, more out in the street, maybe holding back. This boy was not at ease but fidgety. Catlett remembered them in the Gold Dollar.

Now the one close said, "What was it you did over there in Cuba?"

Meaning a colored man. What did a colored man do. Like most people the boy not knowing anything about Negro soldiers in the war. This one squinting at him had size and maybe got his way enough he believed he could say whatever he pleased, or use a tone of voice that would irritate the person addressed. As he did just now.

"What did I do over there?" Catlett said. "What everybody did, I was in the war."

"You wrangle stock for the Rough Riders?"

"Where'd you get that idea?"

"I asked you a question. Is that what you did, tend their stock?"

Once Catlett decided to remain civil and maybe this boy would go away, he said, "There wasn't no stock. The Rough Riders, *even* the Rough Riders, were afoot. The only people had horses were artillery, pulling caissons with their Hotchkiss guns and the coffee grinders, what they called the Gatling guns. Lemme see," Catlett said, "they had some mules, too, but I didn't tend anybody's stock."

"His brother was a Rough Rider," Macon said, raising one hand to hook his thumb at Wayman. "Served with Colonel Teddy Roosevelt and got killed in an ambush—the only way greasers know how to fight. I like to hear what you people were doing while his brother Wyatt was getting killed."

You people. Look at him trying to start a fight.

"You believe it was my fault he got killed?"

"I asked you what you were doing."

It wasn't even this kid's business. Catlett thinking, Well, see if you can educate him, and said, "Las Guásimas. You ever hear of it?"

The kid stared with his eyes half shut. Suspicious, or letting you know he's serious, Catlett thought. Keen eyed and mean; you're not gonna put anything past him.

"What's it, a place over there?"

"That's right, Las Guásimas, the place where it happened. On the way to Santiago de Coo-ba. Sixteen men killed that day, mostly by rifle fire, and something like fifty wounded. Except it wasn't what you said, the dons pulling an ambush. It was more the Rough Riders walking along not looking where they was going."

The cowboy, Macon, said, "Je-sus Christ, you saying the Rough Riders didn't know what they were *do*ing?" Like this was something impossible to believe.

"They mighta had an idea *what* they was doing," Catlett said, "only thing it wasn't what they *shoulda* been doing." He said, "You understand the difference?" And thought, What're you explaining it to him for? The boy giving him that mean look again, ready to defend the Rough Riders. All right, he was so proud of Teddy's people, why hadn't he been over there with them?

"Look," Catlett said, using a quiet tone now, "the way it was, the dons had sharpshooters in these trees, a thicket of mangoes and palm trees growing wild you couldn't see into. You understand? Had men hidden in there were expert with the rifle, these Mausers they used with smokeless powder. Teddy's people come along a ridge was all covered with these trees and run into the dons, see, the dons letting some of the Rough Riders pass and then closing in on 'em. So, yeah, it was an ambush in a way." Catlett paused. "We was down on the road, once we caught up, moving in the same direction." He paused again, remembering something the cowboy said that bothered him. "There's nothing wrong with an ambush—like say you think it ain't *fair?* If you can set it up and keep your people behind cover, do it. There was a captain with the Rough Riders said he believed an officer should never take cover, should stand out there and be an example to his men. The captain said, 'There ain't a Spanish bullet made that can kill me.' Stepped out in the open and got shot in the head."

A couple of cowboys looking like the two who were mounted had come out of the Chinaman's picking their teeth and now stood by to see what was going on. Some people who had come out of the hotel were standing along the steps.

Catlett took all this in as he paused again, getting the words straight in his mind to tell how they left the road, some companies of the Tenth and the First, all regular Army, went up the slope laying down fire and run off the dons before the Rough Riders got cut to pieces, the Rough Riders volunteers and not experienced in all kind of situations—the reason they didn't know shit about advancing through hostile country or, get right down to it, what they were doing in Cuba, these people that come looking for glory and got served sharpshooters with Mausers and mosquitoes carrying yellow fever. Tell these cowboys the true story. General Wheeler, "Fightin' Joe" from the Confederate side in the Civil War now thirty-three years later an old man with a white beard; sees the Spanish pulling back at Las Guásimas and says, "Boys, we got the Yankees on the run." Man like that directing a battle. . . .

Tell the *whole* story if you gonna tell it, go back to sitting in the hold of the ship in Port Tampa a month, not allowed to go ashore for fear of causing incidents with white people who didn't want the men of the Tenth coming in their stores and cafés, running off their customers. Tell them—so we land in Cuba at a place called Daiquirí . . . saying in his mind then, Listen to me now. Was the Tenth at Daiquirí, the Ninth at Siboney. Experienced cavalry regiments that come off frontier station after thirty years dealing with hostile renegades, cutthroat horse thieves, reservation jumpers, land in Cuba and they put us to work unloading the ships while Teddy's people march off to meet the enemy and win some medals, yeah, and would've been wiped out at El Caney and on San Juan Hill if the colored boys hadn't come along and saved Colonel Teddy's ass and all his Rough Rider asses, showed them how to go up a hill and take a blockhouse. Saved them so the Rough Riders could become America's heroes.

All this in Bo Catlett's head and the banners welcoming Capt. Early hanging over him.

One of the cowboys from the Chinaman's must've asked what was going on, because now the smart-aleck one brought his claybank around and began talking to them, glancing back at the porch now and again with his mean look. The two from the Chinaman's stood with their thumbs in their belts, while the mounted cowboy had his hooked around his suspenders now. None of them wore a gun belt or appeared to be armed. Now the two riders stepped down from their mounts and followed the other two along the street to a place called the Belle Alliance, a miners' saloon, and went inside.

Bo Catlett was used to mean dirty looks and looks of indifference, a man staring at him as though he wasn't even there. Now, the thing with white people, they had a hard time believing colored men fought in the war. You never saw a colored man on a U.S. Army recruiting poster or a picture of colored soldiers in newspapers. White people believed colored people could not be relied on in war. But why? There were some colored people that went out and killed wild animals, even lions, with a spear. No gun, a spear. And made hats out of the manes. See a colored man standing there in front of a lion coming at him fast as a train running down grade, stands there with his spear, doesn't move, and they say colored men can't be relied on?

There was a story in newspapers how when Teddy Roosevelt was at the Hill, strutting around in the open, he saw colored troopers going back to the rear and he drew his revolver and threatened to shoot them—till he found out they were going after ammunition. His own Rough Riders were pinned down in the guinea grass, the Spanish sharpshooters picking at them from up in the blockhouses. So the Tenth showed the white boys how to go up the hill angry, firing and yelling, making noise, set on driving the garlics clean from the hill. . . .

Found Bren Early and his company lying in the weeds, the scrub—that's all it was up that hill, scrub and sand, hard to get a footing in places; nobody ran all the way up, it was get up a ways and stop to fire, covering each other. Found Bren Early with a whistle in his mouth. He got up and started blowing it and waving his sword—come on, boys, to glory—and a Mauser bullet smacked him in the butt, on account of the way he was turned to his people, and Bren Early grunted, dropped his sword, and went down in the scrub to lay there cursing his luck, no doubt mortified to look like he got shot going the wrong way. Bo Catlett didn't believe Bren saw him pick up the sword. Picked it up, waved it at the Rough Riders and his Tenth Cav troopers, and they all went up that hill together, his troopers yelling, some of them singing, actually singing "They'll Be a Hot Time in the Old Town Tonight." Singing and shooting, honest to God, scaring the dons right out of their blockhouse. It was up on the crest Catlett got shot in his right hip and was taken to the Third Cav dressing station. It was set up on the Aguadores River at a place called "bloody ford," being it was under fire till the Hill was captured. Catlett remembered holding on to the sword, tight, while the regimental surgeon dug the bullet out of him and he tried hard not to scream, biting his mouth till it bled. After, he was sent home and spent a month at Camp Wikoff, near Montauk out on Long Island, with a touch of yellow fever. Saw President McKinley when he came by September third and made a speech, the President saying what they did over there in Cuba "commanded the unstinted praise of all your countrymen." Till he walked away from Montauk and came back into the world, Sergeant Major Catlett actually did believe he and the other members of the Tenth would be recognized as war heroes.

He wished Bren would hurry up and get here. He'd ask the hero of San Juan Hill how his heinie was and if he was getting much unstinted praise. If Bren didn't come pretty soon, Catlett decided he'd see him another time. Get a horse out of the livery and ride it up White Tanks.

THE four Circle-Eye riders sat at a front table in the Belle Alliance with a bottle of Green River whiskey, Macon staring out the window. The hotel was across the street and up the block a ways, but Macon could see it, the colored man in the suit of clothes still sitting on the porch, if he tilted his chair back and held on to the windowsill. He said, "No, sir, nobody told me they was niggers in the war."

Wayman said to the other two Circle-Eye riders, "Macon can't get over it."

Macon's gaze came away from the window. "It was *your* brother got killed."

Wayman said, "I know he did."

Macon said, "You don't care?"

The Circle-Eye riders watched him let his chair come down to hit the floor hard. They watched him get up without another word and walk out.

"I never thought much of coloreds," one of the Circle-Eye riders said, "but you never hear me take on about 'em like Macon. What's his trouble?"

"I guess he wants to shoot somebody," Wayman said. "The time he shot that chili picker in Nogales? Macon worked hisself up to it the same way."

CATLETT watched the one that was looking for a fight come out through the doors and go to the claybank, the reins looped once around the tie rail. He didn't touch the reins, though. What he did was reach into a saddlebag and bring out what Catlett judged to be a Colt .44 pistol. Right then he heard:

"Only guests of the hotel are allowed to sit out here."

Catlett watched the cowboy checking his loads now, turning the cylinder of his six-shooter, the metal catching a glint of light from the sun, though the look of the pistol was dull and it appeared to be an old model.

Monty the desk clerk, standing there looking at Catlett without getting too close, said, "You'll have to leave. . . . Right now."

The cowboy was looking this way.

Making up his mind, Catlett believed. All right, now, yeah, he's made it up.

"Did you hear what I said?"

Catlett took time to look at Monty and then pointed off down the street. He said, "You see that young fella coming this way with the pistol? He think he like to shoot me. Say you don't allow people to sit here aren't staying at the ho-tel. How about, you allow them to get shot if they not a guest?"

He watched the desk clerk, who didn't seem to know whether to shit or go blind, eyes wide open, turn and run back in the lobby.

The cowboy, Macon, stood in the middle of the street now holding the six-shooter against his leg.

CATLETT, still seated in the rocker, said, "You a mean rascal, ain't you? Don't take no sass, huh?"

The cowboy said something agreeing that Catlett didn't catch, the cowboy looking over to see his friends coming up the street now from the barroom. When he looked at the hotel porch again, Catlett was standing at the railing, his bedroll upright next to him leaning against it.

"I can be a mean rascal too," Catlett said, unbuttoning his suit coat. "I want you to know that before you take this too far. You understand?"

"You insulted Colonel Roosevelt and his Rough Riders," the cowboy said, "and you insulted Wayman's brother, killed in action over there in Cuba."

"How come," Catlett said, "you weren't there?"

"I was ready, don't worry, when the war ended. But we're talking about *you.* I say you're a dirty lying nigger and have no respect for people better'n you are. I want you to apologize to the colonel and his men and to Wayman's dead brother. . . ."

"Or what?" Catlett said.

"Answer to me," the cowboy said. "Are you armed? You aren't, you better get yourself a pistol."

"You want to shoot me," Catlett said, " 'cause I went to Cuba and you didn't."

The cowboy was shaking his head. " 'Cause you lied. Have you got a pistol or not?"

Catlett said, "You calling me out, huh? You want us to fight a duel?"

"Less you apologize. Else get a pistol."

"But if I'm the one being called out, I have my choice of weapons, don't I? That's how I seen it work, twenty-four years in the U.S. Army in two wars. You hear what I'm saying?"

The cowboy was frowning now beneath his hat brim, squinting up at Bo Catlett. He said, "Pistols, it's what you use."

Catlett nodded. "If I say so."

"Well, what else is there?"

Confused and getting a mean look.

Catlett slipped his hand into the upright end of his bedroll and began to tug at something inside—the cowboy watching, the Circle-Eye riders in the street watching, the desk clerk and manager in the doorway and several hotel guests near them who had come out to the porch, all watching as Catlett drew a sword from the bedroll, a cavalry saber, the curved blade flashing as it caught the sunlight. He came past the people watching and down off the porch toward the cowboy in his hat and boots fixed with spurs that chinged as he turned to face Catlett, shorter than Catlett, appearing confused again holding the six-shooter at his side.

"If I choose to use sabers," Catlett said, "is that agreeable with you?"

"I don't have no *saber.*"

Meanness showing now in his eyes.

"Well, you best get one."

"I never even had a sword in my hand."

Irritated. Drunk, too, his eyes not focusing as they should. Now he was looking over his shoulder at the Circle-Eye riders, maybe wanting them to tell him what to do.

One of them, not Wayman but one of the others, called out, "You got your .44 in your hand, ain't you? What're you waiting on?"

Catlett raised the saber to lay the tip against Macon's breastbone, saying to him, "You use your pistol and I use steel? All right, if that's how you want it. See if you can shoot me 'fore this blade is sticking out your back. You game? . . . Speak up, boy."

* * *

IN the hotel dining room having a cup of coffee, Catlett heard the noise outside, the cheering that meant Capt. Early had arrived. Catlett waited. He wished one of the waitresses would refill his cup, but they weren't around now, nobody was. A half hour passed before Capt. Early entered the dining room and came over to the table, leaving the people he was with. Catlett rose and they embraced, the hotel people and guests watching. It was while they stood this way that Bren saw, over Catlett's shoulder, the saber lying on the table, the curved steel on white linen. Catlett sat down. Bren looked closely at the saber's hilt. He picked it up and there was applause from the people watching. The captain bowed to them and sat down with the sergeant major.

"You went up the hill with this?"

"Somebody had to."

"I'm being recommended for a medal. 'For courage and pluck in continuing to advance under fire on the Spanish fortified position at the battle of Las Guásimas, Cuba, June twenty-fourth, 1898.' "

Catlett nodded. After a moment he said, "Will you tell me something? What was that war about?"

"You mean why'd we fight the dons?"

"Yeah, tell me."

"To free the oppressed Cuban people. Relieve them of Spanish domination."

"That's what I thought."

"You didn't know why you went to war?"

"I guess I knew," Catlett said. "I just wasn't sure."

Moment of Vengeance

At midmorning six riders came down out of the cavernous pine shadows, down the slope swept yellow with arrowroot blossoms, down through the scattered aspen at the north end of the meadow, then across the meadow and into the yard of the one-story adobe house.

Four of the riders dismounted, three of these separating as they moved toward the house; the fourth took his rope and walked off toward the mesquite-pole corral. The horses in the enclosure stood and watched as he opened the gate.

Ivan Kergosen, still mounted, motioned to the open stable shed that was built out from the adobe. The sixth man rode up to it, looked inside, then continued around the corner and was out of sight.

Now Kergosen, tight-jawed and solemn, saw the door of the adobe open. He watched Ellis, his daughter, come out to the edge of the ramada shade, ignoring the three men, who stepped aside to let her pass.

"We've been expecting you," she said. Her voice was calm and her smile, for a moment, seemed genuine, but it faded too quickly.

She touched her dark hair, smoothing it as a breeze rose and swept across the yard.

"Where is he?" Kergosen said.

Her gaze lifted, going out across the open sunlight of the meadow to the far west corner, to the windmill that stood out faintly against a dark background of pines.

"He's at the stock tank," Ellis said. "But he'll come in now."

Mr. Kergosen's hands were gripped one over the other on the saddle horn. He stared at his daughter in silence, his mustache hiding his mouth, but not the iron-willed anger in his eyes and in the tight line of his jaw.

"Whether he does or not," Kergosen said, "you're going back with me."

"I'm married now, Pa."

"Don't talk foolish."

"Married in Willson. By a priest."

"We'll talk about that at home."

"I am home!"

"Girl, this isn't going to be a public debate."

"Then why did you bring an audience?" She was sorry as soon as she said it. "Pa, I don't mean disrespect. Phil and I were married in Willson five days ago. He bought stock, drove it here, and we intend to raise it." Her father stared at her, saying nothing, and to fill the silence she added, "This is my home now, where I've come to live with my husband."

Leo Pyke, one of the three men standing near her, the curled brim of his hat straight and low over his eyes, said, "Looks more like a wickiup. Someplace a 'Pache would bring his squaw." He grinned, leaning against a support post, staring at Ellis.

Mr. Kergosen did not look up, but said, "Shut up, Leo."

"It's no fit place," Pyke said, straightening. "That's all I'm saying."

"Phil has work to do on it," Ellis said defensively. "He's already put on a new roof." She looked quickly at her father. "That's what I mean. We didn't just run off and get married. We've planned for it. Phil paid down on the house and property more than a month ago at the Dos Mesas bank. Since then we've been making it livable."

"Behind my back," Kergosen said.

Ellis hesitated. "Phil wanted to ask your permission. I told him it wouldn't do any good."

"How did you suppose that?" her father asked.

"I've lived with you for eighteen years, Pa. I know you."

"Can you say you know Phil Treat as well?"

"I know him," Ellis said simply.

"As far as I'm concerned," Kergosen said, "he qualifies as a man. But certainly not as the man who marries my daughter."

Ellis asked, "And I have nothing to say about it?"

"We're not discussing it here," Kergosen said.

He had hired Treat almost a year ago, during the time he was having trouble with the San Carlos Reservation people. He lost two men that spring and roughly two dozen head of beef to raiding parties. The Apache police did nothing about it, though they knew his stock was being taken to San Carlos. So Ivan Kergosen went to Fort Thomas and hired a professional tracker whose government contract had expired, and went after them himself. They turned out to be Chiricahuas and the scout ran down every last one of them.

The scout's name was Phil Treat. He had been a soldier, buffalo hunter, and cavalry guide, and had earned a reputation as a gunfighter by killing three men: two of them at Tascosa when they tried to steal his hides; the third one at Anton Chico, New Mexico—an Army deserter who drew his gun, refusing to go back to Apache land. Only three, but the shootings were done well, with witnesses, and it took no more than that to establish a reputation.

And after the trouble was past, Phil Treat stayed on with Mr.

Kergosen. He was passing fair with cattle, a good horsebreaker, and an A1 hunter; so Kergosen paid him top wages and was pleased to have such a man around. But as a hired hand; not as a son-in-law.

All his life Ivan Kergosen had worked hard and prayed hard, asking God for guidance. He built his holdings according to a single-minded interpretation of God's will, respecting Him more as a God of Justice than a God of Mercy. And his good fortune, he believed, was God in His justice rewarding him, granting him success in life for adhering to Divine Will. It had taken Ivan Kergosen thirty years of working and fighting—fighting the land, the Apache, and anyone who tried to take from his land—to build the finest spread in the Pinaleño Valley. He built this success for his own self-respect, for his wife who was now deceased, and for his daughter, Ellis—not for a sign-reading gunfighter who'd spent half of his life killing buffalo, the other tracking Apache, and who now, somehow, contrary to all his plans, had married his daughter.

He heard Leo Pyke's voice and he was brought back to the here and now. "Fixing the house while he was working for you, Mr. Kergosen," Pyke was saying. "No telling the amount of sneaky acts he's committed."

The man who had gone to the corral came out, leading a saddled and bridled dun horse. He looked back over his shoulder, then at Mr. Kergosen, and called, "He's coming now!"

Ellis was aware then of the steady cantering sound. She saw Leo Pyke and the two men with him—Sandal, who was a Mexican, and Grady, a bearded, solemn-faced man—look out past the corral, and she said, "In a moment you can say it to his face, Leo. About being sneaky."

She looked up in time to see her husband swing past the corral, coming toward her. She watched him dismount stiffly. He let the reins drop, passed his hand over his mouth, then up to his hat brim, and loosened it from his forehead. He turned his back to the three men in the ramada shade as if intentionally ignoring them; then looked from Ellis to her father and said, "Well?"

And now Ivan Kergosen was faced with the calm, deliberate gaze of this man. He saw that Phil Treat was not wearing a gun: he saw that he was trail dirty and had moved slowly, to stand, now, tall but stooped, with his hands hanging empty.

He could handle this man. Kergosen was sure of that now, but he respected him and he had planned this meeting carefully. Leo Pyke, who openly disliked Treat, and Sandal and Grady, who had been with him longer than any of his other riders, would deal with Treat if he objected. No, there would be no trouble. But he formed his words carefully before he spoke.

Then he said, "You made a mistake. So did my daughter. But both mistakes are corrected as of this moment. Ellis is going home and you have ten minutes to pack your gear and get out. Clear?"

"And my stock?" Treat said.

"You're selling your stock to me," Kergosen said, "so there'll be nothing to delay you." His hand went into his coat and came out with a folded square of green paper. "My draft on the Willson Bank to cover the sale of your yearling stock. Thirty head. When you draw the money, the canceled draft is my receipt." He extended his hand. "Take it." Treat did not move and Kergosen's wrist flicked out and the folded paper floated—fell to the ground. "Pick it up," Kergosen said. "Your time's running out." He looked at Ellis then. "Mount up."

ELLIS almost spoke, frightened, angry, and unsure of herself now, but she looked at her husband and waited.

Treat stood motionless, still gazing up at Kergosen. "You have five men and I have myself," he said. "That makes a difference, doesn't it?"

"If this is unjust," Kergosen said, "then it's unjust. I'll say it only once more. Your time's running out."

Treat's eyes moved to Ellis. "Do what he says." He saw the bewildered look come over her face, and he said, "Go home with him, Ellis, and do what he tells you." Treat paused. "But don't speak one solitary word to him as long as you're under his roof. Not till I come for you." He said this quietly in the brittle silence that hung over the yard, and now he saw Ellis nod her head slowly.

He looked up at Kergosen, who was staring at him intently. "Mr. Kergosen, we can't argue with you and we can't fight you, but take Ellis home and you'll know she isn't just your daughter any more."

"You don't threaten me," Kergosen said.

"No," Treat said, "you've got iron fists, a hundred and thirty square miles of land, and you sit there like it's the high seat of judgment. But you live with Ellis now, if you can."

Kergosen said, "Pick up that draft."

Treat shook his head.

"As God is my judge, I mean you no harm," Kergosen said. "But you don't leave me a choice."

He nodded to Leo Pyke as he reined his bay in a tight circle and rode out. Ellis had mounted and now she followed him, looking back past the two riders who fell in behind her as she passed the corral and started across the meadow.

They were not yet out of sight, but nearing the aspen stands when Pyke said to Sandal and Grady, "So he won't pick it up."

Treat looked at him, then stooped, without loss of dignity, unhurriedly, and picked up the draft. "If it bothers you," he said.

Pyke grinned. "He's not so big now, is he?"

The Mexican rider, Sandal, said, "Like a field hand. I thought he was something with a gun."

"A story he made up," the third man, Grady, said.

Pyke said to Sandal, "Move his horse out of the way."

Sandal winked at Grady. "And the Henry, uh?" He led Treat's claybank to the corral and lifted the Henry rifle from the saddle boot as he shooed him in. He walked back to them, studying the rifle, holding it at belt level. Without looking at them, as if not aiming, he flipped the lever down and up and fired past them, and the right front window of the adobe shattered.

Sandal looked up, smiling. "This is no bad gun."

Across the meadow two of Kergosen's riders were moving the herd away from the stock tank. Treat watched them, turning his back to Sandal. There was time. These men would do as they pleased, whether he objected or not. Wait and say nothing, he thought. Wait and watch and keep track of the score.

He remembered a patrol out of Fort Thomas coming to a spring, and a Coyotero Apache guide whose name was Pesh-klitso. The guide had said to him in Spanish, "We followed the barbarian for ten days; two men died, three horses died; we have no food and we killed no barbarian. Yet we could have waited for them here. Our stomachs would be full, the two men and the horses would still be alive, and we would take them when they came." He'd asked the Coyotero how he knew they would come, and the guide answered, "The land is not that broad. They would come sooner or later." Which meant, if not today, then tomorrow; if not this year, then the next.

He had known many Pesh-klitsos at San Carlos, and at Tascosa, when they carried Sharps rifles and hunted buffalo—hunted them by waiting, then killed them. And the more patience you had, the more you killed.

Treat waited and watched. He watched Grady go into the adobe and saw the left front window erupt with a spray of broken glass as a chair came through. He saw Sandal break off two of the chair legs with the heel of his boot, then walk into the adobe, and a moment later the Henry was firing again. With the reports, with the ear-ringing din and the clicking cocking sound of the lever, he heard glass and china shattering, falling from the shelves. Then the sound of a Colt and a dull, clanging noise; sooty smoke billowed from the open doorway and he knew they had shot down the stove chimney.

Grady came out, fanning the smoke in front of him. He mounted his horse, sidestepped it to the ramada, fastened the loop of his rope to a support post, and spurred away. The post ripped out, bouncing, scraping a dust rise, and the mesquite-pole awning sagged partway to the ground. Sandal came out of the adobe, running, ducking his head. He watched Grady circle to come back, went to his own horse, fastened his rope to the other support post, and dragged it away. The ramada collapsed, swinging, smashing, against the adobe front, and the mesquite poles broke apart.

Watching Treat, Leo Pyke said, "You letting them get away with that? All this big talk about you, and you don't even open your mouth."

Grady and Sandal walked their horses in. Treat glanced at them, then back to Pyke. "I don't have anything to say."

"Listen," Pyke said. "I've put up with that closemouth cold-water way of yours a long time. I've watched men stand clear of you, afraid they'd step too close and you'd come to life. I watched Mr. Kergosen, then Ellis, won over to your sly ways. But all that time I was seeing through you—looking clean through, and there was nothing there to see. No backbone, no guts, no nothing."

Sandal was grinning, leaning over his saddle horse. "Eat him up, Layo!"

Pyke's eyes did not leave Treat. "If you were worth it, I'd take my gun off and beat hell out of you."

Treat's eyebrows raised slightly. "Would you, Leo?"

"You damn bet I would."

Sandal said, "Go ahead, man. Do it."

"Shut your mouth!" Pyke threw the words over his shoulder.

"The vision of being segundo returns with the return of the daughter," Sandal said, grinning again. To Grady, next to him, he said, "How would you like to work for this one every day?"

Grady shook his head. "She can't marry him now. And that's the only way he'd get to be Number Two."

"I think she married him," Sandal said, nodding at Treat, "just to escape this one."

"I said shut up!" Pyke screamed, turning half around, but at once he looked back at Treat. "You ride out, right now. And if I ever see you this close again, I'll talk to you with a gun. You hear me!"

NINE days after that, R. C. Hassett, the county deputy assigned to Dos Mesas, was told of the disappearance of two of Ivan Kergosen's riders. On Saturday, two days before, they'd spent the evening in town. They started back home at eleven o'clock and had not been seen since.

Hassett thought it over the length of time it took him to strap on his holster and take a Winchester down from the wall rack. Then he rode out to Phil Treat's place. Entering the yard, he heard a hammering sound coming from the adobe. He saw that a new ramada had been constructed. As he reined toward the adobe, Phil Treat stepped out of the doorway, a Henry rifle under his arm.

"So you're rebuilding," Hassett said. "I heard about what happened."

His eyes held on Treat as he stepped out of the saddle, letting his reins trail. He brushed open his coat and took a tobacco plug from his vest pocket, bit off a corner of it, and returned the plug to the pocket. His coat remained open, the skirt held back by the butt of his revolver. He had been a law officer for more than two dozen years and he was in no particular hurry.

"I wasn't sure you'd be here," said Hassett. "But something told me to find out."

"You're not looking for me," Treat said.

"No; two of Mr. Kergosen's boys."

Treat called toward the adobe, "Come out a minute!"

Hassett watched as Grady and Sandal appeared in the doorway, then came outside. Grady's bearded face was bruised, one eye swollen and half closed, and he limped as he took the few steps out to the end of the ramada shade. There was no mark on Sandal.

"These the men?" asked Treat.

Hassett nodded. "Ivan reported them lost."

"Not lost," Treat said. "They quit him to work for me."

"Without drawing their pay?"

"That's none of my business," Treat answered.

Hassett's gaze moved to the adobe. "Grady, I didn't know you were a carpenter."

The bearded man hesitated before saying, "I'm swearing out a complaint on one Phil Treat."

Hassett nodded, moving the tobacco from one cheek to the other. "It's your privilege, Grady; though I'd say you got off easy."

"This man forced us—" Grady began.

Hassett held up his hand. "In my office." He looked at Treat then. "You come in, too, and state your complaint. I make out a writ and serve it on Ivan. The writ orders him to court on such and such a date. You're there to claim your wife with proof of legal marriage."

"And if Mr. Kergosen doesn't appear?" asked Treat.

"He's no bigger than I am," Hassett said. "I see that he does next time."

"But that doesn't calm his mind, does it?"

"That's your problem," Hassett said.

Treat almost smiled. "You said it as simply as it can be said."

"All right," Hassett said. "You've been told." He moved around his horse, stepped up into the saddle, then looked down at Treat again. "Let me ask you something. How come Grady looks the way he does and there isn't a mark on Sandal?"

"I talked to Grady first," Treat said.

"I see," Hassett said. "I'll ask you something else. How come Ivan didn't come here looking for these two?"

"I guess he doesn't know I'm still here."

Hassett looked down at Treat. "But he'll know it now, won't he?" He turned and rode out of the yard.

That afternoon, after they had finished the inside repairs, Sandal and Grady were released. They rode out, riding double, and watching them, Treat pictured them approaching the great U-shaped adobe that was Mr. Kergosen's home, then dismounting and standing in the sunlight as Ivan came down the steps from the veranda.

Sandal would tell it: how they were ambushed riding back from Dos Mesas, how Treat had appeared in front of them, coming out of the trees with the Henry; how Grady's horse had been hit when they tried to run, and had fallen on Grady and injured his ankle; how they had been taken back to his adobe and forced to rebuild the ramada and patch the furniture and the stove. And Sandal would describe him as some kind of demon, a nagual who never slept and seldom spoke as he held them with a Henry rifle for two days and two nights.

Ivan Kergosen would turn from them, his eyes going to Ellis sitting on the shaded veranda, reading or sewing or staring out over the yard. She would not look at him, but he would detect the beginning of a smile. Only this, on the tenth day of her silence.

You have a woman, Treat thought, picturing her. You have one and you don't have one. He thought of the time he had first spoken to her, the times they rode together and the time he first kissed her.

And now they'll come again. But not Grady, because his ankle will put him to bed. Outwait an old man, he thought. Wait while an old man realizes he is not God, or God's avenging angel, or God's right hand. Which could take no longer than your lifetime, he thought.

He took dried meat, a canteen, a blanket, the Henry, and a holstered Colt revolver and went out into the corral to wait for them.

THERE were five that came. They reached Treat's adobe at dusk, spreading out as they approached it, coming at it from both sides of the corral, two of the riders circling the stable shed and the adobe before entering the yard. Sandal dismounted and went into the adobe. He came out with a kerosene lantern and held it as Pyke struck a match and lit it.

"Who's going to do it?" asked Sandal.

"You're holding the fire," Pyke said.

"Not me." Sandal shook his head.

"Just throw it in. Hit the wall over the bed."

"Not me. I've done enough to that man."

"What about what he did to you?"

"He had reason."

Pyke stepped out of the saddle. He jerked the lantern away from Sandal and walked to the door. His hand went to the latch, then stopped.

"Layo!" Sandal's voice.

Pyke looked over his shoulder, saw Sandal not looking at him, but staring out toward the corral, and he turned full around, holding the lantern by the ring handle.

He saw Treat crossing the yard toward him. In the dusk he could not see the man's features, but he knew it was Treat. He saw Treat's hands hanging empty and he saw the revolver on his right leg. Now Sandal was moving the horses, holding the reins and whack-slapping at the rump of one to force both of them to the side. The horses of the three riders still mounted moved nervously, and the riders watched Treat, seeing him looking at Leo Pyke. Then, thirty feet from the ramada, Treat stopped.

"Leo, you tore my house down once. Once is enough."

Pyke was at ease. "You're going to stop us?"

"The last time you stated that you'd talk with a gun if I ever came close again." Treat glanced at Sandal when Pyke said nothing. "Is that right?"

"Big as life," the Mexican said.

Treat's gaze returned to Pyke. "Well?"

"You got me at an unfair advantage," Pyke said carefully. "A lantern in my hand. All the light full on me."

"You came here to burn down my house," Treat said, standing motionless. "You're holding the fire, as you told Sandal. You've got four men backing you and you call it a disadvantage."

"Three men backing him," Sandal said.

Beyond him one of the mounted riders said, "This part of it isn't our fight."

And Sandal added, "Just Layo's."

"Wait a minute." Pyke was taken by surprise. "You all work for Mr. Kergosen. He says run him out, we do it!"

"But not carry him out," the one who had spoken before said. "You threatened him, Leo; then it's your fight, not ours. And if you think he's got a unfair advantage, put the lantern down."

"So it's like that," Pyke said.

"You got two feet," Sandal said. "Stand on them. Show us how the segundo would do it."

"Listen, you chili picker! You're through!"

"Sure, Layo. Now talk to that boy out there."

"Mr. Kergosen's going to run every damn one of you!" Pyke half turned to face them, shifting the lantern to his left hand, the light swaying across Sandal and the chestnut color of his horse.

"We'll talk to him," Sandal said.

Pyke stared at him. "You know what you done, you and the rest? You jawed yourself out of jobs. You see how easy a new one is to find. Mr. Kergosen's going to be burned, but sure as hell I'm going to"—his feet started to shift—"tell him!"

As he said it, Pyke was spinning on his toes, swinging the lantern hard at Treat, seeing it in the air, then going to his right, but seeing Treat moving, with the revolver suddenly in his hand, and at that moment Treat fired.

Pyke was half around when the bullet struck him. He stumbled back against the front of the adobe, came forward drawing, bringing up his Colt, then half turned, falling against the adobe as Treat fired again and the second bullet hit him.

The revolver fell from Pyke's hand and he stood against the wall staring at Treat, holding his arms bent slightly, but stiffly against his sides, as if afraid to move them. He had been shot through both arms, both just above the elbow.

Treat walked toward him. "Leo," he said, "you've got two things to remember. One, you're not coming back here again. And two, I could've aimed dead center." He turned from Pyke to Sandal. "If you want to do him a good turn, tie up his arms and take him to a doctor. The rest of you," he said to the mounted men, "can tell Mr. Kergosen I'm still here."

HE was told, and he came the next morning, riding into the yard with a shotgun across his lap. He rode up to Treat, who was standing in front of the adobe, and the shotgun was pointing down at him when Kergosen drew in the reins. They looked at each other in the clear morning sunlight, in the yellow, bright stillness of the yard.

"I could pull the trigger," Kergosen said, "and it would be over."

"Over for me," Treat said. "Not for you or Ellis."

Kergosen sat heavily in the saddle. He had not shaved this morning and his eyes told that he'd had little sleep. "You won't draw a gun against me?"

"No, sir."

"Why?"

"If I did, I'd have to live with Ellis the rest of my life the way you're doing now."

"So you're in a hole."

"But no deeper than the one you're in."

Kergosen studied him. "I underestimated you. I thought you'd run."

"Because you told me to?"

"That was reason enough."

"You're too used to giving orders," Treat said. "You've been Number One a long time and you've forgotten what it's like to have somebody contrary to you."

"I didn't get where I am having people contrary to me," Kergosen stated. "I worked and fought and earned the right to give orders, but I prayed to God to lead me right, and don't you forget that!"

"Mr. Kergosen," Treat said quietly, "are you afraid I can't provide for your daughter?"

"Provide!" Kergosen's face tightened. "An Apache buck provides. He builds a hut for his woman and brings her meat. Any man with one hand and a gun can provide. We're talking about my daughter, not a flat-nosed Indian woman—and you have to put up a damn sight more than meat and a hut!"

Treat said, "You think I won't make something of myself?"

"Mister, all you've proved to me is that you can read sign and shoot." Kergosen paused before asking, "Why didn't you sign a complaint to get Ellis back? Don't you know your rights? That's what I'm talking about. You can track a renegade Apache, you can stand off five men with a Colt, but you don't know how to live like a white man!"

"Mr. Kergosen," Treat said patiently, "I could've got a writ. I could've prosecuted you for tearing down my house. I could've killed Leo Pyke with almost a clear conscience. I could've done a lot of things."

"But you didn't," Kergosen said.

"No, I waited."

"If you're waiting for me to die of old age—"

"Mr. Kergosen, I'm interested in your daughter, not your property. We can get along just fine with what we're building on."

"Which is nothing," Kergosen said.

"When you started," Treat asked, "what did you have?"

"When I married I had over one hundred square miles of land. Miles, mister, not acres. I was going on forty years old, sure of myself and not a kid anymore."

"I'm almost thirty, Mr. Kergosen."

"I'll say it again: And you've got nothing."

"Nothing but time."

"Listen," Kergosen said earnestly. "You don't count on the future like it's nothing but years to fill up. You fill them up, good or bad, according to your ability and willingness to sweat, but you're sure of that future before you ask a woman to face it with you."

Treat said, "You had somebody picked for Ellis?"

"Not by name, but a man who can offer her something."

"So you planned her future, and it turned out different."

"Damn it, I try to do what's right!"

"According to your rules."

"With God's help!"

"Mr. Kergosen," Treat said, "I don't mean disrespect, but I think you've rigged it so God has to take the blame for your mistakes. Ellis and I made a mistake. We admit it. We should've come to you first. We would've got married whether you said yes or no, but we still should've come to you first. The way it is now, it's still up to you, but now you're in an embarrassing position with the Almighty. Ellis and I are married in the eyes of the same God that you say's been guiding you all this time, thirty years or more. All right, you and Him have been getting along fine up to now. But now what?"

Kergosen said nothing.

"We could probably argue all day," Treat said, "but it comes down to this: You either go home and send out some more men, or you use that scattergun, or you come inside and have some coffee, and we'll talk it over like two grown-up men."

Kergosen stared at him. "I admire your control, Mr. Treat."

"I've learned how to wait, Mr. Kergosen. If it comes down to that, I'll outwait you. I think you know that."

Kergosen was silent for a long moment. He looked down at his hands on the shotgun and exhaled, letting his breath out slowly, wearily, and he seemed to sit lower on the saddle.

"I think I'm getting old," he said quietly. "I'm tired of arguing and tired of fighting."

"Maybe tired of fighting yourself," Treat said.

Kergosen nodded faintly. "Maybe so."

Treat waited, then said, "Mr. Kergosen, I'm anxious to see my wife."

Kergosen's face came up, out of shadow, deep-lined and solemn, but the hard tightness was gone from his jaw. He shifted his weight and came down off the saddle, and on the ground he handed the shotgun to Treat.

"Phil," he said, "this damn thing's getting too heavy to hold."

From his pocket Treat brought out the bank draft Kergosen had given him. He handed it over, saying, "So is this, Mr. Kergosen."

They stood for a moment. Kergosen's hand went into his pocket with the bank draft and when they moved toward the adobe, the bitterness between them was past. It had worn itself to nothing.

Saint with a Six-Gun

Inside the hotel café Lyall Quinlan sat at the counter having his breakfast. Every once in a while he would look over at Elodie Wells. Elodie had served him, but now her back was to him; she was looking out the big window over the lower part that was green painted and said REGENT CAFÉ in white—looking across the street to the Tularosa jail. Horses and wagons were hitched there and down the street both ways, and behind the jailhouse in the big yard where everybody was now, that's where they were hanging Bobby Valdez.

Out on the street there wasn't a sound. Inside now, just the noise of Lyall Quinlan's palm popping the bottom of the ketchup bottle until it flowed out over his eggs. Elodie scowled at him as if she was trying to hear something and Lyall was interrupting the best part. Lyall just smiled at her, a young-kid smile, and began eating his eggs. Elodie, like about everybody in Tularosa, had been excited all week long waiting for this day to come—a whole week while Bobby Valdez sat in his cell with Lyall Quinlan guarding him. Elodie was mad because she had to work this morning. Lyall felt pretty good, so he just went on eating his eggs. . . .

* * *

BOHANNON, the Tularosa marshal, brought in Bobby Valdez on a Thursday afternoon and right away sent a man to Las Cruces to fetch Judge Metairie. Bohannon didn't have a doubt Valdez would not be bound over for trial, and he was right. Friday morning a coroner's jury decided that one Roberto Eladio Viscarra y Valdez did willfully commit murder—judging from the size hole in the forehead of one Harley Tanner (deceased) and the .41-caliber Colt gun found on the accused when he was apprehended the next day. A witness testified that he saw Bobby Valdez pull this same Colt and let go at Tanner in a fashion that in no way resembled self-defense.

Everybody agreed it was about time a smart-aleck gunman like Bobby Valdez was brought to justice and made to pay the penalty. The only ones who'd cry would be some of the girls who couldn't see his handgun for his brown eyes. It was a shame he had to hang, being only twenty-two, but that's what would happen. He didn't have to be bad.

Saturday morning, Criminal Sessions Court, the Honorable Benson Metairie presiding, was called to order in the lobby of the Regent Hotel. The courthouse at Las Cruces would have been better, but that meant transporting Bobby Valdez almost a hundred miles. A year ago he'd gotten away when they were taking him there from Mesilla, and Mesilla was like just across the field.

VALDEZ waived counsel, though there wasn't an attorney in Tularosa to defend him if he'd wanted one. Judge Metairie said it was just as well. Since the case was cut and dried, why waste time with a lot of litigating?

The court called up a witness who swore he'd seen Bobby Valdez plain as day come out of the Regent Café that Wednesday evening, which established the accused's presence in town the night of the shooting.

The star witness took the stand and said he was crossing the street to have a word with his friend Harley Tanner, who was standing right in front of this hotel, when Bobby Valdez came out of the shadows of the adobe building, called Tanner a dirty name, and, when Tanner came around, pulled his gun and shot him. Then Valdez lit out.

Bohannon suggested stepping outside to reenact the crime, but Judge Metairie said everybody knew what the front of the Regent Hotel looked like and the fierce sun this time of day wasn't going to make it any plainer. "Just close your eyes, Ed, and make a picture," the judge told Bohannon.

It was stated that the next morning Bohannon's posse followed Valdez's sign till they caught up with him about noon near the Mescalero reservation line. Valdez's horse had lamed and left Bobby out in the open, as Bohannon said, "with his pants down, so to speak."

Judge Metairie called a man who was referred to as a character witness and this man described seeing Bobby Valdez shoot two men during the White Sands bank holdup last Christmastime. Another character witness was on the Butterfield stage that was held up last June between Lordsburg and Continental. Surer'n hell it was Bobby Valdez who'd opened the door with that .41 Colt gun in his hand, and no polka-dot bandana over his nose was going to argue it wasn't. Two more men sat down on the Douglas-chair witness stand with like stories.

Judge Metairie looked at his watch and asked what time was the stage back to Las Cruces, and when somebody told him not till three o'clock, he said that they might as well adjourn for dinner then and let the jury reach their verdict over a nice meal—though he didn't see where they'd have much thinking to do.

Court reconvened at one-thirty. The jury foreman stood up, waited for the talking to die, then said how they allowed Bobby Valdez sure couldn't be anything else but guilty.

Judge Metairie nodded, gaveled the register desk to restore

order, waited until the quiet could be felt, then in the voice of doom sentenced Roberto Eladio Viscarra y Valdez, on the morning one week from this day, to be hanged by the neck until dead.

Criminal Sessions Court was closed and most people felt Judge Metairie had turned in a better-than-usual performance.

Saturday evening Lyall Quinlan went on duty at the Tularosa Jail.

It came about because Bohannon was scheduled to play poker and Quinlan arrived just at the right time. He came looking for the job; still, he was taken by surprise when Bohannon offered it to him, "temporarily, you understand," because he'd been turned down so many times before. Lyall Quinlan wanted to be a lawman, but Bohannon always put him off with the excuse that he already had an assistant, Barney Groom, and Barney served the purpose even if he was an old man.

But Bohannon was thinking maybe an extra night man ought to be on with Valdez upstairs, a man to sit up there and watch him. He was supposed to play cards tonight, which disallowed him. Then, lo and behold, there was young Lyall Quinlan coming in the door!

"Lyall, you musta heard me wishin' for you." Then, seeing the astonishment come over the boy's face—a thin face with big, self-conscious eyes—he thought: Hell, Lyall's all right. Even if he don't pack much weight, he's honest. And he rode in the posse that brought in Valdez. An eager boy like him'd make a good deputy! For what he considered would be a temporary period, Bohannon convinced himself that Quinlan would do just fine. Tomorrow he could always kick him the hell out. . . .

"Barney, give Lyall here a scattergun and tell him what to do," and Bohannon was gone.

Lyall Quinlan sat up all night watching Bobby Valdez. That is, most of the time he sat in the cane-bottom chair—it was in the hallway facing the one cell they had upstairs—he was keeping his eyes on Valdez, who hardly paid him any attention. Whenever Lyall would start to get sleepy, he'd get up, crook the sawed-off scattergun under his arm, and pace up and down in the short hallway.

The first time he did it, Bobby Valdez, who was lying on his back with his eyes closed, opened them, turned his head enough to see Lyall, and told him to shut up. It was his boots making the noise. But Lyall went right on walking up and down. Valdez called on one of the men saints then and asked him why did all keepers of jails wear squeaky boots? The lamp hanging out in the hall didn't seem to bother him, only Lyall's boots.

When Lyall kept on walking, the Mexican said something else, half smiling—a low-voiced string of soft-spoken Spanish.

Lyall edged closer to the cell and said through the heavy iron bars, "Hush up!"

Valdez went to sleep right after that and Lyall sat in the chair again, feeling pretty good, not so tense anymore.

Let him try something, Lyall thought, watching the sleeping Mexican, feeling the shotgun across his lap. I'd blast him before he got through the door. He practice-swung the gun around. Cut him right in half. Boy, it's heavy. Only about fifteen inches of barrel left and it's really heavy. Imagine what that'd do to a man!

He kept watching the sleeping man, his eyes going from the high black boots to the lavender shirt and the dark face, the composed, soft-featured dark face.

How can he sleep? Next Saturday he's going to swing from the end of a rope and he's laying there sleeping. Well, some people are built different. If he wasn't different he wouldn't be in that cell. But he ain't more'n a year older than I am. How could he have already done so much in his life? And killed the men he has? Two at White Sands, one in Mesilla. Tanner. Lyall's thumb went over the tips of his fingers. That's four. Then two more way over to Pima County. At least six, though some claim nine and ten. And

Elodie thrilled to death because she served him his dinner the night he shot Tanner. They say he was something with the girls—which about proves that they don't use their heads for much more than a place to grow hair.

Well, he just better not try to come out of that cell. About a minute later Lyall went over and jiggled the door to make sure it was still locked.

Barney Groom came up when it was daylight, and seeing Lyall just sitting there he blinked like he couldn't believe what his eyes told him. "You awake?"

Lyall rose. "Of course."

"Son, you mean you've been awake all night?"

"I thought I was hired to watch this prisoner."

Old Barney Groom shook his head.

"What's the matter?"

"Nothin'," Barney said. Then, "Bohannon's downstairs."

Lyall said, "He want to see me?"

"When you go out he won't be able to help it," said Barney.

"Well, and when should I come back?"

"I ain't the timekeeper. Ask Bohannon about that."

They heard footsteps on the stairs and then Bohannon was in the hallway, yawning, scratching his shirtfront.

Barney Groom said, "Ed, this boy stayed awake all night!"

Bohannon stopped scratching, though he didn't drop his hand. He looked at Lyall Quinlan, who nodded and said, "Mr. Bohannon."

The marshal squinted in the dim light. It was plain he'd been drinking, the way his eyes looked filmy, though he stood there with his feet planted and didn't sway a bit. Finally he said, "You don't say!"

"All night," Barney Groom said.

Bohannon looked at him. "How would you know?"

"He was awake when I come up."

Bohannon said nothing.

"Mr. Bohannon," Lyall said, "I didn't go to sleep."

"Maybe you did and maybe you did not."

Bobby Valdez had been watching them. Now he swung his legs off the bunk. He stood up and moved toward the bars. "He's telling the truth," the Mexican said.

Bohannon put his cold eyes on Valdez for a moment, then looked back at Lyall Quinlan.

Valdez shrugged. "It don't make any difference to me," he said. "But make him grease his boots if he's going to walk all night."

Barney Groom moved a step toward the cell as if threatening Valdez. "You got any more requests?"

"Yes," the Mexican said right away. "I want to go to church."

"What?" Barney Groom said, then was embarrassed for having looked like he'd taken the Mexican seriously, and added, "Sure. I'll send the carriage around."

Valdez looked at him without expression. "This is Sunday."

Bohannon was squinting and half smiling. "Any special denomination, Brother Valdez?"

"Listen, man," Valdez said, "this is Sunday, and I have to go to mass."

Bohannon asked, "You go to mass every Sunday?"

"I've missed some."

Bohannon, with the half smile, went on studying him. Then he said, "Tell you what. We'll douse you with a bucket of holy water instead."

Bohannon and Groom left right after that. Lyall was to stay until one or the other came back from breakfast.

When he was alone again, Lyall looked at Valdez sitting on the bunk. Even after the words were ready he waited a good ten minutes before saying them. "The nearest church is down to White Sands," he told Valdez. "You can't blame the marshal for not wanting to ride you all the way down there."

Valdez looked up.

"It's so far," Lyall Quinlan said. He looked toward the window at the end of the hallway, then back to Valdez. "I appreciate you telling the marshal I was awake all night. I think something like that sets pretty good with him."

Bobby Valdez looked at Lyall curiously. Then his expression softened to a smile, as if he'd suddenly become aware of a new interest, and he said, "Anytime, friend."

When Bohannon came back he sent Lyall across the street to the Regent to get Valdez's breakfast. After he'd given the tray to Valdez, Bohannon deputized him, but mentioned how it was a temporary appointment until the Citizens Committee passed on it. "Now, if you was to keep an extra-special eye on Brother Valdez, I'd have to recommend you as fit, wouldn't I?" He patted Lyall's shoulder and said now was as good a time as any to start the new appointment. "We'll see how you handle yourself alone."

Lyall thought it was a funny way to do things, but he'd have plenty of time for sleep later on. When opportunity knocks on the door you got to open it, he told himself. So he stayed on at the jail, sitting downstairs this time, until midafternoon when Bohannon came back.

"Now get yourself some shuteye, boy," the marshal told him, "so you'll be in fit shape for tonight."

Lyall's mother told him they were making a fool out of him, but Lyall didn't have time to argue. He just said this was what he'd always wanted to do—a hell of a lot better than working behind a store counter, though he didn't use quite those words. Lyall's mother used mother arguments, but finally there was nothing she could do but shake her head and let him go to bed.

HE went back on duty at nine, sitting in the cane-bottom chair, not hearing a sound from Barney Groom downstairs. Bobby Valdez was more talkative. He talked about horses and girls and the terrible fact that he hadn't gotten to church that day; then made a big to-do admiring Lyall for the way he could go so long without sleep. That was fine.

But pretty soon Bobby Valdez went to sleep and that night Lyall walked up and down the little hallway even more than he had the first night. Two or three times he almost went to sleep, but he kept moving and blinking his eyes. He found a way of propping the shotgun between his leg and the chair arm, so that the trigger guard dug into his thigh and that kept him awake whenever he sat down to rest.

In the morning Bohannon came up the stairs quietly, but Lyall heard him and said, "Hi, Mr. Bohannon," when the marshal tiptoed in.

Lyall slept all day Monday and after that he was all right, not having any trouble keeping awake that night. Bobby Valdez talked to him until late and that helped.

Tuesday he ate his supper at the Regent Café before going to work. He mentioned weather to Elodie and how the food was getting better, but didn't once refer to the silver deputy star on his shirtfront. Elodie tried to be unconcerned, too, but finally she just had to ask him, and Lyall answered, "Why, sure, Elodie, I've been a deputy marshal since last Saturday. Didn't you know that?"

Elodie had to describe how Bobby Valdez came in for dinner the night he shot Tanner. "He sat right on that very stool you're on and ate tacos like he didn't have a worry in the world. Real calm."

Lyall said, "Uh-huh, but he's kind of a little squirt, ain't he?" and walked out casually, knowing Elodie was watching after him with her mouth open.

TUESDAY night Valdez told Lyall how his being in the cell had all come about—how he'd started out an honest vaquero down in Sonora, but got mixed up with some unprincipled men who were chousing other people's cows. Bobby Valdez said, by the name of a saint, he didn't know anything about it, but the next thing the *rurales* were chasing him across the border. About a year later, in Contention, Arizona, he killed a man. It was in self-defense and he was acquitted; but the man had a friend, so he ended up killing the friend too. And after that it was just one thing leading to another. Everybody seemed to take him wrong . . . couldn't get an honest job . . . so what was a young man supposed to do?

The way he described it made Lyall Quinlan shake his head and say it was a shame.

Wednesday night Bobby Valdez only nodded to Lyall when he came on duty. The Mexican was sitting on the edge of the bunk, elbows on his knees, staring at his hands as he washed them together absently.

He's finally realizing he's going to die, Lyall thought. You have to leave a man alone when he's doing that. So for over an hour no one spoke.

When Lyall did speak it was because he wanted to make it a little easier for Valdez. He said, "All people have to die. That's the best way to look at it."

Valdez looked up, then nodded thoughtfully.

"You got to look at it," Lyall went on, "like, well, just something that happens to everybody."

"I've done that," the Mexican said. "What torments me now is that I have not confessed."

"You didn't have to," Lyall said. "Judge Metairie found out the facts without you confessing."

"No, I mean to a priest."

"Oh."

"It is a terrible thing to die without absolution."

"Oh."

It was quiet then, Lyall frowning, the Mexican looking at his hands. But suddenly Bobby Valdez looked up, his face brightening, and he said, as if it had just occurred to him, "My friend, would *you* bring a priest to me?"

"Well—I'll tell Mr. Bohannon in the morning. I'm sure he'll—"

"No!" Valdez stood up quickly. "I cannot take the chance of letting him know!" His voice calmed as he said, "You know how he makes fun of things spiritual—that about the holy water, and calling me 'Brother.' What if he should refuse this request? Then I would die in the state of mortal sin just because he does not understand. My friend," he said just above a whisper, "surely you can see that he must not know."

"Well—" Lyall said.

"In White Sands," Valdez said quickly, "there is a man called Sixto Henriquez who knows the priest well. At the mescal shop they'll tell you where he lives. Now, all you would have to do is tell Sixto to send the priest late Friday night after it is very quiet, and then it will be accomplished."

Lyall hesitated.

"Then," Valdez said solemnly, "I would not die in sin."

Lyall thought about it some more and finally he nodded.

He woke up at noon for the ride to White Sands. He'd have to hurry to be back in time to go on duty; but he would have hurried anyway because he didn't feel right about what he was doing, as if it was something sneaky. At the mescal shop the proprietor directed him, in as few words as were necessary, to the adobe of Sixto Henriquez. Lyall was half afraid and half hoping Sixto wouldn't be home. But there he was, a thin little man in a striped shirt who didn't open the door all the way until Lyall mentioned Valdez.

After Lyall had told why he was there, Henriquez took his time rolling a cigarette. He lit it and blew out smoke and then said, "All right."

Lyall rode back to Tularosa feeling a lot better. That hadn't been hard at all.

When he went on duty that night he said to Bobby Valdez, "You're all set," and would just as soon have let it go at that, but Valdez insisted that he tell him everything. He told him. There wasn't much to it—how the man just said, "All right." But Valdez seemed to be satisfied.

Friday morning Lyall stopped at the Regent Café for his breakfast. Elodie was serving the counter. She was frowning and muttering about being switched to mornings just the day before Bobby Valdez's hanging.

Lyall told her, "A nice girl like you don't want to see a hanging."

"It's the principle of it," she pouted. The principle being everybody in Tularosa was excited about Bobby Valdez's hanging whether they had a stomach for it or not.

"Lyall, don't you get scared up there alone with him?" she said with a little shiver that might have been partly real.

"What's there to be scared of? He's locked in a cell."

"What if one of his friends should come to help him?" Elodie said.

"How could a man like that have friends?"

"Well—I worry about you, Lyall."

Lyall stopped being calm, his whole face grinning. "Do you, Elodie?"

And that's what Lyall was thinking about when he went on duty Friday night. About Elodie.

Barney Groom was sitting at Bohannon's rolltop with his feet propped up, looking like he was ready to go to sleep. He said to Lyall, " 'Night's the last night. After the hanging we can relax a little."

Lyall went upstairs and sat down in the cane-bottom chair still thinking about Elodie: how she looked like a little girl when she pouted. A deputy marshal can probably support a wife, he thought.

Still, he wasn't so sure, since Bohannon hadn't mentioned salary to him yet.

Bobby Valdez said, "This is the night the priest comes."

Lyall looked up. "I almost forgot. Bet you feel better already."

"As if I have risen from the dead," Bobby Valdez said.

Later on—Lyall didn't have a timepiece on him but he estimated it was shortly after midnight—he heard the noise downstairs. Not a strange noise; it was just that it came unexpectedly in the quiet. He looked over at Bobby Valdez. Still asleep. For the next few minutes it was quiet again.

Then he heard footsteps on the stairs. It must be the priest, Lyall thought, getting up. He'd told the man to tell the priest to just walk by Barney, who'd probably be asleep, and if he wasn't, just explain the whole thing. So Barney was either asleep or had agreed.

Lyall wasn't prepared for the robed figure that stepped into the hallway. He'd expected a priest in a regular black suit; but then he remembered the priest at White Sands was the kind who wore a long robe and sandals.

Lyall said, "Father?"

That end of the hallway was darker and Lyall couldn't see him very well, and now as he came forward, Lyall still couldn't see his face because the cowl, the hood part of the robe, was up over his head. His arms were folded, with his hands up in the big sleeves.

"Father?"

"My son."

Lyall turned to the cell. "He's right here, Father." Valdez was standing at the bars and it struck Lyall suddenly that he hadn't heard Valdez get up. He turned his head to look at the priest and felt the gun barrel jab against his back.

"Place your weapon on the floor," the voice behind him said.

Bobby Valdez added, "My son," smiling now.

* * *

THE man behind Lyall reached past him to hand the ring of jail keys to Valdez. As he did, the cowl fell back and Lyall saw the man he'd talked to in White Sands. Sixto Henriquez.

Valdez said, "Whether you could get a robe was the thing that bothered me."

"A gift," Sixto said. "Hanging from his clothesline."

Lyall heard them, but he wouldn't let himself believe it. He wanted to say, "Wait a minute! Come on, now, this wasn't supposed to happen!"

Thinking of Bohannon and Elodie and the nights walking in the hallway, suddenly knowing he'd done the wrong thing, and too late to do anything about it. "Wait a minute . . . I was trying to help you!" But not saying it because it had been his own damn, stupid fault, and he was so aware of it now, he had to bite his lip to keep from yelling like a kid.

Valdez came out of the cell and picked up the shotgun Lyall had dropped. He said to Lyall, "Now my soul feels better."

He motioned Sixto toward the stairs. "Go first and see how it is with the old one."

"He sleep," Sixto said, and patted the barrel of his pistol.

"Let's be sure," Bobby Valdez said. He watched Sixto go through the doorway and listened to him start down the stairs. He looked at Lyall again, smiling. "You can mark this to experience."

If Valdez had backed out, holding the gun on Lyall, it wouldn't have happened. Even if he had just warned Lyall not to yell out or follow them—but he just turned and started walking out, *knowing* Lyall wouldn't dare try to stop him. And that's where Bobby Valdez made his mistake.

Lyall saw the man's back like a slap in the face. Even though he was scared, all of a sudden the knots inside him got too tight to stand. No thinking now about how it happened or what might happen—just an overpowering urge to get him!

He lunged at the back that was moving away. Three long

strides and his arms were around Valdez's neck, jerking, swinging him off his feet. He heard the shotgun clatter against the wall and hit the floor.

Tight against him, Bobby Valdez was turning his body. Lyall let go with one arm, brought it down quick, and drove it as hard as he could into the stomach almost against him. Valdez gasped and started to sag. Then footsteps on the stairs. Lyall scrambled for the shotgun, came up with it, and was at the doorway in time to see Sixto partway up the stairs, but as he raised the shotgun there was a swirl of robes and Sixto was at the bottom again. There was the sound of him running through the office, then nothing. Lyall came around fast. Valdez was almost on him, coming in low, diving for Lyall's legs—and he dove right into the shotgun barrel swung hard against his skull.

Lyall just stood there breathing for a minute before he dragged Bobby Valdez back to the cell and hefted him onto the bunk.

"Mr. Valdez," Lyall said out loud, "that's one *you* can mark to experience."

He went downstairs after that. Barney Groom was slouched in his chair, out cold. Lyall went to the doorway; he stepped outside to have a look around, and there was the friar's robe. It was in the road over by the hitch rack. Lyall gathered it up quick. He brought it back in the office and hung it beneath his rain slicker that was hooked on a peg. Then he breathed easier.

ELODIE turned away from the window. "It's over, Lyall," she said gravely. "They're starting to come out on the street."

Lyall glanced at her. "Is that right, Elodie?" he said, then put a little more ketchup on his eggs. Scrambled eggs were good that way; this morning they tasted even better. He ate them, half smiling, remembering Bohannon coming that morning. Bohannon frowning at Barney Groom, Barney trying to figure how he got his head bumped when he was sound asleep.

Then when they went upstairs—that was really something. Bohannon saying, "Maybe he's sick," seeing Valdez's white face and the side of his head swollen like a lopsided melon. And Barney Groom saying, "Maybe the same bug bit me, bit him."

Then what Bohannon said to him when they went downstairs again—that was the best.

"Now, Lyall, you done a fair job, though just sitting up there trying to keep awake wasn't much of a test. Tell you what"—Bohannon pulled a folded sheet of paper from his vest pocket—"last night I got a note from the White Sands marshal telling about the padre there getting his outfit stolen off the clothesline and would I assign a man to it since he's busy collecting taxes." Bohannon chuckled. "Have to keep the padres happy. Now, Lyall, if you could prove to me you're smart enough to get that padre's robe back for him, I'll see you're made a permanent deputy. And that's my solemn word."

Lyall pretended he didn't see Bohannon wink at Barney Groom. He said, "Yes, sir, I'll sure try." Just as serious as he could.

The Nagual

Ofelio Oso—who had been a vaquero most of his seventy years, but who now mended fences and drove a wagon for John Stam—looked down the slope through the jack pines seeing the man with his arms about the woman. They were in front of the shack which stood near the edge of the deep ravine bordering the west end of the meadow; and now Ofelio watched them separate lingeringly, the woman moving off, looking back as she passed the corral, going diagonally across the pasture to the trees on the far side, where she disappeared.

Now Mrs. Stam goes home, Ofelio thought, to wait for her husband.

The old man had seen them like this before, sometimes in the evening, sometimes at dawn as it was now with the first distant sun streak off beyond the Organ Mountains, and always when John Stam was away. This had been going on for months now, at least since Ofelio first began going up into the hills at night.

It was a strange feeling that caused the old man to do this; more an urgency, for he had come to a realization that there was little time left for him. In the hills at night a man can think clearly, and when a man believes his end is approaching there are many things to think about.

In his sixty-ninth year Ofelio Oso broke his leg. In the shock of a pain-stabbing moment it was smashed between horse and corral post as John Stam's cattle rushed the gate opening. He could no longer ride, after having done nothing else for more than fifty years; and with this came the certainty that his end was approaching. Since he was of no use to anyone, then only death remained. In his idleness he could feel its nearness and he thought of many things to prepare himself for the day it would come.

Now he waited until the horsebreaker, Joe Slidell, went into the shack. Ofelio limped down the slope through the pines and was crossing a corner of the pasture when Joe Slidell reappeared, leaning in the doorway with something in his hand, looking absently out at the few mustangs off at the far end of the pasture. His gaze moved to the bay stallion in the corral, then swung slowly until he was looking at Ofelio Oso.

The old man saw this and changed his direction, going toward the shack. He carried a blanket over his shoulder and wore a willow-root Chihuahua hat, and his hand touched the brim of it as he approached the loose figure in the doorway.

"At it again," Joe Slidell said. He lifted the bottle which he held close to his stomach and took a good drink. Then he lowered it, and his face contorted. He grunted, "Yaaaaa!" but after that he seemed relieved. He nodded to the hill and said, "How long you been up there?"

"Through the night," Ofelio answered. Which you well know, he thought. You, standing there drinking the whiskey that the woman brings.

Slidell wiped his mouth with the back of his hand, watching the old man through heavy-lidded eyes. "What do you see up there?"

"Many things."

"Like what?"

Ofelio shrugged. "I have seen devils."

Slidell grinned. "Big ones or little ones?"

"They take many forms."

Joe Slidell took another drink of the whiskey, not offering it to the old man, then said, "Well, I got work to do." He nodded to the corral where the bay stood looking over the rail, lifting and shaking his maned head at the man smell. "That horse," Joe Slidell said, "is going to finish gettin' himself broke today, one way or the other."

Ofelio looked at the stallion admiringly. A fine animal for long rides, for the killing pace, but for cutting stock, no. It would never be trained to swerve inward and break into a dead run at the feel of boot touching stirrup. He said to the horsebreaker, "That bay is much horse."

"Close to seventeen hands," Joe Slidell said, "if you was to get close enough to measure."

"This is the one for Señor Stam's use?"

Slidell nodded. "Maybe. If I don't ride him down to the house before supper, you bring up a mule to haul his carcass to the ravine." He jerked his thumb past his head, indicating the deep draw behind the shack. Ofelio had been made to do this before. The mule dragged the still faintly breathing mustang to the ravine edge. Then Slidell would tell him to push, while he levered with a pole, until finally the mustang went over the side down the steep-slanted seventy feet to the bottom.

OFELIO crossed the pasture, then down into the woods that fell gradually for almost a mile before opening again at the house and outbuildings of John Stam's spread. That jinete—that breaker of horses—is very sure of himself, the old man thought, moving through the trees. Both with horses and another man's wife. He must know I have seen them together, but it doesn't bother him. No, the old man thought now, it is something other than being sure of himself. I think it is stupidity. An intelligent man tames a wild horse with a great deal of respect, for he knows the horse is able to kill him. As for Mrs. Stam, considering her husband one would think he would treat her with even greater respect.

Marion Stam was on the back porch while Ofelio hitched the mules to the flatbed wagon. Her arms were folded across her chest and she watched the old man because his hitching the team was the only activity in the yard. Marion Stam's eyes were listless, darkly shadowed, making her thin face seem transparently frail, and this made her look older than her twenty-five years. But appearance made little difference to Marion. John Stam was nearly twice her age; and Joe Slidell—Joe spent all his time up at the horse camp, anything in a dress looked good to him.

But the boredom. This was the only thing to which Marion Stam could not resign herself. A house miles away from nowhere. Day following day, each one utterly void of anything resembling her estimation of living. John Stam at the table, eyes on his plate, opening his mouth only to put food into it. The picture of John Stam at night, just before blowing out the lamp, standing in his yellowish, musty-smelling long underwear. "Good night," a grunt, then the sound of even, open-mouthed breathing. Joe Slidell relieved some of the boredom. Some. He was young, not bad looking in a coarse way, but, Lord, he smelled like one of his horses!

"Why're you going now?" she called to Ofelio. "The stage's always late."

The old man looked up. "Someday it will be early. Perhaps this morning."

The woman shrugged, leaning in the door frame now, her arms still folded over her thin chest as Ofelio moved the team and wagon creaking out of the yard.

But the stage was not early; nor was it on time. Ofelio urged the mules into the empty station yard and pulled to a slow stop in front of the wagon shed that joined the station adobe. Two horses were in the shed with their muzzles munching at the hay rack.

Spainhower, the Butterfield agent, appeared in the doorway for a moment. Seeing Ofelio he said, "Seems you'd learn to leave about thirty minutes later." He turned away.

Ofelio smiled, climbing off the wagon box. He went through the door, following Spainhower into the sudden dimness, feeling the adobe still cool from the night and hearing a voice saying: "If Ofelio drove for Butterfield, nobody'd have to wait for stages." He recognized the voice and the soft laugh that followed and then he saw the man, Billy-Jack Trew, sitting on one end of the pine table with his boots resting on a Douglas chair.

Billy-Jack Trew was a deputy. Val Dodson, his boss, the Doña Ana sheriff, sat a seat away from him with his elbows on the pine boards. They had come down from Tularosa, stopping for a drink before going on to Mesilla.

Billy-Jack Trew said in Spanish, "Ofelio, how does it go?"

The old man nodded. "It passes well," he said, and smiled, because Billy-Jack was a man you smiled at even though you knew him slightly and saw him less than once in a month.

"Up there at that horse pasture," the deputy said, "I hear Joe Slidell's got some mounts of his own."

Ofelio nodded. "I think so. Señor Stam does not own all of them."

"I'm going to take me a ride up there pretty soon," Billy-Jack said, "and see what kind of money Joe's askin'. Way the sheriff keeps me going I need two horses, and that's a fact."

Ofelio could feel Spainhower looking at him, Val Dodson glancing now and then. One or the other would soon ask about his nights in the hills. He could feel this also. Everyone seemed to know about his going into the hills and everyone continued to question him about it, as if it were a foolish thing to do. Only Billy-Jack Trew would talk about it seriously.

* * *

At first, Ofelio had tried to explain the things he thought about: life and death a man's place, the temptations of the devil and man's obligation to God—all those things men begin to think about when there is little time left. And from the beginning Ofelio saw that they were laughing at him. Serious faces straining to hold back smiles. Pseudosincere questions that were only to lead him on. So after the first few times he stopped telling them what occurred to him in the loneliness of the night and would tell them whatever entered his mind, though much of it was still fact.

Billy-Jack Trew listened, and in a way he understood the old man. He knew that legends were part of a Mexican peon's life. He knew that Ofelio had been a vaquero for something like fifty years, with lots of lonesome time for imagining things. Anything the old man said was good listening, and a lot of it made sense after you thought about it awhile—so Billy-Jack Trew didn't laugh.

With a cigar stub clamped in the corner of his mouth, Spainhower's puffy face was dead serious looking at the old man. "Ofelio," he said, "this morning there was a mist ring over the gate. Now, I heard what that meant, so I kept my eyes open and sure'n hell here come a gang of elves through the gate dancin' and carryin' on. They marched right in here and hauled themselves up on that table."

Val Dodson said dryly, "Now, that's funny, just this morning coming down from Tularosa me and Billy-Jack looked up to see this be-ootiful she-devil running like hell for a cholla clump." He paused, glancing at Ofelio. "Billy-Jack took one look and was half out his saddle when I grabbed him."

Billy-Jack Trew shook his head. "Ofelio, don't mind that talk."

The old man smiled, saying nothing.

"You seen any more devils?" Spainhower asked him.

Ofelio hesitated, then nodded, saying, "Yes, I saw two devils this morning. Just at dawn."

Spainhower said, "What'd they look like?"

"I know," Val Dodson said quickly.

"Aw, Val," Billy-Jack said. "Leave him alone." He glanced at Ofelio, who was looking at Dodson intently, as if afraid of what he would say next.

"I'll bet," Dodson went on, "they had horns and hairy forked tails like that one me and Billy-Jack saw out on the sands." Spainhower laughed, then Dodson winked at him and laughed too.

BILLY-JACK Trew was watching Ofelio and he saw the tense expression on the old man's face relax. He saw the half-frightened look change to a smile of relief, and Billy-Jack was thinking that maybe a man ought to listen even a little closer to what Ofelio said. Like maybe there were double meanings to the things he said.

"Listen," Ofelio said, "I will tell you something else I have seen. A sight few men have ever witnessed." Ofelio was thinking: All right, give them something for their minds to work on.

"What I saw is a very hideous thing to behold, more frightening than elves, more terrible than devils." He paused, then said quietly, "What I saw was a nagual."

He waited, certain they had never heard of this, for it was an old Mexican legend. Spainhower was smiling, but half-squinting curiosity was in his eyes. Dodson was watching, waiting for him to go on. Still Ofelio hesitated and finally Spainhower said, "And what's a nagual supposed to be?"

"A nagual," Ofelio explained carefully, "is a man with strange powers. A man who is able to transform himself into a certain animal."

Spainhower said, too quickly, "What kind of an animal?"

"That," Ofelio answered, "depends upon the man. The animal is usually of his choice."

Spainhower's brow was deep furrowed. "What's so terrible about that?"

Ofelio's face was serious. "One can see you have never beheld a nagual. Tell me, what is more hideous, what is more terrible, than a man—who is made in God's image—becoming an animal?"

There was silence. Then Val Dodson said, "Aw—"

Spainhower didn't know what to say; he felt disappointed, cheated.

And into this silence came the faint rumbling sound. Billy-Jack Trew said, "Here she comes." They stood up, moving for the door, and soon the rumble was higher pitched—creaking, screeching, rattling, pounding—and the Butterfield stage was swinging into the yard. Spainhower and Dodson and Billy-Jack Trew went outside, Ofelio and his nagual forgotten.

No one had ever seen John Stam smile. Some, smiling themselves, said Marion must have at least once or twice, but most doubted even this. John Stam worked hard, twelve to sixteen hours a day, plus keeping a close eye on some business interests he had in Mesilla, and had been doing it since he'd first visually staked off his range six years before. No one asked where he came from and John Stam didn't volunteer any answers.

Billy-Jack Trew said Stam looked to him like a red dirt farmer with no business in cattle, but that was once Billy-Jack was wrong and he admitted it himself later. John Stam appeared one day with a crow-bait horse and twelve mavericks including a bull. Now, six years later, he had himself way over a thousand head and a jinete to break him all the horses he could ride.

Off the range, though, he let Ofelio Oso drive him wherever he went. Some said he felt sorry for Ofelio because the old Mexican had been a good hand in his day. Others said Marion put him up to it so she wouldn't have Ofelio hanging around the place all the time. There was always some talk about Marion, especially now with the cut-down crew up at the summer range, John Stam gone to tend his business about once a week, and only Ofelio and Joe Slidell there. Joe Slidell wasn't a bad-looking man.

The first five years John Stam allowed himself only two pleasures: he drank whiskey, though no one had ever seen him drinking it, only buying it; and every Sunday afternoon he'd ride to Mesilla for dinner at the hotel. He would always order the same thing, chicken, and always sit at the same table. He had been doing this for some time when Marion started waiting table there. Two years later, John Stam asked her to marry him as she was setting down his dessert and Marion said yes then and there. Some claimed the only thing he'd said to her before that was bring me the ketchup.

Spainhower said it looked to him like Stam was from a line of hardheaded Dutchmen. Probably his dad had made him work like a mule and never told him about women, Spainhower said, so John Stam never knew what it was like *not* to work and the first woman he looked up long enough to notice, he married. About everybody agreed Spainhower had something.

They were almost to the ranch before John Stam spoke. He had nodded to the men in the station yard, but gotten right up on the wagon seat. Spainhower asked him if he cared for a drink, but he shook his head. When they were in view of the ranch house—John Stam's leathery mask of a face looking straight ahead down the slope—he said, "Mrs. Stam is in the house?"

"I think so," Ofelio said, looking at him quickly, then back to the rumps of the mules.

"All morning?"

"I was not here all morning." Ofelio waited, but John Stam said no more. This was the first time Ofelio had been questioned about Mrs. Stam. Perhaps he overheard talk in Mesilla, he thought.

IN the yard John Stam climbed off the wagon and went into the house. Ofelio headed the team for the barn and stopped before the wide door to unhitch. The yard was quiet: he glanced at the house, which seemed deserted, though he knew John Stam was inside. Suddenly Mrs. Stam's voice was coming from the house, high pitched, excited, the words not clear. The sound stopped abruptly and it was quiet again. A few minutes later the screen door slammed and John Stam was coming across the yard, his great gnarled hands hanging empty, threateningly, at his sides.

He stopped before Ofelio and said bluntly, "I'm asking you if you've ever taken any of my whiskey."

"I have never tasted whiskey," Ofelio said and felt a strange guilt come over him in this man's gaze. He tried to smile. "But in the past I've tasted enough mescal to make up for it."

John Stam's gaze held. "That wasn't what I asked you."

"All right," Ofelio said. "I have never taken any."

"I'll ask you once more," John Stam said.

Ofelio was bewildered. "What would you have me say?"

For a long moment John Stam stared. His eyes were hard, though there was a weariness in them. He said, "I don't need you around here, you know."

"I have told the truth," Ofelio said simply.

The rancher continued to stare, a muscle in his cheek tightening and untightening. He turned abruptly and went back to the house.

The old man thought of the times he had seen Joe Slidell and the woman together and the times he had seen Joe Slidell drinking the whiskey she brought to him. Ofelio thought: He wasn't asking about whiskey, he was asking about his wife. But he could not come out with it. He knows something is going on behind his back, or else he suspicions it strongly, and he sees a relation between it and the whiskey that's being taken. I think I feel sorry for him; he hasn't learned to keep his woman and he doesn't know what to do.

Before supper Joe Slidell came down out of the woods trail on the bay stallion. He dismounted at the back porch and he and John Stam talked for a few minutes looking over the horse. When Joe Slidell left, John Stam, holding the bridle, watched him disappear into the woods and for a long time after, he stood there staring at the trail that went up through the woods.

Just before dark John Stam rode out of the yard on the bay stallion. Later—it was full dark then—Ofelio heard the screen door again. He rose from his bunk in the end barn stall and opened the big door an inch, in time to see Marion Stam's dim form pass into the trees.

He has left, Ofelio thought, so she goes to the jinete. He shook his head thinking: This is none of your business. But it remained in his mind and later, with his blanket over his shoulder, he went into the hills where he could think of these things more clearly.

He moved through the woods hearing the night sounds which seemed far away and his own footsteps in the leaves that were close, but did not seem to belong to him; then he was on the pine slope and high up he felt the breeze. For a time he listened to the soft sound of it in the jack pines. Tomorrow there will be rain, he thought. Sometime in the afternoon.

He stretched out on the ground, rolling the blanket behind his head, and looked up at the dim stars thinking: More and more every day, *viejo,* you must realize you are no longer of any value. The horsebreaker is not afraid of you, the men at the station laugh and take nothing you say seriously, and finally Señor Stam, he made it very clear when he said, "I don't need you around here."

Then why does he keep me—months now since I have been dismounted—except out of charity? He is a strange man. I suppose I owe him something, something more than feeling sorry for him which does him no good. I think we have something in common. I can feel sorry for both of us. He laughed at this and tried to discover other things they might have in common. It relaxed him, his imagination wandering, and soon he dozed off with the cool breeze on his face, not remembering to think about his end approaching.

TO the east, above the chimneys of the Organ range, morning light began to gray-streak the day. Ofelio opened his eyes, hearing the horse moving through the trees below him: hooves clicking the small stones and the swish of pine branches. He thought of Joe Slidell's mustangs. One of them has wandered up the slope. But then, the unmistakable squeak of saddle leather and he sat up, tensed. It could be anyone, he thought. Almost anyone.

He rose, folding the blanket over his shoulder, and made his way down the slope silently, following the sound of the horse, and when he reached the pasture he saw the dim shape of it moving toward the shack, a tall shadow gliding away from him in the half light.

The door opened. Joe Slidell came out, closing it quickly behind him. "You're up early," he said, yawning, pulling a suspender over his shoulder. "How's that horse carry you? He learned his manners yesterday . . . won't give you no trouble. If he does, you let me have him back for about an hour." Slidell looked above the horse to the rider. "Mr. Stam, why're you lookin' at me like that?" He squinted up in the dimness. "Mr. Stam, what's the matter? You feelin' all right?"

"Tell her to come out," John Stam said.

"What?"

"I said tell her to come out."

"Now, Mr. Stam—" Slidell's voice trailed off, but slowly a grin formed on his mouth. He said, almost embarrassedly, "Well, Mr. Stam, I didn't think you'd mind." One man talking to another now. "Hell, it's only a little Mex gal from Mesilla. It gets lonely here and—"

John Stam spurred the stallion violently; the great stallion lunged, rearing, coming down with thrashing hooves on the screaming man. Slidell went down covering his head, falling against the shack boards. He clung there gasping as the stallion backed off; the next moment he was crawling frantically, rising, stumbling, running; he looked back seeing John Stam spurring and he screamed again as the stallion ran him down. John Stam reined in a tight circle and came back over the motionless form. He dismounted before the shack and went inside.

Go away, quickly, Ofelio told himself, and started for the other side of the pasture, running tensed, not wanting to hear what he knew would come. But he could not outrun it, the scream came turning him around when he was almost to the woods.

Marion Stam was in the doorway, then running across the yard, swerving as she saw the corral suddenly in front of her. John Stam was in the saddle spurring the stallion after her, gaining as she followed the rail circle of the corral. Now she was looking back, seeing the stallion almost on top of her. The stallion swerved suddenly as the woman screamed going over the edge of the ravine.

Ofelio ran to the trees before looking back. John Stam had dismounted. He removed bridle and saddle from the bay and put these in the shack. Then he picked up a stone and threw it at the stallion, sending it galloping for the open pasture.

The old man was breathing in short gasps from the running, but he hurried now through the woods and did not stop until he reached the barn. He sat on the bunk listening to his heart, feeling it in his chest. Minutes later John Stam opened the big door. He stood looking down at Ofelio while the old man's mind repeated: Mary, Virgin and Mother, until he heard the rancher say, "You didn't see or hear anything all night. I didn't leave the house, did I?"

Ofelio hesitated, then nodded slowly as if committing this to memory. "You did not leave the house."

John Stam's eyes held threateningly before he turned and went out. Minutes later Ofelio saw him leave the house with a shotgun under his arm. He crossed the yard and entered the woods. Already he is unsure, Ofelio thought, especially of the woman, though the fall was at least seventy feet.

* * *

WHEN he heard the horse come down out of the woods it was barely more than an hour later. Ofelio looked out, expecting to see John Stam on the bay, but it was Billy-Jack Trew walking his horse into the yard. Quickly the old man climbed the ladder to the loft. The deputy went to the house first and called out. When there was no answer he approached the barn and called Ofelio's name.

He's found them! But what brought him? Ah, the old man thought, remembering, he wants to buy a horse. He spoke of that yesterday. But he found them instead. Where is Señor Stam? Why didn't he see him? He heard the deputy call again, but still Ofelio did not come out. He remained crouched in the darkness of the barn loft until he heard the deputy leave.

The door opened and John Stam stood below in the strip of outside light.

Resignedly, Ofelio said, "I am here," looking down, thinking: He was close all the time. He followed the deputy back and if I had called he would have killed both of us. And he is very capable of killing.

John Stam looked up, studying the old man. Finally he said, "You were there last night; I'm sure of it now . . . else you wouldn't be hiding, afraid of admitting something. You were smart not to talk to him. Maybe you're remembering you owe me something for keeping you on, even though you're not good for anything." He added abruptly, "You believe in God?"

Ofelio nodded.

"Then," John Stam said, "swear to God you'll never mention my name in connection with what happened."

Ofelio nodded again, resignedly, thinking of his obligation to this man. "I swear it," he said.

The rain came in the late afternoon, keeping Ofelio inside the barn. He crouched in the doorway, listening to the soft hissing of the rain in the trees, watching the puddles forming in the wagon tracks. His eyes would go to the house, picturing John Stam inside alone with his thoughts and waiting. They will come. Perhaps the rain will delay them, Ofelio thought, but they will come.

The sheriff will say, Mr. Stam this is a terrible thing we have to tell you. What? Well, you know the stallion Joe Slidell was breaking? Well, it must have got loose. It looks like Joe tried to catch him and . . . Joe got under his hooves. And, Mrs. Stam was there . . . we figured she was up to look at your new horse—saying this with embarrassment. She must have become frightened when it happened and she ran. In the dark she went over the side of the ravine. Billy-Jack found them this morning. . . .

He did not hear them because of the rain. He was staring at a puddle and when he looked up there was Val Dodson and Billy-Jack Trew. It was too late to climb to the loft.

Billy-Jack smiled. "I was around earlier, but I didn't see you." His hat was low, shielding his face from the light rain, as was Dodson's.

Ofelio could feel himself trembling. He is watching now from a window. Mother of God, help me.

Dodson said, "Where's Stam?"

Ofelio hesitated, then nodded toward the house.

"Come on," Dodson said. "Let's get it over with."

Billy-Jack Trew leaned closer, resting his forearm on the saddle horn. He said gently, "Have you seen anything more since yesterday?"

Ofelio looked up, seeing the wet smiling face and another image that was in his mind—a great stallion in the dawn light—and the words came out suddenly, as if forced from his mouth. He said, "I saw a nagual!"

Dodson groaned. "Not again," and nudged his horse with his knees.

"Wait a minute," Billy-Jack said quickly. Then to Ofelio, "This nagual, you actually saw it?"

The old man bit his lips. "Yes."

"It was an animal you saw, then."

"It was a nagual."

Dodson said, "You stand in the rain and talk crazy. I'm getting this over with."

Billy-Jack swung down next to the old man. "Listen a minute, Val." To Ofelio, gently again, "But it was in the form of an animal?"

Ofelio's head nodded slowly.

"What did the animal look like?"

"It was," the old man said slowly, not looking at the deputy, "a great stallion." He said quickly, "I can tell you no more than that."

Dodson dismounted.

Billy-Jack said, "And where did the nagual go?"

Ofelio was looking beyond the deputy toward the house. He saw the back door open and John Stam came out on the porch, the shotgun cradled in his arm. Ofelio continued to stare. He could not speak as it went through his mind: He thinks I have told them!

Seeing the old man's face, Billy-Jack turned, then Dodson.

Stam called, "Ofelio, come here!"

Billy-Jack said, "Stay where you are," and now his voice was not gentle. But the hint of a smile returned as he unfastened the two lower buttons of his slicker and suddenly he called, "Mr. Stam! You know what a nagual is?" He opened the slicker all the way and drew a tobacco plug from his pants pocket.

Dodson whispered hoarsely, "What's the matter with you!"

Billy-Jack was smiling. "I'm only askin' a simple question."

John Stam did not answer. He was staring at Ofelio.

"Mr. Stam," Billy-Jack Trew called, "before I tell you what a nagual is I want to warn you I can get out a Colt a helluva lot quicker than you can swing a shotgun."

OFELIO Oso died at the age of ninety-three on a ranch outside Tularosa. They said about him he sure told some tall ones—about devils, and about seeing a nagual hanged for murder in Mesilla . . . whatever that meant . . . but he was much man. Even at his age the old son relied on no one, wouldn't let a soul do anything for him, and died owing the world not one plugged peso. And wasn't the least bit afraid to die, even though he was so old. He used to say, "Listen, if there is no way to tell when death will come, then why should one be afraid of it?"

TROUBLE AT RINDO'S STATION

CHAPTER ONE

There was a time when Bonito might have fired at the rider far below on the road, and for no other reason than to test his carbine, since the rider was a white man. He had done this many times before—sometimes for a shirt, or a fresh horse, usually for ammunition, though a reason was not necessary. But now there was something on the Mescalero's mind. He held his fire and urged his pony down the piñon slope.

From high up he had recognized Ross Corsen—the lank figure slouched in the McClellan saddle, head down against the glare, hat low over his eyes. And now, as the Mescalero closed in, Corsen looked up, though he had seen him long before, when Bonito was still high up the slope.

"*Sik-isn,*" Bonito said. The word was a hiss between his lips. Strands of hair hung from the shadow of a high-crowned hat, thick, glistening hair accentuating the yellowish cast of his skin and the pock scars that roughened heavy-boned features. A frayed, sweat-stained shirt covered his chest, but his legs were naked, for he wore only a breechclout, and the curled toes of his moccasins hung beneath the pony's belly, ridiculously close to the ground. A carbine was across his lap.

Ross Corsen smiled at the Apache's greeting and studied the broad, ugly face. "Now you call me *brother*," he said in Spanish. "You must want something." He had not seen the Mescalero in almost a year, not since the four-day chase down to the border, and a glimpse of Bonito far off, not running any longer because he was safely in Mexico. Bonito had killed two Coyotero policemen during a tulapai drunk. That had started it. On the run for the border, he killed two more men, plus four horses that didn't belong to him. Now he was back and Corsen studied him, wondering why.

The Apache spoke a slow, guttural Spanish and said, as if in the middle of his thoughts, "We have suffered unfairly from your hand; all of us have"—he used the Apache word *tinneh*, which meant all of the people and in its meaning described the blood tie which bound them together—"and from the other man, the one who directs you. You think only of yourselves."

"And when did you begin thinking of others?" Corsen said.

"Those are my people at Pinaleño," Bonito answered him.

Corsen shrugged. "I won't argue with you. What you do now is no concern of mine. I can't do a thing to you or for you, but maybe suggest you go home and get drunk, which is what you'll probably do anyway."

"And where is our home, Cor-sen?"

"You know as well as I do."

"At San Carlos, where there is little to eat?"

Corsen nodded to the Maynard carbine across the Apache's lap. "Maybe in Mexico. You can't have one of those at San Carlos."

"Yes, in Sonora and Chihuahua where it is a business of profit to take the hair of the Apache, the government paying for our scalps."

Corsen shook his head. "Look, I no longer am in charge of the Pinaleño Reservation. The government man has discharged me." He thought for words that would explain it clearly to the Apache.

"He is the one, Mr. Sellers, who has taken your guns and decided that you live on government beef."

"Some of the government beef," Bonito corrected. "He sells most of it to others for his own profit."

"That is not true of all reservations. You know I treated your people fairly."

"But you are no longer there and soon it will be true of all reservations."

The words were familiar to Corsen. No, not so much the words as the idea: he had argued this very thing with Sellers three days before, straining his patience to explain to the Bureau of Indian Affairs supervisor exactly what an Apache is. What kind of thinking animal he is. How much abuse he will take before all the peace talks in the world will not stop him. And he had lost the argument because, even if reason was not on Sellers's side, authority was. He threw it in Sellers's face, accusing him of selling government rations for his own profit, and Sellers laughed, daring him to prove it—then fired him. He would have quit. You can't go on working for a man like that. He decided that he didn't care anyway.

For that matter it was strange that he should. Ross Corsen knew Apaches because he had fought them. He had been in charge of the Coyotero trackers at Fort Thomas for four years. And after that, for three years—until the day before yesterday—he had been in charge of the Mescalero Subagency at Pinaleño, thirty miles south of Thomas.

He didn't care. The hell with it. That's what he told himself. Still he kept wondering what had brought Bonito back. He thought: Leave him alone. If he came back to help his people, let him work it out his own Apache way. You tried. But instead he asked carefully, "Why would a warrior of Bonito's stature return now to a reservation? They haven't forgotten what you did. If you're caught, they'll hang you."

"Then I would die—which the people are doing now on the

reservation, under Bil-Clin who calls himself their chief." Bonito's eyes half closed and he went on. "Let me tell you a story, Cor-sen, which happened long ago. There was a young man of the Mescalero, who was a great hunter and slayer of his enemies. From raids to Mexico he would return to his rancheria with countless ponies and often with women who would then do his bidding. And many of these he gave to his chief out of honor.

"One day he returned from war gravely wounded and his hands empty, but he noticed that still this chief, who was the son of a chief and he the son of one before him, received more spoils than anyone, yet without endangering himself by being present on the raid. Now this grieved the warrior. He would not offend his chief, but he was beginning to think this unjust.

"On a day after his wound had healed, he was walking in a deep canyon with this in his thoughts and as it grew unbearable he cried out to U-sen why should this be, and immediately a spirit appeared before him. Now, this spirit questioned the warrior, asking him how a man became chief, and the warrior answered that it was blood handed from father to son. And the spirit asked him where in the natural order was this found? Did one lobo wolf lead the pack because of his blood? The warrior thought deeply of this and gradually he realized that chieftainship of blood was not just. It was the place of the bravest warrior to lead—not for his own sake, but for the good of all.

"You know what he did, Cor-sen?" Bonito paused then. "He returned to the rancheria and challenged his chief and fought him to the death with his knife. Two others opposed him, and he killed these also. With this the people realized that it was as it should be and the warrior was acclaimed chief of Mescaleros.

"That was the first time, Cor-sen, but it has happened many times since. When one is no longer deserving to be chief, then another opposes him. Sometimes the opposed chief steps aside; often it is settled with a knife."

Corsen was silent. Then he said, "At Pinaleño Bil-Clin is still a strong chief. And he is wise enough not to lead his people in a war he cannot win."

Bonito's heavy face creased into a grim smile. "Is he strong . . . and wise?" Then he said, his tone changing, "Do you go away from here?"

"Perhaps." Corsen looked at the Apache curiously.

"It would be wise," Bonito said, "if you went far from here." He turned his pony then and loped off.

ROSS Corsen followed the road to Rindo's and the Mescalero's parting words hung in his mind like a threat, and for a while the words made him angry. The running of their tribe was no concern of his. Not now. But it implied more than just Bonito opposing Bil-Clin. There was something else. Bonito was a renegade. He was vicious even in the eyes of his own people. Not the type to be followed as a leader unless the people were desperate. Unless he came just at the right time. And it occurred to Corsen: like now, with a man they don't know taking over the agency . . . and with unrest on every reservation in Arizona, I'd like to stay, just to handle Bonito. . . . But again, the hell with it. Working under Sellers wasn't worth it.

He planned to go up to Whipple Barracks and talk to someone about a guide contract. He would leave his horse at Rindo's and catch the stage there, and while he was waiting he'd have a while to be with Katie.

CHAPTER TWO

The Hatch & Hodges' Central Mail section had headquarters at Fort McDowell. From there, one route angled northwest to Prescott. The Central Mail swung in an arc southeast. From McDowell the route skirted the Superstitions to Apache Junction, then continued on, changing teams at Florence, White Tanks, Gila Ford, and Rindo's. Thomas was the last stop, the southern terminal.

Rindo's Station had been constructed with the Apaches in mind. An oblong, thick-walled adobe building had an open stable shed at one end. The corral, holding the spare stage teams, connected behind the stable. And circling the station, out fifty-odd yards, was an adobe wall. It was thick, chest high. At the east end of the yard a stand of aspen had been hacked down and only the trunks remained. Beyond the wall the country was flat on three sides—alkali dust and heat waves shimmering over stubbles of desert growth—but to the east the ground rose gradually, barren, pale yellow climbing into deep green where piñon sprouted from the hillside.

Corsen had skirted the base of the hill and now he was in sight of Rindo's. He nudged his mount to a trot.

Someone was in the doorway. Another figure came from the dark line of the shed and moved to the gate which was in the north side of the wall. He could make out the man in the doorway now—Billy Teachout, the station agent. And as the gate swung open there was the Mexican, Delgado, in white peon clothes.

"Hiiiii, man!"

"Señor Delgado, keeper of the horses!"

Corsen reached down and slapped the old Mexican's thin shoulder, then dismounted.

"God of my life, it has been months!"

"Three or four weeks."

"It seems months."

Corsen grinned at the old man, at the tired eyes that were now stretched open showing thin lines of veins, smiling at the sight of a friend.

Billy Teachout moved a few steps into the yard, thumbs hooked behind his suspender straps. "Ross, get in here out of the sun!"

"Let the keeper of the horses take yours," Delgado said, still smiling. "We will talk together after."

"I will look forward to it," Corsen said.

Corsen followed the station agent's broad back into the house and opened his eyes wide to the interior dimness. It was dark after the sun glare. He pushed his hat brim from his eyes and stood looking at the familiar whitewashed walls, the oblong pine table and Douglas chairs at one end of the room, the squat stove in the middle, and the red-painted pine bar at the other end. Billy Teachout edged his large frame sideways, with an effort, through the narrow bar opening.

"You wouldn't have beer," Corsen said.

"It's about six months to Christmas," Billy answered, and leaned his forearms onto the bar. He was in no hurry. Time meant little, and it showed in his loose, heavy build, in his round, clean-shaven face that he most always kept out of the sun's reach unless it was stage time. He had worked in the Prescott office until Al Rindo's death two years before, then had been transferred here. Al Rindo had died of a heart attack, but Billy Teachout said it was sunstroke and he'd be damned if he'd let it happen to him. He had Katie to think of, his sister's girl who had come to live with him after her folks passed on.

It wasn't a bad life. Five stages a week for him and Katie; Delgado and his wife to take care of. Change horses; keep them curried; feed the passengers. Nothing to it—as long as the Apaches minded.

"You can have yellow mescal or bar whiskey," Billy said.

"One's as bad as the other." Corsen put his elbows on the bar. "Whiskey."

"Kill any bugs you got."

Corsen took a drink and then rolled a cigarette. "Where's Katie?"

"Prettyin'. She saw you two miles away. After Delgado all week, you don't look so bad."

CORSEN grinned, relaxing the hard line of his jaw. A young face, leathery and immobile until a smile would soften the eyes that were used to sun glare, and ease the set face that talked eye to eye with the Apache and showed nothing. Corsen knew his business. He knew the Apache—his language, often even his thoughts—and the Apache respected him for it. Corsen, the Indian agent. He could make natural-born raiders at least half satisfied with a barren government land tract. The Corsens were few and far between, even in Arizona.

"Billy, I just saw Bonito."

"God—he's returned to the reservation?"

"I don't know—or much care. I'm leaving."

"What?"

"Sellers fired me day before yesterday. He's got somebody else for the job."

"Got somebody else! Those are Mescaleros!"

"I'm through arguing with him. Sellers is reservation supervisor. He can run things how he likes and hire who he likes. I should have quit long ago."

"Who's taking your place?"

"A man named Verbiest."

"Somebody looking for some extra change."

"He might be all right."

Billy Teachout shook his head wearily. To him it was another example of cheap politics, knowing the right people. Agency posts were being handed out to men who cared nothing for the Indians. There was profit to be made by short-rationing their charges and selling the government beef and grain to homesteaders, or back to the Army. Even that had been done.

"Sellers has been trying to get rid of you for a long time.

Finally he made it," Billy Teachout said. He shook his head again. "Your Mescaleros aren't going to take kindly to this."

"Verbiest might know what he's doing," Corsen said. Then, "But if he doesn't, you better keep your windows shut till he hangs a few of them and they calm down again."

"Where you going? I might just close up and go with you."

"What about the stage line?"

"The hell with it. I'm getting too old for this kind of thing."

Corsen smiled. "I'm going up to Whipple to see about a guide contract."

"So if you can't nurse them, you fight them."

"Either one's a living."

"Ross—"

He turned to see Katie standing in the doorway that led to the kitchen. His gaze rested on her face—tanned, freckled, clear eyed, a face that smiled often, but now held on his earnestly.

"Ross, I heard what you were telling Billy."

"I can't work for that man anymore."

"Can't you find something else around here?"

"There isn't anything."

"Fort Thomas. Why can't you guide out of there?"

Corsen shrugged. "There's a chance, but I'd still have to go through the department commander's office at Whipple."

"Ross . . ." Her voice was a whisper.

It showed on her face that was not eager now and seemed even pale beneath the sun coloring. The face of a girl, sensitive nose and mouth, but in her clear, blue, serious eyes the awareness of a woman.

Katie was nineteen. She had known Ross Corsen for almost three years, meeting him the day after she had arrived to live with her uncle. And she expected to marry him, even though he never mentioned it. She knew how he felt. Ross didn't have to say a word. It was in the way he looked at her, in the way he had kissed her for the first time only a few weeks ago—a small, soft, lingering, inexperienced kiss. She loved Corsen; very simply she loved him, because he was a man, respected as a man, and because he was a boy at the same time. Perhaps just as she was girl and woman in one.

"Are you coming back?"

"Of course I am."

"What if you're stationed somewhere far away?"

"I'll come and get you," he answered.

Billy Teachout looked at them, from one to the other. "Maybe I've been inside too much." To the girl he said, "Has he behaved himself?"

"Billy," Corsen said, "I was going to ask you. This is all of a sudden—" Then, to Katie, "I'm taking the stage." He smiled faintly. "If I leave my horse here, I've got to come back."

"THE stage!" Delgado was in the doorway momentarily. The screen door banged and he was gone.

It came in from the east, a thin sand trail, a shadow leading the dust that rose furiously into a billowing tail.

Delgado was swinging out with the grayed wooden gate.

Then the stage, rumbling in an arc toward the opening, and the hoarse-throated voice of Ernie Ball, the driver,

"Delgadooo!"

The little Mexican was in front of the lead horses now, reaching for reins close to the bit rings.

"Delgado, you half-a-man! Hold 'em, *chico*!"

Ernie Ball was off the box, grinning, wiping the back of a gnarled hand over his mouth, smoothing the waxed tips of his full mustache. His palm slapped the thin wood of the coach door, then swung it open to bang on its hinges.

"Rindo's Station!"

Billy Teachout came out carrying a paintbrush and a bucket half full of axle grease. Ross and Katie were already outside.

"You're late," Billy told the driver.

Ernie Ball pulled a dull gold watch from his vest pocket. "Seven minutes! That's the earliest I've been late." He replaced the watch and dipped a thumb and forefinger daintily into the grease bucket, then twirled the tips of his mustache between the fingers.

"Ross, how are you? Katie, honey." He touched his hat brim to the girl.

Ross Corsen was looking past the stage driver to the man coming out of the coach—the familiar black broadcloth suit and flat-crowned hat. The man reached the ground and there it was, the bland expression, the carefully trimmed mustache. He carried a leather business case tightly and carefully under his arm.

W. F. Sellers. Field supervisor. Southwest Area. Bureau of Indian Affairs.

"Fifteen minutes," Ernie Ball was saying, "for those going on. Time enough for a drink if the innkeeper's feelin' right. Hey, Billy!" His voice changed as he turned to Sellers. "End of the line for you and your friend."

Another man was out of the coach. He stepped down uncertainly and moved next to Sellers. Two others came down, squinting at the glare—thin-hipped, sun-darkened men in range clothes. They stretched and looked about idly, then moved beyond the back of the stage, walking the stiffness from their legs.

Sellers had not taken his eyes from Corsen.

"I thought you might have had the politeness of staying to meet your successor."

Corsen looked at the other man now. "Mr. Verbiest," he said, "I hope you know what you're doing."

"I've instructed Mr. Verbiest on how the agency should be run," Sellers said.

"Then you both ought to make a nice profit," Billy Teachout said mildly.

Sellers stared at him narrowly. "All we want from you is a couple of horses."

"What for?"

"None of your damn business."

Verbiest said, smiling, "We're riding north to the San Carlos Agency. I'd like to take a look at how a smooth-running reservation operates."

"Sellers'll learn you without riding way up there," Ernie Ball said. "All you need is some spare weights to heavy your scale for when you're passing out the 'Paches their beef." Ernie laughed and looked at Teachout. "Hey, Billy?"

"You're insinuating something that could get you into a great deal of trouble in court," Sellers told the stage driver.

"Insinuatin'!"

Sellers turned on Billy Teachout. "I said two horses. Good ones!"

"I'm not the stable hand. Wait for Delgado or get them yourself."

Sellers's face showed no reaction. But he said quietly, "Mr. Teachout, you're through here—as of the next time I get to Prescott."

The station agent shrugged. "While I'm waiting, I'll go inside and pour drinks for those that wants."

Corsen relaxed, exhaling slowly, and watched them all go inside. It was a relief not to have to put up with Sellers anymore. Just seeing him had made his stomach tighten. He glanced at Katie.

"This is a poor way to say good-bye."

"For how long, Ross?"

"Maybe a few months."

The screen door slammed. Corsen remembered the two men in range clothes then. They must have just gone in. Then he was looking at Katie, at the expression changing on her face, eyes alive, looking at something behind him. He turned sharply.

Standing a few feet away was one of the men in range clothes. He stood with his legs spread, as if bracing himself, a short man in faded Levi's, holding a pistol dead on Corsen's stomach.

CHAPTER THREE

"Raise your hands up." He motioned with the pistol. "You too, honey." He came forward slowly.

"I'm not armed," Corsen said.

"Take your coat off and drop it."

Corsen took off the worn buckskin and let it fall. He backed up as the man motioned with the pistol, then watched him trample on the coat to make certain there was no gun in it.

"Inside now," the man said.

His partner stood one legged, his left boot on a chair, leaning slightly, elbow on knee, hand holding the pistol idly.

Billy Teachout was behind the bar. Ernie Ball, Sellers, and Verbiest stood in front of it, all with their arms raised. Three pistols were on the floor, along with the business case Sellers had been carrying. Ygenia, Delgado's wife, stood in the kitchen doorway, unable to move.

The one on the chair waved Ross and Katie toward the others. They moved across the room and stood by the front window. "Buz," he said then, "round up that Mexican. He's outside somewhere."

Ernie Ball was squinting at the gunman. "Your face is starting to ring a bell, but your name don't register."

"How would you know my name?"

"You entered Ed Fisher in the book when you paid your fare at Thomas."

The gunman shrugged. "That'll do. . . . What're you carrying this trip?"

"Mail."

"That all?"

"Swear to God. It's on the rack if you want to look."

The one called Buz came in through the kitchen, pushing past the Mexican woman.

"He ain't in sight. Not anywhere."

Corsen glanced out at the yard. Just the stage was there. The horses had been taken away, but the change team had not yet been harnessed.

"That's all right," Fisher said. "Hand me your gun and go through their pockets. We got to move."

He watched Buz search them, stuffing bills and coins into his pockets as he went along. "About how much?" he asked when he had finished.

"Not more than a hundred and fifty."

"What about that satchel there?" He pointed to the business case on the floor.

INSTANTLY Sellers said, "Those are government papers!" More calmly he said, "Bureau statistics."

Ed Fisher said, "Buz, open it up."

The gunman lifted the case and looked at Fisher with surprise. "If there's writin' in here, it's cut on stone." He carried it to the table and unfastened the straps and opened it. He brought out something folded in newspaper and unwrapped it carefully. A leather pouch. He pulled the thongs quickly, eagerly, and dumped the pouch upside-down on the table. The coins came out in a shower.

"Ed! Mint silver!"

Fisher was grinning at Sellers. "How much, Buz?"

"Four, five, six pouches . . . about two thousand!"

Corsen was looking out of the window. There was something, a movement high up on the slope. Then, hearing Buz, he glanced quickly at Sellers. That was it, plain enough. Sellers didn't make that kind of money with a Bureau job. It could only come from selling Indian rations. But now, as the others watched Buz at the table, Corsen's eyes narrowed, looking out into the glare again, and now he could make out the movement. Far out, coming down from the slope, reaching the flat stretch now, were tiny specks, dots against the sand glare that he knew were riders. They were coming from where he had seen Bonito that morning, and suddenly, abruptly, Corsen realized who the riders were.

Ed Fisher was saying, "Get two horses and run off the others. One's saddled already." He looked at the men in front of him. "Whose mount is that in the shed, the chestnut?"

Corsen looked from the window as the screen door slammed behind Buz going out. "The chestnut's mine," he said.

"Thanks for the use."

"You're not going anywhere."

Fisher looked at him quickly, then smiled, his eyes going to Katie. "If you want to play Mister Brave for your girl, wait for when I got more time."

"It's not me that's stopping you," Corsen said, "but I'll tell you again—you're not going anywhere."

"You can talk plainer than that."

"All right. Call to your partner."

"What'll that prove?"

"Just see if he's still there."

Fisher yelled. "Hey—Buz!"

There was a silence, then boot scuffing and Buz was at the door. "What?"

Fisher looked at Corsen, then back to Buz. "Nothing. Hurry up." Buz looked at him queerly and moved off again.

"Now what?" Fisher said.

"It'll come," Corsen said. "He hasn't seen them yet."

"Seen who?"

And there it was, as if answering his question—the sound of running, boots on packed sand. Buz's voice yelling, hoarse with panic. Then he was at the door, stumbling against it. " *'Paches!*"

"STAY where you are!" Fisher held his pistol on the men at the bar and backed toward the door. He glanced out. "How many?"

"Six of them! Let me in!"

"Keep watching!"

Through the window Corsen could now see the cluster of riders plainly, walking their ponies. They were in no hurry—not six, but five, coming across the flat stretch.

"They're peaceful." It was Sellers who said this. "There hasn't been a war party around here in over a year."

Corsen looked at him. "They're twenty miles over the reservation boundary."

"They've been known to wander, but when they do, they have to be taught a lesson. That was your trouble, Corsen—too easy on them. Verbiest, you come along with me and see how it's done."

Corsen said quietly, "Bonito doesn't learn very fast."

"Bonito!" Sellers showed surprise. "He's down in the Madres."

"He wasn't this morning when I talked to him."

"And you're just now telling me?"

"I was fired."

Fisher glanced out the door again, then back, his eyes stopping on Sellers. "Have you got something to do with them?"

Sellers did not answer, but Teachout said, "He's with the Bureau of Indian Affairs."

"Then this is your party, mister," Fisher said, looking at Sellers.

"I'm not obligated to confront known hostiles. That's common sense."

Fisher moved out of the doorway. "You don't have a choice. Get out there and find out what they want." He waved the long-barreled pistol. "Come on, all of you except the women. They stay here."

In the yard Corsen glanced back once at the two outlaws in the doorway. Then they had reached the adobe wall and his gaze swung back to the five Mescaleros who had reined in a hundred paces beyond the wall.

Bonito was a pony's length ahead of the others. He did not resemble the man Corsen had talked to earlier. The flop-brimmed hat was gone and now his coarse face was paint streaked—a line of ochre from ear to ear crossing the bridge of his nose, another over his chin. His headband was yellow, bright against long hair glistening with oil. Only one thing about him was the same—the Maynard across his lap.

Behind him were Bil-Clin, chief at the Pinaleño Agency, Bil-Clin's son, Sunshine, and two other Indians. All four were armed with old-model carbines.

Corsen's eyes remained on the Mescaleros, but he said to Sellers, "Let's see you go out and teach them a lesson."

Sellers did not reply at first. He kept his eyes on the five Apaches, waiting, expecting them to make a move. Then he said, "All right. Ask him what he wants."

Corsen hesitated. He wanted to make it hard for Sellers, not offer any assistance, but there was Katie and the others to think of.

He boosted himself over the wall, then motioned to the Apaches to come on.

They moved forward, Bonito still in the lead, and when they were less than ten feet from the wall Bonito raised his arm and they stopped there.

"Corsen, we speak to each other again."

"But this time not by accident."

"You told me before that you were not with this one now." Bonito's eyes shifted to Sellers.

"These are unordinary circumstances," Corsen answered. "Tell me why you are here and I'll relate it to him."

Bonito waited, then nodded toward Sellers. "There is the reason."

"What would you have me tell him?"

"Tell him that he will come with us, until *pesh-e-gar*—many of them—are brought here tomorrow."

"Rifles!"

"Enough for as many of us that could stand in line from here to the house there. And many bullets for the *pesh-e-gar*. This one"—he nodded again to Sellers—"will remain with us until they are brought and the ones who bring them depart again. Then he will be released and my people will go with me from Pinaleño across the Bravos and there we will fight the Nakai-yes."

Corsen turned to the others. "He says he needs guns to make war on the Mexicans." Then to Bonito. "You would, of course, not use the guns on this side of the Bravos."

Bonito nodded solemnly.

"The guns would have to be acquired at Fort Thomas. How do you know the Army would let you have them? Perhaps this man isn't worth a hundred rifles."

Bonito's face barely moved as he spoke. "Killing this one would be a reward in itself."

Corsen paused. "What if he refuses to go with you?"

"At Pinaleño you would find only the women and the children." He turned his head, indicating the dense pines of the higher slope. "The warriors are here, Cor-sen. You are six. Then two men in the house and two women. If he does not come with us, then we will come into your house there—"

Corsen concealed his surprise. "You observe our number well."

Bonito said. "I have been here longer than a full day, waiting for this time. And you see I did not count the Mexican man. He has agreed to remain with us until this one comes to take his place."

Corsen glanced at Billy Teachout. "He says they've got Delgado."

"Oh-my-God—"

Sellers moved closer to Corsen.

"What else does he want?"

"He wants you."

"Me!"

"We get you back in exchange for about a hundred rifles," Corsen added. "I don't know what makes him think you're worth that many."

"Tell him," Sellers said evenly, "that if he doesn't get back to Pinaleño by sundown he'll be shot. Along with Bil-Clin and his boy."

"Pinaleño has moved here," Corsen answered. "The braves are up in the pines. If you don't go with them they'll swarm down all over us."

"They wouldn't get across the wall," Sellers sneered. "There aren't a dozen rifles among the pack of them."

"You forgot, we don't have any."

Sellers was silent. Then, "All right. When the stage doesn't arrive at Gila Ford this evening they'll know something's wrong and send help."

Corsen said, "There are three men at the Gila Ford Station."

"Then they'll get more help!" Sellers said angrily.

"In what—three or four days?"

"What's the matter?" Sellers taunted. "You scared?"

Corsen ignored the remark. "What about Delgado?"

Sellers shrugged. "One thing at a time. Tell him we'll go back and think it over, and let him know."

Corsen told him, and as they were turning to go he looked at

Bil-Clin. "Now the chief of the Mescaleros follows the words of a bandit."

Bil-Clin shifted his eyes and did not reply.

CHAPTER FOUR

Katie came out from the kitchen, edging by Buz, who was in the doorway, and went to Corsen. She had served them food and had now finished washing the dishes. Corsen was at the front window, looking off to the east, watching for a movement to change the monotony of the plain.

She stood close to him and he asked in a low voice, "How's Ygenia?"

"She's praying."

He wanted to say something consoling that she could take to Ygenia, but there was nothing. The Apaches had Delgado. They would keep him until Sellers turned himself over to them. And that was not likely to happen.

KATIE'S face was close to his. Serious, searching eyes repeating the question he could not answer. She had been in the kitchen most of the time and she did not know all that had happened since the men had returned. Fisher was in the doorway, a silhouette against the faint outside dusk. Buz was by the kitchen door, holding his gun on the others at the bar end of the room, keeping an eye on Billy Teachout, who was in the kitchen watching the corral and yard.

"Ross, why doesn't he force Sellers to go to the Indians?"

"Fisher would have to shoot him first," Ross said quietly. "This business about the rifles is the long chance. Bonito would like to have them, but I think he'd just as soon have Sellers—for one long day. Sellers knows it. You can't force him to go. No matter what he's stolen, he's a white man. Handing him to Bonito wouldn't be right."

"How long will he wait, Ross?"

"Bonito? He'll send us a message tonight, most likely. And if we don't act on it he'll come at sunup."

"The outlaw would have to give you guns then." Katie said.

Corsen nodded. "He's holding off as long as he can, waiting for a miracle. I feel kind of sorry for him. He can't fight off Bonito with just one man, but if he gives us guns he's through. He loses either way."

They were silent then, standing close to each other.

Corsen's gaze would come in from the dim plain and go about the room.

Fisher, in the doorway, glanced now and then at Sellers. You have to give him credit, Corsen thought. Sitting on the edge of his nerves until the last possible minute.

Buz looks hard, but he leans on Fisher. He could never do this alone. They thought they had something good, and it turns out to be the worst jackpot they could fall into. Let them stew in it.

Billy and Ernie are men who know patience because they do more than just live here: they're part of the country. They'll sit through something like this and not show it.

Verbiest is afraid to open his mouth. His voice would give him away. He's so scared, he can taste it.

And Sellers. He'll never believe he's through—and maybe he isn't. He's got his life at stake, plus a government post and two thousand dollars in government silver. The money must have come from selling agency stores. He'll scheme, confident that he'll think of something to pull him out of this.

Bonito has nothing to lose. With a hundred warriors, and nothing to lose, he will probably win.

Strips of gray light crossed the room from the doorway and the windows. Outside, the moonlight showed the station yard in dim, unmoving stillness, bounded by the adobe wall, a pale line against the darkness beyond. Corsen looked out of the window again, then moved toward Fisher. He saw the dull gleam of a pistol barrel bear on him and he said, "Ed. A word with you."

"Come ahead," Fisher said quietly.

"It'll be dark in a few minutes," Corsen said. "You'd better give us our guns."

"I'll take my chances for a while."

"You won't be able to watch us in the dark—and you're not going to use a lamp with Bonito outside."

Fisher was silent. Then, "I'm trying to think it out," he said wearily.

"You don't have a choice," Corsen told him. "Those are Mescaleros. You're old enough to know how they behave when they're up."

"No, I don't. Not the way I know what would happen if you people had guns. Buz and I would turn our backs once—"

"All right," Corsen said. "Then give back all the money you took."

"Tell them I was just kiddn', eh?"

"I'm thinking about two women being here," Corsen said, "and a hundred Mescaleros out there. Make up your mind one way or the other—but do it before it's too late."

THE sound came to them gradually. It came faintly, growing out of the darkness, at first a muffled sound, now the unmistakable clop of a horse moving at a slow walk. A chair scraped in the room. Fisher's voice rasped, "Quiet!"

In the stillness Fisher cocked his head, listening, then whispered close to Corsen's cheek, "It's stopped."

Corsen waited. "At the gate," he said.

"It's a trick." Fisher was talking to himself. "A damn Apache trick."

"Maybe it is." Corsen paused. "And maybe it isn't, Ed," he said quietly. "If I was to go out there, would you hold your gun that way?"

"You're crazy."

"Let's find out." Corsen pushed through the screen door without a sound and was moving across the yard. He walked unhurriedly, because if Bonito was behind the wall, running would not make a difference; the yard was open, and gray with moonlight. He reached the gate and stood with his hand on the heavy latch.

Fisher watched him tensely. He felt someone close to him and glanced to see the girl. Billy Teachout was behind her. They looked at Fisher, then out toward the gate, and they did not speak.

In the darkness someone said, "What is it?" excitedly.

At a window Ernie Ball's voice hissed. "Shhhhh!"

They watched Corsen lift the iron latch. Then the shadowy figure pushed against the gate and the squeak of the hinges was a mournful screech with no other sounds in the night. Corsen went through the opening, and for the moment he was out of sight Katie held her breath. Then the gate swung wide and he was there again, leading the larger, darker shadow of a horse. A rider was atop the horse, head down, swaying gently with the movement of the horse's shoulders and flanks. Corsen closed the gate and came on, holding the horse close under the muzzle by a hackamore.

"Who is it?" from inside the doorway.

Fisher was in the yard now. He looked at Corsen, then toward the rider, questioningly.

Corsen went to the rider, raised his arms, and said gently, "Come, *viejo.*" The small figure toppled hesitantly, stiffly, into Corsen's arms.

He heard someone behind him say, "Delgado—"

They carried him inside to a bedroom and eased him down onto the bed. And when the lamp was lighted next to the bed, no one recognized Delgado.

"Mary, Virgin and Mother," Ygenia said, close to Delgado's cheek, kneeling on the floor and stroking her hand gently over his head. When Katie came in with a basin of water, she mopped his face, washing the blood away. She moved the cloth over his eyes very gently and when she took it away she gasped and uttered the name of the Mother of God again.

Delgado's face was knife scarred, small marks crisscrossing his cheeks. His nose was broken, that was evident, and his right eye was no longer in the socket.

His head came off the blanket, then fell back as the thin lines of his face tightened. He said, almost inaudibly, "Ross."

"I'm here," Corsen said close to his cheek. "Don't talk now. Say it in the morning."

Delgado breathed. "Bonito did this to me. There were others who beat at me and stuck me with their knives, but it was Bonito who did this." His hand waved close to his face.

"As I gathered the fresh team, one of them broke away and I went after it afoot because this one was a friend and would come if I approached with gentleness. But this time he went a greater distance. When he was near the piñon he stopped and let me approach, and at that moment the barbarians came from out of the pines. Almost as if this friend had lured me to them—"

CORSEN said gently, "Tell this in the morning."

Delgado turned his head, opening his left eye. "If you are here to listen." He waved his hand again. "Bonito did this to me. He impressed upon me that when he comes he will take the remainder of my sight. I would not like that to happen. He said that you had failed him. Now he will enter this house with the coming of the sun. . . ."

Silence then. Corsen rose as Ygenia began to stroke Delgado's head. Fisher appeared in the doorway.

"Your guns are on the table," he said quietly.

CHAPTER FIVE

Corsen pushed his gun belt lower on his hips and picked up the Winchester leaning against the support post. He heard the screen door close softly and peered into the darkness around the coach, which they had pushed into the stable shed. A figure was moving along the front of the house toward him.

It was Fisher. "There better be two of us out here. The east side of the house is a blind spot. And when the shootin' starts," he added, "I don't hanker to be in the same room with that thievin' government man. He could swing his barrel two feet and let go, easy as not." He looked at Corsen's carbine and holstered pistol. "You had them out here?"

"With the saddle," Corsen said.

"Where's your horse? It was here."

"I took it around to the corral. I'd rather have it run off than hit."

They rolled straw bales from the back wall of the shed to the front and piled them three high for some protection. There were no doors on the stable shed. It was built out from the station house four wagons wide. Ernie's coach was in the first stall nearest the house. Corsen went to the small window at the far end of the shed and Fisher stopped near him, looking out into the night.

"Might they come before dawn?"

"I've never heard of it," Corsen answered. "But don't put that down in your book as a rule. Bonito might have told Delgado dawn to put us off guard."

"That was something, what he did to him."

Corsen said quietly, "Delgado was lucky. Bonito's showing off. He wants us to think he's got full control of the situation. Even to letting a prisoner go, knowing he'll get him back again."

"He could convince me."

"I'm not so sure he has." Corsen paused. "If I could talk to Bil-

Clin—I don't see how he could help but resent this renegade's coming up and taking over. If we could get Bil-Clin alone. . . ."

Fisher said nothing.

Sometimes when you wait, the time goes slow, Corsen thought, but now it is going fast, so fast it isn't time anymore, but something else. That was a month ago that I told Katie I would come and get her. And Billy was surprised because he hadn't known what was going on. It seems like a month, but it was yesterday afternoon. Now he pictured himself with Katie at night, her face in soft shadows. She was in the room with Ygenia and Delgado, and a pistol. The door was bolted. If they broke through the door, then she would fire the pistol until it was empty. Then, in a timeless time she would pray. Pray that it would not take long for Ygenia and for herself. She would not use the gun on herself to make it quick. Even if he had asked her to, she would not. She doesn't even show this. There may be a little of it in her eyes, but it isn't in her voice. You're lucky, Ross. But how can you be lucky and unlucky at the same time?

But now more time had passed and there was an orange streak in the east and the sky was no longer full dark, and suddenly shadows were coming over the wall. Shadows that were the shapes of men, but without sound and without the gleam of weapons. They dropped and clung close to the wall. Now some were coming forward!

"Oh, my God!" Fisher had seen them.

From the house, "They're coming!" and the hurried report of a rifle. A pause, now a staccato of rifle fire and suddenly the station yard erupted into wild sound—whining gun reports and the full-throated scream of the Mescalero war cry and the whinnying of horses.

Down the carbine barrel Corsen squinted at three warriors coming zigzagging toward the shed. Then the outside two were out of vision and he fired. The Mescalero fell in his tracks. As he levered, the other two turned abruptly and were back to the wall as he aimed again. One of them was on the wall, and he brought the barrel up an inch and squeezed the trigger, and the warrior dropped to the other side. The third one was over, out of sight. And as suddenly as the firing had started, it stopped.

Corsen glanced both ways, surprised. Two, three, four of them were down and the rest had retreated. They're feeling us out, he thought. Seeing how many guns we have.

Fisher exhaled a long sigh. "We drove them off."

"The first time," Corsen said. "Now Bonito knows what we have and he'll scratch his head till something comes out of it."

Fisher looked up suddenly. "There!"

It was the Apache Corsen had hit first, now crawling toward the wall, dragging his left leg. Fisher raised his pistol.

"Hold it!" Corsen squinted hard at the Apache. "That's Bil-Clin's boy!"

Corsen waited until Sunshine reached the wall. Then, as the Apache raised himself slowly, painfully, with his weight on his right leg, Corsen raised the carbine and fired.

The bullet sang, ricocheting off the wall, and white dust spattered above the boy's head as he sank down.

Corsen levered a shell into the breech, his eyes on Sunshine. Watch him. Watch him like a hawk. He's got a broken leg, but he can be over that wall in one jump.

The next moment Sunshine was pushing up with his arms and his one good leg. But it was a feint, for he lunged suddenly to the side. Corsen was ready. He swung the barrel and placed the next shot a foot in front of Sunshine. Pieces of adobe splattered on the Apache's hair, and now he sat down and stared toward the shed.

Corsen said, "Watch along the wall, Ed. I'm going out. You edge toward the house."

Fisher said, "What?"

"If this works," Corsen said hurriedly, "I'll give you a signal. When I do, bring the men out. Just the men!"

Sunshine had not moved, and now Corsen said, "Here we go." He handed the Winchester to Fisher and pushed over the straw bales. Going over them, he drew his pistol and walked out into the open yard with the handgun pointed toward Sunshine. When he was in the middle of the yard he stopped.

"Bil-Clin!"

There was no answer, though he knew they were on the other side of the wall.

He shouted again, "Bil-Clin!" Then he said in Spanish, "My gun is on your son!" His eyes shifted above Sunshine. Stillness. A bare line of adobe—and then Bil-Clin was standing a dozen paces to the left, head and shoulders above the wall. Corsen's eyes went to him.

"Come over the wall."

Bil-Clin's arms came up and he raised himself to the top of the wall and dropped to the inside. He did not look at his son, but approached Corsen.

"Bil-Clin," Corsen said, "call Bonito and the others."

The Apache said a word in Mescalero and suddenly his warriors were at the wall. They had stood up and were now a line of bare chests and war paint and thick blue-black hair with cloth bands over the foreheads. Bonito stood among them, but he was alone. He lifted his Maynard and rested it on the wall.

"Come in, Bonito," Corsen said. And when the renegade did not move he glanced at Bil-Clin, then cocked his pistol. "Order him to come in—if you're still chief."

Bil-Clin looked at his son now, for the first time. The boy's eyes, between stripes of yellow paint, were on Corsen. Bil-Clin spoke again in Mescalero and it was evident that his words were for Bonito. But Bonito did not answer.

Corsen tightened. He could feel it in his stomach, but he made his voice sound calm. "Bonito, you are now chief?"

Still the Apache said nothing.

"Yesterday you told me that chieftainship of the Mescalero is not a thing of heredity, but a position earned by the one most capable in war. In fighting. So, Bonito, are you chief?"

Bonito did not move. Corsen was looking at him now, but he glanced away momentarily toward Ed Fisher, and nodded to him.

"Let me tell you something, Bonito. There are others who live here now—some with authority that seems to contradict yours. How can you be a chief if you have opposed only this old man, Bil-Clin?"

HE glanced toward the house and saw them coming out now.

"What about the government man, Bonito? He tells me you are a woman—a filthy pig of a woman with the diseases of animals. Unfit to live. And he has much authority. Perhaps he is the true chief here?"

Bonito's eyes had gone to Sellers as he appeared in the doorway. The eyes held on the man, narrowing, and then Bonito was over the wall.

"How would you have it, Cor-sen?"

"Whatever is customary."

"With the knife, then."

"I'll tell him." Corsen turned to the men in front of the station house. "Sellers, Bonito says you're afraid to fight him alone."

Sellers was startled. "You're crazy!"

"Ask him."

"Fight him with what?"

"Knives."

"Now I know you're crazy."

"You want to convince him you're boss, don't you? Beat him in a fair fight, the way they have to pick their chiefs sometimes."

Fisher moved a step toward Sellers and, as he did so, brought the Winchester up and down in a short motion and Sellers's pistol was out of his hand. He looked at Fisher with complete surprise, watching the outlaw pick up the pistol.

"I'll hold it for you while you're teaching that red son a lesson."

"Corsen! Tell him I won't fight him, that we don't do this in our government."

"Bonito," Corsen translated, "he says he does not have a knife."

BONITO reached behind him and drew a dull-gleaming blade from his waistband. His arm swung low. The knife scraped, bouncing over the sand to stop near Sellers.

"Corsen, tell that savage—"

"Listen," Corsen said, "this started because of you and Bonito. So you and he are going to finish it."

"He's fought this way all of his life. I wouldn't have a chance!"

Corsen shrugged. "You can't tell."

Bonito was handed a knife and without hesitating he stepped toward Sellers.

Fisher stooped, picked up the knife at Sellers's feet, and put it in his hand. "If you make it, I'll buy you a drink."

"Wait a minute, Ross!" Sellers backed up. "Ross, tell him I won't do it—"

But Bonito was in front of him now.

The Mescalero lowered his head, hunching his shoulders, and brought the knife up in front of him, looking up at Sellers's face through half-closed eyes.

"Ross!"

The blade flashed, a short swipe of naked arm that was out and in before anyone could see what had happened.

Sellers screamed. His left cheek was slashed from ear to mouth.

"Ross!"

Bonito feinted toward Sellers's head. Going back, Sellers brought up his arm, but the blade dropped. It flashed low under his guard and flicked a short arc across the sucked-in stomach. Sellers's vest opened from pocket to pocket and he screamed again and this time turned and started to run. But he came up short, pushed, jolted back to face Bonito by Teachout, who stood behind him.

"You're going the wrong way," Teachout said.

"Let me go!"

Bonito stood waiting.

Corsen's gaze went from him to Sellers. "Are you through?"

Sellers, blood smeared over his face, was breathing hard, holding his stomach. "Ross." He gasped. "Shoot him! Now, while he's still!"

"Are you quitting?" Corsen said.

"God! Shoot him!"

Corsen said calmly, "Fight him, or else get out."

Sellers looked at him strangely, taken by surprise. "Get out?"

"That's right. Ride out of here and take Verbiest with you. Forget you ever worked for the Bureau. There are seven people here to testify you're not fit for the job. Now, either fight him or write yourself off."

Sellers hesitated, fingering the cut across his stomach, his eyes on Corsen. Then his gaze went slowly to Bonito, who stood unmoving, watching him. Gradually Sellers's grip loosened around the knife, and as it dropped from his hand he turned abruptly and walked to the station house. The screen door banged.

"Now," Bonito said coldly, "there is no more doubt."

"It is still in my mind," Corsen said mildly. He lowered the pistol he'd been holding on Sunshine and turned to Bonito. He added, pointedly, "I have seen women fight before. Usually it proves nothing."

Bonito's eyes narrowed. "Say your words straight, Cor-sen."

Corsen stopped a stride from the Apache. He raised his hand and swung the open palm hard against Bonito's face. The Apache was taken off guard and staggered back, but he did not go down.

"Is that straight enough?"

Corsen looked back at Ed Fisher and swung the pistol underhand toward him, and as he turned back to Bonito he shifted his feet suddenly and came around with his right fist smashing against the Apache's face. And this time Bonito went down.

"Maybe that's a little straighter." Then, looking toward Bil-Clin, Corsen said, "Is this your chief?"

Bonito came to one knee. His mouth was half open with numbness, but he smiled and said, "All right. Corsen."

Behind him he heard Fisher say, "Here's the knife." Corsen half turned as if to look at Fisher, but it was a short movement. He pivoted, swinging his left hand, and again caught Bonito on the face as he was rising.

The Apache went down, rolling away from Corsen's reach, but as he came up Corsen was there. He swung a right and then a left to the Apache's head to beat him down again.

Bonito looked up at him, propping himself with his elbows; his face was cut at both eyes and his mouth swollen. And now he considered what to do next—how to fight this man whose not using a weapon was an insult. He brought his knees up under him, then one foot, watching Corsen closely.

Corsen moved a step closer, clenching his fists. Bonito will pull something this time, he thought. Bonito was rising, then suddenly throwing himself at Corsen's legs. Corsen dodged and kicked out, but his boot caught Bonito's shoulder and now the Apache was rolling. Corsen started after him, then stopped dead as Bonito jumped to his feet.

Fisher yelled, "You want it now, Ross?"

Corsen shook his head. This was the way to beat him, if it could be done. He started toward Bonito, thinking: Carry it to him. Once he starts calling the play, you're through. Watch his eyes. They'll tell you a snap second before he moves. He moved close to Bonito, tensed, watching the yellow-filmed eyes, smelling the animal smell of the man, seeing the eyes now and not the face.

Corsen drew his arm back slowly, knotting the fist. He shifted his weight suddenly, swinging the fist—*the eyes*—then just as suddenly threw himself to the side. Bonito's knife jabbed viciously, but Corsen was not there. And as the Apache came around to find him, in that split second Corsen was ready. He went back on his left foot, his body balanced, and then his weight shifted and his boot kicked savagely into Bonito's loins. The Apache gasped and stopped dead in his tracks, bending, holding his stomach.

And that was it. Corsen hit him with one fist, then the other, and as Bonito started to sag he caught the Apache's arm and drove his right fist straight into the paint-streaked face. The Apache went down, dropping the knife, and landed heavily on his back.

"There, Bil-Clin, is your chief," Corsen said. He went over to Sunshine and knelt beside him, examining the shinbone that his bullet had broken.

Bil-Clin was standing next to him now. It was hard for him to speak, even if it was not an outright apology, for he was Mescalero, but he said, "What would you have us do?"

Corsen rose and looked at Bil-Clin. "If you wish, we will get an American doctor for your son. But now go back to Pinaleño . . . and take your dead."

"And you will come, Cor-sen?"

CORSEN'S gaze went over the line of Apaches at the wall. Immobile faces, streaks of vermillion and bright yellow, and looking at them he was angry. But he thought: These are Mescaleros. You know what they are. You know what they can do. You were lucky today, but don't push your luck, and perhaps because of it make some cavalry patrol officer, who isn't even out here yet, push his. And he nodded slowly, wearily, to Bil-Clin and said, "Yes. I will come."

The others were standing almost in a line. Teachout and Ernie Ball, Ed Fisher and his partner and Verbiest.

Maybe this will straighten Fisher out, Corsen thought. He's a man you'd buy a drink for, even after he's robbed you. Verbiest made a mistake, but he knows it and he won't make it again. . . .

And then he did not think of them anymore. Katie was in the doorway and he walked toward the house.